Totally Bound Publishing books by C.J. Burright

Music, Love and Other Miseries
Every Kiss
Every Minute
Every Breath
Every Step

Hearts and Haunts
Now and Always
Wherever, Whenever

I0662168

Hearts and Haunts

WHEREVER, WHENEVER

C.J. BURRIGHT

Wherever, Whenever
ISBN # 978-1-80250-741-6
©Copyright C.J. Burright 2024
Cover Art by Kelly Martin ©Copyright July 2024
Interior text design by Claire Siemaszkiewicz
Totally Bound Publishing

Published in 2024 by Totally Bound Publishing, United Kingdom.

WHEREVER, WHENEVER

Dedication

To the wolves in the world, who weave magic
and fire for the girls who've lost themselves.

Chapter One

As far as Violet Keller knew, no one had ever died while getting a miniature tattoo of a pink skull. The giant biker in the chair had obviously heard otherwise.

"*Garg.*" Spike squeezed his eyes shut. He dug his massive fingers into his thigh, making his leather chaps creak. Perspiration glistened on his bald head. "You're trying to kill me, Magic. Admit it. You dulled them needles, didn't you? This tattoo's taking longer than a computer software update."

Vi glanced up again from her sketchpad and bit her lip to keep from smirking. Ruby, aka Magic Mamba, leaned over the last client of the night, her favorite tattoo gun gripped expertly in a gloved hand. By the set line of her plum-stained lips, she was deciding whether to finish the tattoo or stab Spike in the eye.

"Keep talking, scumbag, and I'll show you the definition of dull." Ruby used her sugary-sweet voice, which meant violence was a single wrong move away.

With a sigh, Vi set aside her sketchpad. Since she owned the tattoo parlor, any lawsuit would be on her head. She preferred to keep her reputation pristine and the cash coming in.

"He's kidding, Ruby." Vi added a hint of warning to her tone. "Aren't you, Spike?"

He drew his eyebrows down. "I may not be the smartest cracker in the package, but I'd never insult my tattoo artist while she's holding iron to my skin." Spike flashed his teeth at Ruby. "I love pink. It's my favorite color."

For a tense moment, Ruby held his gaze, her blue eyes glittering dangerously. The tattoo gun pressed against his flesh, ready to wound or finish the artwork already in motion. She suddenly grinned, wide and feral. "And there's nothing sexier than a man with a pink skull on his arm, am I right?"

"You're the artist, Mamba. I trust you." By his goofy grin, he had a lot more than trust for Ruby. He looked at her as if she alone ruled the world, and her tattoo gun was a scepter of power, not a tool with needles.

"Awww." Ruby pivoted, and her four-inch heels squeaked on the tile floor. "He trusts me, Vi. I think I'll keep him."

"Just don't break anything." Violet uncrossed her legs, stood from the couch, and stretched. A chill crept beneath her black sweater and jeans, a sign she'd have to drag out the Halloween decorations soon. Nothing was more fun than a few rubber spiders dangling from the rafters to scare jumpy customers. She swiped her sketchbook and colored pencils. No way was she sticking around to witness Ruby's next tattoo victim turn romantic. "And clean up when you're done."

"You got it, boss." Ruby wriggled her eyebrows and turned back to her work.

The buzz of the gun resumed as Vi shut the door behind her and strolled to the lobby, where Emma cleaned up for closing. Of all her employees, Emma was the most recent addition, attending the same tattoo artist program Vi had graduated from. When she'd shown up at the parlor looking for work, she'd reminded Vi so much of herself five years before, when she'd been the one desperately searching for a job, a purpose, a place to belong. Sponsoring Emma's education hadn't even been a question.

"Did you finish your latest design?" Emma paused from sweeping and glanced at Vi's sketchbook. "I can't wait to see it."

"Not yet." Vi snapped the book shut. She never shared her designs until they were one hundred percent perfection. "Maybe tomorrow. Spike and Ruby were too distracting."

Emma laughed and hooked a lock of eggplant-colored hair behind her ear. "You think talking is all they're going to do tonight?"

"Please, I just ate."

"You were in there so long, I thought maybe you finally let Ruby finish your tattoo. It's better than imagining you doing the three-way tango with Spike and Ruby."

"Again, *ew*. And I'll wrap up my tattoo when I'm ready." The incomplete design inked on Vi's shoulder seemed to tingle, as if the mere mention of it activated some sort of voodoo. Vi rested one elbow on the front counter and bumped a large envelope resting askew between a design book and a box of temporary tattoos Ruby insisted they keep for the occasional wimp who decided needles were too scary. "What's that?"

Emma shrugged and resumed sweeping, the sparkling polish of her ebony fingernails glittering like a night sky. "A courier dropped it off half an hour ago.

Since it says 'personal' and 'confidential', I didn't open it."

"Maybe it's a bomb." Vi frowned at the label on the envelope and picked it up. No return address listed, and it felt no lighter than a letter.

"Then give me a minute to finish before you open it," Emma said between sweeps. "I'm too young to die, and if I'm going to bite it, I want to be doing something exciting. Wielding a broom definitely won't cut it."

"It's probably just laced with poison." Vi ripped open the manila envelope. "Nothing you need to worry about. I prefer to be cremated—you know, just in case I fall to the floor and start frothing at the mouth."

"You got it." Emma set the broom aside and leaned one hip against the counter as Vi pulled a plain white envelope free. "Do you think it's a love letter from that guy you sketched a Gothic castle scene for? He freakin' adores you, especially since Ruby inked it perfectly on his twin brother's back."

Vi snorted. "If I could figure out what a man might do, I wouldn't have to worry about charging people for tattoos. I'd already be insanely rich."

She turned the envelope over and paused. A single, purple violet had been drawn on the back flap...familiar, unmistakable. Her heart surged into race-car speed. Only one person drew that bloom on every birthday card, on her bedroom dresser, once on her face while she'd been sleeping.

Dahlia. The sister she hadn't seen in five years.

"Vi, you okay?" Emma lightly gripped her wrist, her forehead lined. "Do you need some water?"

An entire ice bath sounded great. "No, I'm fine. It's fine." Ignoring how her hands trembled, she gently peeled the envelope open, careful not to rip the paper. "It's from my sister."

10

"Oh, boy." Emma's eyebrows lifted. "I wonder how she found you?"

How Dahlia had found her didn't matter so much as *why*. Her throat dry, Violet slid the folded letter from the envelope and set it on the black marble counter. She opened it and smoothed the paper with her palm. Dahlia's delicate handwriting flowed over the white, her words filling from margin to margin.

Vi shoved the letter at Emma and turned away. "You read it. Tell me the important parts."

"Are you sure?"

Not at all. "Absolutely."

Blood pounding in her head, Vi paced the lobby as Emma scanned the letter. She paused at the glass door and stared out into the night, unseeing. She'd known one of her family members would eventually track her down, and even though five years stretched between now and when she'd left, seeing her sister's penmanship erased those days and made her feel like the same, vulnerable teenager who'd ditched the only life she'd known. She'd fled the father whose expectations killed her dreams, the sister she loved better than any best friend, the small, quirky town that never felt like home…

And Max.

She rested her forehead against the cool glass pane and closed her eyes. Max, her first kiss, first heartbreak, first everything. He'd been too good for her in every way, deserved a girl who wouldn't tear him from the home and life he adored. Leaving and never looking back had been the greatest gift she could offer to both Max and Dahlia, the two best people she knew, a chance to find love together without her there, muddying the waters.

Whatever she could do to make her sister happy, she'd do it, no questions asked, even if losing Max still felt like a knife in her chest. Her heart had simply grown over the blade, claiming the pain as a permanent part of her being.

"Vi, you need to go home." Emma's voice held a sympathy that jerked her straight up and around, like a puppet on strings. Tears shone in her progeny's eyes as she lifted the letter to her. "You should read this."

She shook her head and shoved her hands into her back pockets to keep from reaching for it, her ribs tightening, making it hard to breathe. "Just tell me the highlights, Em."

"The letter is from your sister. She hired a private investigator to find you."

That Dahlia had resorted to using a PI wasn't surprising. Beyond the yearly Christmas card and no return address letter to assure her mom that she still breathed, Violet had done her best to lie low and stay out of the spotlight. Going home had never been on the agenda. Direct contact would open the door to some serious guilt trips, so like any good daughter and sister who'd slithered away, she'd severed all other communication. Kicking ass behind the scenes and letting Ruby steal the show as Magic Mamba worked perfectly. Together, they'd made the tattoo parlor wildly successful.

"She's begging you to come home to help out at the café during the October swarm. They're down a cook and three waitresses, and with your dad being sick—"

Her stomach twisted into a hundred knotted waterweeds, dragging her back to Devils Hollow. "Dad's sick?"

"Vi." Emma took her hand and squeezed hard, her fingers graveyard cold. "You need to go home."

The image of her sweet, kind sister, handling the family business all alone came to stark life. Vi didn't need to hear more, didn't need to make her usual checklist to figure out her next steps. If Dahlia needed her, she wouldn't refuse. The dreaded day had finally come to face her disquieting past in Devils Hollow.

Even if it slowly killed her to see the man she loved happily attached to her little sister.

* * * *

A bouquet of wildflowers in his hand, Max strode across the packed café parking lot. Only the first day of October and already the tourists poured in for the month-long Halloween festivities. As much as he appreciated the enthusiasm of both visitors and citizens of Devils Hollow, it interfered with his weekly cherry pie fix. Dahlia may not like it, but he preferred to eat his pie in quiet, only the sound of his own fork scraping the plate, his moment of personal contemplation for the days behind and ahead.

Through the line of windows, Dahlia fluttered through Keller's Killer Café like a bright butterfly, balancing a tray of dishes in each hand. Nearly every table was taken. Worse, a trio of pale-skinned, black-haired girls wearing red cowls huddled at his favorite corner spot in back.

Tourists — a necessary evil. Tomorrow, he'd drop off the special carving Gramps had whittled last season. Shaped into a graveyard cross, the 'reserved' sign had been engraved with a dire warning to trespassers. A man needed to at least have a place to briefly take a load off while scarfing down his treats, and by God, he wasn't above pushing tourists out of the way for his one fleeting moment of bliss.

A cheery sign painted with sunflowers dripping blood held the door open and announced the daily special. As he approached, Dahlia flashed him a smile. He didn't take it personal. No matter how busy she may be, she always made sure each customer felt special the second they stepped inside. She laughed at something a customer said before heading for the kitchen. For a blinding moment, with her hair up, she looked exactly like her sister.

Violet. His traitorous heart skipped a beat, and he scowled. Five long years had passed since she'd abandoned him, and she still infected his thoughts like an immortal venom.

He reached the café entrance as the kitchen door swung open. A woman pressed her back to the wall to let Dahlia and her trays pass. She swiped her golden hair back, offering a glimpse of winding, blood-red roses tattooed on her forearm, and turned his way. Their gazes met, and they both froze. Her dark eyes widened.

His heart stopped beating altogether. The world came to a complete halt.

Vi. Violet.

Over the last five years, Max had fantasized about running into Vi again. He'd carefully prepared hundreds of speeches, some meant to blister her skin with shame, others to make her beg for forgiveness, a few to hurt her as deeply and permanently as she'd hurt him. In his spun dreams of vengeance, her reactions ranged anywhere from pleading on her knees for him to stay while he walked away to hot, punishing makeup sex and vows of forever.

None of those imaginings had prepared him for reality.

Her thick, blonde hair was piled on top of her head in a messy bun, long bangs swiped to the side. Though she only came up to his collarbone in boots with heels, she maintained the impression that she'd kick in his teeth if he smarted off. The tattooed sleeves in rich, deep colors added a vibrant touch to that wildcat effect. *Burning hell.* Why did she still have to be so damn cute with an unreasonable shot of sexy?

A shiver of longing crashed through him like a tidal wave, fierce and unstoppable. *Violet.* She was finally home.

A customer stopped to speak to Violet, blocking his view, and time began ticking again.

Max drew a deep breath. His damaged wrist ached from the stranglehold on Dahlia's half-crushed flowers, and he forced his fingers to relax. Devils Hollow was a small town, and even with the influx of tourists, the odds of running into Vi often were high if she planned to stick around for longer than a day. Avoiding her would be nearly impossible—and glaringly obvious. Then she'd know the secret he kept, that even after what she did all those years ago, she alone colored his dreams.

He wiped his moist palm on his jeans. He'd never been a coward and had no intention of starting down that road today. No matter her reasons for being back in Devils Hollow, he wouldn't go out of his way to avoid her, wouldn't allow her to have that power over him again. In fact...

A tiny smile worked its way onto his mouth as the perfect plan wove to life. He wouldn't avoid Vi at all. If she was back in town, it must be because she had nowhere else to go. This was the chance he'd been waiting for, to show her what she'd missed out on by leaving him behind. He'd charm her socks off, enthusiastically share every one of his triumphs, pretend her absence had been the best possible outcome for his incredibly happy, amazingly successful life.

So what if the adjectives leaned toward exaggeration? He had more than enough to be happy about, and Vi had relinquished the right to the full, unadulterated truth the second she'd left town without a goodbye, taking his heart with her. He wouldn't waste this opportunity to get over her once and for all…to finally forget her throaty laugh, the nimble glide of her fingers as she drew her latest designs, how her hair had felt like silk in his hands.

He shook the details off, fantasies inspired by no closure. All old news, just like the Max plus Vi heart carved on their rock by Lake Forsaken.

The customer occupying Violet moved away, and Max forced himself to hold her gaze. Straightening, he widened his smile and headed into the café, his violent pulse a war hammer against his T-shirt collar. By the time he was through with her, Violet Keller would know the full meaning of remorse.

And maybe then his heart would finally mend.

Chapter Two

As Vi's universe shattered and reformed in the next second, she gulped a breath, unable to look away from the man aiming straight for her like a military tank on a one-lane street.

Maximus Carter.

The sizzling aromas from the kitchen, humming conversations and clanking utensils on plates faded into the background as the past collided with the present. Dahlia's plea for help had been the catalyst for her returning to Devils Hollow, the main reason why Vi had agreed to suck it up and cross the border into the town that held her history in its clawed hand. But she'd also decided, in that irrevocable moment, that if she went back, she'd make the trip count on every level. She'd face all her demons, fight them to the death and leave completely free...free of guilt, regrets or heartbreak.

Her pulse roared in her ears, drowning out all other noise. One of those personal demons resided in the body of the Roman warrior statue brought to full life and coming closer with every heartbeat.

She'd mentally prepared herself to cross paths with Max—eventually, not within the first crazy-busy hour upon arrival in Devils Hollow. The same bad luck that had clung to her back while in her hometown returned, fast and vengeful—not a promising sign that her fate had changed with time.

Or that her storm-strong emotions for Max had faded at all in the time apart.

As he drew near, it was as if the last five years rewound with each step. One look into his blue eyes and her heart sang. That confident, crooked smile awakened every coma-induced butterfly in her stomach, and when he stopped right in front of her, bringing a draft of the outdoors and autumn, all the feelings she determined to block and avoid came rushing back.

Max was here, sharing the same air, and she had to deal with everything that went along with it. She intended to mend what bridges she could in the next month, to free herself of the chains shackling her to the past and the dark secrets of this town. And that included, somehow, getting over the only man she'd ever loved. *Still* loved.

"Vi, sweeting." The endearment he'd always used for her, said in that rough voice that haunted her steamiest dreams, curled hot through her blood, and she resisted a shiver. "It's *so* marvelous to see you again."

His slight emphasis on the word 'so' and the fierce, familiar gleam in his eyes that indicated he was on the path of some sort of personal challenge cut through her daze and brought her back to the present with an icy splash. Oh, he definitely hadn't forgiven or forgotten.

This particular bridge clearly had a troll waiting for its pound of flesh.

This month is going to be simply splendid.

Vi forced a smile as bright as his. "Max. You're looking really good."

"So I hear." His eyes sparkled.

She couldn't stop a laugh. "Nice to know your self-esteem remains in full force."

"Some qualities can't be killed, no matter the destruction others leave behind." The slight narrowing of his eyes gave his mild tone away, and her stomach dipped.

But he wasn't wrong on either account. Even wearing a plain black T-shirt, faded jeans and work boots, he turned more than a few heads from the October café crowd. The *Twilight* wannabes in the back openly stared. And she knew firsthand about natures that couldn't be killed, no matter how hard others tried to drown, stab and pitchfork them into the grave.

Max pivoted and leaned his hip against the counter. When she'd first locked gazes with him, he looked like he'd come face to face with a tormented spirit at Lake Forsaken and considered screaming for the hills. Now, he seemed completely at ease, fully prepared to have a long, friendly catch-up session.

Part of her wanted that more than anything, *needed* it. The other part kicked her in the shin and told her to smarten up. Max was simply being polite, using his small-town manners on her, now an outsider since she wasn't a resident anymore. The only way to survive a month in Devils Hollow was to apologize, hope he accepted it, then keep the talk superficial and the distance between them as wide as possible.

A solid plan. If she stuck to it, she might manage to escape Devils Hollow again, somewhat intact.

Max leaned in next to her ear. His warm breath fluttered a stray tendril of her hair, slid over her skin like the best memory. "Did you miss me, Vi?"

So much for escaping unscathed. Her pulse skittered into a twisted, erratic dance. *Every second of every day.* But he wasn't hers. He'd never really been hers. And what was he doing, flirting with her when he was attached to —

"Hey, you two."

Dahlia.

At her sister's cheerful voice behind her, Vi jumped back and bumped into the counter. She steadied herself on an empty barstool, guilt sweeping through her. Thinking about Max as anything more than an old friend was a mistake that she couldn't make.

When she'd walked into the café an hour ago, Dahlia had been slammed with customers, and Vi had leaped in to help after a quick, unexpected welcome-home hug. No time for awkward apologies or explanations. Nothing at the café had changed in the last five years, and it was like she'd only been off for the weekend. Waiting tables was the same as riding a bike, a skill scarred on the brain. They hadn't had a free moment to talk about anything important, but she wasn't going to mess up her sister's life…again.

"Sorry to scare you, sis." Dahlia threw an arm around her shoulders and squeezed, hard. Vi swore her bones popped beneath the pressure. Behind that sunshine act, her sister clearly harbored some serious venom. Not that she blamed her. "Can you believe it, Max? Vile's back."

If anyone else had used that nickname, Vi would have slugged them in the face. But it was Dahlia, so she let it slide. "Gone five years and still no respect."

"This month is going to be epic." Dahlia jumped up and down, her excitement contagious. *Almost*. If not for the dagger-sharp gleam in her eyes, Vi would have believed her. "You have no idea how glad I am to have you home."

"Me, too." Max hooked a thumb into his jeans pocket, all casual and composed.

The sly edge to his smile should have troubled her. Instead, it quickened her blood and reawakened sparks of magic she'd never forgotten. She'd expected a tirade, a cold shoulder, maybe the silent treatment and glares, not...*this*. He'd worn that same expression when he decided to teepee his baseball coach's house after being benched for mouthing off. A decade later, that crafty grin hadn't changed.

His easygoing presentation was a performance. Some scheme was afoot, and she'd just stepped into the steaming middle of it. She needed to figure out what that was before it bit her — or Dahlia — in the butt. It had nothing to do with the challenge lighting his eyes. Nope, nothing at all.

"Oh, I almost forgot." Max pulled a bedraggled bunch of asters, sweet Williams and coneflowers from behind his back. A yellow ribbon tied around the stems kept the flowers together. He handed them to Dahlia. "For you, doll. I forgive the sin of allowing tourists to occupy my sacred spot in back. You have until tomorrow to remedy the situation."

"Aw, Max." Dahlia clasped her hands together and sighed dreamily. "Thank you, sweetie." She rose on tiptoes and kissed him on the cheek.

All the colors dimmed at the edges, and Vi's chest tightened. She focused on a man seated by the window sporting devil horns and a greasy mustache, chowing down on Dahlia's daily special, Shepherd's Eye Pie.

Telling herself she could survive, find a way to get over him, didn't quite prepare her for the reality of seeing Max and Dahlia together, being near them, enduring the exchange of flowers and kisses.

So the month of nightmares begins.

"Miss." Mr. Devil hailed Dahlia with an air-jab of his pitchfork. "More water, when you get a moment."

Dahlia's dimples appeared. "Coming right up, hon." She patted Max on the arm. "Duty calls. If you want to wait for a seat, I'll bring your pie. Extra whipped cream for sharing your seat with the peasants."

Vi forced her spine straight. The more she immersed herself in their love, the more she'd grow numb to it. A good theory, anyway. She forced her attention back to Max.

Instead of gazing adoringly at Dahlia as she expected, his glittering eyes studied her, as if he couldn't decide if she was human or a body snatcher using Violet Keller's colorful skin as a hideout. But no matter the truth, he'd dig it out. Slowly. Painfully. With the biggest smile.

"Thanks for the offer, doll, but I promised Gramps I'd be home for dinner. You know how he is if I'm late. Duke will get all my grub, no leftovers." He lifted his eyebrows, leaned in, and lowered his voice to a secret-sharing hush. "Missing pie *and* lasagna night would be an utter tragedy."

"Dogs before tardy dudes and damsels." Gramps' motto rolled automatically off Vi's tongue. She always loved the low-key dinners with Max's grandpa and his obnoxious black lab, Duke. A single, unguarded plate moment was all the opening Duke needed, leaving only a trail of slobber as evidence. Those meals had been nothing like the formal events at her own house. She'd whine, barter and fib at every possible chance to stay with Max and Gramps rather than go home.

Max laughed, and the sound ribboned through her, silky and warm. "He still says that, even though Duke has enough fat rolls to keep him warm through a dozen zombie apocalypses. You should drop by. But be warned—neither one can hear very well. And being licked to death is a very real possibility." He winked at Dahlia. "Later, doll." He held Vi's gaze as he turned toward the door. "Welcome back, Violet."

His hands tucked into his jeans' pockets, he strolled through the exit and headed toward—she couldn't hide a smile—Gramps' puke-green Oldsmobile parked on the grass beside the road. She couldn't believe that monster hadn't died yet. It wasn't surprising Max chose to drive it instead of some shiny new car. He took good care of what he had and never wasted his resources, a skill learned directly from Gramps. He'd clearly taken good care of himself, too. She wasn't usually one to ogle men, but when it came to Max, she couldn't seem to control herself.

"You can breathe now." Dahlia nudged her playfully in the ribs.

Vi blinked. Max climbed into the car and shut the door. He'd crossed the entire parking lot while she'd stared like an idiot—in front of Dahlia. So much for staying cool and collected.

"He hasn't changed much, has he?" Even her voice betrayed her, the words all rough and raspy. She coughed into her elbow, pretending to clear her throat.

"If Max changed, that would be a grave loss to the world of women everywhere." Her sister's smile made the last rays of sunlight look like a dying lightbulb. She nabbed the water pitcher off the counter and aimed for the devil cradling his pitchfork. "Grab a coffee. There's your favorite mint creamer in the back fridge. I'll catch you up on everything once the dinner rush is over."

"Can't wait." Vi marched toward the kitchen, ignoring a woman wearing batwings and fangs waiting to be seated, her arms crossed, toe tapping. It was super-awesome to be home.

* * * *

The dinner rush lasted all the way to closing. It was only after the door deadbolted, the lights turned low and the blood-dripping, sunflower-decorated *Shut Down Until Dawn* sign hung in the front window that Vi slouched into a plastic booth table with an overfull glass of red wine in her grip.

She sighed, relaxed into the cushioned backrest and gazed into the night. Her black, lifted pick-up looked out of place all alone in the parking lot beneath the sick lamplight glow.

Her feet ached, and she kicked off her boots. Toes free to wiggle in her fuzzy socks felt better than sex — at least better than her last, temporal experience with the man who'd gained her fleeting attention. She'd never been much good at separating her emotions from the physical act, and since her heart remained muzzled and caged, partners had been few, far between and extremely short-lived.

"Take this." Dahlia slid a plate holding a generous wedge of her infamous slain-by-chocolate cake across the table. "You earned it."

"Trying to kill me on the first day home." Vi grabbed a fork and stabbed the cake straight in the gut. Chocolate goo laced with red sprinkles oozed over the silver. "I approve."

"Bribery, my darling Vile." Dahlia plopped onto the bench across from her, scooted in until her back hit the wall and stretched her legs out on the cushioned seat. "Whatever works to get you to stay until November."

"Already promised to stay." Vi shoved cake into her mouth and moaned. "Oh. Dang. This is better than I remembered."

"New and Dahlia-improved recipe." She waved, as if baking cake this glorious was as easy as waking up. "Not everything in Devils Hollow stays the same. Have I told you yet how happy I am you came home to help me out?"

Vi licked her fork. "That's number thirteen, not that I'm keeping track. And you're welcome…again."

"How many checklists did you pin to your wall and destroy before deciding to come?" Dahlia smirked, settling right back into the routine of teasing her. Vi's devotion to her checklists and planning had always been an endless source of humor for her family.

"Zero. Didn't need one." She set her fork down and looked her sister square in the eyes. "For you, anything."

Dahlia's eyes widened. She glanced frantically around and patted her peony pink apron with the café logo of a knife stabbing a heart. "Where's my phone? I need you to repeat for recording and later sabotage."

Vi snorted and stuffed her mouth again. Getting all gushy wasn't her style, and even though she'd cave for her sister to make amends, she'd avoid it as long as possible. Pretending nothing had happened suited her just fine. She'd deal with it later—on October thirty-first at midnight, just before heading back to Kickin' Ink.

"Honestly, even shorthanded, I can keep up with the café on my own. It's the mandatory Hallowtoberfest business activities that I need help with." Dahlia leaned over and squeezed her hand, hard enough to bruise. Vi refused to wince. "Your mission, which you have already naively accepted without knowing any details, is representing Keller's Killer Café at every required community event, from passing out monster cookies, volunteering at the haunted corn maze and assisting in the narrated ghost tour through the woods."

"Dammit." Vi tossed the fork aside, and it clattered on the plate like bones on concrete. "Can't I just hide out in the back and cook until grease slicks my hair to my head?"

Dahlia grinned, all teeth and evil. "Payback's a wicked witch, sis. And Dustin wouldn't give up his spatula and apron, even if you kicked him in the face. He lives to cook for me."

"Destroying all my fantasies." But Dahlia was right. She had some groveling to do, mistakes to make up for, an absence to repay. If that meant suffering through crowds of zombies playing laser tag and wandering the freaky-as-frick forest to amuse tourists, she'd suck it up and deal.

"Just keeping it real. Mrs. Beasley scheduled the initial meeting tomorrow at seven sharp. As my official rep, you'll be there to get all the details."

"Beasley? Gah. When did you get so bossy?"

"Someone had to fill your shoes after you left." Dahlia batted her eyelashes. She swiped the fork, delicately separated a perfectly sized bite of cake and popped it into her mouth.

"Saucy wench." Vi grabbed the utensil back and pulled the cake closer, resisting a possessive growl. It wasn't right that someone could eat such sinful cake and look like a perfect princess while doing it.

"I suppose I should summarize all the gruesome details of the last five years." Dahlia leaned back with a sigh. "There's too much that's happened to go into full detail in one setting, so I'll keep to the important stuff."

"Dad?" Vi swallowed, the cake losing its flavor.

"He's in treatment, a very exclusive and insanely expensive clinic at a secret location, but his liver is shot." Tears glimmered in Dahlia's eyes. "Going dry will give him another year or so…maybe."

"Dang." Her heart ached. Even though she always butted heads with her dad, loathed the man he became when he drank, he was still her father.

"It took him driving his car into the lake to finally get him to admit that he might need help."

"He drove into the lake?" A shiver of cold slithered through Vi—Lake Forsaken, the local haunted hot spot with an urban legend staked to its dark shores…and the source of her worst nightmares. Those wicked-sharp dreams had tapered off since leaving Devils Hollow. She didn't want them—or the premonition that inspired them—back.

"Straight through Beasley's fence—and by some miracle missed every tree trunk along the way. Made a big splash, too."

"You don't go to the lake anymore, right?" Vi tightened her fingers around the fork, waiting for the answer.

"If I had any time to waste, it wouldn't be in that leech-infested pond." Dahlia absently rubbed at a scratch in the lacquered tabletop. "Mom, of course, refused to let him face treatment alone. She probably assumed he'd push away every doctor, nurse and caretaker."

"Fair theory."

"It's been rough on everyone, especially when the staff keeps quitting. If I believed in curses, I'd say someone—or some*thing*—is out to get the Keller family."

"Not even funny. I'm the only one who's cursed…obviously." Vi had always felt more of a connection with the supernatural-seeking tourists who believed in the unknown than the citizens of Devils Hollow, who manipulated those beliefs for monetary gain. The weird and uncanny bit back with fangs and venom that were very much real, and no amount of cash was worth that.

"I've borrowed a few crosses from Gramps to hang around the house, just in case." Dahlia winked, not as concerned as she should be, the perfect example of a Devils Hollow resident. "And Max has been beyond great, supporting me as much as possible."

Max. Vi swallowed hard. She'd almost forgotten. Ha, who was she kidding? She never forgot that she'd left him behind so he could find the life he had now.

"How about a happy subject?" Dahlia stretched her hand across the table and wriggled her fingers. A diamond glittered on her ring finger, almost as dazzling as Dahlia's smile. "I'm engaged. Can you believe it?"

Vi straightened her shoulders. Here it was, the subject she dreaded. Dahlia and Max, together forever, the Devils Hollow super couple. "I'm glad he makes you happy."

"He does." She sighed and gazed at her treasure, shifting it back and forth. The jewel gleamed like ice in unexpected winter sunshine. "So happy."

"You and Max deserve each other, truly." Thank God her voice didn't waver in time with her thundering pulse or the ringing in her ears. "You're the two best people I know."

"Max?" Dahlia's eyebrows drew together. She lifted her gaze from admiring her rock. "I'm engaged to Brian."

Vi blinked. "Brian? Who the hell is Brian?"

"He moved to Devils Hollow a year ago." Slowly, she shook her head, gauging her with a scrutiny that made Vi want to squirm—which she didn't. Vi Keller did *not* squirm. "All this time, you thought I hooked up with Max, didn't you?"

Dahlia and Max aren't together. Vi denied the sudden urge to slump into a puddle of relief. Instead, she kept her expression blank. Dahlia always could read her soul better than anyone else...except Max. "It was a valid assumption." She sniffed. "You've always adored Max, and why wouldn't he fall in love with you? You're the sweetheart of Devils Hollow."

Dahlia snorted, mischief glinting in her eyes. "You're a bonehead, Vile. Just because I crushed on him for a hot minute never meant I danced to wedding bells. He's loved you since second grade, testament by the frog he put down your shirt. Then you left, and that was that. But me and Max?" She shook her head. "Never in a million years, whether or not you were around."

Vi could hardly breathe—one of her nightmares shattered with no more than a few simple words. But even without being in love with Dahlia, the best she could hope to get from Max was an acknowledgment of her apology. And he still deserved the best, a girl who could give him everything he wanted—a future and family in Devils Hollow. That girl absolutely wasn't her.

Hell. Years under the bridge and still her heart hurt.

"You've had a long day and are obviously tired. We have all month to catch up." Dahlia slid out of the booth and stood. "With the tourist season in full swing, every inn, hotel, bed and breakfast, campsite and empty space within fifty miles is booked, including our house. I'm sharing my room with a woman who believes she's possessed by the spirit of Elvis."

"Crap." Being homeless for a month wasn't part of her game plan. She hadn't had time to arrange for accommodations. After Dahlia's letter, she'd left Ruby in charge of Kickin' Ink, thrown necessities into a duffel bag, hopped into her truck and driven until she got to Devils Hollow.

"Worry not, my sister. I've got you covered. You even have options."

"So I won't have to sleep in my truck and sneak into the gym to shower? Good to know."

"I'm not saying they're options you'll like." Dahlia's smile was sweet with a touch of evil. "You might keep the truck stop in your back pocket."

"Splendid. I'm all aflutter with anticipation."

"Option one—you can share the living room at home with a family who identify as orcs."

"Hard pass." Breathing the same air with tourists for a month, no personal space to escape to? She'd go insane and create a new Devils Hollow urban legend. "I'll take option two. Don't even need to hear what it is."

"Excellent. Done, no takebacks. Gramps offered his last spare room." She winked, every ounce of the sweet and innocent act gone, nothing but wicked witch on the rise. "You'll be right across the hall from Max."

Chapter Three

Parked in the field posing as an improvised lot behind Gramps' home, Vi gripped the steering wheel and forced herself to take a few steady breaths. Night had swept in hours ago, bringing a clear sky and enough stars to glimpse the landscape she knew by heart in both daylight and darkness.

Ward House was exactly as she remembered, all grim storybook goodness, a towering, three-story structure meant to hold secrets and shadows. She'd loved it at first sight and had never looked back. The people inside merely confirmed what her heart had recognized that first day.

Brickwork in variegated colors of tan, gray and red covered the exterior, a perfect Gothic complement to the outer banisters, arched windows and pointed gables. The unique porch, roof rounded as if it were a mouth gaping open for visitors to willingly waltz inside, sported just enough moss to give it a fairy-tale edge. The balcony on top had always reminded her of a wicked king's crown. A single birch tree shielded the corner column of windows with bare, clawing branches.

Ward House was the one place from Devils Hollow she'd missed.

Beyond the fake cobwebs fluttering in the fir trees — and Fred the giant spider undoubtedly stuffed somewhere in the depths — Gramps never decorated early. He kept his cards up his sleeve for the haunted house grand finale at the end of the tourist season. Competition with the local historian, Mrs. Beasley, was fierce, the rivalry between them savage.

She couldn't deny a smile. Maybe Gramps had beaten the odds and won once while she'd been gone.

Her smile faded as she slid down from her truck and grabbed her bag and rolling suitcase from the back seat. She faced the house, took another fortifying breath, and marched for the porch. If it was time to suck it up — better to go down with a snarl, not a snivel.

The uneven ground made her suitcase bounce more than roll, and she dragged it along behind her. Without permission, her gaze rose to the last second floor window by the birch tree. A dozen memories she'd kept locked down — mostly — for five years flashed to full, vivid life, sweeping through her like a tidal wave.

More than a few times she'd tossed pinecones at that window in the middle of the night. Max would sneak down, meet her in the dark, and they'd talk in the back field until dawn, about nothing and everything.

The lattice alongside the house, heavy with glistening ivy, made for a perfect ladder when it had been too cold or wet. Max would open the window for her, she'd crawl through and they'd huddle under the blankets, trying hard not to laugh or talk loud enough to wake up Grams and Gramps.

Later, it became just Gramps.

She climbed up the porch steps and slid the spare key Dahlia had given her into the lock. The velvet purple ribbon attached to the decorative bow of the key whispered over her wrist as she slowly opened the door.

Warmth washed over her. A vintage iron lamp brightened the foyer and the stairwell leading upstairs to her room. The grandfather clock beside the stairs ticked into the silent house. It was an hour past midnight. If she were super-lucky, the wonder dog Duke would be dead asleep and everyone would be in bed already, not gathered deeper in the house for a nightcap, palm-reading or horror stories.

In October, more than a few citizens of Devils Hollow opened their homes to tourists and rented every inch of spare room. Historic Ward House with its dark, Gothic charm was booked years in advance, a tourist favorite. With more than a dozen bedrooms and only Gramps and Max living there, some serious cash was made during the season. Filling the big house with voices and life was his joy, no matter how much he groused. She had no idea how he had a vacancy for her last-hour, unexpected visit.

But right now, only quiet filled the corners as she carefully pulled her suitcase over the threshold, shut the door behind her and shouldered her bag. Thank God. Everyone must have hit the sack.

Vi turned from the door and jumped to find a man near the stairs, his sexy lean too familiar, his nearness perturbing all the butterflies in her stomach. She gripped the strap of her bag to prevent the instinct to either punch him or leap into his arms.

"Max." She huffed out a breath and arched an eyebrow, playing it cool. *Calm down, heart.* "Trying to scare me?"

"Did it work?" His smirk didn't help.

"Depends on the perspective. I didn't break your nose, so it's a total fail on my part."

"Aw, same ol' Vi, all bite and no bark."

"I've learned to bark." She sniffed. "I just prefer to hit only dirtbags who deserve it."

"Good to know I'm not in the dirtbag category...yet." His smile widened, and before she could move, he snatched her bag from her shoulder. The trail of heat left by his fingertips sank through her T-shirt, imprinting her skin. "As the assigned concierge of Gramps' Group Home for Halloween Enthusiasts, I'm expected to show late-arrival guests to their rooms."

She scowled. "Dahlia called you, didn't she?"

"Maybe." He shrugged, his blue eyes glittering, and after a brief struggle, wrangled her suitcase from her death grip. "Either way, it would be my pleasure to assist you with your baggage." He held her gaze and dropped his chin, casting his face in shadows. "And see to your every need while you're here."

The deep, sexy rumble of his voice curled through her blood like molten lava. Before she could fully process his meaning, Max lifted her suitcase and climbed the stairs. Having his fine ass at eye level wasn't helpful to her cause.

The last five years had been good to him. He'd never needed help in the looks department, but the boy he'd been was all man now—broad shoulders, supple roll of muscles as he hefted her suitcase, lean hips...

Stop looking.

Vi forced her gaze to the polished banister beneath her hand. As usual, Gramps stayed true to his reputation and kept up the Gothic charm of the house. From the carved woodwork of the balustrade to the damask wallpaper in black and navy, he made sure the guests got the full-meal-deal when they rented a room that once belonged to the original founder of Devils Hollow.

"Here we are." Max stopped outside the last door at the end of the hall and deposited her luggage. "The key Dahlia gave you works for both the front door and your room. With all the riff-raff—and I mean the usual residents, not the tourists—it's probably best to keep it locked." He winked.

The familiar ebony door with its etched ravens and roses was refreshing water to her tired brain. "You're giving me the Raven Room?" A thrill fluttered through her. "It's *always* booked for October."

"Must be serendipity. Steamy dreams, sweeting." His crooked smile appeared as tucked his hands into his jeans' pockets and turned away. "Enjoy the honey-heavy dew of slumber."

She blinked, and he was already gone, down the stairs…quoting Shakespeare. The man obviously plotted something. Tomorrow, she'd figure out what that might be. Tonight, she didn't have the extra brain cells to manage it.

Vi flicked on the light switch, dragged her suitcase and bag inside, and nearly swooned into a puddle of goo. She'd always loved the Raven Room, but Gramps had invested some serious time and thought revamping the décor. It was everything a Gothic-loving girl could want in a bedroom.

A crystal chandelier hung from the ceiling, scattering soft reflections like water in moonlight. Wallpaper of ravens and skeletal trees scratching for the sky made it seem like she'd stepped into an endless woodland in winter. A Victorian chair in dark wood and blood-red velvet rested crookedly by the window, completed by a throw pillow embroidered with a flock of ravens rising on shadowy wings.

She turned toward the window as she closed the door. A mural of leaves in various shades of red and a sign reading 'Welcome, Foolish Mortals' hung beside a mirror circled in decorative iron, all whorls and wings. Even the small desk in the corner oozed with detail, ebonized inlay, raven emblem on the drawer, and topped in silver-veined marble.

And the bed…

Good God. The bed. She sighed and leaned back against the door, a bit woozy. Its obsidian wood frame, four-posters rising like twisted horns in the air, and elegant canopy at the ceiling, made her want to sink into the mattress and fall into eternal sleep until true love's vampiric kiss awakened her. Sable silk flowed almost to the floor and Victorian-style pillows with red tassels and damask lined in a neat row at the headboard.

As if in a trance, she wandered deeper into the room. Vintage sconces hung on each side of the bed, adding soft, intimate light to the chandelier. One pillow leaned forward from the rest, set in a position to be noticed. It read 'I, myself, am strange and unusual'.

Vi couldn't hold back a smile. It was as if this room had been created for her, as if Gramps had known all along that she'd be back, needing this room.

She snorted softly and ran her hand lightly over the smooth comforter. Of course, he'd known. Dahlia had probably phoned him the moment she'd agreed to return to Devils Hollow, figuring she'd never want to stay in a tourist commune. Not that she could complain. Even the rose-scented candles set in a clawed, iron candelabrum called to her.

Home.

The unexpected thought shook her. Devils Hollow had never been her home. She'd created a life for herself at Kickin' Ink, a niche where she could be herself. She'd never belonged in Devils Hollow, even in October when other unabashed freaks flocked to town, and she didn't stick out quite so much.

But to be fair, she'd always felt centered at Gramps' house...with Max.

Not going there. With Max sleeping right across the hall, a door and a few steps away, she couldn't let her thoughts stray to what it might be like to knock on his door and talk until dawn like they used to, once upon a happier time.

The mere memory of curling up beneath the covers with him shot heat through her veins. She closed and locked the door. Needing to cool off, she slipped out of her T-shirt and jeans and dug her pajamas from her suitcase. Dawn would slap her sooner than she wanted, and tomorrow would bring enough trouble of its own. She needed rest to face the battles coming her way.

Red cami and black-cat sleep shorts on, she settled her notebook and colored pencils on the desk and pinned the checklist she'd made while on her way to Devils Hollow below the autumn leaf mural. Helping Dahlia in any way she required was Priority Number One, but she refused to waste the opportunity by not adding a few ulterior motives and goals of her own. Vi drew up one knee and ran down her list.

Make up with Dahlia and make a vow to never lose touch again.

Apologize to Mom.

Attempt to make peace with Dad — at least try.

Hug Gramps and tell him how much he impacted me growing up.

Convince Max to forgive me.

Face my fear of the lake, rational or not.
Leave Devils Hollow with no regrets.

She crossed off the goals pertaining to her parents with a red pencil. Since Mom and Dad were out of town indefinitely, those would have to be added to another list down the road. The other objectives would be hard enough to achieve. Earning back the trust necessary to make them possible in a single month wouldn't be a cakewalk, maybe wasn't even achievable. But she'd give it everything she had.

Next to her list, she lined up a calendar for October and pinned it carefully to the wall. A slash of her red pencil, and October first was marked as dead. *One day down. Thirty more to go.* The ominous graveyard picture on the calendar, of headstones and mist, seemed grimly appropriate.

Vi opened the window to let in the autumn breeze and paused. Across the field, beyond the woods, the water of Lake Forsaken glistened through gaps between the trees, moonlight dancing on its dark surface.

Face my fear of the lake, rational or not.

Goosebumps prickled on her arms. Ward House was the one place in Devils Hollow she'd always felt safe, accepted and seen. Being so close to the lake was the only element that ever lessened the sense of safety. She'd done her best to ignore its presence, had avoided going near whenever possible, but being away from it for five years, she'd forgotten the impact of its gravity. Lake Forsaken pulled at her like a black hole, drawing her back to its wasted banks and dark waters.

Closing her eyes, Vi took a deep breath. Since departing Devils Hollow, her nightmares had faded. The bad luck that kept her in a chokehold had fallen away like shackles freed. She'd made a vow to face all her demons, to try her damnedest to mend what bridges she could…and conquer her greatest terror.

Lake Forsaken.

She lifted her chin in defiance and stared at the glints of moonlight and water. *I shall not fear.* Tomorrow morning before heading to the café for the breakfast rush then representing Keller's Killer Café at the Hallowtoberfest business meeting at seven, she'd go down to those barren banks. She'd do whatever she had to in order to slay the demon that still whispered in her ear, claiming something more than water lurked beneath the surface. Then, when she split from Devils Hollow in the wee morning hours on November first, she could leave the lake behind, too.

Chapter Four

Max gave up trying to sleep and shoved his fleece blanket back. He gazed up at the shadowed ceiling, unable to shake off thoughts of Vi in the room across the hall. Knowing she'd returned to Devils Hollow, that he'd cross paths with her, had been enough of a torment. Having her beneath the same roof for an entire month, only steps away, might be more than he could take.

Gramps was keeping secrets. Somehow, he'd known that she'd be back. Why else would he reserve the Raven Room during tourist season? It hadn't been surprising that Gramps redecorated the room. It was always the first to be reserved, and keeping it updated made sense. The Devils Hollow founder, Godric Ward himself, had slept between those same walls. In the last year, some guests swore that, during the darkest hours of night, they woke up to his mutterings and heavy footsteps in the hallway, a distraught father searching for his missing daughter.

He doubted Vi cared about those details. She'd always just loved the ravens...and the resident owl that haunted the woods and lake. Might be worth some brainstorming with Gramps to create another themed room surrounding owls and superstition. *Would probably be a hit with the tourists.*

He sat up and scrubbed his scratchy jaw as if he could itch away thoughts of Vi. Earlier, at the café, he'd felt in control. His scheme for revenge had been solid, an anchor to keep his emotions in check. How many times had they shared that same space at the bottom of the stairs, laughing, horsing around, making plans? No manner of preparation prevented how easily she unbalanced him. To his heart, it seemed as if she'd never left. But his brain knew better, keeping careful track of the days since she'd abandoned him with no goodbye, no 'Dear Max' letter, not even a deuced handshake. Nothing but a boy's broken heart.

He hitched up his black pajama pants, strode to the window and opened it. Cool air brushed the bare skin of his chest, and he leaned against the windowsill, closing his eyes. As much as he wanted Vi to regret leaving him behind so easily, he couldn't pretend having her close didn't remind him of everything he'd wanted before she'd gutted him and left him to bleed out on the side of the road, drop by slow drop.

What a disaster. Flirting with her had only reawakened emotions he didn't want to revisit, emotions he'd thought he had under wraps. *I need a drink.*

Sliding his feet into the fuzzy sheep slippers Gramps had given him for Christmas and tossing on a shirt, Max carefully opened his bedroom door to keep it from squeaking and paused in surprise. Vi silently closed the door to Raven Room and turned. Her eyes went wide, and she jumped, her hand on her heart.

He'd always loved how he could startle the cutest badass he knew without barely trying, but that wasn't why his mouth went dry. *Burning hell.* Vi was midnight-snack gorgeous. In only a red camisole with thin straps and black shorts showcasing her toned legs and colorful tattoos, she made his deepest fantasies stand up straight. *Oh, wait.* That was a different appendage paying her homage. Casually, he clasped his hands over his groin and leaned against the doorframe.

"Don't tell me that on your first day back you're planning to sneak a shot of Gramps' apple-cider whiskey," he whispered, shaking his head as if disappointed in her morals. "Pathetic, Vi."

"Maybe." Her smile was brilliant in the shadows and set his pulse to unsteady. "I'm legal now, so the excitement factor has faded somewhat."

"There's always the risk of Gramps catching you. Duke's gone deaf and mostly blind, limiting his already-sketchy watchdog skills—unless it's the refrigerator opening, of course. But Gramps still sleeps with his shotgun."

"Challenge accepted." She rubbed her hands together, and her eyes sparkled with mischief, so much like the Vi he knew and loved all his life that his chest squeezed. Joining her was a no brainer.

Her bare feet and his slippers made only the faintest hush on the carpeted stairs. The faint, familiar scent of roses drifted from Vi. Her choice of perfume hadn't changed, unlike the designs inked on her skin. The camisole exposed her upper back and left the blood-red roses with black thorns twisting in vines across her shoulder blades clear to admire.

Her father would hate the artwork on her body. It wasn't a surprise that she'd chosen to stay at Ward

House instead of the home where she grew up. Even with her parents gone, she might not want to relive all the tumultuous memories. Not that he blamed her for that. While Dahlia had always been the perfect daughter, adored and accepted, Vi had butted heads with her father...hard.

He followed her through the shadows and moonlight to the liquor cabinet in the study. Neither one of them turned on a light, the routine practiced and unforgotten. Without a word, he took two shot glasses from the sidebar decorated with cobwebs and preserved spiders pinned to cards. Silently, he set them on the counter.

"Nice slippers," she whispered.

"Don't be hatin' on my wardrobe choices."

"Not at all. I'm going to steal those later." She smirked secretively, as if the perfect plan to do it had already come to mind and there was no stopping her.

"Paws off my slippers. But paw me anywhere else, and we'll see what happens." Burning hell, he was pathetic. The mere arching of her eyebrow got him all hot and bothered. He jerked his chin at the locked liquor cabinet. "You do the honors. If we're caught, you'll get in less trouble than I will."

She glanced at the elegant sign in black calligraphy affixed to the cabinet that read 'All Trespassers of Liquor Will be Shot'. "Wimp."

"I'll hunker down behind you if Gramps shows up. You'll scare him off." He grinned. "I believe in you, even if you haven't kept practiced up with your skills for five years."

She crossed her arms and cocked a hip. "I'll be happy to give you a demonstration of exactly how well I've stayed in practice...after my whiskey."

Fire coiled low in his gut as she knelt and stuck her hand beneath the liquor cabinet, searching for the key Gramps always hid there. Her shorts stretched over the curves of her delectable hips and ass. There were a few different skills he wouldn't mind demonstrating with her now and later. They could practice until every step together was nothing short of a perfect rhythm in nature.

Waxing poetic after a few measly minutes with her. *Pull yourself together, man.*

"Ta-da." Vi lifted the key in triumph and brushed off the real spiderwebs clinging to its edge. "I'm shocked you haven't put in a security system on this puppy to keep Gramps out of jail, considering all the strangers always coming to Ward House."

"Both old and new." He couldn't keep the snarf from his voice.

"You have something to say, Max?" She gazed up at him from where she still knelt, a new challenge lighting her eyes. "I'll listen."

Then you'll run. He almost said it aloud, but if he wasn't careful, she'd bolt from Devils Hollow tomorrow and never return. No matter how she'd hurt him, he wasn't ready for that, not yet. He had revenge to exact. Nothing more, nothing less.

"Just sayin' you haven't been around for a while." He shrugged and took the key from her. "People change."

"Yeah, they do." Holding his gaze, she stood, ballerina graceful. "I'm definitely not the same stupid girl from five years ago."

He couldn't argue with that. Vi had left as a teenager, a person who knew who she was, what she wanted and was done trying to fit into someone else's box. The future she dreamed of wasn't in Devils Hollow — or with him, obviously.

She'd returned as the woman he always knew she'd be — confident and colorful, sexy and sassy, every part of her a work of art from her full, pouty lips to her brown eyes always touched of sadness. It wouldn't have mattered if she'd gained twice her weight, grew a hump on her back and walked with a limp. She'd still be the girl of his fantasies.

"You're lucky. I'm basically the same stupid boy, except that I'm only on the field to guest coach the high school team." He unlocked the cabinet and grabbed the jug of Gramps' special apple-cider whiskey. "Broke my wrist in a motorcycle accident and poof. My baseball career ended before it began."

"Damn," Vi whispered. She watched him pour the whiskey, and he pretended she wasn't examining his wrist for scars, ignored the sympathy in her voice. "Sorry. I didn't know. That...sucks. Big time."

"It does." He handed her a glass. Their fingertips touched, and heat zipped through his nerves. "But I wouldn't be able to be with Gramps now, and I found a new career as backup innkeeper and 'Max of All Trades' at Ward House. My laundry and landscaping skills rock. Gotta look at the rainbow, not the storm, right?" He put the whiskey bottle back in the cabinet before slamming his shot of cider. The liquor left a pleasant burn down his throat, all the way to his belly.

"Oh, I don't know. I always kind of liked the storms." She propped her ass against the sideboard and took a delicate sip of her whiskey. "Remember when we used to watch the lightning storms from the hayloft?"

As if he could ever forget Vi sitting close enough that their thighs touched, the hay soft and scratchy beneath them, the barn cat snuggled in her lap. She'd watch breathlessly for each strike of summer lightning, her eyes blazing with excitement.

He hadn't cared about the storm outside, every sense attuned instead to the girl beside him. He'd count the seconds with her between lightning and the follow-up boom of thunder, simply because she did. He'd wait for her wide, wild smile when the rumble hit less than a heartbeat after the lightning, the sign that they were in the midst of the storm. She'd always be a little disappointed when Devils Hollow remained standing afterward, that the lightning hadn't at least left a few smoking holes, blackened as a warning.

Stop reminiscing, idiot. Remind her why she should regret leaving.

Max pivoted and leaned on the table next to her, close enough that their arms brushed. "I remember everything." He lowered his voice to a soft rumble and eased nearer to her ear, taking wicked pleasure in her shiver. "How the electricity would make the hair on your neck stand up straight. How you'd jump every time the thunder rolled, even though you expected it. How you'd use it as an excuse to grab my very muscled, incredibly sexy biceps."

She snorted and took another sip of her whiskey. "You wish."

"Oh, sweeting." He gently hooked a stray tendril of hair behind her ear, the barest touch on her skin, and she went still. "You have no idea all the things I've wished for these last five years."

Vi anchored her focus on the amber whiskey gleaming in her glass. Her slender throat worked, and she turned her head slightly his way, as if reluctantly pulled by invisible strings. Slowly, her eyelashes lifted, and her gaze found his, dark and deep in the gloom. Her lips parted, as if she couldn't decide whether to respond with words or a kiss.

Words weren't what he wanted right now, no matter how stupid the choice or any later regret. He'd dreamed of tasting those lips again, to determine if they were as soft and sweet as he remembered, to exorcise the memory from his soul. Max refused to move, his pulse drumming faster as she lifted her chin. Her mouth hovered less than an inch from his, and her breath brushed his chin, warm and velvet.

Do it, Vi. Kiss me. Show me you haven't forgotten what we had.

The squeak of footsteps on the stairs erupted in the quiet. For one long moment, Max held Vi's wide-eyed stare. In complete sync, they both dove behind the thick, floor-length curtain draping the narrow window, old habits and instinct kicking into high gear.

Somehow, Vi didn't spill her whiskey. Shot glass tight in her grip, she pressed against his side, needing every inch of available space to stay hidden. He wasn't a teenager anymore and took up more room than he used to. The windowpane bit cold through the fabric of his thin T-shirt as he pushed back as far as he could and held his breath. Moonlight spilled in through the window, illuminating the mischief in Vi's lovely grin and painting her tattoos with soft color.

More than once during their rebellious teen years, Gramps had heard them break into his liquor cabinet. He never looked behind the curtain, the most likely hiding spot for trespassers and thieves of his prize homemade apple-cider whiskey. The danger of being caught had always been worth the thrill of hiding with Vi, co-conspirators in a small-town heist. It had always been them, scheming to escape the rest of the world.

It seemed as if time rewound, and she'd never left. Every sense twanged on high alert. Her full breasts flattened against his ribcage, his arm around her shoulder holding her, tight and protective. The silken brush of her hair on his skin shot straight to his gut.

Soft, feminine laughter echoed beyond the curtain, followed by the wet smack of kisses and a low, throaty moan. Vi bit her lip, holding in a snicker. Whoever had ventured into the study hours after midnight definitely wasn't Gramps.

The scrape of items being shoved off the table followed a gasp and the rustle of clothing.

"Burning hell," he mouthed, unsure what to do. Two guests were getting it on mere feet away, having no idea they had an audience. Gramps would be ticked if he knew they violated his antique sideboard.

"Scandalous," she mouthed back, her dark eyes dancing.

And just like that, the slurps and groans beyond the curtain faded into nothingness, every sense focused instead on the woman molded so perfectly against him, soft curves against his growing hardness and heat. Holding her gaze, he slid a hand from her shoulder to her spine and tugged her even closer.

Vi had to either straddle his leg or expose their hiding place. She planted a palm on his chest for balance. Her thighs pressed on each side of his, a warm, welcome trap. Shivers tripped up his back as her breath fanned his shoulder. He inhaled her faint, floral scent. Raw desire flooded his entire body, yearning a corrosive need barely contained.

Despite the chilled glass against his back, the air had become very warm, the whiskey hot in his blood. Vi's pulse caused the thin strap of her camisole to vibrate ever so slightly, but she didn't struggle to escape or withdraw. When her lips parted, the promise of an invitation, it was all he could do not to surrender all dignity and attack like a starved beast.

A steady beat rose from beyond the curtain, a stifled mewl of pleasure, a soft grunt barely registered in the haze of lust surrounding Max. He ached in time with the lovers beyond sight in the study. This was his particular version of hell, Vi caging him, nothing to do but resist every instinct or risk exposure. If she had any idea of how close he was to reminding her of their last night together, bringing one of his vengeance fantasies to life and taking her against the windowpane until she begged for forgiveness, panted for more, she'd probably rip the curtains aside and storm back to wherever she'd been the last five years.

As if reading his thoughts and intent on torturing him, she lowered her hand down his chest, somewhere between a careless brush and a caress. Her fingertips made a delicious trail along his abs and ribcage, leaving a ribbon of fire on his skin. She stopped at his hip, a light touch anchoring them together. Her heavy-lidded gaze held his, a dare or plea, he wasn't quite sure. The rise and fall of her breasts against his side betrayed her quickening breaths.

The moment expanded, stretched, twisting into timelessness. Max waited for her next move, both fascinated and unnerved at how easily she stepped through his defenses and made him want to forget how she'd hurt him, forgive so they could pick up where they'd left off.

As the beat beyond the curtain grew stronger, faster, headed toward climax, Vi averted her gaze, her eyelashes dark against her pale skin. She bit her lip, and he nearly groaned along with the unseen paramours. If she would only hook her hand around his neck and pull him down to her, touch him or press her lips to his skin, give the merest hint that she wanted him the way he wanted her…

Something heavy fell to the rug in the study with a muted thud, followed by strangled laughter. The rustle of hastily replaced clothing preceded retreating footsteps.

Vi blinked, and the bubble surrounding them burst back into reality. Time began ticking again, the midnight charm broken.

"Thanks for the nightcap." Faster than he could follow, she slipped free of his hold and ducked out of the curtain, gone before he could reach for her and pull her back into his arms where she belonged.

Max thunked his head back against the glass, his vision somewhat blurred. His skin and bones burned as if a furnace erupted in his blood, hot and roaring, an unfulfilled desire only Vi could satisfy. *I'm an imbecile.* Instead of driving her mad with need and regret, he only tortured himself.

He straightened and blew out a long, ragged breath. Clearly, he sucked at vengeance. When it came to Vi, he was helpless to help himself. He pushed the curtain aside. Decorations littered the floor and an antique lamp lay askew on the rug, evidence of the romp they'd involuntarily witnessed. He crouched and began rearranging Gramps' decorations. At least someone had gotten lucky. He had a feeling that only a miracle would get him what he wanted.

Violet. God help him. He wanted Vi, in his arms, his life, his forever. And since he wouldn't be sleeping any time soon, he had hours to figure out a new game plan to win her over...for good.

Chapter Five

By the time dawn hit, Max had launched his canoe and finished his morning rowing session of five laps across Lake Forsaken. Some people considered it to be more of a pond, but it was deep in the middle and wide enough to offer a workout, either swimming or paddling. He stopped in the center of the lake, wiped the sweat from his eyes, and lifted his face to the rising sun.

This was always his favorite time of day, when quiet spilled across the water and through the trees. A few birds chirped from the surrounding branches, distant, nothing but echoes from another world. For this fleeting second, he could pretend no worries darkened his doorstep, that Gramps would be fine for another dozen years, not—

He closed his eyes long enough to shake the thought away. A breeze whispered along his heated neck, carrying the scent of leaves, moisture and decay. A dragonfly skittered over the water's surface, a bright dancer on dark glass, and he traced its progress toward the barren line of charred soil circling the lake. Nothing had ever grown on the banks of the tiny lake, confirmed by Beasley's historical archives, another layer to the urban legend that all the tourists loved to contemplate.

The dragonfly flitted over the shoreline, headed for the trees…and the blonde woman curled up with a sketching pad a safe distance from the water.

Sunlight glowed golden in Vi's thick hair piled into a messy bun. She wore a black hoodie, plaid pajama pants and slip-on boots, as if she'd jumped out of bed and thrown on whatever was closest in time to make it to the lake before sunrise. By the way she furiously scribbled, oblivious to anything but her drawing, that was probably exactly what she'd done.

Finding her near the water was a shock. She'd avoided the lake ever since coming oh-so-close to drowning a couple years before leaving Devils Hollow, when it all began to roll down to hell on a hairball. The nightmares had started afterward, and her already-volatile relationship with her father had deteriorated to unbearable. Max had spent uncountable nights with her in the field beyond Ward House, talking through dreams and fears, watching the stars with her until morning.

He couldn't deny the need to observe her openly from afar. Even a hundred yards away, every line of her face was familiar, scarred on his heart, etched on his brain. Good Lord, she was adorable, small and furious behind her sketchpad. She still chewed her bottom lip when she concentrated. Five years ago, he would have paid in organs to be the one nibbling her lip instead. Now, he'd up the ante with a sliver of his soul, no hesitation.

Keeping his movements smooth and silent, he slipped his oar into the water and glided slowly in her direction. She faced the lake at an angle and hadn't noticed him. He wasn't even sure she *would* notice him, focused as she was on her art. Sneaking up on her wasn't all that hard.

Max had made it to within a dozen feet of the shoreline before Vi glanced up from her work. She blinked and rubbed her eyes, as if she didn't trust her senses and questioned if he were truly there.

She lowered her sketchbook as he banked his canoe and stepped onto shore, his water shoes squelching. "Are you stalking me?"

"Of course."

"Did you bring coffee?" Her tone, so hopeful, almost brought a smile.

"Not even a question." He set his paddle down and lifted his travel cup. "Enough for me, anyway."

Her expression serious, Vi lithely rose and crossed the distance between them. She stopped just short of bumping toes. Her nearness kicked his pulse into full speed. It took every ounce of self-control not to brush her bangs from her eyes, tilt her chin up and kiss her like he'd wanted to last night.

She used his momentary distraction to swipe the cup from his grip. Giving him a dare-you stare, she took a swig. His pilfered cup held tight, she stalked back to her sketchbook and settled onto the ground.

"Rude." Max spread his empty hands, denying the urge to laugh. It was such a typical Violet thing to do that he shouldn't have been surprised. "Stealing the right of first sip from my miserly grasp."

Vi took another long drag from his cup and sighed. "Heavenly. Since when do you like cinnamon in your coffee?"

Since you introduced me to it. "'Tis the season." He shrugged and sauntered to her chosen spot in the space between two lacy ferns on the pine-needle strewn ground a few inches from the barren soil circling the lake. "Are you drawing the sunrise or the lake?"

She flipped the pages over, tucked the sketchpad against her chest and held it close. "None of your business."

"No need to be so cagey...or embarrassed. I'm completely fine with you drawing me in all my glory, slicing through the water like some island god heading into battle to defeat my fierce enemies and rescue my queen from the erupting volcano."

"No self-respecting queen would wait around to be rescued." She quirked an eyebrow. "And for an island god, you're sorely lacking tribal tattoos."

He lifted his chin. "I have a tattoo."

"Really?" Her eyes brightened. "Where?" Her gaze drifted over his T-shirt and sweats, clearly curious, but he wasn't about to reveal his secrets, especially this particular one.

"None of your business." He smirked.

When she smirked back at him, his throat went dry. There she was, the Vi he'd fallen in love with decades ago. He steeled himself, shook off the memory. If she'd ever loved him at all, as a friend or in any other capacity, how could she have left the way she did, a complete cutoff from the person she'd claimed to connect with on the deepest level? Forgiving that was hard, forgetting even harder.

All humor faded from Vi's expression, as if she read his mind and hated his thoughts. She settled her sketchpad on her lap. "Max," she said in the smallest voice he'd ever heard from her. "I —"

She cocked her head, clearly listening. The sudden intensity, the way she sat motionless and silent like prey sensing a predator, sent a chill down his back. Max eased closer to her, the need to protect her a living, breathing need, even if he couldn't see or hear the danger.

Something wild flashed in her eyes, and she whispered, "Do you hear that?"

Max focused on his surroundings, attune to anything out of the ordinary. The birds had gone quiet. Only the breeze hushed through foliage and water lapping the shore. Except…

He faced the lake and gazed across its darkly glinting surface. Nothing moved on the far shore or in the immediate tree line, but the barest hint of a murmur drifted from that direction, as if someone beyond sight chanted a prayer.

Or a curse.

He nodded slowly, searching in the shadows between tree trunks for any sign of people. "I hear it. Pushy tourists. We gave the guests staying at Ward House explicit instructions not to go to the lake unless accompanied by me. No one ever believes the 'No Trespassing' signs apply to them."

"Those signs just represent a challenge to the determined. You know that." Still facing the lake, Vi rose and inched closer to him, her sketchbook clutched like a shield. She trembled slightly, as if her hoodie no longer kept out the autumn morning chill. "Rules are meant to be broken, especially in October."

"Maybe, but if they're idiot enough not to listen and drown while searching for contact with restless spirits, wicked sprites or lingering demons, at least Gramps is somewhat protected from frivolous lawsuits."

"Right." Vi released a quick breath and gathered her art supplies. "Gotta go. I have to check in with my crew at home, make sure no one has set anything on fire or stabbed anyone in the day I've been gone. Either one is likely. And Dahlia's expecting me in half an hour. I'm not going to be late and miss out on her Evil Booberry Muffins hot from the oven — or make Beasley's day by being late to the instructional Hallowtoberfest meeting at seven."

Pride curled in Max's chest, bright and warm. Of course, she ran her own tattoo parlor, had found success outside of Devils Hollow. She'd always been driven, even when some of the people closest to her did their best to hold her down. He knew why she'd always loved storms. They reminded her that strength sometimes arrived in a whisper before rising to a thunderous shout to shake the sky.

"Yeah, I have work to do, too." He stuffed his hands into his pockets. He wasn't ready to tell her that his responsibilities at Ward House had quadrupled…or why. The majority of grocery shopping, laundry, cleaning, repairs and landscaping were all on him. He left the cooking and guest entertainment to Gramps, when he had the energy for it. "Important work. Might not be done until midnight."

"Awesome." Avoiding his gaze, she collected the last of her colored pencils from the leaf-strewn ground and shoved them into her hoodie pocket. She took off at a speed-walk along the worn path toward Ward House and didn't look back.

Max watched her go until the trees swallowed her tiny frame, then turned again toward the lake. The surface shone like glass in the early morning light, a dark mirror leading to a world of tormented spirits and murders without justice. The supernatural had never bothered him. Growing up in Devils Hollow, you either believed or pretended to believe. Even though he'd never experienced the same things others claimed to, the idea that *something* else existed beyond the physical realm, beyond the detection of dull, human senses was more a comfort to him than fear or folly.

Vi had never wanted anything to do with any of it, especially after her near-death experience. She believed and wished she didn't, but she'd never let it slow her down. She kept a pocketful of salt handy, and he'd spotted the iron ring she'd worn since forever. Any spirit that threatened her would get its ass royally kicked.

But something in the woods or water had shaken the bravest woman he knew, given her another reason to run. Whoever lurked around the lake wasn't going to scare her off. He'd make sure of it, even if it required casting a curse of his own. If anyone—or anything— was going to torment Violet Keller, they'd have to get in line behind him.

Chapter Six

Since downtown Devils Hollow was less than a mile from Ward House, Vi opted to walk to the morning meeting for Hallowtoberfest volunteers. During October, Main Street was closed off to vehicles, giving the crowds of pedestrians safe passages to all the best local merchants. She'd made it to the café in time to nab a warm Evil Booberry muffin from Dahlia and strolled the last few blocks to the community hall, where she'd discover all the insufferable deeds she had to perform to get back into her sister's good graces.

The wind carried a chill, and she tightened her scarf and tucked her free hand into the pocket of her wool peacoat—black scarf, black coat, black jeans, black boots, her hair up in a wild bun. She'd dressed the part for the meeting, the hometown girl who never really belonged to Devils Hollow, the theory irreversibly confirmed when she'd left.

Gold and orange leaves scattered the cobblestone sidewalk, blown in from the ancient maples and oaks bordering the town and suburbs. Dry as old bones, they cracked and snapped beneath her boot heels. The architecture of Devils Hollow reflected the age it had been built, all bladed angles, decorative bargeboards and iron lampposts. While beautiful, the small town had a sharp edge beneath the details, like teeth hidden behind a closed smile.

Not much had changed in her time away. No new buildings joined the old, and the only improvements were repairs to keep an original wall standing or a roof intact. If a business wasn't on Main Street, it might as well shut down. Five stoplights, ten straight blocks and the citizens had no desire to expand. Families born in Devils Hollow didn't leave, and they did their best to keep outsiders at a safe distance. They wouldn't want the world to discover the fake behind their smiles, the grabby hands spread open in hearty welcome for one exclusive month every year.

Hallowtoberfest, when ghosts, ghouls and anything in between were gobbled up and spit out on November first—as long as they brought cash to burn. It was the single event that kept Devils Hollow afloat for the rest of the year.

Vi paused outside the door leading to the community hall. Spiderwebs, both real and fake, decorated the doorframe. Several husks of doomed insects dangled in their midst. A skeleton in a suit and tie leaned against the wall, its arms crossed, as if waiting for a ride. The band of his fedora matched the peacock blue of his tie. Vi snorted. *Beasley House colors. Figures.*

Widow Beasley and Gramps had squared off as fierce competitors in every Halloween haunted house contest for as long as she could remember. While

Gramps had the advantage of the ancestral Ward House, Widow Beasley was the local historian and had no life other than her delightful herd of cats. She spent the entirety of the year scheming and planning for this month and beating Gramps...always. She took her duties as Hallowtoberfest Coordinator very seriously. Just as seriously, Gramps had always referred to her by last name only, like a curse word. *Beasley.*

The Keeper of Devils Hollow dirty secrets had never forgiven Vi for sneaking into her poison garden and planting plastic delphiniums the night before her morning garden tour. Beasley had made it quite clear that when it came to the Keller family, other than Dahlia, contempt was all she felt.

This is going to be perfectly fun. She squared her shoulders and opened the door.

Faces, all familiar if five years older, turned her way as she slipped inside, obviously not subtly enough. The chatter slowly died until she alone became the focal point of the entire room. Even though she suspected everyone had heard she was back the moment she'd called Dahlia — small-town gossip spread faster than a volcano exploding — expressions ranged from raised eyebrows to narrowed eyes.

Vi bared her teeth in greeting. "I'm here for the free coffee."

"You're one minute late." From the front of the crowded room, Beasley lifted her pert nose higher and shifted the stack of papers in her arms. "All volunteers are expected to be timely and cooperative. If we don't all pull our weight, Hallowtoberfest will fail." Her black-dyed beehive bounced with each marching step on her four-inch stilettos to Vi. She shoved a thick, stapled manual into her free hand.

Vi nearly dropped it, catching a handful of pages just in time. The manual was heavier than an old school textbook.

"That is your only copy." Towering over her, Beasley adjusted her wire-rim glasses — fifty-something and still wielding the fierce librarian vibe from decades of practice. "For this month, it's more important than your Bible. I suggest you study up on both."

"I'm hosting Bible study at Ward House on Tuesday." Vi added a bite to her tone. "I hope you'll be there, Mrs. Beasley. I'm making devil's food cookies for the séance afterward."

Beasley's smile turned poisonous, and her dark eyes glittered, cold and dangerous. "Suggestion number two — read the manual before making any commitments. Free time for volunteers is limited, and there are times when even God's work must take a back seat for a spell."

Oxymoron. The word had never fit another person so perfectly.

"As I was saying before interrupted," Beasley continued, locking the door to the community hall to keep any stray, early rising tourists out of Devils Hollow's secret business, "the manual, as always, contains the schedule of events, the responsibilities each of you have agreed to and every rule and regulation to keep the festival running smoothly." She spun on Vi. "Miss Keller, if you would kindly take a seat? You're making me nervous, standing behind me like a gargoyle waiting to pounce."

"Anything to make you feel better about yourself." Vi scanned the full room for an empty chair and found one near the back row. *One.* Next to Max, who grinned like a demon making the best crossroads deal ever. He patted the waiting seat. This day got better by the minute.

Refusing to look at him, she strolled through the aisle as Beasley continued yapping. She plopped into the hard, plastic seat, set the manual on her lap and broke off a warm piece of muffin. If she was going to suffer, she might as well eat.

Max leaned in. "I know you wouldn't be so cruel as to devour that in front of me. I haven't had breakfast yet, and I saved a seat for you. Give me some sugar. I'm starving."

Somehow managing not to roll her eyes, she handed him the bite she'd been about to take. "That's all you're getting."

He popped it into his mouth and smiled. For a second, she couldn't look away. A delicious tremor spiraled down her back, as if they were again behind the curtain in Gramps' study, their bodies pressed together, Max's hand gliding over her too-sensitive skin.

"This is orientation, not a discussion." Beasley paused and gave them both an evil eye, killing any spark of heat. "It's important for everyone to pay attention, no distractions. If you have questions, you may ask them after I'm through speaking."

"Of course, Mrs. Beasley." Max used his honeyed voice, the one that charmed every kid and old lady from Texas to Toronto. "My apologies."

"Thank you, Mr. Carter." A flush invaded Beasley's cheeks. She smoothed her gray cashmere cardigan and continued with instructions and protocol.

Vi barely managed not to snicker. It took considerable effort not to whisper a snarky comment. It seemed at least *one* thing had changed since she'd been gone. While Beasley looked prim-and-proper fantastic and ageless as always—she claimed yoga kept her young—apparently, she'd noticed that Max had grown up. It also seemed the fine widow wondered if that man might just be the catnip she and her feline horde had been waiting for since her husband had died years ago.

Not that she could disagree. The boy she'd known most of her life, the boy who'd been her best friend and first everything, had become the man she'd always suspected he would be. His scrawny frame had filled out with lean muscle. The peach fuzz that he used to call facial hair had thickened into a sexy scruff. He held an air of confidence that suggested he knew what he wanted from life and wasn't afraid to go get it.

Max shifted slightly, and his knee brushed hers. That single, innocent touch, even separated by two layers of jeans, shot tingles along her thighs.

She pressed her legs together, partly to avoid further contact, partly to tamp down on her body's ridiculous response. If she couldn't figure out how to control her own instincts, living under the same roof with him for the month would be beyond torture. She'd survive, but there might be nothing left of her already-shredded heart.

"And that brings me to the team assignments." From the front of the room, Beasley flipped over a whiteboard. "I hand-selected team leaders. Partner assignments were made through the usual, technical method—names randomly drawn from a witch's hat."

A few people chuckled while Vi resisted crushing the remains of her muffin in her fist. Dahlia hadn't mentioned partners and teams. She worked better alone...always. Even at her tattoo parlor, she managed the business end while keeping a comfortable distance from her employees, even Ruby and Emma. She usually created designs in the solitude of her studio, popping in occasionally during tattoo sessions to assure the others she was still alive and kicking.

She'd promised herself she'd be nice this month—at least as nice as a snarky introvert out of her element could be. But handling Hallowtoberfest duties with someone who'd be watching her every move would push her right over the edge into snarling mode.

"The activity schedule and each team's responsibilities are listed here, as well. I suggest you take a picture of it to keep in your phone for future reference." Beasley smiled. Vi almost shielded her eyes from its brilliance, every perfect tooth whitened to glaring. The effect would be perfect with fangs. "If you have questions or concerns, consult your team leaders. As coordinator and leader of my own team, I'll be far too busy to field anything more than major issues. It is imperative to follow the chain of command."

Vi remained in her seat as the other volunteers gathered around the whiteboard, chattering with excitement. Unfortunately, Max stayed put, too.

"Randomly selected, my ass." His arms folded, he bumped her shoulder with his. "How much do you want to bet I got teamed up with Dean Walker?"

"Tough times." Dean ran the mortuary, and it was rumored he enjoyed his job a bit more than appropriate, not that she believed all rumors. "But I doubt it. You'll be on Beasley's team, guaranteed. I saw the way she looked at you."

His eyebrows bunched. "What do you mean?"

"Hubba hubba." She let her wicked smile slide free. "You're into cats, aren't you?"

He gasped in mock outrage and lowered his voice to a conspiratorial hush. "How dare you imply that

Widow Beasley is anything but impartial? I understand I'm irresistible in every way, but our beloved coordinator is beyond reproach, no matter what Gramps says. Take it back."

"Not until I'm proven right." She handed him the last of her crumbled muffin. "Take this as a consolation prize. You're going to need the sustenance." She winked.

"Sick, Vi." He shook his head but didn't pass up the muffin remains. "Can't say I haven't missed it."

Warmth bloomed in her chest as she stood, needing space between them. He just had to add that final bit, didn't he? His open friendliness was too suspicious, had to be a ploy to test her for weak points. When it came to Max, those weaknesses were everywhere. There was no way he had just forgiven and forgotten. She left him and the muffin behind, headed for the whiteboard.

Most partners and teams had figured out where they belonged and gathered in knots, leaving the board with the list of names and duties relatively clear. Vi stopped in front of it and scanned for her name.

A wall of heat rolled over her back a heartbeat before Max's particular, outdoor cologne curled around her. His breath tickled the shell of her ear. "Whadd'ya know?" He reached over her shoulder and pointed at the very bottom of the whiteboard. "We're partners on Team Orange."

Vi barely avoided groaning aloud. Obviously, the universe was out to get revenge for all her misdeeds, to balance the scales, her bad luck returning with a kick to the head. What were the odds of not only being on the same team as Max, but partnered up with him? The selection *had* to be random. Beasley would never put them together on purpose. She knew they'd been tight, conducted more than a few Devils Hollow shenanigans while growing up. Keeping them apart would be in the best interests of the well-oiled Hallowtoberfest machine.

With her team gathered around her like adoring Frankensteins, Beasley met Vi's gaze. Her mouth twitched, as if fighting off a smirk — which wouldn't be proper at all for the local Mistress of Manners to showcase in a room full of her inferiors.

Or maybe Beasley knew exactly what she'd been doing. Partnering her with Max would mean eventually dredging up the past, dealing with the pain she'd inflicted. And Widow Beasley would be the shoulder waiting for Max to bump, cry on or wrap his strong arms around to hold on tight.

Boo-frickin'-hoo.

"This is going to be epic, sweeting." Max's low, honeyed voice brought her back to the more pressing problem at hand, and when he looped his arm through hers and pulled her against his side, she almost tripped, nowhere to go but into his solid, sexy form. "Spending every day together conducting our obligations as dutiful volunteers, then spending every evening under the same roof. There are only a few other things I can think of that would be more fun."

Those words, said in that low, bedroom tone, sparked more than a dozen scenarios to life. All of them included Max, various body parts, and minimal clothes.

"Suck it, Max."

He chuckled. "Careful what you wish for."

Vi ignored the heat invading her cheeks as best she could and growled to throw him off. Maybe she wasn't any better than Beasley, fantasizing over the man right in her face and yet completely out of reach.

Thirty days left. I can handle this.

"Let's go canoodle with the rest of Team Orange and get ready for tonight." He towed her relentlessly toward a group gathered loosely by the door.

"What's tonight?" She'd been too distracted to check the daily activity list or the duties she's stupidly signed up for. Earning forgiveness was a bitch. Avoiding the festivities in her years at Devils Hollow by working at the café hadn't prepared her at all.

"The graveyard ghost walk, of course." Max winked. "I expect the most sinister and notorious ancestors of Devils Hollow to show, maybe even Miss Abigail Ward herself. It'll be a hoot."

Abigail Ward was the most notorious of the town's ancestral lineage. Daughter of the founding father, history claimed she cursed her own sister and took her own life, tethering their spirits to the mortal coil, doomed to haunt Devils Hollow for eternity — all over a boy, of course. Tourists slavered over the tragic, unrequited love story gone to the dark, supernatural side with blood and a whole lot of hate. Team Abigail T-shirts sold out every year.

"Awesome. Can't wait." If only her sarcasm had the power to kill the sudden shiver clawing down her back.

Chapter Seven

"You totally tricked me." Vi tossed her scarf at the line of coat hooks beside the back door of the café. When it missed and slithered to the floor, she didn't bother picking it up, too busy glaring at Dahlia. "I want to trade. I'll handle the café, and you can attend all the Hallowtoberfest activities. You love that stuff."

Dahlia set down the platter of food balanced in her hand, threw her head back and laughed, so much like a cackle that Vi paused. Her sweet, innocent sister rarely revealed her tiniest of wicked sides, and never in public. That she did it now? *Beyond suspicious.* Dahlia had known exactly what she was doing when she guilt-tripped Vi into taking the Hallowtoberfest duties. She'd be lucky to have any free time to swipe a snack, let alone check in on Kickin' Ink.

Folding her arms, Vi waited for her sister's shoulders to stop shaking and watched, straight-faced, as Dahlia dried tears of laughter from her eyes.

"Payback's a wicked witch, isn't it, Vile?"

"I can still change my mind, jump into my truck and ditch Devils Hollow for good."

"And break your sacred vow?" Humor shimmered in Dahlia's dark eyes. "You wouldn't."

No, I wouldn't. Not after sucking it up to come home and face her failures, see what she could fix. But at the moment, it was tempting. "Might be worth being cursed."

"You're already cursed, remember?" Dahlia picked up the platter again. She slung an arm around Vi's shoulders and pulled her deeper into the kitchen. "And you'll never break it if you slink away again."

"I didn't slink," Vi grumbled. "I snuck. It's far more dignified."

Enough bacon to feed an army sizzled on the stove, filling the air with deliciousness. Dustin, the café cook since forever, stood watch with his spatula in one hand, the other kneading a giant lump of dough. He glanced over his meaty shoulder, grunted and returned to his work. Still grumpy, one of the reasons Vi got along so well with him, even if he hadn't quite forgiven her for ditching the family.

"You're making Bat Eggs in a Basket sandwiches for tonight's special, aren't you?" Vi didn't bother hiding the accusation in her voice. "Knowing full well I won't be here when they're done because I have to help with the stupid graveyard summoning ceremony."

The end of Dustin's sinister black mustache twitched up on one side, the only confirmation she'd ever get.

"You're both evil. I've tried recreating the recipe for the Kickin' girls and never got it right." Dahlia's culinary café masterpieces were to die for, one of the things she'd missed most while gone. Eggs-in-a-hole sandwiches using bat cookie-cutters, adding bacon and four different cheeses, and including the local dairy's famous handmade brie were perfect for the tourist season. They'd be demolished by the time she got back...guaranteed.

"Dammit." She resisted stomping her foot.

"I'll save you one, whiner." Dahlia released her and kept going toward the swinging door leading to the dining area. "Sit outside with me on my one-minute break. It's slow right now. An entire table is free."

"But I have to go—"

"Be back in a sec." Dahlia winked and sailed away, disappearing out of the door.

"Nothing has changed, has it? Nobody ever tells her 'no', do they?" She didn't bother waiting for Dustin to respond. He'd knock down cities in Dahlia's honor, and she didn't need the answer. If she'd slowed enough to say goodbye to her sister five years ago, she never would have made it out of Devils Hollow, wouldn't be the woman she was today. And everyone else who'd be impacted by her staying?

Scary thought.

Vi grabbed her scarf from the floor and returned to the chilled October air. She plopped onto an upturned plastic crate and wished she'd nabbed a coffee. But she was already peopled out, and dealing with Dustin's accusing looks wasn't worth the effort, even for the caffeine powerup.

A second later, the door opened, and Dahlia joined her, her ski jacket covering her café T-shirt and a paper coffee cup in hand. She perched on a second crate, handed Vi the coffee and swiped her bangs from her eyes. "So how do you feel about being partnered with Max?"

Vi paused, the cup halfway lifted to her mouth. Even with years apart, she recognized the trickery in her sister's tone. "You dirty dog. You bribed Beasley to put us together, didn't you?"

"If I tried to bribe the esteemed Widow Beasley, we'd be kicked out of the festivities and blacklisted… ruined. I'd never give her that satisfaction."

"You're not answering the question, D." A sip of her coffee didn't help her dry throat. "Why do I get the impression that you're setting me up to be bombed by Max? Are you two working together to sabotage me?"

"Who…me?" Dahlia laid a hand on her heart and batted her eyelashes. The innocence proclamation wasn't even remotely believable. "Why would I do that to my favorite sister, only recently returned from her five-year bout of silence?"

Vi snorted. "*Only* sister. And vengeance, obviously."

"My darling Vile." Dahlia reached across and squeezed Vi's hand. "I love you, even when you're a turd."

"Thanks. Appreciate it."

"I only want what's best for you, and I believe I can see that far more clearly than you can."

"So you want Max to destroy me." She made it a statement, not a question. It all started to make sense, Max's easygoing attitude instead of the expected anger — Dahlia's residence arrangements, her demand that Vi handle the festivities rather than help out at the café. They were in cahoots against her, setting her up for…what? An epic plan to get even? A way to take her down when she least suspected it? Convince her to let her guard down, only to be cut to ribbons?

Dahlia had the nerve to laugh. She released Vi's hand and stood. "I want you to be happy, sister mine. And if that takes wading through the wreckage of what's left of you and Max to find your happy ending? Yeah. Prepare to be destroyed. But, Vi?"

Vi could only gaze up at this sister who had a hidden scheming side she couldn't help but admire, even if it would be better aimed at someone else.

"When you get back up and dust yourself off, don't leave without finding me." Her grin was sly. "I'll be waiting with an 'I told you so'."

* * * *

"Aren't you thrilled the graveyard ghost walk got moved to the historic cemetery closest to the lake? Someone with icy cash wanted the real deal, so here we go into the deepest part of the forbidden forest." Max swung his lantern and managed not to laugh at Vi's answering scowl in the dim glow, shadowed by the hood halfway shoved back from her face. She was adorable, dressed in all black as if she intended to melt into the night at the first sign of trouble. "Don't worry, sweeting. The woods make a buffer between us and the most haunted places, but if anything comes lurching, groaning or demanding brains, I'll protect you."

"Lies." She eyed him up and down, one eyebrow raised, and ducked a low-hanging branch invading the narrow path leading to the original plots of Devils Hollow's graveyard. "You'd trip me and leave me behind as a noble sacrifice."

"Probably." He let his grin slide free. With Vi here, beside him, ribbing him as if they were still best friends, flirting with the idea of more, he couldn't help himself.

"You're tastier than I am, like dessert before the main dish."

"Nah, my flesh is stringy, no flavor."

"No, it's not." Not a lie or a guess. He remembered every detail of their time together, from the sweet taste of her skin to the bruising way she gripped his shoulders, holding on as if he alone tethered her to the ground.

She averted her gaze to the staggered line of cowled tourists ahead of them, an end to the subject and the memories that went with it.

Max tightened his hold on the metal lantern handle. Were the memories imprinted on her mind, heart and soul like they were on his? For so long, he'd wondered, believed she'd sacrificed what they had together for her ambitions and freedom, that he wasn't enough for her to stay. Now, with her back in Devils Hollow, full in his face, he only knew for certain that she held on to some serious secrets.

And he wanted to discover every single one.

He had to hand it to Dahlia, using her charm and popularity to finagle his status as Vi's partner this month. She'd convinced him so easily it was embarrassing, that she was on board with him teaching Vi a lesson, to make her regret leaving them behind to face an uncertain future without her.

He was beginning to have a sneaking suspicion that maybe he'd seriously underestimated both Keller women.

"Think you can handle herding nerds to the cemetery without any going rogue and making a run for it to the lake?" Vi kept her voice below normal speaking volume, not quite a whisper, but low enough that said nerds following their team leader ahead couldn't hear. Playing rear guard had its benefits.

The majority of Devils Hollow residents might find their reliance on tourists annoying, but they weren't stupid. Keeping the masses happy in October was necessary to survival. But there were a handful of places that remained off limits to even the deepest pockets, and there had been too many unexplained incidents at Lake Forsaken to give tourists free rein of its barren shores. Dead bodies didn't always make for great tourist attractions.

"Nothing to worry about in this crowd. They're all sheep. See the guy with the green-dyed beard?" He waited for her to spot the dude's hair glowing neon beneath a solar lamp as the path curved through a stand of white-barked birches. "He meticulously filled out the entire waiver, sanitized the pen and replaced it in the holder. And the pixie with red braids? She hasn't strayed from her gaggle of witchy friends, all of whom screeched when the wind made the shutters bang open in the community hall. Lambs to the slaughter, every single one."

Vi's smile took on a mischievous edge. "Gotta love easy victims."

"You know it."

"So who bought the extra-special ride to the Ward family graves?"

He shrugged. "Beasley didn't say."

The path opened up into the historic section of the Devils Hollow graveyard. Moonlight glittered on crooked granite crosses and crumbling headstones, cold and lifeless as the founders and their descendants buried in the soil. Solar lights glowing in shades of blue, purple, and green scattered at the edges of the rusted iron fence. Bare-limbed trees leaned in on all sides, protective and listening for rumors to silence.

As the team leader unlatched the bent gate and antique hinges groaned, an owl glided from a branch, ghost-pale. The girl with the braids shrieked, clinging to her chittering, imitation Wednesday-Addams girlfriends. One of them waved her EMF meter wildly, as if it was a weapon, not a prop for detecting magnetic fields.

Max watched the bird until it blended into the trees once more. As much as he loathed the October invasion, he loved the season, witnessing others high on the chills and thrills of the mere possibility of brushing eyebrows with the supernatural. There was an extra energy when the veil between worlds was at its thinnest, at least in Devils Hollow. The air itself seemed to hold its breath, expecting *something* to happen, and the closer to the lake, the deeper and fiercer the sense became, like thorns forming beneath the skin.

"I hate Halloween," Vi muttered, joining him in following the tourists through the gate. She skirted an angel statue veined with moss and missing its nose. "What is wrong with people that they have nothing more productive to do than come here and hope some dark spirit swallows their souls? Do you know how many starving orphans could be fed with the money they toss down the deep well of Devils Hollow greed? And why would anyone with half a brain sacrifice perfectly good cookies to wicked sprites and think their wishes were heard when those cookies are gone in the morning? Don't they realize the squirrels are their only appreciative but completely powerless gods?"

"Hey, don't blame the squirrels. Those ceremonial cookies are tasty. And have you ever been bitten by a squirrel?" He stuck out his front teeth, curled his upper lip and chittered like a chipmunk. "Not utterly powerless, I promise."

Vi stared at him for a moment, her eyebrows lifted. "Impressive, on so many levels." Damn, he'd missed her dry humor. "The squirrels are a lot smarter than the majority of the people who come here. It's why the forest always goes quiet when danger stalks the shadows."

"Well, when you say it like *that*..." He nudged her with an elbow. "Don't be such a hard ass, Vi. Give them a break. They're poor, desperate humans searching for something more in a mundane world that has lost most of its magic. You can't blame them for trying to find that spark, even if they're misguided."

"What they find might not be what they're looking for," she muttered darkly.

"And there's nothing wrong with us banking on people who choose to spend their cash on the frivolous. We might as well be the ones to take their money and give them something to remember."

If the residents of Devils Hollow who owned businesses didn't rake in the dough during October, the rest of the community suffered. Last year, numbers had been down. The rental income from Ward House had felt the pinch. They couldn't risk having a lean year. Gramps didn't need the extra stress. If he wanted his final days to be filled with nothing but his favorite things, Max would make it happen.

A stab of sorrow made his chest ache, and he waited for it to fade. Death came for them all, eventually. The best he could do was make Gramps comfortable, happy and cater to his every whim until the end.

Vi snorted, regaining his full attention. "Speaking of something to remember..." She ducked behind a headstone and crouched, motioning for him to join her — which he did, no question. He'd go anywhere she asked him to, anytime, anyway. "What do you say to a replay of paranormal investigators gone wild?"

The glitter in her eyes, the familiar smirk that hinted at mischief and mayhem to come lit up every need inside him like firecrackers. This woman, even though missing from his life for five long years, still managed to take him back to when the future was wide open and true love was only a kiss away, if he dared.

His gaze drifted to her full, lush mouth. The memory of his lips tangled with hers hadn't faded in the least. He wasn't that same boy anymore, awkward and unsure, pretending as best he could that he knew what he was doing to impress the girl he'd loved at first sight.

Her smile faded at the corners, and Vi absently scratched her knee. Her short fingernail rasped on her black jeans, like a nervous cricket unable to keep a rhythm. The others conversing in solemn whispers drifted from farther in the graveyard. The scent of moisture, decaying leaves and mossy stone blended with her rose perfume.

This. The word curled through him, sure and solid, settling deep. *This is what I need to fully breathe.* Moments with her trailing into forever. No matter what they might be doing, he wanted to be doing it with Violet.

Only Violet.

Yes, they had issues to clear up, hurts to mend, but Gramps' pragmatic reaction to his recent diagnosis had reminded him that life was far too short to allow the past to barricade happiness. Growing up, he'd held back with Vi, hid his emotions — an awkward, insecure boy completely out of his element with the feisty, broken girl who made his life right. He'd waited too long to make a move, to let her know what she meant to him.

He'd like to believe he was somewhat wiser now. Repeating the same mistake, playing it cool while he burned alive for her wouldn't be happening. Satisfaction for vengeance could be worked out along the way. It was the perfect plan.

"I have a better idea," he whispered. He planted one palm on the cold stone and leaned in, close enough that her breath warmed his jaw. "Let's ditch, slip away while everyone's distracted by the bones of Devils Hollow forefathers and wondering which spirit might make an appearance to scare them shitless."

He didn't miss the slight part of her lips, the quick, barely-there inhale, the flickering depths of her dark eyes. All good signs in his favor. No matter how cool and collected she pretended to be, he affected her, a tool he'd use to the full extent.

"The meadow behind Gramps' house isn't far. With a moon like this?" He glanced up at the crescent glowing softly among the stars. "Imagine how magical it would be, tangled in the grass, me moaning your name, you gasping mine, drenched in dew and silver. We can pretend it's a dream, a secret to keep between us in the morning. No one needs to know, if that's what you want. We'll be back before anyone notices."

Vi hesitated, and at that pause, his heart stuttered, his breath caught. She'd thought about him, too, remembered the hours beneath the stars, hours before she left without a goodbye. Their time together hadn't been a moment easily forgotten for her, either, unimportant, lost in youth and broken dreams.

It was everything he needed to know.

Say yes, sweeting. If Beasley discovered they'd slipped away, he'd concoct a rational explanation. If Vi gave him the chance, he'd show her—in slow, sensual detail—every reason why they belonged together.

Her midnight eyes gleamed with a feral light, as if the moon and cemetery called her to commit dark acts to slake her thirst. Her heavy-lidded gaze drifted down his face, lingered on his lips, lowered to his throat, as if fascinated by the rapid beat of his pulse.

Blood thrummed in his veins, hot and fast, and his entire body tensed in anticipation. It took every ounce of effort not to drop his lamp, push his hands into her hair and kiss her the way he'd wanted to since she left Devils Hollow, to feel the slide of her skin against his again, her mouth greedy on his, her fingers pressed into his back, words of need and love gasped in his ear. Burning hell, he needed that again. He needed *her*.

Her gaze lifted again to his lips, and she eased closer.

Max held completely still, waiting. The darkness held them close, hiding whatever the gravestone didn't. Murmured conversation from the others floated from another world, unimportant. Only he and Vi existed in this moment. Any wrong move and the night-spell would be broken. He'd lose her again.

Vi's eyelashes fluttered shut, and she leaned in, a bare inch away, each centimeter erasing the years apart. Max didn't look away, afraid if he blinked, she'd vanish. She tilted her head—

A scream rent the air, followed by breaking glass. In the next second, Vi and any hope of a life-giving kiss were gone.

Again.

Chapter Eight

Vi's pulse raced, incited by Max and his somewhat indecent, very tempting proposal. The tourist's scream kicked that beat into violent, saving her from making another mistake by kissing him.

She jumped from behind the gravestone, all thoughts of pranks and moonlight trysts with Max cut short. Two of the tourists — the girl with red braids and one of her friends — ran by in a blur of dark, flying cloaks as if Satan himself gave chase. Their lanterns trembled wildly in their hands, sketching spidery shapes on the grass, and they were gone, swallowed by the forest.

Vi swung back around to the cemetery. Max stood beside her, his light lifted, peering into the darkness ahead. It seemed she'd missed a lot in the moments she'd hidden with Max, wavering between mischief and life-ruining mayhem.

Lanterns formed a crooked circle at the far edge of the cemetery where the remains of Devils Hollow forefathers rested in eternal peace. Bare-limbed ash trees loomed over them in silent menace, their bark gleaming like bones in the moonlight. Half a mile beyond those branches, out of sight, the murky depths of Lake Forsaken waited.

It didn't take a genius to figure out the particular grave at the center of the lanterns. Abigail Ward was the star of Devils Hollow's darkest urban legend – the girl rumored to have cursed her sister in death, all over the unrequited love of a selfish boy…so the stories said.

But most legends contained a grain of truth, and Vi wasn't about to go near that grave to test those particular waters. The tourists could knock themselves out on that one. Plotting pranks at the edge of the graveyard while the main group performed whatever rituals idiots did to call up phantoms was far preferable to the alternative.

Encountering a spirit once was plenty, thank you very much, whether or not she'd been delusional, oxygen-deprived or reeling from a brush with death at the time. The real-as-life premonition thereafter merely confirmed it, the follow-up nightmares warnings she dared not deny. It could be mere coincidence that those barbed dreams faded when she'd left Devils Hollow, but she didn't believe in coincidences. Their message was loud and clear.

Stay away.

Max jumped over a grave, headed for the tourists. He must have realized she wasn't following because he spun back to her.

"You coming, Vi?"

"Hell to the no." She retreated a step. Escorting the fleeing girls sounded like a smart move. Something had terrified them enough to run, and since people came to

Devils Hollow in October for chills and thrills, copping out early was a blood-red flag.

He was back at her side in a heartbeat, lamp lifted face-level. He furrowed his brow as he studied her.

She answered the question in his eyes before he could ask. "Cemetery, spirits and idiots? The combination is toxic."

"Someone might be in trouble."

"How is that my fault? They're the ones who chose to venture into a graveyard at midnight in the hopes of dancing with demons, even paid money for it. I'm just a volunteer, and I didn't sign any waiver. It's safer to stay here. We're the lowly rear guard, remember? Not in charge."

"Funny, the Violet Keller I remember kicked ass first and asked questions later. She wasn't afraid of anything...besides Lake Forsaken." He cocked his head and arched an eyebrow in challenge. "What changed?"

Sonuvabitch. Why did he have to remind her of the vows she'd made, vows she hadn't told anyone else? *Face my fears.* If she backed out now, she might never find the courage to take that step forward—even if it was pitch-black and energy tingled over her skin like a premonition of wicked things waiting for her in the trees. She clenched her jaw, threw back her hood, and scowled.

"Nothing has changed." She swiped the lamp from where it sat in the grass beside the headstone. "I don't remember reading in our volunteer packet that we're responsible for figuring out who died or got possessed."

His teeth flashed in the gloom, white and sharp. "That's the fun of it. Come on."

She followed his zig-zagging rush through the headstones and twisted crosses, their lanterns casting misshapen shadows on the grass and cracked stone. Her breath came faster than she wanted. Running was her go-to way to de-stress, and a barely-more-than-a jog usually wouldn't be a problem. But her heart slammed against her ribs the closer she got to the circles of lanterns, the tourists — and Abigail Ward's grave.

Max looked over his shoulder a few times, probably making sure she hadn't wimped out and followed the two smarter tourists who'd taken off at the first sign of trouble. Which put her in the idiot category, but she wasn't about to let Max think she was a coward or let him run headfirst into danger. She'd always have his back, even if it meant being scared out of her wits and facing her worst fear.

They reached the circle of lanterns without cracking a shin on a crumbling headstone or tripping and getting impaled by sharp iron crosses rusted with age. Dave, fearless leader of Team Orange, crouched beside the green-bearded man. The remaining tourists hovered around them, some clinging to each other, wide-eyed.

"What happened?" Max shouldered his way through and knelt with Dave.

"I don't even know." Dave clenched his shaking fist on his thigh. "One second, we were setting up to see if we could communicate with any present spirits, and the next, he was on the ground, out cold."

Vi slipped past two tourists for a better look. Greenbeard laid spread-eagled, his head a few inches beneath a stone cross fuzzed with moss, blackened by age and weather. His booted feet centerpunched between twin five-foot iron gargoyles. She sucked in a breath. Greenbeard sprawled on Abigail Ward's grave like a sacrifice.

"His EMT went crazy." A rainbow-haired girl wearing iridescent gossamer wings cleared her throat and continued. "All the lights went on, full blast, then he...flew backward and landed here." Fear gleamed in her eyes. "We were standing over there, by the rose bush."

Vi turned and looked to where she pointed. The rosebush was at least twenty feet away, its crimson blooms gleaming velvet in the lantern light.

"I saw it, too," added a man dressed as a pilgrim, his face stark and pale against his black costume. "He was beside Kari, then it was like something picked him up and tossed him, so fast I would've missed it if I hadn't been right there."

Vi studied their faces, hoping for a sign of trickery, a single hint that someone had set up this elaborate prank and they were all in it together. All she found was surprise, shock and fear.

"Larry." The rainbow-and wings girl threw herself beside Greenbeard — Larry, apparently — and shook his shoulder. She held her lantern in his face. "Wake up!"

Larry's eyelashes fluttered. He opened his eyes and stared into the lantern. The flames writhed in his dark irises. He blinked several times and finally turned his gaze to the fairy girl leaning over him. "Kari?"

As Kari cooed over Larry and Dave helped him sit up, cold shot straight to Vi's bones. She gripped Max's forearm without meaning to. When Larry had snapped out of it, his eyes had been black as oil. Now, they were summer-sky blue. It could have been a trick of the light, a reflection off the fake jewels on Kari's filmy dress, but Vi never dismissed her gut instincts.

Something so isn't right.

"You okay?" Max whispered. He slipped his arm around her shoulders and pulled her close. She couldn't muster up a protest, too grateful for his sturdiness.

Larry suddenly yiped, shrugged free of Dave and Kari, and scrambled to his feet. His hand shaking, he pushed up his sleeve. Fresh blood glistened in the lantern's glow. Two ragged words scrawled over his skin, as if carved by knife-sharp claws.

Free me.

* * * *

The unexplained skin carving was enough to end the graveyard ghost walk. Dave rounded up the ghosthunters and sent them off with another Team Orange volunteer to the van waiting in the cemetery parking lot to return them to their various lodgings. He paused long enough for the last straggler to be out of earshot before turning to Max and Vi.

"It would be smart to take a look around, see if there's any evidence of…hell, I don't even know." Dave ran his fingers through his thinning hair. "In all the years I've been leading this ghost walk, I've never seen anything like that. Just see if you find anything strange. Widow Beasley will want a report, and I'd love to give her some explanation as to why tourists are too scared to pay for tomorrow's walk."

"Sure thing, boss." Max grabbed his lantern from where it hung from one gargoyle's open, snarling maw. "Vi and I are on it. We'll check back in when we're done." He turned to Vi, a challenge in his eyes. The dirtbag. He knew she'd never back down from a dare. "Right?"

Hell to the double no. "If we must."

"Stay together." Dave gave them both a warning look. "This isn't a horror movie, but you know what happens to loners." He took off, taking another slice of light with him, sacrificing more strength to the shadows.

Vi fought to keep her breathing even. *Shit. Shitshitshit.* Volunteers didn't get paid enough to deal with this kind of crap.

"What, exactly, are we looking for?" She held the lantern close to her body to keep the light near. If something slipped through the cemetery gloom, something with enough power to slice someone's arm and throw a hefty man at the very center of Abigail Ward's grave, she didn't want to see it. She'd already had her fair share of nightmares. Living one wasn't on her goals list.

"Voodoo dolls, skeletons, traces of blood... You know, the good stuff."

"You're the worst."

He grinned at her. "I know."

Vi trailed him to Abigail Ward's grave, her boots heavy as concrete. With the exception of the lake, this was the last place she wanted to be, in any graveyard, let alone hovering over the buried bones of Devils Hollow's darling.

"Do you believe the stories?" Max asked quietly, trailing his fingers over the cracked headstone. "That Abigail cursed her sister as she died? That the lake sprung up from her blood and her spirit stalks the woods and water, sometimes in the form of a woman in white, other times an owl?"

"Screw off, Max." She ignored his low chuckle. "Besides, owls represent guidance and protection, not dark spirits in animal form. If you read the right books instead of harassing tattoo artists, maybe you'd know that. Luckily, I'm more of a raven girl."

"The intelligence and cunning of a raven with its survival instincts? Always knew your spirit animal, raven girl." He winked. "I also know that owls are believed to serve as a bridge between the living and the dead, gatekeepers of the underworld. Their task is to protect straying souls."

She narrowed her eyes at him as he frowned again at the faded script on Abigail's headstone. "Since when do you know anything about spiritual symbols and signs? You always made fun of me when I read that stuff."

"Maybe I saw the light." He shrugged, so casual it was suspicious. "It never made sense to me, how you avoided anything supernatural in Devils Hollow but had no problem stuffing your brain with other kinds of spiritual lore."

"Says the guy who embraces all October terrorists but laughs off everything else from numerology to empaths." She snorted. "And God doesn't count as lore. Just ask Gramps. He'll fight you on my behalf."

"Not taking that bait." Max's mouth twitched. "Speaking of Gramps, you're not slithering out of breakfast with him tomorrow at daybreak. Sneaking out before dawn, coming back after everyone is asleep isn't a solution. You can't avoid him forever, and I'm not about to let him be disappointed two days in a row."

"I don't slither or sneak, and I'm not avoiding him." She sniffed, hating the stake twisting in her chest. As much as she couldn't wait to see Gramps again, she wasn't sure if she could bear his thoughts on her disappearance. "I've been seriously busy...obviously."

"Not busy enough to let down an old man more than once."

She released a quick-shot breath. "I'll be there."

"Yes, you will." He swung his lantern gently, scattering shadows from the grass and cracked concrete. "But getting back to the topic at hand, what I failed to realize while you were still living in Devils Hollow, I see clearly now." He didn't look away from Abigail's grave, his voice soft. "You were scared. You wanted answers, whether rational or not. You wanted some sliver of assurance that there was more to life than the present, that a better future waited for you, that you'd find it as long as you kept believing."

Vi went still. *Yes.* She'd been so tired of not belonging, of never living up to the expectations of others, of pretending to be someone she wasn't. She'd been scared that if she stayed in Devils Hollow, she'd surrender her dreams and identity to live unhappily ever after. She'd been terrified of what that future would bring to Max and Dahlia if she'd stayed, terrified to witness her premonition become true.

With the constant nightmares after almost drowning, she knew, down to the bone of her pinkie toe, that if she hadn't fled from Devils Hollow, something terrible would have happened, either to her or someone she loved too dearly to lose. Seeing Max and Dahlia kiss had simply been the heart-wrenching catalyst she needed.

"You know what else I learned about owls?" Max turned from the grave and stepped close enough that the toes of his boots brushed hers. "An appearance indicates that it's time to make an important decision, to stop dithering and move forward, to grasp a new beginning."

Vi's mouth went dry, and any thoughts of spirits and slash marks faded into the background. Max's particular scent of crisp air and autumn leaves held her in his gravity. No hint of humor shone in his blue eyes. A teasing Max was hard enough to resist, but serious Max discussing the symbolism of owls? *Irresistible.*

"A white owl is even more specific," he said, his voice low and husky. His gaze drifted over her face and landed on her mouth. "They're the very symbol of change and transformation. When you see one, you're supposed to make a wish."

"Did you see the white owl tonight?" Maybe she shouldn't have asked, but it felt as if she was right back behind the curtain with him in Gramps' parlor, where nothing and no one else existed besides them.

He nodded, still focused on her prickling mouth.

"What did you wish for?" she whispered, helpless to stop her tongue.

Max eased an inch closer, and it was all she could do not to fist his coat and pull him down to her. Last night, while trapped behind the curtain, the tourists had saved her skin by making a racket, a slap back to reality. Tonight, alone with Max in a private graveyard shown by reservation only, she had no one to rescue her from herself.

"That's a very personal question, sweeting." He brushed her cheek with the back of his hand, and her skin tingled, warming beneath his touch. "The real question is what will you give to know the answer?"

Anything. She swallowed hard. *Nothing.* While they had both changed in the five years apart, the reasons that kept them apart hadn't. Max belonged in Devils

Hollow, tied to Gramps and Ward House, the town he loved. She didn't. And even though nothing bad had happened — yet — whatever force that wanted her gone remained, patiently waiting to strike.

"What are you two doing here?" A bright light shone in her face, and Vi shielded her eyes with her hand. "The cemetery closed five minutes ago."

"Hey, Greg. Didn't know you were on duty tonight." Max pointed to the neon-orange sticker on his jacket. "Team Orange."

"Don't care, Max. We're closed to everyone at midnight on the dot. You know that." The security guard lowered his flashlight, and Vi blinked, adjusting to the sudden darkness. "We don't bend the rules, not even for Old Biddy Beasley."

Vi snickered. She couldn't help it, even when Greg glowered at her.

"Keller." He nodded. "Heard you were back in town."

"Not for long."

"But long enough to join the Team Orange Investigative Team." Max used his snake-charmer voice, smooth and convincing. "We stayed behind to hunt for clues of any shenanigans or foul play from tonight's graveyard walk."

"Foul play?" Greg's frown deepened. "What happened?"

While Max relayed the incident, leaving nothing out, Vi watched Greg. His expression never changed, as if strange happenings in the graveyard weren't out of the ordinary at all — or he didn't believe them, which wouldn't be surprising. Greg had been the graveyard guard since forever. He'd undoubtedly seen and heard a lot of things that she had no desire to experience. How he put up with all the tourists over the years and still had a full head of dark hair, she couldn't fathom.

By the time Max finished the story, Greg had folded his arms over his thick chest. He tapped his thumb in an impatient beat on the flashlight handle. "Hallowtoberfest doesn't change the rules, and being appointed to a team doesn't give you any authority within cemetery grounds to do what you want. This is my territory, kids, and you can tell Widow Beasley to limit her tricks and treats to the streets of Devils Hollow."

"But—"

Max's protest was cut short as Greg tucked his flashlight into his belt, took them each by the arm and guided them firmly and briskly away from Abigail Ward's grave and toward the front gate. "Any investigation will be conducted by Team Graveyard. I'll let you know if I find anything."

"If you do find anything," Vi managed, trotting to keep pace without having her arm yanked out of its socket, "will you tell us instead of Beasley?"

Greg suddenly stopped. He shone the beam of his flashlight in her face again, and she threw up an arm to save her eyes. He grunted and pushed them both past the front gate and into the parking lot. The iron gate slammed shut with a clang and chains rattled as he locked them out.

"I'd better not see you again past visiting hours, no matter what team you're on." He paused, his eyes shining and iridescent like a nocturnal animal's. "And who I tell will depend on what—if anything—I find."

Since she wasn't in any position to argue, Vi nodded and turned away. Max might be grumbling beneath his breath about being kicked out of the graveyard, but she couldn't deny a flood of relief. Let Greg search between crumbled tombstones and grass above old bones for signs of anything supernatural. He seemed better suited to the job and would probably scare even Abigail Ward back to the other side of the veil.

"Oh, and...kids?" At Greg's voice, they both pivoted toward the great iron gate. He stood behind the bars, his flashlight shining beneath his chin and casting his face in sinister shadows. "Before you go home, I'd suggest burning some sage. Grab a protective crystal or two and keep them close. Hang a cross over your bed before going to sleep. You never know what might follow you out."

With that, the flashlight blinked off. As he melted into the gloom, Vi swore something slithered in the shadows, past the gate and back into the heart of the cemetery where worms burrowed in the earth among the bones and decay.

Chapter Nine

The sun was still an hour from rising when Vi gave up trying to sleep through the tourists arguing somewhere outside. No matter how many pillows she'd held over her ears, their voices had filtered through the window, as if on speakers. Every time she'd looked outside, the conversation had stopped. Night had hidden them, but now that morning was here, she'd find them and shut them up.

No one messed with her snooze time and got away with it.

She jerked on yoga pants and a jacket, shoved her feet into her boots. Her favorite scarf wrapped around her throat, she grabbed a flashlight, ready for a fight. If neither caretaker of Ward House was going to do something about it, she would.

Tiptoeing out of her bedroom, she eased the door shut, careful not to make any noise. Annoyance didn't instantly turn her into a compassionless monster who wanted to wake up other people to suffer the same fate.

"Where do you think you're going, sweeting?"

Vi whirled at Max's whisper, her heart jackrabbiting. He stood by his door with a coffee mug in hand, fully dressed in faded jeans, a long-sleeved T-shirt and tennis shoes, his hair damp and smelling of mint shampoo. No matter the time of day or what he wore, that initial sighting always made her stomach flip.

She forced herself to scowl. "How do you keep sneaking up on me so easily?"

"That's an insulting question." He lifted his chin. "I practice my skulking skills regularly. It's my superpower."

Doubtful. If she had to guess, his superpower would be charming anyone in his path. Which was why she couldn't fall under his spell. Someone had to keep him honest.

"You might consider working on more useful skills," she said, pointing her flashlight at him, "such as keeping loud trespassers out. Their stupid argument has been going on since an hour after we got back from the graveyard. Even with my window shut, I could still hear them. Zero sleep for me means victims are inevitable."

All humor fell from his expression. "I didn't hear anything."

"Maybe you should borrow Gramps' hearing aids. I lost every minute of my much-needed life-giving sleep. Now someone has to pay. Dahlia said if I'm grumpy to a single customer or tourist while representing the café, I'll be assigned to Beasley's personal supervision. Trust me when I say no one would survive that." She shouldered past him, swiped the coffee mug from his hand, and swept down the stairs.

"Guests aren't allowed to freely explore the premises, Vi. You know the rules." He followed her, a wall of heat at her back, and she bit back a curse. Being distracted by Max was the last thing she needed after a night of zero shuteye.

"Then I suggest you pretend you didn't see me." Slowing only enough to open the door, she marched outside.

"No can do." Max grabbed his jacket from the coatrack, still on her heels. "I can't leave other innocent guests at the mercy of irascible, sleep-deprived tattoo artists. It would be irresponsible."

"Your choice. If you get hurt, that's on you." Vi rolled her eyes and stomped across the field, her steps infuriatingly quiet on the wet grass. There was nothing worse than dealing with fake-fang-wearing wannabe ghosthunters attempting to make contact with the dead while trying to sleep so she could act halfway normal in the daylight hours.

"So." His hands stuffed inside his jacket pockets, Max strolled next to her, easily matching the furious strides of her much shorter legs. *The jerk.* "What do you plan to do once you find these wicked interlopers?"

"Kill them." She cast him a sidelong look. "Obviously. That's the only sure way to keep them from coming back again tonight."

He shook his head, that sexy dimple coming to life. "Vi, sweeting, your plan is missing one very key point."

She stopped suddenly and gazed forlornly at her flashlight. "You're right. I forgot a knife. Be back in a sec—"

He grabbed her arm before she turned back for the house. "No pointy weapons. If you want to kill them, you'll have to work at it. Get creative."

"Bludgeoning with a flashlight? I can totally handle that."

"Holy hell, you're a terror."

For the first time since she'd returned to Devils Hollow, Vi's smile came naturally, free and without restraint. She allowed Max to guide her into the woods that formed a buffer around the lake. Leaves and pine needles crunched beneath her black boots. The early morning chill snaked through her ebony scarf embroidered with a quote from *The Tell-Tale Heart* in blood-red thread.

"They who dream by day are cognizant of many things which escape those who dream only by night."

It had seemed appropriate, considering she hadn't slept enough to dream last night at all, but now, slipping along a path between ferns glistening with dew, gray, predawn light smudging the sky, an unearthly tingle swept over her. The woods held a surreal quality, more dreamy than real. Mist curled between tree trunks and mossy logs half-hidden by ivy. A poison-green frog hopped from a pale toadstool close to Max's shoe and leaped into a prickly holly bush, out of sight.

With Max beside her, she felt as if she walked inside one of her own uncountable dreams from the last five years, her senses hyperaware of his every detail. His jacket whispered against his over-loved jeans, and a stray branch raked along his shoulder with a hiss of denial when he shoved it aside. Moisture shimmered on his skin and glinted in his dark hair like a crystal crown. He resembled a fey prince returning under the hill with the dawn. And she was the foolish, besotted human woman seduced into going with him wherever he went, even being fully aware of the danger to her heart and soul.

"In case you didn't read the full registration when you rented your room, all guests are required to participate in the downtown business Spooktacular contest tonight." Even his voice bled into her dream, all low and husky, weaving another spell over her. "Gramps won't make the semi-finals without placing in the window display competition, so feel free to terrorize tourists into voting for him."

"No need to ask me twice to frighten innocent people. Does Gramps stand a chance of winning? If I remember right, Beasley beat him out every year."

"This year, he's going to win." Max's throat worked as he gazed into the trees ahead. "He's done so much for me over the years. Helping him win in whatever way possible is the least I can do."

The rasp in his voice reminded her too much of her own when she'd called her mom after she'd ditched Devils Hollow, a goodbye. Vi's chest tightened. Imagining a world without Gramps firing it up...she couldn't. Without Gramps and Grams taking Max in when his alcoholic mother had dumped him on their doorstep at the tender age of five... She didn't want to think about that, either. Gramps and Grams had molded the one man who'd kept her sane, the one man who'd been her first friend, confidant, lover.

The one man who would always own her heart, even if he could never forgive her. Even if they could never be together.

She stuffed the thought down, out of sight beneath other worries that she had some measure of control over. "What are we talking about when you say 'whatever way possible'? Sabotage and schemes? Mischief and mayhem?"

His mouth twitched. "You know it."

"Then count me in."

His smile blinded her, and God help her, she couldn't resist smiling back, a perfectly natural response to the sunshine breaking through winter clouds. Even her soul stretched out and basked in the warmth that was Max.

He rubbed his hands together, looking somewhat evil. "Beasley is really the only competition."

"I remember." Beasley lived with her cat horde in Adams House, a historic monument second only to Ward House, where Caleb Adams once resided. Caleb was the man who broke Abigail's heart, chose her sister Anna instead, and caused the curse, according to local legend. The structure seemed to be crafted purely for Halloween. Pointed gables and decorative iron rods on the windows offered endless opportunities for hanging skeletons, devils, and giant spiders. Beasley was the black, pulsing organ of Halloween in Devils Hollow and had all the town history at her fingertips to back it up.

"This year," Max said, solemn, "Beasley and her cats can suck it."

"Oh yeah. Grandma's going down." Vi brandished her flashlight like a sword. "Team ViMax takes no prisoners."

Max laughed softly and shook his head. "Damn, I've missed you, Vi."

She swallowed the knot suddenly blocking her windpipe. "Ditto."

Without intending to, she slowed among the ferns and pine needles. Max stopped and pivoted her way, his eyebrows up. Instead of sidestepping him, she halted and met his gaze. An emotion flickered in his eyes, there and gone before she could name it, replaced by a quick-fire blaze that scorched her to the marrow, a memory resurrected.

Her heart squeezed at everything she wanted and couldn't have. Maybe she should have kept going, because the only thing she wanted to do was lift on tiptoes, hook her hands around his neck, and pull him down for a kiss that went into forever. Whatever schemes he spun, being sweet and sexy to her when there remained so much unsaid between them, unforgiven and unhealed, she couldn't bring herself to care. She'd take any pain he wanted to inflict, as long as it included a fleeting moment of being in his arms again, pretending they had a future.

The fir trees created a shelter, making it seem as if nothing else existed outside, that she and Max were the only people in a quiet realm of mist and shadow. His dark head tipped forward, so slow and deliberate it could only be a dare. She should step away, stop him while she still had some semblance of dignity and self-control. If only she had the strength.

She moistened her lips, and his gaze fixed there. A delicious shiver rolled down her spine. If he planned to make her life a burning hell of want and need, he succeeded gloriously.

Whispers interrupted the stillness, drifting from afar. Usually, only a bloody murder scream would be enough to distract her from Max's mouth inches away from hers, but goosebumps erupted on her skin and the tiny hairs on her arms prickled in warning. The words were too hushed and distant to decipher, and she couldn't say she was sorry for it. Sibilant, the voice echoed as if rising from a deep, watery well.

Together, they slowly faced the lake.

Chapter Ten

Lake Forsaken's lifeless shoreline made a stark barrier, a warning to anyone wise enough to notice. In the barely-there gray of dawn, the water looked like glass darkened by smoke. No breeze or insect disturbed the surface. But at the very center of the lake, something white floated, big enough to be an animal — or one of the owls that nested in the trees.

Or a child.

Vi absently rubbed the faded silver line around her wrist. Years ago, she had ignored that instinct to resist summer fun with friends in the lake. The scar offered a reminder to always trust her gut, whether it seemed rational or not. Right now, every sense screamed that whatever floated in the water was better left unknown.

"What the hell is that?" Max gripped her arm and tugged her slightly behind him, protective.

"No idea." She pressed closer to him, thankful for his solid strength. "But it looks like a shirt." *Please let there be no body attached.*

"I'm going to see what it is." Max's canoe remained anchored on the shoreline from yesterday morning, and he headed for it. "It'll only take a couple minutes."

"You're not going alone." Vi took several deep breaths as she followed him, every step a clanging bell in her skull. As much as she hated to be near the lake, the need to stay beside Max outweighed the fear. It didn't matter that the lake was closer to the size of a pond or that he'd be in sight the entire time, less than a football field away. She wouldn't — *couldn't* — let him go on the water alone. Something felt off, wrong, and she wouldn't watch safely from the bank, wringing her hands like a damsel in distress while he tackled the danger head-on.

Something had made those whispers, whispers that had now stopped.

He paused at the canoe and looked at her. "You sure? I know how you feel about bodies of water, this one in particular."

"Positive. One hundred percent. Going with." *Breathe.* If she couldn't make it with the crutch of a canoe, crossing off her vow to swim in the dark waters would be even more of a challenge. Wimping out wasn't an option.

You can do this.

"You'll be fine in the canoe," he said, his confidence palpable. "I won't let you fall out. Promise."

"What sort of idiot falls out of a canoe?" It was easier to focus on other people who toppled into the water and survived without supernatural encounters. She climbed into the canoe, carefully settled into the far end, and gripped the edges in a white-knuckled hold. Tumbling out wouldn't be possible.

"It happens." Max pushed the canoe into the water and hopped gracefully in at the last second, so smooth the canoe barely rocked. "Hunters fall in and drown all the time."

"Not helpful, Max."

One side of his mouth twitched. "Your odds are up since you're not hunting."

She glared at him as he slid the oar into the water, nearly soundless. Giving him the evil eye was better than looking down into the smoked glass of the lake, thinking about the depths beneath or whatever floated in the distance.

Or what lurked at the bottom.

The canoe cut through the water like an eel, sleek and quiet. Vi focused on keeping her breaths even as the shoreline drew further away. Once she'd left Devils Hollow, she'd forced herself to take swimming lessons, determined to never again be afraid of drowning. Swimming pools and hot tubs — in daylight — she could handle. Shallow creeks and water parks? Totally fine. Anything deeper or murkier reminded her too much of tangling in the slick milfoil, dragged deeper by cold, invisible hands.

But she'd purposely faced larger bodies of water, even when her steps dragged and her heart threatened to punch out of her chest. She'd swam in everything from water holes with cascading waterfalls to oceans, and each one had earned a petal on her rose tattoo.

Only one remained — one petal, one last lake. The final frontier.

Breathe, idiot.

"I have a specific goal this month," Max said casually, the distraction she desperately needed. "I knew you were wondering."

Focusing on the easy, practiced movements of his arms as he paddled, Vi managed to fill her lungs. He didn't watch her as if she was some sort of freak or frail, desperate girl shackled by fear. Instead, he focused past her, as if teetering on the verge of a breakdown was nothing more than a round of hiccups. She couldn't help but love him more for it. He always knew how to calm her crazy.

"No need to share your weird secrets," she wheezed.

"I'll happily share every single one of my secrets with you, sweeting. All you have to do is ask." The husky rumble of his voice, backed up by his dimple, made her much-needed breath hitch. "But this particular goal is no secret."

A chilled breeze kissed her neck, cooling skin that had risen a few degrees. "Same old Max. You get my hopes up then kill them in the same minute."

He stopped rowing, rested his elbows on his knees and leaned forward, his eyes bright. "I'd never kill your hopes, and if we're talking about getting things up, I think you could help me with that."

She lifted her eyebrows. "Subtle much?"

"I mean getting up the decorations for Gramps' big win, of course." He assumed a scandalized expression, but his mouth was all mischief. "I hate to imagine what sordid images just ran through your demented brain."

"Right." Vi hoped the sudden heat in her face wasn't obvious. He wasn't wrong, and he knew it. The tricky bastard. Her mind had immediately rewound to the night before she'd left Devils Hollow — Max's hands in her hair, his hungry lips on hers, the surge of his muscles as he'd stolen the last fragment of her heart.

No man since had even a chance of comparing to her first and only time with Max. Without her heart involved, the physical act just didn't cut it, a temporary tattoo in black and white that only he could color.

Her chest caved. Even though he made it increasingly clear that he wasn't uninterested in exploring where they'd left off—whether his intentions were sincere or not—the elements that kept them apart hadn't changed. He deserved someone who could make him happy, someone equally invested in his heritage and ties to Devils Hollow...and that wasn't her.

"Here we are." He stopped paddling and the canoe slowed, drifting to a stop near the object floating in the water.

Vi turned her head, careful not to move any other part of her body or rock the canoe. The white material, no larger than a handkerchief, draped the surface of something solid, obscuring whatever the murky water hid.

"Keep your death grip on the sides of the canoe." Max hefted the paddle. "We're gonna rock a bit."

Crap.

"But, Vi?"

"Yeah?" She hated that her voice cracked.

"I make a solemn vow to not let you fall, at least not into the water." He winked. "And I always keep my vows."

Touche. At least drowning was off the agenda, but if falling for him counted, she was already a goner. He didn't even have to try.

Vi forced her eyes to stay open as Max reached over the side of the canoe with the paddle and poked at the material. The water stirred and bubbled, as if some great beast below woke up.

"It's stuck on something. Might just be a tree branch snagged in a piece of cloth."

One could hope. "Left behind by whoever kept me up all night." She tensed as he tossed the paddle aside and leaned farther out over the water, his fingers stretching. The canoe shifted with him. "Be careful."

"Always. Just another inch and —"

The canoe jerked hard. Water spilled in and sloshed Vi's boots as she braced herself and held on for dear life. With a grunt and splash, Max plunged into the lake.

"Max!" Vi nearly lost her balance and followed Max into the water as the canoe righted itself. Sliding off the seat into the bottom of the vessel and her life preserver grip on the sides were all that saved her from the same fate.

Cautiously, she pushed herself upright and inched back onto the seat. The paddle floated in the water between the canoe and the unidentified object Max had been trying to rescue. No sign of Max.

Her pulse took off at a sprint and her legs trembled, her blood going icy. Nothing else broke the surface, and the dark water kept its underworld secrets close. Max was an excellent swimmer, but what if slimy tendrils and dead, clammy hands chained him at the bottom?

Carefully, she leaned over the side and peered into the space he'd disappeared, searching for any sign of him. *Come on, Max.*

A gasp erupted on the other side of the canoe, and she jumped, nearly losing her balance once more. Max bobbed above the surface, his hair plastered to his head and water sluicing down his face. She could suddenly breathe again.

The second after he nimbly climbed back into the canoe, she tackled him. It didn't matter that the canoe wobbled precariously again or that he was drenched and cold. He'd come back from the depths, safe.

Vi wrapped her arms around his neck and pressed her face into his throat. She didn't care that she trembled or that she sprawled on top of him. "Don't do that to me ever again, Max." Her voice broke. "I thought I'd lost you."

For a heartbeat, he went very still, then he clung to her like a lifeline to sanity. "You can never lose me, sweeting," he whispered against her hair. "It's about time you realized that. No matter where you go or what you do, I'll always be waiting for the moment you come back to me. Of course, I wouldn't have to wait at all if you'd do the decent thing and invite me to go with you. Wherever, whenever, I'll always say yes."

Wherever, whenever. She squeezed her eyes shut as her heart seemed to stretch, straining at her ribcage. His skin was moist and chilled against her cheek, and the dank scent of decaying reeds stuck to his shirt. She never wanted to leave the comforting strength of his arms around her, keeping her tucked tight to his pounding pulse. What she wouldn't give to tell him the truth, how she'd been...*less* without him these last five years, that he was the only man she ever wanted yesterday, today and tomorrow.

"Vi." Max slipped his hands over her shoulders to her face and eased her back enough to meet his gaze. "You don't need to hide or pretend with me. I'm on your side." He traced her cheekbone with his thumb, brutally gentle. "Eternally. Nothing you say or do has the power to change that, no matter what fear tells you."

"Why can't you cooperate with my plans and just be a jerk for the next month?" She refused to let her smile wobble. If she let that happen, he'd sense her weakness and she'd be done, completely lost to his magic.

"I never was great at conforming to what anyone else wanted me to be."

"Likewise."

His huff of laughter brushed her mouth, warm. "One of the uncountable reasons why I can't seem to ever get enough of you."

The truth rested on the tip of her tongue, waiting, the apology she'd replayed in her mind a thousand times, the rational explanation for leaving Devils Hollow without saying goodbye, for never calling, writing or visiting. But with him looking at her as if all her flaws were stars, bright and burning endlessly, she couldn't bring herself to say a single word. She had no idea how he could forgive her or why, and she didn't want to ruin it with more hurt.

She eased out of his hold. On hands and knees, she carefully inched back to her side of the canoe. The boat wobbled with each move and water sloshed against its sides, sounding like ethereal laughter. She couldn't deny the sense that the lake taunted her, a message that next time wouldn't be so easy...or lucky.

But as long as Max and Dahlia weren't there at the same time, her premonition couldn't come true. And she'd do everything in her power to keep it that way.

With a sigh, Max lifted himself onto the seat and shook out his wet hair, scattering drops of moisture everywhere. He picked up the object she hadn't noticed earlier sitting by his boot and tossed it to her. "Check out our prize."

Wet, white material—a pillowcase—tangled in her fingers as she caught the bundle and almost dropped it. Slimy tendrils of water weeds made it slippery. The linen ripped, exposing a pale, slender...limb.

"Gah!" Vi dropped it, and it landed with a heavy thud. The pillowcase snagged on the corner of the canoe seat and tore further, revealing an eye, matted hair and the line of a mouth set into a small, permanent smile.

"Gramps is going to perform his happy dance when he sees this." Max picked up the doll and carefully stripped the rest of the pillowcase from its body. Pale porcelain flecked with age and pockmarks marred the slender limbs. The remnants of a dress, its original color indiscernible and faded with time, clung with the slick, green weeds wound around the doll's torso. Max brushed the long, blonde hair from its face. The brown, marble eyes were open and stared back at them, watchful and aware. Ancient.

It was the freakiest doll she'd ever seen.

"I say we toss it back in the lake and pretend we never found it." Vi rubbed her arms. A chill infused the air, but nothing close to the ice tumbling over her skin. How the hell had it floated? Wet stuffing and porcelain would sink. Right?

"And relinquish this treasure?" Max tucked the doll behind his back as if Vi might rip it from him. "I bet it's been buried in the lake for at least a century. It's antique, probably priceless."

"More likely haunted…or cursed."

"All the better."

"No, it's not, Max." How could he be so blasé about the supernatural after the happenings last night at the graveyard? "I bet a tourist threw it in the lake last night to get rid of it and let someone else take on its evil. I can see it now, a witching hour ceremony on the opposite shore, casting the doll into the lake, hoping another victim would find it and assume the curse." She arched an eyebrow at him. "That makes you the victim in this situation."

His eyes sparked with excitement, completely inappropriate for the gravity of the situation. "I thought you said you heard an argument on repeat last night, not a ceremony."

"Maybe the cursed person couldn't bear to part with it and put up a fight. How should I know?" He was definitely not taking the situation as seriously as he should be. Just because he seemed immune to the supernatural didn't mean he couldn't be affected...or hurt. "But it seems too much of a coincidence, don't you think?"

Max pulled the doll from behind his back and frowned at it for a moment before carefully setting it down. "Let's check out the woods, see if we can find any sign of what might have happened last night to make you so grumpy this morning. Gramps makes the final decision on keeping the doll."

A shiver rolled through her, and she had to rein in an urge to lunge past him, grab the doll and throw it across the lake as far as she could. Max would probably dive in after it. "Just humor me, and don't bring it into the house, okay?"

Holding her gaze, he leaned forward and brushed his knuckles over her knee, turning the shiver into a shot of heat. All thoughts of dolls and hauntings, lakes and curses flew away on the morning wind. "Whatever you want, Vi."

Whatever she wanted? She looked away, to the safety of the shoreline and trees beyond. If only that were possible.

Chapter Eleven

After a quick shower to scrub the lake from his skin and hair, Max headed downstairs to the private breakfast nook in the sunroom where tourists were trespassed upon consequences of beating, maiming and potential death. Gramps loved to share Ward House with fellow history and spook enthusiasts, but speaking to him before he'd had his morning sludge coffee spiked with the Ward family secret homemade apple whiskey? Almost as dangerous as Vi without a proper night's sleep.

He slipped through the empty foyer and into the corridor leading to the back of the house. *Vi. Burning hell.* Simply breathing the same air with her lured him into temptation. When she'd thrown herself on him and clung to him as if he mattered to her survival, he'd been utterly undone. Yes, she had some explaining to do, but he wouldn't reject a groveling session that led to more, such as dark, unbreakable vows of forever. Only day three of her return to Devils Hollow, and he crumbled.

Smitten. That was the word for his weakness. Vi smote him, and despite the hurt she'd caused, he couldn't stop wanting to be near her, talking to her, wanting her. Oh, he'd have his pound of flesh, one way or another, but in the end, all he wanted was...

Violet...always.

Laughter drifted from the sunroom, Gramps' deep chuckle, followed by Vi's cute, unrestrained giggle. He paused beside the faded painting of Ward House in its first days, his heart swelling with warmth. Two of his favorite sounds, sounds he thought he'd never hear again together. He closed his eyes and let it weave into his soul, a memory he could hold tight in the harder days to come. He wasn't ready to lose Gramps.

He'd never be ready. When Gramps was gone, all he'd have left was Ward House, promises and memories.

Shaking off the sadness, Max pushed forward and turned the corner. The twin doors were open wide in invitation, the octangular wall of windows and clear ceiling allowing October sunshine to spill in from all angles. Mullions of Gaboon ebony framed the glass and gabled roof, a touch of darkness to balance the light and remind the occupants of the shadows always waiting in Ward House.

Gramps sprawled in his usual spot in the corner rocking chair, dressed in overalls, flannel shirt and rubber boots to keep his thin frame warm. The remaining tufts of his white hair hid beneath his favorite black-and-red handkerchief, and as he lifted his coffee cup to his mouth, steam fogged up his glasses, there and gone. Duke snored softly by his feet on a dog cushion, gray as Gramps and deaf to the world. As much as he wanted to paint the image permanently on his mind, his attention pulled to Vi.

She was curled up in one of the cushioned iron chairs, her elbow on the armrest closest to Gramps, chin on her fist as if ready for another story. Her golden hair was coiled in a tight braid on the top of her head. She'd changed into ripped jeans and a short-sleeved T-shirt. Dawn limned the bright tattoos on her arms in silver.

Vi had always believed she didn't belong in Devils Hollow, that she was more like one of the tourists, a temporary visitor in a place that didn't fit her quite right. But seeing her small smile in the ancient sunroom where city founders once gathered, a vibrant force of rebellion and resolve, she'd never looked more at home. Ward House had suited her years ago. That had never changed.

"Stop lurking in the doorway and staring, boy. You're making me nervous." Gramps raised his bushy eyebrows. "Breakfast waits for no man."

"I see that." Max slipped his hands into his jeans' pockets and strolled over the floor of gray river rock. Two empty plates waited on the small table. The slice of toast on the third had a bite out of it.

"Can't blame an old man for getting hungry again while you took your sweet time getting purdy." Gramps sipped his coffee. "You're lucky Duke already ate."

"Doubt he'd protest second breakfast." Vi shook her head, her eyes shining with amusement. "Look at the belly on that thing. I can't believe he hasn't eaten any guests yet."

"The three teeth he still has makes that a challenge." Max settled into the chair next to Vi and nabbed his plate before Duke woke up. "Not that he doesn't try."

Duke squinted one eye open, groaned and rolled onto his side.

Vi laughed. "Such a vicious beast."

"Of course, he is. I won't settle for some namby-pamby watchdog." Gramps scowled, personally offended on behalf of his pooch and best companion.

"I've seen better watchdogs in the aquarium section of the pet store." Vi slid from her seat and slouched on the floor beside Duke. He stretched out and sighed as she scratched his floppy ears. "But I could see a murderer tripping over him on the way to conducting his dirty deeds."

"A single misstep is all it takes." Gramps pointed a crooked finger and straightened in his chair. "My faithful shotgun will take care of the rest."

"What if he came for your apple pie whiskey or Baleful Blackberry Beastea?" Vi grinned.

"Mark my words." An evil glitter entered his narrowed eyes. "No one would ever find the body."

"And Duke would be eating meat for a month," Max added between a bite of eggs.

"Gross." Vi made a face.

"Justice." Gramps leaned back in his rocker. "No one steals the Ward whiskey or specialty tea blend."

"But many a soul have tried," Max said at the same time as Vi. He caught her gaze and wriggled his eyebrows. Each time after they'd stolen a shot of whiskey, the moment Vi next escaped to Ward House, Gramps had herded them to the sunroom. Each time, he gave the same threats, the same speech.

Burning hell, I'm going to miss this.

"Did you see what little Violet got up to while she's been gone?" Gramps pointed his chin at the vines and blooms twining down Vi's arms. "She turned herself into a walking stained-glass window. I should hang her up in the front room of Ward House. Maybe she'd stay put for a spell, eh?"

Max didn't miss Vi's slight wince at the veiled accusation. *Good.* She may not regret the rest of the innocent bystanders getting blasted by her dust, but at least she felt guilty for abandoning Gramps for five years.

"I like the colors." With a jab of his cane, Gramps indicated the blood-red bloom right beneath her sleeve. "They make your shadows all the deeper."

"Aw, Gramps. That's the nicest thing I've heard in years." Vi flashed her teeth in a saccharine-sweet smile. "Speaking of deep shadows, I hear you're willing to bend rules to take Beasley down this year in the haunted house competition."

"Damn straight." His white eyebrows quivered. "That insufferable, self-righteous witch has reigned as queen of Devils Hollow for too long, and her cats are a menace to the community. If I have to spend the last of my miserable days listening to her gloating in that cackle she calls a voice, I might as well kick the bucket now."

"Settle down." Max managed to keep his tone calm, despite the chill coiling in his gut. "No one's kicking anything before Halloween."

"I might," Vi said, scratching a spot that made Duke's leg twitch. She held up a hand and Gramps gave her a high five.

"Vi and I are on top of it, Gramps. No need to get upset."

"Upset? Who said I'm upset? Determination is a fire in my blood, the steel in my bones." Gramps lifted his cane in the air. "Mark my words—" Gramps choked and one of his coughing spells started.

Max was at his side in an instance, pounding his back. His hacking breaths were like razor blades to his heart. Helpless to do anything, all he could do was watch, hover and hope.

Gramps swiped the handkerchief from his head and covered his mouth with it as great, wracking coughs shook his thin shoulders. Vi rose to a kneel and rested her hands on his knees, worry in her dark eyes. Gramps hated to appear weak, hated asking for help and refused to trade his independence for what may or may not give him a few extra days. He wanted to die in Ward House, the house he'd lived and loved in, and Max would do whatever it took to make that wish come true.

"I've got it." Gramps finally wheezed and took a long swig of coffee. He waved Max away and wiped tears from his eyes. "I'm fine."

"You don't look fine." Vi studied his face, as if noticing for the first time the deep bags beneath his eyes, the gray hue of his skin, the bones too close to the surface of his skin. "Do you need a doctor?"

"I'm old, not an invalid." Gramps snorted and set his handkerchief on the end table. Vi scooted back as he stood with the assistance of his cane. His thin, white hair, freed from the handkerchief, rose in all directions. "And I have things to do. Since you're determined to stay only until the end of the month, I expect you to be present every morning for breakfast." His eyes glittered with fond menace as he pointed at Vi. "No excuses, and if you disappear again, I'll skin your colorful hide."

Without another word, Gramps hobbled out of the sunroom. Duke groaned, scrambled up and waddled after him.

"Fine, my ass," Vi said the second Gramps was out of view. She looked up at Max. "How long has this been happening?"

He'd hoped to put off telling her about Gramps' condition until other troubles had been sorted out, but hiding it now, after she'd seen the evidence? She'd never believe him if he minimized it, and he'd never been any good at lying to her.

Max slumped into the chair and swept a hand down his face. "Doc gave him another year, at best. He's elected not to take treatment, to die naturally instead of prolonging life only to be miserable, filled with chemicals and sick all the time. He wants to die with dignity, and I promised to do everything in my power to make that happen."

Vi turned her gaze out into the garden beyond the glass panels of the sunroom, not before he caught the bright sheen of tears. Her throat worked, and she wrapped her arms around herself, as if suddenly cold.

In a heartbeat, Max was on the floor beside her. Vi was so much like Gramps in that she hated anyone to think she was weak or incapable of handling herself. She resisted revealing her emotions, allowing others to know her on that level, a level that could be used to hurt her. But he wasn't just anyone, and he knew her better than anybody else. Five years apart didn't change that.

He pulled her close, her back to his chest, and folded her in his arms, his legs on either side. She didn't need his protection, but even a badass girl needed a rare moment of comfort, to feel safe and seen. And since she'd never ask, he never offered. He just gave.

Vi melted into him, and when he rested his chin on her shoulder, she leaned her head against his. For a minute, two, they sat in silence, like they used to do after a long discussion of dreams and pain, too drained to speak more. Some of his dreams had changed over the years. The baseball career he'd hoped for was gone, his aspirations to hit the big leagues, never worry about finances or Gramps losing Ward House flushed down the tubes. But his dream to share his life with Vi had never wavered.

"Well." Vi released a heavy sigh. "I guess there's only one thing left to do."

"What's that?"

"Make this the best Hallowtoberfest ever." She turned sideways, her shoulder digging into his chest, and met his gaze. "And cause any mischief and mayhem necessary so Gramps kicks Beasley straight in her bony, uppity ass."

Chapter Twelve

Vi trudged up the front steps to Gramps' place, still reeling from the news that he'd soon be gone. Cancer should be a cuss word. She understood why, at his age, he didn't want to undergo treatment, chose to instead live his final days as comfortable and content as he could in the house he loved, Max by his side until the end.

But it still sucked.

She opened the door and swept inside in a swirl of orange leaves. Excited voices drifted from another room. Hallowtoberfest activities and the café had kept her so busy that she hadn't yet met the other Ward House occupants. She couldn't avoid them forever. Might as well get the introductions over with so she could return to being an introvert.

Vi hung her coat by the door, her off-the-shoulder sweater more than warm enough. Keeping her steps quiet, she crept to the doorway leading to the living room and peered inside. A vampire, a dark fairy and three witches — she shouldn't stereotype what could be a simple propensity to dress in black, black and more black — huddled around the coffee table. Max assumed his sexy lean against the wall and observed from a safe distance, his arms folded across his chest. On the table sat The Doll.

A chill slithered past her wool coat and invaded her skin. Max had promised he wouldn't bring that thing into the house.

As if sensing her presence, Max glanced her way and jerked his head in a come-join-the-fun gesture.

Why the hell not? It wasn't like he'd listened to her advice when she told him to leave the doll outside. Now, if there was a curse attached to the monstrosity, it would find a new victim to cling to. If that happened to be Max or Gramps, she'd have to be the one to protect them. Clearly, they had no survival skills of their own to rely on when it came to the supernatural.

Vi joined Max against the wall and listened in on the conversation happening around the table.

"You've got it all wrong, Victor," the dark fairy said, jabbing a finger at the vampire, his gaze fixed on the doll. "I don't feel any vibrations of a possession. It's something else. Something stronger."

"We should conduct a séance." One witch clapped and bounced, clearly thrilled by her suggestion. Her flouncy lace dress swung around the buckles of her thigh-high leather boots. "Under a waxing gibbous moon. What could be more perfect?"

Vi elbowed Max in the ribs and gave him a purposeful frown. *Hell to the no.* If idiots chose to open doorways to other dimensions, it would be done elsewhere, far from people she cared about.

He elbowed her back and grinned, absolutely no help. Typical. As much as he grumbled about the tourists and the energy the residents of Devils Hollow put into the October festivities, he never stopped hoping to experience the barest hint of paranormal. He'd be over the moon at even an unexplained drop in room temperature but refused to pretend. Nothing ever happened to him. How he wasn't a skeptic, she had no clue.

Another witch shook back her sable curls. "We should consult the stars. Chiron is in play, triggering past wounds and self-perception." She trailed her paisley corset and smoothed her gauzy skirt, as if needing to assure herself that her image remained in proper place. "From what we know of Abigail Ward, these elements may call to her spirit more strongly, especially with Pluto pushing to detox negative emotions. Meditation, reaching her on a psychic plane, may be a more suitable approach."

"There's no need for a séance, examination of the planets or out-of-body connections," the third witch said in a low, honeyed voice.

Vi went still and her face heated. She recognized that sultry tone. Witch number three had been one of the enthusiastic participants near the whiskey cabinet the other night while she'd been hiding behind the curtain with Max, a reluctant eavesdropper. She didn't need to look at him to know he wriggled his eyebrows like mad at her. She didn't need to ease closer to him to feel the temperature of his skin rising. She didn't need to know if he heard her heart beating faster, harder.

The mere memory of his hands on her back, his breath on her throat made her temperature rise. His outdoor autumn scent in her nose made her blood race, too quick.

"I've been researching Lake Forsaken for a decade now and know its tragic history, the secrets that hide beneath its waters." Witch number three lifted her chin, an empress addressing the imbecile peasants. "This is no mere doll. This belonged to Abigail Ward herself."

The rest of the group inhaled and began talking over one another.

Max leaned close to Vi's ear. "The vampire is Victor, of course. Vamps are nothing without a Victorian name."

Vi rolled her eyes. It was better than focusing on the brush of his shoulder against hers, the thrum of his voice against the shell of her ear.

"The fairy's name is Greg, but while in Devils Hollow, he goes by Oberon."

"Seriously?" Vi snorted. King of the fairies. Short and squat, Greg didn't seem to have any royal qualities about him. Even his wings sagged.

Max chuckled softly, barely heard above the others arguing several feet away. "Oh yeah. It gets better. Guess the names of the three witches."

"Winifred, Sarah and Mary?" Even the most serious of tourist witches were *Hocus Pocus* fans. As they should be.

"Excellent guess, but no. Miss corset astrologist is Sabrina. The one in the pointy hat is Raven and the know-it-all queen is…"

"Hecate." Vi couldn't hold back a smile.

"Picked up on my hint, didn't you?"

"You know it." Falling back into a familiar rhythm with Max was so easy, so natural. It had been years since she felt in sync at all with anyone, just one of the many things she'd missed while away—one of the many things she'd leave behind again in November.

"Their collective name is Dimensions. They've been together for three years, traveling to haunted places, investigating rumors and urban legends all over the country. This year, Devils Hollow is the place to be."

"Lucky you."

"Lucky us," he agreed. "Dimensions has a growing online presence, and whatever they post will be excellent advertising for Ward House. Odds are they know more about our random discovery in the lake from this morning than we do—or will at least pretend to." He shrugged as Raven readied the video on her phone. "Either way, Ward House wins."

"I told you not to bring that thing into Gramps' house." Vi lifted on tiptoes to bring her mouth next to his ear. "Don't you know anything about old dolls? They're always cursed, haunted or evil-creepy."

"We're not sacrificing any edge if it might mean a win for Gramps. The moment he saw it, his eyes lit up and he made grabby hands like a kid in a candy store. I wasn't going to deny him."

Vi didn't bother arguing. In the stubborn department, Gramps beat out Max every time.

"Wallflower time is over." His eyes glittering with mischief, Max pushed away from the wall, grabbed her wrist and dragged her toward the arguing group of supernatural seekers. "I don't believe you've yet had the privilege of meeting the last-minute Ward House guest." He snaked an arm firmly around her waist, more a chain than a comfort. "Everyone, this is Violet Keller. Her sister gets away with calling her Vile, but if you value your unbroken noses, it's safer to stick to Vi."

There were few situations more awkward than being stared at by a vampire, fairy and three witches. Wearing a tight smile, Vi wriggled her fingers in a halfhearted greeting and rammed her elbow into Max's side. She may have enjoyed his grunt a bit more than proper.

"Wicked cool tattoos." Her gaze fixed on the roses peeking out from Vi's sweater, Sabrina moved closer, her gauzy skirt swishing around her legs. She reached out, as if to touch the lifelike blooms. Inches away from making contact with Vi's skin, definitely invading her personal space, she paused. Her eyelashes lifted, revealing green eyes, bright with life. "May I?"

Usually, Vi avoided physical contact with strangers. She wasn't a touchy-feely type of girl, even with her closest friends. But the awe in Sabrina's voice, the excitement in her expression reminded her too much of Dahlia admiring another chef's work, dying to taste and discover the masterpiece, layer by layer. How could she refuse?

Vi pushed the scooped neckline of her sweater farther off her shoulder.

"True art," Sabrina whispered, lightly tracing her fingertip along the barbed thorns and delicate petals. "Where did you get these?"

"The best tattoo parlor in the state, Kickin' Ink." Vi couldn't keep the pride from her voice. No matter how many complements she received from both her own tattoos and those of her customers, hearing it never got old.

Sabrina's finger hesitated on the bare spot of the unfinished design, a single petal waiting to be inked. Every petal had been earned, symbols of victory when she'd faced her fear of water and emerged safely on the other side, another step toward freedom. The first rose, fully open, had been after she'd graduated from swimming lessons, surviving the deep end and a few jumps off the high dive. Every bud in between had been after a swim. Each petal in the biggest bloom represented a body of water she'd conquered — river, reservoir, ocean — but the space on her shoulder was reserved for the final chain to be broken.

Lake Forsaken. Only after she plunged into its depths would that emptiness be filled.

Sabrina sighed dreamily. "I've always wanted a tattoo, but never decided what I'd want permanently on my skin." She stepped back and turned toward her friends. "It's like a marriage."

"A bond," Victor said solemnly.

Raven nodded. "A vow."

"A covenant." Apparently, Oberon didn't want to be left out.

"There are so many threads of coincidence gathered here, I'm all atwitter." Hecate remained by the doll. Her black eyes glittered like obsidian in moonlight as she whipped out a leatherbound notebook the size of her palm. Pages crackled as she thumbed through them. With a triumphant chirp, she set the notebook on the table, her finger marking the spot. "Yes, my memory didn't mislead me. Abigail Ward had a porcelain doll, a gift from Anna. When Abigail sought her death, her beloved doll went missing."

Vi exchanged a glance with Max. She didn't believe in coincidences, and the darkness in Hecate's words bled with knowledge. The rest of the gang leaned near the notebook.

"Do any of you remember what she named her doll?" Hecate snapped the book shut.

The others shook their heads, looking as if they'd failed their leader.

"We came to investigate the past of Lake Forsaken and free its lingering spirits. It's imperative to keep a log of every discovery. Even the smallest detail may be of the utmost importance to our case." Hecate gave each of her crew a pointed look. She then set her stare on Vi.

A chill tripped down Vi's spine, as if icy fingertips tapped each vertebra in sequence, playing a tune with her bones.

"Violet," Hecate said with a sharp smile. "The doll's name was Violet."

Chapter Thirteen

Another day gone, another red X on the calendar. Vi set the color pencil down on the desk in her room at Ward House. Technically, she had a few more minutes before October seventh was dead and gone without any tragedies, but since she wouldn't be getting more than a few hours of sleep tonight, she wasn't one to argue deadlines.

Night blackened the sky beyond the window, any sliver of moon hidden by clouds. It was an ideal night for slithering, skulking and shenanigans.

She slipped on her black beanie and carefully tucked her single braid beneath it. In black boots, jeans and jacket, she finished her uniform with an ebony scarf, courtesy of Max. Even with the cloud cover and shadows, pale skin could be easily spotted by anyone vigilantly watching. Getting caught would be a disaster for everyone.

Except Beasley.

Vi wrapped the scarf around her neck, and the scent that always made her heart pound harder drifted near. She closed her eyes, lifted the cashmere to her nose and inhaled. *Max.* He managed to torture her without even being present.

Being assigned to partner with him on Team Orange had been out of her control, but now she had only herself to blame. She'd signed up to help him ensure Gramps won the haunted house contest this year, no hesitation. And if that included spending even more time with Max...

She exhaled long and slow, expelling his scent from her nose. It came right back with the next breath, a taunting reminder of how close he was, within reach if she dared. Every second she spent with him, that challenge became harder to resist.

When it came to Max, resistance had never been her strong suit.

Her cell phone buzzed.

12:05 a.m. Time to move.

Vi found Max easily enough, leaning against the leafless maple tree near the driveway, gazing up at the starless heavens as if he'd been patiently waiting for her for hours. Years. Centuries.

The scarf tightened like a noose ready to close, depending on what path she chose to take. At her approach, that slow, crooked grin she'd loved at first sight came to life.

"You're late." His whisper seemed to be part of the shadows, a murmur among the branches.

Fireflies fluttered in her stomach, and for a second, she was back in high school, the girl stealthily infatuated with the boy she knew was never meant for her. Dressed like a night assassin from his long, lean legs to his broad shoulders and dark hair, Max was a vision from her steamiest dreams. He'd managed to break into her heart when he'd been a skinny boy with only shy smiles and secrets to keep. The man he'd become? Her heart didn't stand a chance.

Resistance is futile. Maybe she should stop trying so hard and just go along for the ride. He understood she'd be gone again on November first. They were both adults, reweaving their tentative friendship while flirting with fire.

It could work. If his schemes — and she *knew* he had schemes — included seducing her only to reject her later, it would be a deserving punishment...and worth every second, being close to him, creating memories she could take with her when she once again traded Devils Hollow for Kickin' Ink. She could handle it. No matter the in-betweens, she was destined to be without him.

One night five years ago wasn't enough...would never be enough. If he offered more, with full disclosure, no expectations, there wasn't any reason she shouldn't take him up on it.

A weight seemed to fall from her shoulders, leaving her steps lighter as she crossed the dew-glistening grass to him. Life was short. Gramps was proof of that. If the rest of October was all she had left with him and Max, she was going to live it to the fullest, no more regrets.

And that meant an apology. Groveling. Probably tears. Ugh, she hated to cry. But it was a price she'd already determined to pay when Dahlia's letter had arrived.

"You said twelve-o-five," she said, stopping beside him. "I set my alarm for that time, and here I am."

"It's twelve-o-seven." He shook his head. "Two minutes could be the difference between being caught or not."

"So why are you still flapping your mouth and not moving?"

His teeth flashed. "Ready for an adventure?"

She rolled her eyes, fighting a smirk, feeling more alert and alive than she had in months. "Always —"

Before she could say more, Max shoved from the tree and took off at a sprint, straight into the woods surrounding Lake Forsaken.

Dammit. Vi chased after him and clicked her flashlight on. She followed the bobbing, blue glare of his cell phone. Her steps crunched on dry leaves as she ducked tree branches and hopped over fallen logs. Soon enough, she recognized the trail that circled the lake.

Beasley's property lay to the east, its boundary the creek rumored to have sprung up after Abigail's curse and death. Beasley also mentioned that detail in her tours, convincing visitors that the reason the water smelled of sulfur was because the creek flowed from a portal leading to hell. Couldn't be the natural minerals in the area. But tourists ate it up, and Beasley had a knack for twisting history with urban legend, anything to line her cat-hair-infested pockets.

By the time she caught up with Max, she gasped for air and her side ached. Canoeing, apparently, was far more effective at getting into shape than drawing and an occasional jog.

"Warmed up yet?" Max barely breathed hard, the jerk.

"I was born" — she wheezed and coughed — "ready."

Laughing, he threw an arm around her shoulders and tugged her onward. Ferns rustled against their shoes and a moth fluttered in the beam of light like a man falling to his death. The lake glimmered darkly through the trees, a watchful, waiting presence. Vi tightened her grip on the flashlight as the woods opened.

Without moon and stars to give life to its surface, the water resembled a black pit, ready to devour whatever or whoever foolishly strayed into its gaping maw. Moisture and a hint of decay laced the night air. The forest seemed to hold its breath, the graveyard quiet, deep and eternal. A bit of white broke from the trees across the water and glided off on silent wings.

The hair on the back of Vi's neck stirred as she tracked the owl, Max's insights about signs and symbols echoing anew. *Stop dithering. Move forward. Make a wish.*

Wishes had no power to change anything, not like action did. She'd learned that the hard way. But the dithering? Moving forward? As much as she'd progressed in her career, her personal life was a different story. So, she was a ditherer. She'd been called worse. And a wish? It couldn't hurt.

The owl blended into the tapestry of tree limbs and night. *I wish —*

"We're almost there." Max jerked his chin toward the path and what lay ahead. The faint burbling of running water splintered the stillness, the boundary between Ward and Adams land. Beasley may not be an Adams by blood, but she took her deceased husband's heritage very seriously.

Gramps, on the other hand, was a true Ward, the house inherited down the line from the original founder of Devils Hollow to him. He also cherished his family legacy and did everything in his power to preserve and share it with visitors. Yet another reason losing to Beasley galled him to no end. It didn't help that she was the queen of gloating.

Her breathing normal again, Vi nudged Max in the hip with her flashlight. "What, exactly, is this brilliant plan of yours? Other than meeting you outside after midnight and going to Adams Mansion," — she air-quoted — "cloaked by the darkness of night, you've been sketchy on the Grand Max Mastermind Plot details."

"That's on a need-to-know basis."

"I need to know." She added a bit more power to her flashlight nudge in his stomach.

"*Ooof.* Fine." He lifted his hands in surrender and stuffed his phone in his pocket, killing the blue light. "Since you've willingly joined my team without coercion."

"You didn't tell me coercion was an option. I would have resisted if I'd known."

"Feel free to resist later, when we're back home." His voice turned sultry with velvet promise. "I'll put up just enough of a fight to make you want it more."

Home. The word almost drowned out the flare of heat low in her belly at the thought of playing hard to get with Max. *Home and Max.* She couldn't afford to think of the two elements intertwined, but damn it was easy. The temptation to let it go and pretend it was possible might break her black heart, but she'd be pushing her luck to stay more than a month. If not for Dahlia's desperate plea for help, she never would have come back. Risking her sister and Max for her own happiness, her own selfishness wasn't an option, no matter how superstitious the reason.

The underground spring separating the properties emerged less than a hundred feet from the lake and spilled into the murky depths. A narrow ravine channeled the creek to the larger body of water. Vi used to play in that ravine with Max and Dahlia in the summer, when the water levels were low and lazy. They'd crawl inside as far as they could and pretend they hunted orcs and magical rings.

She'd welcome an orc battle any day over what she'd encountered in the lake years ago. *Thought* she'd encountered. The certainty had faded over the years, and while lying in bed alone, in the dark and quiet, it was far more comforting to believe that her fear inspired visions of impossible things.

But being back in Devils Hollow? That initial certainty grew stronger by the day.

"Beasley doesn't allow anyone inside Adams Mansion until the night of the haunted house contest, which always makes her theme a surprise." Max followed the path back into the woods, to a spot where the ravine ended and the earth closed above the creek. "She doesn't trust anyone else with the decorations, handles it all herself. She's so adamant about keeping snoops and potential spies out this year that she hired guards to patrol the grounds."

"And you know this how?"

He grinned, evil, and winked. "Don't you worry about it, sweeting. The guards keep a regular schedule and shift change is at twelve thirty."

Vi glanced at her phone. "We have five minutes."

"Then we'd better move."

Crap. She kept on his heels as he broke into another sprint. No way was she going to let him think she'd gone soft since leaving Devils Hollow.

An eight-foot chain-link fence barricaded Beasley's property from the Ward riffraff, a stark contrast to the elegant iron posts that circled the front property for public inspection. A thick stretch of thorny rose shrubs tight to the wire worked on any thrill seekers who dared to face the ugly side of Adams property and trespass upon Devils Hollow royalty outside of business hours.

Vi couldn't hide a grin as Max veered off and headed south along the fence. She knew his ultimate destination. Years ago, they'd found a chink in Beasley's chain, a rusted-out hole hidden by the shrubs. A bit of creativity with pruners made a tunnel through the thornbushes big enough to low-crawl through.

Beasley's conniption fit when she'd discovered her poison garden had been invaded had been epic. Worth every scratch and thorn.

Max carefully lifted the loose section of wire and hooked it to stay open, the squeak like fingernails scrabbling against the inside of a coffin lid. "Ladies first."

She cocked an eyebrow. "So, what are you waiting for, Maxie?"

A glimmer entered his eyes, sharp in the flashlight beam, and he stepped close, the toes of his boots knocking hers. "If you believe I'm too feminine for you, sweeting, you haven't been paying attention." His gaze drifted to her mouth, and her lips tingled as if brushed by a phantom caress. "Feel free to test me whenever you want. I promise I'll blow your mind." His crooked grin appeared. "If you can take it."

Challenge accepted. Fireflies fluttered in her stomach and a thrill roller-coasted down her spine as she lifted on tiptoes and brought her mouth to his.

Before contact, Max ducked away and dropped to the ground. On elbows and knees, he shot through the opening faster than should be humanly possible.

She grinned as his bootheels disappeared into the shrubs. He'd been practicing. Or maybe he'd been spying on Beasley a lot longer than she knew. Probably both. She'd bet her ink supply that he'd started the day Gramps' diagnosis came back. And she couldn't help but love him more for it.

The Max-made fox tunnel was a lot smaller than she remembered. Thorns snagged in her jacket, and she had to stop to retrieve her beanie more than once. Max waited for her at the end of the hedge, where a hiding spot large enough for two had been groomed in the roses.

Vi settled next to him and peered out between the branches. Beasley had been busy in the last five years. A long stretch of green lawn separated the fence from the mansion. Statues and benches, sundials and arches scattered about the edges of the lawn in creative display, all to showcase the true gem of the landscape.

Where Ward House was a masterpiece of Gothic architecture, its details meant to charm and inspire, Adams Mansion had been built to impress. It rose three stories and sprawled from end to end of the wide lawn. From the outside, it gave the impression of elegance and old money. On the inside, Beasley molded it into a house of horrors for Hallowtoberfest guests, turning her home into a tourist attraction, all to win a contest and the bragging rights that went with it.

"The guard will be passing by any second now," Max whispered. His breath brushed her ear, curling warmth to her toes. "Once he's out of sight, we make a run for it to the gargoyle by the swing on the east side."

Vi nodded. A seven-foot stone gargoyle stood sentry over a wooden swing beneath an archway of ivy. She had zero doubt it would make for great cover, that Max had already tested his plan and ensured it worked.

"Once we're there, we have two minutes to make it to the mansion before the next guard shows." Max kept his gaze ahead to the lawn and the waiting house beyond. "Beasley never locks the basement."

"The basement. Great."

He glanced at her and grinned. "What? You thought we'd waltz in through the front door and you'd steal through the house spying while I distracted Beasley and her cats?"

"That, sir, is an awesome plan." She couldn't hold back a pirate smile. "And I know exactly how Beasley would want you to distract her."

He leaned close to her ear, close enough his lips brushed her lobe. "I'd rather distract you."

Vi sucked in a breath, her heart stalling.

At the steady beat of approaching footsteps, she froze. Even though hidden by leaves and a weave of thorny branches, she couldn't help but feel like a rabbit hiding in a thicket, hoping the wind drove her scent in the opposite direction of the predator.

Scuffed boots and a flashlight beam came into view only inches away from their faces and paused. *Shit.* If he decided to crouch and shine his light in the shrubs, they'd be seen, no question. And any hope of Gramps winning would be gone. He'd be eliminated from

Hallowtoberfest activities, out of the competition for good. He'd die without having his last wish fulfilled.

Vi held her breath. Beside her, Max could have been one of the statues in Beasley's garden, still as stone.

The guard crouched. A hand came into view.

Her stomach sank. Maybe she could make a scene and Max could get away, clearing Gramps of any wrongdoing. But that would mean Dahlia would be accused of foul play, a connection to her. She couldn't let that happen, either.

"Stupid birds." The guard picked up a white feather from the ground that Vi hadn't noticed. "Idiotic I have to clean up after them or get fired. Beasley's such a troll." With that, the guard strolled onward.

Vi waited long enough for the soft beat of his steps to disappear before releasing a breath. She exchanged a glance with Max, but instead of the relief she expected to find, his smile was wide and wicked.

"Time to move." He scrambled out of the shrubs into the open and disappeared into the darkness.

She hurried after him, and as she got to her feet, her beanie caught in a branch and tore off her head. The bobbing flashlight beam of the guard following the path paused and swung slowly back her way. *Crapcrapcrap.* Her blonde hair would be like a spotlight, impossible to miss in the gloom.

Vi ripped her knit hat from the thorns, and the branch broke. The snap blared in the quiet, loud as any alarm. She stuffed the beanie back on her head as she sprinted along the shrub border rather than straight across the lawn. With any luck, she'd blend in with the roses and night.

"You there! Stop!" The guard's command ricocheted off the statues and trees.

Her lungs burning, Vi ran harder, faster, driven by adrenaline. She hoped Max had a backup plan. She cut between a grove of willow trees, ducked behind an arborvitae hedge, and veered back toward the gargoyle. At the very least, the guard wouldn't know for sure which direction she went.

The second Max saw her, he took off toward the house at a flat-out sprint. She had no choice but to follow him and hope he knew Beasley's landscape well enough to avoid the guard.

A boxwood hedge taller than Max stretched the full length of the building. He darted between two shrubs as she caught up. She understood why he'd slowed for her. Beasley had installed a hedge maze since she'd last invaded the Adams property. Smart move. At the very least, it would slow down trespassers long enough to get caught.

"Keep up, Keller." Max's whisper and a flash of his teeth were her only warning before he leaped away, headed deeper into the maze.

Holy crap. She'd never be able to get a full breath again, and she sucked at puzzles. If she lost Max, she'd be caught for sure.

A flash of light cut across the hedge, and heavy footsteps pounded closer. No rest for the wicked.

Max was nothing more than a shadowed blur, the soft blue light of his phone a magical lamp guiding her on. She caught glimpses of him just as he turned corners, always several steps ahead. Blood thundered in her head, and her gasps filled her ears. If the guard followed, she'd never hear him.

The maze split into three directions, and she skidded to a stop, unsure. Max was nowhere in sight.

The glow from the guard's flashlight bobbed across green leaves above her head, there and gone as he turned a corner, coming closer. No matter which way she chose, she couldn't stay here.

Vi darted to her right and clicked her flashlight off. If she could see signs of the guard's flashlight, he could undoubtedly see her, too. But not being able to see meant she had to slow down or risk tripping — she got a face full of bristly leaves as she ran straight into a shrub and bounced back — or fumbling into a dead end.

Nearly blind without her flashlight, she felt along the border, letting the shrubs guide her. Her wheezing sounded like a dragon snoring, and she fought to steady her breathing. If she could hear herself, the guard probably could, too.

Where are you, Max? This was bad. So, so bad. Getting caught would ruin everything. Dahlia would disown her for good. Beasley would make sure her family never participated in Hallowtoberfest again, and her parents would lose the café. She'd left her family voluntarily before. There'd be nothing voluntary about round number two.

A glimmer of light shone on the shrubs ahead, offering a glimpse of the hedge and another split. She picked up speed until her hands met leaves and dashed to the left. With light and speed at his disposal, it wouldn't be long until the guard caught her. The shrubs were planted too close, their branches woven together, for her to squeeze between them, too tall and spindly to climb over. Her heart pounded. Maybe she should just risk turning her flashlight back on and hope she didn't find another dead end.

A scuff of pebbles came from the darkness, and she froze. Was that the guard sneaking up on her? Or Max in another section of the labyrinth? It was impossible to tell. Maybe it would be smarter to simply stay in one place, still and quiet, and hope she wasn't found rather than blindly fumbling about and making noise.

A silence fell across the maze, and she held her breath. Obviously, the guard followed her train of thought and waited for her to make a move, a sound that he could trace. But if that was right, then he didn't know her location in the hedge, either.

Soft as a whisper, another scrape came from ahead. Vi strained her eyes for any movement or shape. The boxwood made it impossible to discern anything between its borders.

Leaves rustled behind her, and her pulse jumped. Trapped. No matter which direction she ran, either to the guard or to Max, she'd be heard and followed. And she didn't know which direction led to Max. The guard could have circled around a different way to cut her off, which would mean Max was behind her, not ahead.

Dammit, I hate mazes.

A hand came around her mouth and a warm body pressed to her back. Only the familiar scent of autumn and outdoors kept her from driving an elbow in Max's stomach, flipping him onto his back and stomping a heel in his throat.

"This way," he murmured in her ear. "It's the unfinished part of the maze, all shrubs and no direct paths. Take off your shoes and carry them. Reduce noise."

Her boots were off in two seconds. He grasped her hand in his and guided her through the maze, in the opposite direction she would have gone. She'd been right—the guard had circled around. The thought of how she almost went that way and destroyed everything made her stomach turn. Bad luck dragged at her in Devils Hollow. Made alone, her decisions led to trouble.

And Max had a knack for always pulling her back out.

Grass soon replaced the tiny, round pebbles lining the path beneath her stockinged feet and untamed shrubs pressed in on them. Soon, a light from the mansion came into view. Max's long fingers around hers were warm, strong and sure. She should've known he'd never leave her behind, that he'd made careful preparations and had a backup plan on board.

He was…everything—everything she yearned for and could never keep. But for this moment and maybe a few of the next, she'd savor the dream.

A draft of air brushed her face, a sign the maze opened ahead. Unless the guard knew of a shortcut, there was no way he'd make it to the exit in time to intercept them. And he'd have to guess which way they went, forward or back. They might just make it out of this unscathed.

Still holding her hand, Max tugged her close and brought his mouth next to her ear. "Your skulking skills are definitely rusty, sweeting. Where did you go? One second you were behind me and gone the next. I thought I'd lost you."

"You know how I hate mazes and puzzles. I *was* lost."

"Not anymore." The rasp in his voice felt like a caress on her cheek, warm and intimate as his breath. His grip tightened on her hand, almost painful. "Once we reach the exit, run along the fence line to the eastern corner of the house. That's where the basement is."

She resisted rolling her eyes. "I haven't been gone that long. I remember the ins and outs of Beasley's house. It's the landscape that's changed."

"That's not all that's —"

Without warning, the ground dropped out from beneath their feet. Ripped from Max's hold, Vi tumbled into a black hole.

Chapter Fourteen

Max landed on his back and the air burst from his lungs. His boots went flying. A millisecond later, Vi smacked on top of him, all bony elbows and delicious curves. If he had any breath, he'd be able to fully appreciate her ass pressed against his groin and her hair tossed in his face. She rolled off before he could command his limbs to hold her fast to him.

Other than a wedge of night a dozen feet above, they were in complete and utter darkness.

"What the hell?" Vi's whisper shook. "Are you hurt?"

"Just my pride," he wheezed. "Give me a moment."

He couldn't help but wonder if Beasley had purposely set this trap, or if the cavern they'd fallen into was merely a result of her renovations. Over the last five years, she'd turned the Adams homestead into a delicate trap to keep the uninvited at bay. The maze had been the last impressive expansion, one he'd memorized on the midnight sly. Maybe he hadn't been as discreet as he imagined.

He pushed himself to a sit and pulled his cell phone from his back pocket. A swipe of his finger brought nothing. "Burning hell. I think I killed my phone in the fall."

Material rustled. A second later, the glaring beam of Vi's flashlight blinded him.

"Put that thing down." He blinked away the bright dots burned onto his eyeballs. "We don't want to tip the guard off."

"Pretty sure he'll figure it out once he sees that part of the path fell in."

"But not for a while. I sent him on a wild goose chase with a few well-thrown pebbles. And since we're in the unfinished section of the maze, we'll be harder to find. We'll get out before anyone's the wiser. Promise."

The light swept to the ground, illuminating Vi's dirty purple socks decorated with black cats, skulls and crescent moons. His mouth twitched. Even her stockings made his nerve endings thrum with awareness.

"What is this place?" The enclosure seemed to flatten Vi's whisper to barely heard words. The light swept over a small, natural cavern. Roots veined the sides. Grass and soil from their fall littered the floor. The scent of moist earth filled the air. Luckily, the ground had softened the fall.

"Looks like Beasley's got a sinkhole in her yard. The price of her keep-off-the-grass transformations." Max pushed to his feet, his bones aching from tumbling down a rabbit hole. "She's going to love hearing this so close to her garden tour."

Vi snorted. "She probably dug this herself to trap tourists and sacrifice them."

"Or feed her cats."

Her teeth flashed in the gloom. "I bet they'd all find you tasty."

"That's because I am." No situation, no matter how grim, would stop him from taking advantage of every opportunity to flirt with her. He wriggled his eyebrows. "Feel free to test it out whenever you want, sweeting."

Surprisingly, she didn't look away. Instead, she held his gaze. "Maybe I will."

Was that a challenge or a dare? His body didn't seem to care the reasoning behind her answer. All the blood headed south, hot and thrumming in his veins. Never breaking eye contact, he stepped closer until she had to crane her neck to look up at him.

Burning hell, she was beautiful. Whether in sunshine, moonlight, or the beam of a flashlight she never failed to catch and hold his attention. Like a vivid suncatcher, its colors separated by dark, iron lines, he'd never get tired of looking at her.

"Max?" Her voice whispered over him, warm and velvet. Her gaze drifted to his mouth and stayed there. The tip of her tongue darted out, wetting her lips, and it took every ounce of control not to throw her down and take her like a beast in heat.

"Yes?" The word was hardly more than a rasp.

"How are we going to get out of here?"

"Don't ruin this moment with reality, sweeting." He brushed the strands of escaped hair from her face and tucked them behind her ear. A delicate tremor shuddered beneath his fingers. Her hat must have fallen somewhere in the darkness. "At least reward me with a few seconds of fantasy for playing your landing pad. You're heavier than you look."

She narrowed her eyes, a sign that her nasty throat-punch gathered for delivery.

"All muscle, except the delectable parts that are supposed to be soft." He winked. "Feel free to roll on top of me anytime you want."

"You're incorrigible."

"Determined. Not the same."

"With you, they are."

"Just another reason why you love me." He meant the words as teasing, but the flash of emotion in the deep darkness of her sad eyes felt like fireworks exploding in his heart. For several seconds, he couldn't breathe. *She still loves me.*

"And yet I fail to see how your qualities or how I feel about them have any power to climb twelve feet up or tunnel our way out of this rabbit-trap before the guard finds us here." Vi always did have a knack for avoiding the real subject, issues that would drudge up painful emotions or topics that would force her to reveal parts of herself that she preferred to keep hidden, secret and safe.

And he was done letting her dive, dodge or duck him.

Max took her face between his hands, holding her captive, gentle but firm. "When are you going to trust me enough to know that I'll never let you down? I'll always be right beside you." He caressed the corner of her mouth with his thumb, and her breath snagged. "Or behind you. Or right in your face. But no matter the location, I'm here for you, sweeting. No matter the rollercoaster of our history, what hills, valleys and hairpin curves the track takes, it will always be you."

With a tiny mewl that sounded dangerously close to desperation, Vi wrapped her arms around his neck, pressed her slender frame tight to his and pulled his mouth down to hers.

Resisting didn't even cross Max's mind. At the second of contact, electricity swept from his scalp to the ends of his toes. He'd dreamed of kissing Vi again, and while the range of reasons why ran from one wild extreme to the other, from punishment to temptation to making her regret ever leaving him for a single second, one element remained solid and unchanging. She was the only woman he wanted to torment and seduce, fight with and forgive. He kissed her back as if he could imprint himself on her soul and delete any past pain. Vi had managed to escape once. He wouldn't let it happen again.

He slid his free hand behind her head and fisted her braid, holding her captive. She trembled and opened her mouth beneath the demand of his. The sweet taste of her filled his senses, and he couldn't get enough, would *never* get enough.

With a gasp, Vi pulled back, just enough to look at him. Her ragged breaths brushed his chin, matching the quick rhythm of his own. Max's heart thrummed a war drum beat in his chest as she studied him for a moment, a fine line between her eyebrows.

"Don't say this is a mistake." His shoulders heaved, and he kept his hold on her braid. Even in the dim glow of the flashlight aimed at the floor, her thoughts flitted in her expression, easily read by someone who knew her. The pull to either move forward or hide in the past was unmistakable. "Don't push me away. Don't—"

She cut off his sentence with another kiss and laid her palm on his face, possessive. Never had he been kissed with such heat and carnal need, the awkward girl Vi had been five years ago now a woman who knew what she wanted and how to get it. The fire in his gut spiraled upward, unstoppable, and when she gripped his shoulder as if he alone were her anchor to this world, whatever control he still had snapped. In the next second, he had her on the ground, her frame beneath his. She dropped the flashlight beside her, and the beam settled on the wall in a false moonlight glow. Curling her arms around his neck, she fisted his hair as if she were the one making sure he didn't escape.

He couldn't stop touching her, needed her closer. Max slid a hand down her thigh and pulled her leg around his waist, snugging her heat against his hardness. The clothes between them created a delicious, frustrating friction.

Vi rolled on top of him, never breaking the kiss, and straddled his hips. He slipped his hand beneath her jacket and shirt, the contact of skin on hot skin exactly what he sought. The curves of her back, her shoulder, her delectable ass brought all the memories of their first and only night together back to wild, exotic life.

Any danger of being caught faded away. Gramps, the contest, and the intricate, delicate knot of his relationship with Vi vanished into meaningless. She was everywhere and everything, the single focus of his moment, and he planned to savor every second to the fullest.

Max groaned deep in his throat, a snarl built up from years of lust, longing and love. The silken slide of her tongue on his made his body throb and ache with growing need. With fumbling fingers, he unzipped his jacket then hers, the urge to be closer a driving force he had no ability to fight. Her frame melded to his, curves to planes, soft to hard, a perfect fit. He pushed his hips up, and her fingernails grazed his scalp as she hissed into his mouth. Briefly, her legs tightened around him, trapping him in exquisite agony. The next second, she ripped away, leaving him in the cold.

Vi rolled off Max's lap like an action hero. It took every ounce of willpower, the last drop of her strength to pull away from him and his hot, mind-blowing kisses. She'd mark it on her calendar as a miraculous victory, a day her determination to make things right conquered her desire for the only man who had ever made her burn.

Max grabbed her wrist and dragged her back. He pulled her tight against his chest and wrapped his arms around her, his heat surrounding her. Nuzzling her neck—dammit, the sensitive spot that called her to arch and purr—he squeezed her between his legs, another layer to his net. The hard press of him against her back urged her to squirm even closer.

"No more ditching me when it gets deep, sweeting." He grazed the side of her throat with his teeth and licked the sting away. "Right now, there's nowhere to go. Give up denying that you want me."

Of their own accord, her eyes drifted shut in pleasure as he slid a hand beneath her clothes and skimmed up her ribs. The direct contact sent tingles radiating over her skin, all the way to the soles of her feet. "Wanting you has never been an issue." She swallowed hard and fisted her hand to deny the urge to touch him somewhere, anywhere. "I'm not trying to ditch." A gasp broke free as he filled his hand with her breast and rubbed a thumb directly over her nipple. "I'm trying to mend whatever bridges I possibly can before doing all the things I've been dying to do since forever. If you want revenge sex, at least I can say I tried to make you stop hating me before letting you have your way with me."

Max went still, his breath a hot, ragged caress on her throat. His hold relaxed. "I don't hate you, Vi."

She used his surprise to wriggle free. The flashlight glowed against the cavern wall, reflecting enough light to see the gleam in his eyes, the handsome lines of his face. "How can you not hate me? At least be mad at me? *I* hate me."

"I did. I was. I am." He scrubbed his fingers through his hair, leaving it all bedroom-sexy mussed. "Vi, when you left me..."

At his long pause, her chest constricted. For years, she'd prepared for this moment, when he told her how she'd hurt him, that he could never forgive her. No matter how sorry she might be, she chose to leave him without a goodbye. It had been a choice, a decision, at the price of his heart. How could she have ever expected him to forgive her for that?

Dammit, she couldn't breathe.

He gazed up at the thin slice of night sky, into the shadows as if drifting back into the dark past. "When you left, it broke a part of me. Of all the people in the world, I never expected to be betrayed by you."

She forced herself to keep her eyes open, on him, to absorb his pain until it blended with hers, becoming a piece of her soul. She deserved every ounce of it.

"Sit with me." He patted the ground next to him. When she didn't immediately obey, he scooched to her, his knee and thigh brushing hers. He took her hand, his fingers warm on her skin. "I went a little...feral, I guess. For a while, I didn't care about anything. I robbed

Gramps' liquor cabinet too much, went off on my own too much, did far too many reckless things way too much."

Vi could only sit there, still and silent, imagining Max heartbroken, finding ways to numb the pain and forget. She'd done the same thing for longer than she wanted to admit. Blending his agony with her own brought all the days she'd spent alone and terrified that she'd fail to full life.

"Then I got into my motorcycle wreck." He fisted his left hand and released it, stretching his fingers. "Ruined my wrist and any shot I had at the baseball career I dreamed of."

Vi squeezed her eyes shut, her ribcage threatening to crack beneath the building pressure. That she'd been even partly responsible for ruining his dreams… It was exactly what she'd wanted to prevent when she'd left Devils Hollow and him.

And the darkness had found him, anyway. What if her gut instinct had been wrong, telling her to flee Devils Hollow and the two people she loved most in the world? A shiver rolled down her back. No, if she'd stayed, something much, much worse would have happened.

"As much as it sucked, that wreck was my come-to-Jesus moment." He stroked her inner wrist with his thumb, comforting her when she should be the one doing the comforting. "I couldn't blame you for my own actions and the consequences. I figured out that no matter how much I wanted to, I had no control over what you did or didn't do." His mouth twitched. "It was a sad day."

She wanted to smile at the humor in his voice, but she was too afraid she'd sob instead.

"The only thing I or any of us can control is how we respond to the world around us, what it throws our way, both good and bad and everything in between. In the hospital, with every thought I ever had of my future—you and baseball—gone, I decided I didn't want to live the rest of my life on the rollercoaster of hating you, wanting you, wondering why you left me. It was pointless, and I was sick of ruining the good things in my life because I was too much of a dumbass to let you go."

The noose around her neck tightened, and it was all she could do not to jump up, claw her way up to the surface, run and keep running. *Max, let me go.* Whatever love he'd had for her had been diluted by her actions, diminished in her lingering absence and was now only a memory.

It was fitting, a Karma backlash. It felt like dull razors sawed through her heart.

"When I first saw you, back in the café, I admit my thoughts were less than honorable," he continued quietly, as if the remains of her heart weren't dissolving to ash. "I wanted you to hurt as much as you'd hurt me. I wanted you to want me as much as I wanted you. I wanted you to grovel, beg for my forgiveness...and give you a month to wallow in regret."

She nodded, her tongue not working. *Hurt? Been there, done that. Want? Every minute of every day.* Wallowing in regret had become her favorite pastime. If Max wanted her to beg and grovel, she'd do it, even if he couldn't bring himself to forgive her. It was the least she could do.

"That first day, I decided to seduce you," he confessed. "To win you back only to push you away. Give you a taste of your own medicine."

She clenched her hand into a fist to hide the trembling and cleared the nails from her throat. "Good revenge plan."

"Thank you." His mouth twitched into a half-smile. "I thought so, too. But it backfired on me. Less than twenty-four hours with you, and I remembered too much of the good times we had. I found myself slipping back into *us* so easily, so naturally, that I kept forgetting. I gave up on day two." He shrugged. "Never was much good at holding a grudge."

"A grudge?" The word rasped from her mouth, ghoulish. She'd left for his own good, for Dahlia's, but he didn't know that. No explanation would have been enough, so she'd vanished and let them write their own stories about her. He thought she betrayed him, broke his heart as if he didn't matter to her. How could he water it down to a mosquito bite wound? "That's what you call it? Nothing more than a grudge?"

"It doesn't matter what I call it, sweeting." He continued rubbing the inside of her wrist with his thumb, gentle circles over her rapidly beating pulse. "I choose to not live in the past, to not let what happened destroy my future happiness." He laughed, low and warm. "Staying mad at you is impossible. I like you too damn much."

The noise that came out of her mouth sounded garbled, wounded, an animal on the verge of death. All these years she'd clung to the pain, let it claw inside her soul and nest there like a vampire, ready to rise for blood in a century. And all this time, Max had already forgiven her.

"And I can't fully regret being apart. It gave us both time we needed to become the people we are today, and I kinda like those people." His sigh fluttered a loose strand of her hair. "Before, I never believed I was enough for you. You were always so strong. I was in awe of you, and frankly, a little scared."

Her hands trembled. Max had always been enough, then and now. It killed her that he had ever thought otherwise, that she'd made him feel that way. She was the one who wasn't enough, and somehow that had spilled over onto him. "Max—"

"Vi, sweeting, I know why you had to go. Now." He shifted and threw his leg over both of hers and hooked the other behind her back, facing her, holding her fast. "If you'd stayed in Devils Hollow, you would have eventually crumbled. The girl you were, your colorful dreams and fire, would have extinguished beneath responsibilities and the box other people kept pushing you into. You would have done it not because you're weak, but because you love them too much."

Tears burned her eyes, blurring his handsome face. No matter how hard she tried to hide, he'd always been able to see straight into her soul and read every intricate detail of her heart.

"Sometimes," he said softly, "love means letting go."

Unable to bear it any longer, she squeezed her eyes shut. She'd left him. That had been her decision, and she knew there wasn't a future for them. But to hear him say he'd let her go shattered the delicate glass house surrounding her heart. She nodded, not trusting her voice.

Max slid his fingers beneath her chin and gently urged her face up. With a shuddering sigh, she opened her eyes and forced herself to look at him.

"My darling Vi, I'm sorry to tell you this, but you've always been stronger than me." He cupped her face between his big, callused hands. "I'll never be able to let you go."

Chapter Fifteen

Before Vi could respond, Max kissed her again. Unlike his sweet words, there was nothing tender in it, as if a part of him still demanded retribution and would not be denied. He thrust his tongue deep into her mouth, cupped her bottom and pulled her onto his lap. Her mesmerized limbs danced to his hedonistic tune, unable to resist.

She wasn't sure how or when, but when he broke away and trailed hot, open-mouthed kisses down her throat, her arms were locked around his neck, her thighs straddling his hips. Her unzipped jacket spread wide, the sleeves pushed down to her elbows and exposing her T-shirt.

Vi threw her head back and closed her eyes, lost in sensation, as he slipped his hands beneath her shirt. His callused fingers scraped her back, creating a heady friction, and she squirmed on his lap. Holy hell, he was bewitching. Her lips tingled. Blood throbbed fast through her body, pinpointing all the most sensitive places desperate for his touch. The silken material of her bra rasped her nipples, almost painful, and the hard press of him at the juncture of her thighs made her want to rip every stitch of clothes away to feel his skin slide on hers.

"Violet." The raw, vicious need in his voice unleashed the beast she kept chained deep down, and it rose from the darkness to meet him.

With a force close to violence, she pushed his jacket free of his arms, yanked his shirt off and over his head, and tossed it away. Max snarled, and whatever word he said was smothered by her shirt being whipped over her head. The next second, she was on her back, his hard, solid heat stretched over her, cool air brushing the bare skin of her arms and ribs.

"I promised myself," he murmured, licking the space between her breasts, his tongue slow and silky, "that if I ever managed to be in this position with you again, I'd make it last much, much longer than the first time." He lifted his dark head, his expression pained. "I'm not sure I can keep that promise."

"Good." She fisted his hair as he unclasped her bra — with his teeth — and flicked his tongue around her nipple through the silk. *Holy hell.* "A week of foreplay is more than enough for me." She couldn't bring herself to care that the sentence was hardly more than a series of gasps.

His mouth twitched into a smug half-smile. "So my evil scheme worked."

"Bask in your victory later." She clamped her thighs around him, hard, needing his lips on her body, not forming words that required focus. Every inch of her burned, aching for his touch. "Max. Please."

Begging would probably come back to haunt her, but she'd do it again if only to see the same flash of animal hunger in his eyes, an echo of her own desire. He shoved her bra aside and cupped her breasts, squeezing briefly, before sliding down her stomach. Unhurried, he tasted her skin first with his mouth, then his tongue, tracing a fiery path ever downward.

Vi could only hang on and hope she survived. A touch, a kiss, another person shouldn't consume her, make her yearn for the impossible. But Max erased all her boundaries, scattered all her fears and doubts with nothing more than a smile. She longed for a world where she could forever be a part of his.

Max circled her belly button with his tongue, and she squirmed. He dragged his hands along the insides of her thighs, teasing, tantalizing, punishing her with the agonizing wait. His hot breath brushed her abdomen. The top button of her jeans popped free. He grazed the bared skin with his teeth.

Vi bucked her hips. A noise escaped her of frustrated need, and he chuckled, low and wicked. He curled his fingers around the waistband of her jeans and inched them down her hips, tasting, kissing, licking.

She fisted her hands, unable to reach him, and arched her back. "I'm going to kill you, Max." A gasp broke open as he blew on her most sensitive spot. "Later."

"Good things come to those that—"

A light glared down, and Max leaped up. He threw his jacket over her as a man-shaped silhouette darkened the emptiness above.

"You two," came a familiar voice, dripping with disgust. "I should have known." The spotlight shifted out of their faces.

"Greg." Max said the name with a fair amount of relief. "Great to see you. Since when do you moonlight for Beasley? I thought graveyard security was your gig."

"That's none of your damn business, Carter." Greg grunted. "You're lucky Beasley's cat snuck out, and she sent the entire security team looking for it. Even luckier that I'm in charge of this quadrant of her property. Put your clothes back on so I can get you out before the widow comes sniffing around."

A rope tumbled down and the spotlight vanished, leaving only the dim glow of her flashlight on the wall.

Vi was suddenly, excruciatingly aware of the miles of her skin on display. She didn't usually mind showing off her tattoos, but the rest of her was brutally shy. In thirty seconds flat, her bra, shirt and jacket were back in their proper places. She ignored Max's chuckle and the heat in her face as she shoved her feet into her shoes and tugged her beanie down to her ears. Men always seemed amused when they were caught in any state of undress, as if it was some sort of accomplishment to be nude.

"In case you were wondering," Max whispered, leisurely pulling his shirt over his head and hiding all the lean, delicious muscles she'd openly admired moments ago, "I doubt Greg appreciates your tattoos as much as I do."

"Shut your face, Max." She fumbled for the rope in the darkness. Now would be a great time to disappear into the thorns and thistles. If only she could.

Greg waited at the top, his arms folded, shaking his head. He wore the same expression from the cemetery — all glower and grimace. Vi didn't mind that he kept his opinion to himself. She stuffed her hands into the pockets of her jacket and waffled between waiting for Max or getting a head start for Ward House, where she could hide out until her face cooled and pretend that no one else had seen too much of her private bits and pieces.

And forget how close they'd come to being ruined. If anyone besides Greg had found them, she'd never be able to face Dahlia or Gramps.

Max's dark head popped above ground. He gracefully climbed to his feet, smudges on his face, his collar askew. Her heart kicked hard, the heat still simmering in her blood rising a few degrees. Even dirty and disheveled, he was breathtaking. She didn't believe her emotions for him could become stronger, but after tonight, being in his arms with his mouth and hands reverent on her skin? After his confession?

I'm so screwed.

His hair fell in his eyes, and as he swiped it aside, he caught her gaze. His mouth spread into a wide, sly smile, as if he knew exactly the direction of her thoughts.

Vi scowled at him. "This is a very serious situation, Max."

"Definitely is." Mischief sparkled in his eyes.

"Damn straight it is." Greg's face looked like a storm cloud, dark and threatening. He quickly drew up the rope, coiled it and secured it to his belt with an array of other useful items a security guard might need. "If Widow Beasley found out you were here, she'd have your hides, the hides of your next of kin and the bones of your ancestors burned."

"We have a valid reason for being here." Max used his honeyed voice, the one that had old women cooing and crotchety men easing up.

Greg folded his arms over his chest and arched an eyebrow. Apparently, he was immune to Max's charms.

"Over the years, haven't you been at least the tiniest bit suspicious about why Beasley wins the haunted house contest every year? It isn't natural, Greg. You know it, I know it, every devil and fairy who attends Hallowtoberfest on a regular basis knows it."

"Witchcraft… And after the unusual happenings in the graveyard the other night, we figured the two may be connected." Vi simply meant to add some believability to Max's story, but the words rang through her with an uncomfortable vibration. "We just wanted to see if we could find any clue."

"If you gave us a hint about Beasley's theme, it might put our fears to rest." Max smiled, guileless.

"Absolutely would. We could focus on Deadbeat Dean instead. Tourists always claim strange noises come out of his mortuary at night." Vi bared all her teeth.

Max slung an arm around her shoulders. "Or day. And I wouldn't put it past him to stir up concoctions with the embalming fluid…or summon demons."

"You two are pathetic." Greg rolled his eyes. "Go back the way you came, and if I see you on the property again, I won't be so friendly."

"Thanks for not ratting us out," Max said as Vi turned to obey. "You're the last person I expected to see here, not that I'm complaining. Graveyard guard duty not keeping you busy enough?"

Before he'd finished his spiel, Vi had already hurried toward the back fence and freedom. She wasn't so far away, though, that she couldn't hear Greg's response.

"Somebody's got to keep an eye on the evil in this town." His low voice sent a shiver down her arms. "Beasley's theme this year is summoning Devils Hollow's sweetheart herself, Abigail Ward. Now get out of here — and don't come back."

* * * *

Vi was halfway into the secret tunnel of the rosebushes leading out of Beasley's property when Max grabbed her heel, pulling her to a stop.

"Wait," he whispered. "You've got to see this."

After everything that had happened tonight, she didn't want to see anything but her waiting bed at Ward House and the backs of her eyelids. Her dreams would be about Max and hot enough to steam her blood, guaranteed. "Fine."

By the time she'd twisted and squeezed her way back out beneath the space under the hedge that offered a view of the landscape beyond, Max was already lying prone, peering out between the branches and leaves. He pointed to the opposite side of the property from where they'd come, away from the maze, its traps and Greg. "Isn't that Larry, the guy from the graveyard?"

Vi squinted through the screen of roses. Dawn was fast approaching, offering a hint of gray light. The clouds that had covered the sky only minutes ago drifted apart to reveal the fading moon and its light. A glass and iron conservatory glinted across the lawn, heralded by a topiary with short shrubs shaped into various fantasy creatures. Beside an impressive dragon that stretched at least twenty feet, Greenbeard from the graveyard walk fidgeted from foot to foot and glanced at the conservatory door, as if he waited for someone to appear.

"What's he doing here at this hour?" Vi inched closer to the edge of the roses. After he'd been tossed onto Abigail's grave with words etched into his arm, she expected him to beat it out of Devils Hollow the second he was released from the hospital. That he showed up at Beasley's at the witching hour? Something wasn't quite right.

"We need to get closer." Without waiting for her answer, Max slid from the rosebushes and dashed toward a trellis thick with ivy.

"Crap." So much for following Greg's advice. Vi tucked her hair securely beneath her beanie and followed him. The open lawn seemed to stretch for miles, and she was sure the pounding of her boots on the grass would alert not only Greenbeard but Greg back in the maze. A few panicked seconds later, she crouched with Max behind the ivy, gasping.

Max lifted his finger to his lips, and she rolled her eyes. The creak of a door opening sliced into the quiet like a blade. Holding her breath, Vi carefully peeked beyond the trellis.

Beasley strode from the doorway of the conservatory, her glasses on, hair perfectly coiffed. She was fully dressed in a pinstriped pantsuit and heels better suited for a boardroom, not a clandestine meeting in the middle of the night. Clearly, she'd been expecting company. She didn't seem surprised at all to find Greenbeard waiting by the dragon.

Greenbeard jumped and spun when Beasley tapped him on the shoulder, and Vi was fairly sure she heard a squeak come from the big man. But then they were speaking in voices too low to make out the words.

Beasley handed him an envelope, and Greenbeard shook his head, refusing. His response made Beasley glare. She straightened, and Vi swore her words were all angry hisses and buzzing. With each word, Greenbeard seemed to shrink in on himself, slouching, his head bowed. He took the envelope and disappeared into the night.

Beasley watched him go. She smoothed her jacket, lifted her chin and marched back into the conservatory.

Vi exchanged a look with Max, and the same thought she had reflected in his eyes.

What sabotage did Beasley plot?

Chapter Sixteen

By the time Max made it back to Ward House with Vi, dawn crept across the horizon, gray and sparkling. Even without a wink of sleep, life pumped in his veins. Spending the witching hours with Vi, no matter what they did, was better than a full night's snooze.

The walk back through the woods and along the lake had been quiet, the comfortable silence between two people who understood each other and had no need for words. She'd kept close to him the entire way back, their arms brushing occasionally, only shifting into single file when the trail had forced them to. He'd almost taken her hand, twined their fingers together and locked her to him, but he wasn't ready to push his luck.

It felt like they were back in sync...finally. He'd expelled all his heavy realizations and lost dreams from the last five years, exposed his heart. Instead of retreating, she'd basically attacked him with the same desperation that had fueled him since she'd left.

Vi's love language... Words were overrated and unnecessary in some situations. He'd take whatever she offered him, however she wanted to give it.

The trees thinned, and dew glimmered like glass on the lawn stretching to the porch of Ward House. Every so often, the sight of it stunned him with its odd beauty, reminded him of the moment he'd been dropped off to live with Grams and Gramps. Back then, he'd been scared of the unknown. Now, the memory left him only with nostalgia. Ward House would always be his true home.

Baseball had been his only career goal, and when his dreams shattered with his wrist, finding another profession interesting enough to pursue slipped away with the passing months. He'd resigned himself to assisting Gramps at Ward House, resentful at first, bitter with broken dreams. But as days turned to months and months to years, those emotions transformed into the ashes and rose like a phoenix.

Five years later, he found purpose in preserving his family heritage, meaning in shouldering the burdens that Gramps no longer could. He prized Ward House almost as much as Gramps did, and as Gramps slowed, his tragedy turned out to be a blessing.

That never would have happened if Vi hadn't left.

"Gramps will be waiting with breakfast ready." He looped his arm through Vi's and tugged her faster. "Today is cinnamon French toast and caramelized apples. After a night of skulking and shenanigans, I'm starving."

The noise of longing Vi made echoed in his blood, and his body throbbed with a different sort of need. "If he feeds my breakfast to Duke, I blame you."

He lowered his voice to sultry. "Whatever you need, sweeting, I'll make sure you get it."

A lovely pink tinged her cheeks. She wiped a hand across his jaw, so caring that his steps faltered. "You're filthy." The words rasped, raw. "Gramps is definitely going to ask questions."

They reached the porch, and he pulled her to a stop before opening the door. He plucked the knit hat from her head. Trapping her gaze, he casually unfastened the band on her braid. She remained utterly still, her dark eyes glittering. Slowly, he loosened the weave of her hair with his fingers until it spilled over her shoulders like moonlight.

"Trust me." His voice was husky, the sensation of her silken locks on his skin rekindling every spark of heat from hours ago to glowing coals. He dusted a spot of dirt from the tip of her nose. "With your gorgeous hair down, no one is going to notice anything else. We're golden."

Her lips parted, but before he surrendered to the fierce temptation to kiss her, he opened the door and ushered her in with a hand on the small of her back. If he kissed her, he wouldn't want to stop kissing her, that he'd be guiding her upstairs instead and they'd miss breakfast. No matter how desperately he wanted Vi, he wasn't so selfish as to disappoint Gramps.

The delicious aroma of fried eggs, cinnamon and bacon made his mouth water and his steps faster. Laughter and voices drifted from the dining room, one of them Gramps' familiar drawl. Apparently, he'd decided to make breakfast a community affair today.

Max set his jaw. As long as there was enough of his famous cinnamon French toast to go around, he didn't care. But if his slices were sacrificed to Oberon for being a few minutes late, there would be some wicked fairy bargain to break.

Vi entered the dining room in front of him. As predicted, no one else noticed him. The conversation paused, all eyes on Vi. Gramps and the entire Dimensions paranormal investigative crew sat around the table, a feast spread out and waiting. French toast loaded with caramelized apples and dotted with Gramps' homemade whipped cream filled black plates. Coffee steamed from cups, blackberry tea in others, bitter blending with sweet. Duke sprawled on the floor by the hearth, deaf to the snap and pop of the flames.

Max paused. In a child-sized chair beside the fire, The Doll perched, watching them all with staring eyes in its cracked face.

An icy finger trailed his neck, and he couldn't hold back a grin. Vi would be thrilled to know the doll allegedly belonging to Abigail Ward had given him the barest hint of the heebie-jeebies. Maybe there was supernatural hope for him, after all. He'd blame it on Vi and her return to Devils Hollow. She was the one, single factor he needed to make his mundane life magical.

Gramps slowly folded his arms over his chest, bunching up the pocket of his pinstriped denim overalls. "Where have you two knuckleheads been?"

"Predawn zombie walk around the perimeter," Vi said lightly, sliding into the empty chair beside Gramps and grabbing a coffee mug. "Obviously."

"Looks to me that you had a rumble with an entire army of the undead." He snorted and wagged a bony finger beneath her nose. "As long as you got the best of them, girl."

Vi lifted her chin and held her cup out, expectant. "That, sir, is an insulting insinuation."

"Mark my words... If you let one get away, I'll be out there with my shovel tonight to clean up your leftovers." Mischief twinkled in Gramps' eyes as he poured coffee for Vi, and the life there was everything Max could hope for. "Ain't nobody got time for those filthy gravediggers and their hunger for brains. Pesky buggers."

Max settled into the chair between Vi and Sabrina, close enough to Vi that their arms brushed. The single, innocent touch sent a thrill straight to his gut. His cock twitched, and he shifted to ease the sudden tightness in his jeans. *Settle down, beast.*

Sabrina, wearing a velvet funeral hat with translucent veil, matching vest and white silk shirt, planted her elbows on the table and leaned forward. "We are well aware of the spirits haunting Devils Hollow—Lake Forsaken in particular—but I had not heard of the undead. Is that a new problem? It might be due to Chiron and the revival of core wounds, calling the restless to rise and resolve their troubled past."

Hecate snorted into her cup of tea, so soft Max doubted the far end of the table heard. Sabrina straightened in her chair and focused on smoothing her black velvet skirt, color rising to her cheeks.

"There's nothing about the walking dead in our research," Victor said from beside Hecate. He crammed his mouth full of toast and fruit. For a vampire purist, he had no trouble chowing down solid food instead of the red liquid diet some dedicated tourists posing as fang bangers chose. Any man who willingly stuffed lace at his throat and managed not to itch had a strength

Max didn't possess — and deep, dark issues that he had no desire to know about.

"Mr. Carter is joking, of course." Hecate set her teacup down, and the gang went quiet, all focus on their queen. "Even if he wasn't, our purpose is not about the other supernatural creatures abiding in the nooks and crannies of Devils Hollow, but to determine the truth of Abigail Ward's death."

"And free her tormented soul," Oberon dared to add. His teacup, lifted halfway to his mouth, layered his glasses with steam, and he missed the disdainful glare Hecate shot his way.

"Free Abigail Ward?" Gramps waved a dismissive hand. "Her spirit thirsts for vengeance, not freedom."

"Oh no, not this story again." The whine in Vi's words spoke of the great suffering endured by tales told one time too many. "I don't want to hear about ghosts or curses, especially with that thing watching, listening." She pointed at the doll beside the fireplace. "You should burn it."

"We don't burn historical treasures in Ward House, mark me. Lay a finger on her and I'll whip your hide." Gramps' eyes narrowed on Vi. "Test me, girl."

"Chill, Gramps. I promise not to mess with your sick collection of creepy objects. But I make no such promises about trying to convince Max to do it." Vi pushed another piece of French toast onto his plate. "Eat this."

Still watching her with suspicion, Gramps picked up the toast and ripped out a bite.

"We have no need to hear the common legend of Abigail Ward again." Hecate nimbly crooked her knee up and wrapped her arms around it. "We're here to determine the truth, not rumors passed from generation to generation."

"By those who might profit from lies and pain." Oberon nodded as if he alone understood the wisdom of his words. This time, he caught Hecate's pointed stare and quickly took a sip of tea, hiding behind the delicate protection of his fogged glasses.

"The arrival of Abigail's missing doll is no coincidence, but a sign from the universe. Our efforts will not be futile." The secret smile Hecate offered Violet made the hackles on Max's neck rise, and he had the urge to plant himself in front of her, to hide her from Hecate's view. "Only the truth has the power to set spirits—both living and trapped between worlds— free."

Vi held Hecate's black gaze for a good five seconds without blinking before making any response. "Be careful what you wish for. Sometimes, it bites back...with fangs and claws."

"And watch who and what you pray to," Gramps added, his voice gruff. "Not all ears around the hollow are benevolent, if you get my meaning."

Hecate nodded and saluted with her coffee mug, but the sparkle in her midnight eyes reminded Max of an assassin evaluating the weaknesses and strengths of an unwitting mark.

"Gotta go." A piece of toast in one hand, Vi pushed back her chair and kissed Gramps on his grizzly cheek. "Dahlia's expecting me to help out with the breakfast rush before returning to all Beasley's assignments."

"Beasley." Gramps said the name like a curse word, and his eyebrows gathered together, two fuzzy caterpillars fighting for dominance. "Has our sweetheart Dahlia seen the light yet and broken off her engagement to that scumbag traveling salesman?"

Vi froze. "Brian? Whatever you know about him, I want to hear it."

Gramps smacked his lips a few times and waved a hand, dismissing the subject. "Never you mind, girl. Most of the time, your sister's smarter than most and only half as dumb as the rest of us. Let an old man worry about what trifles he wants." When Vi didn't move, he gave her a little push with the end of his cane. "Off with you. Dahlia and Beasley are the last two people you want waiting for you. Present company excluded, of course."

With a final stare that promised the subject would be revisited at a later time, Vi headed from the dining room.

"Coming with." Max folded up his toast, apples and whipped cream like a taco, grabbed his coffee cup and followed on Vi's heels. "Be back in time for dinner, Gramps."

If Gramps heard over the beginning of a thorough Dimensions crew argument about what lesser gods inhabited Devils Hollow, he wasn't sure. When it came to God, religion and all the cracks in between, if Gramps had a captive audience, he could talk for hours.

Good. Whatever fueled his fire and provided reasons to live to the fullest, he'd take it.

"Can't play, Max." Vi paused at the stairwell and gave him a level look. "I have exactly eleven minutes to take a shower, brush my teeth and get to the café."

"Give me two." Setting his elbow on the banister, he leaned down so their faces were at the same height. He lowered his voice an octave. "You won't regret it."

"Already do."

"No need to lie to me, sweeting. Not anymore." He leisurely swept his gaze over her face, from the curves of her golden eyebrows, the line of her cute nose and the planes of her cheekbones. His final destination was her pouty lips, and when she licked them once, he had to fist his hand to keep from tangling his fingers in her hair and pulling her to him. "You wish you were back at Beasley's sinkhole with me to finish what we started."

Her jaw briefly tightened, and her focus lifted from his mouth to his eyes. "That doesn't change the fact that I now have" — she glanced at her watch — "less than ten minutes to get presentable and not be late for Dahlia. I have only a few weeks to redeem myself and can't sabotage that." She looked at his mouth again, eased closer, and spoke in a whisper. "But, Max?"

Burning hell. Every inch of him stood at attention. His voice rasped from his throat in a husky purr. "Yes, Vi?"

She trailed a fingertip along the line of his unshaven jaw, watching as if fascinated. His skin tingled beneath her touch, hot and aching for more. "Just so you know... I'll need a lot more than two minutes."

Then she was gone, up the stairs faster than he could form a sentence. The slam of her bedroom door jolted him back to reality. Heat lingered on his jaw where her finger had been, and a hint of her rose perfume drifted on the air.

Max turned away, his body taut, a smile on his face. Team Orange had a full day of Hallowtoberfest duties, but soon, very soon, he'd find out exactly how many seconds it took him to make Vi moan his name and beg for more.

Chapter Seventeen

Vi adjusted her glowing, neon-orange necklace and kept her smile sewn on tight, even though she faced the danger of her muscles remaining permanently fixed in the unnatural position. She handed a tourist dressed in red leggings and sparkling bodysuit — also unnatural — his tickets to the haunted house contest. Fifty bucks a pop, and they were selling like Dahlia's hellcakes and forbidden molten-blood syrup.

If Gramps won — *when* Gramps won — he could use that money for a final hurrah to do whatever he wanted. Every cent from the ticket sales went to the winner. Almost as good, the team that sold the most tickets got donuts and ice cream on the last day.

Team Orange for the victory.

Costumed tourists crowded Main Street, knotting around food vendors, sloshing drinks as they walked by. The local band, Bloodthirsty Daydream, rocked a decent version of *Evil Woman* several blocks away.

Twilight drifted into evening, and soon the party would begin for real.

"Sold out before seven." Max's low voice next to her ear shot sparks along her nerves. "Must be my charm and pretty face."

"Or maybe, fed up with your annoying jokes and ego, the tourists threw money at you to get rid of you." She pivoted, and her shoulder bumped his chest. Instead of backing up like a normal person would, he steadied her by the elbow and held her close. With his solid heat and outdoors scent reminding her how it felt to be in his arms, his mouth on her skin, she couldn't even pretend to mind.

"Ouch." He clutched his heart, playing his half-smile hard. "Hurting me turns you on. Admit it."

She offered her sweetest smile. "Maybe."

"We'll confirm my theory later." He leaned down, and before she could think about the repercussions of PDA in small-town Devils Hollow, he brushed his lips over hers. "Thoroughly." He nibbled on her earlobe. "Until I'm satisfied with my research."

Vi closed her eyes and swayed into him. Good Lord, the man knew how to push all her best buttons and make them hum.

"If you can manage to resist having your neck sucked, I'd like to buy two tickets, please." Dahlia's voice filtered through her haze of desire, and Vi opened her eyes. Her sister wore a gotcha grin and mischief sparkled in her eyes. "Working hard, I see."

"Doll." Max had her in a bear hug so fast, Vi nearly wobbled at his sudden disappearance. He lifted Dahlia off her feet as she laughed. "Close the café early?"

"*Pfft*. Vampires and devils need to eat, and I'm not about to let them settle for what Slices and Dices down the street pretends are gourmet sandwiches." She shuddered and stuffed her hands into the pockets of her red wool pea coat. "Seriously. Would you rather eat a Poisoned Pickle Reuben or Dahlia Keller's infamous Graveyard Bones Burger complete with fried onion brains? Rhetorical question, of course."

"Obviously." Max slung an arm around Vi's shoulders and pulled her close. It seemed as natural as breathing to lean into him. Somehow, she resisted purring.

Dahlia's smile grew. "What's going on with the two of you?"

"Selling haunted house tickets for the ultimate win of ice cream and donuts...obviously." Vi chose to pretend she didn't understand the real question. "Team Orange plans to pig out, and with Max schmoozing all the gray hairs dressed up as shapeshifting cougars, we've got it in the bag."

"You know it." Max winked. "I'll take a few for the team."

"Always the hero." Vi rolled her eyes.

Dahlia sighed, loud and long. "You have no idea how great it is to see you two joking like old times. I love it."

Me, too. Vi ignored the heat rising to her face and hoped the growing gloom hid it from her sister. Wishful thinking, but better than analyzing her relationship with Max. She wasn't ready to fall from her current high. If she only had a couple of weeks to bask in impossible dreams of Max plus Vi forever, she wouldn't ruin it with reality.

"I only have a couple of minutes. The dinner rush is over, and Dustin promised he could handle it while I grab some things." Dahlia began vibrating like a volcano gathering steam and smoke. "Brian will be back tomorrow." The last sentence was a squeal.

"I finally get to meet my future brother-in-law." A new sensation coiled in her gut, small and hard. Whether or not she believed Brian was worthy of Dahlia, she wouldn't do or say anything to crush her sister's joy. But what if he didn't like her? Odds were not in her favor. "He better be awesome."

Dahlia's eyes sparkled. "He is. You'll love him." She bounced up and down. "Let's do dinner tomorrow night after closing. Can you both make it?"

"Count me in." Her sister's excitement was contagious. If anyone deserved true love and eternal happiness, it was Dahlia.

Max slid his hand into hers and loosely tangled their fingers. A warmth rolled through her, so strong and undeniable that her chest ached. Maybe happy endings, no matter how impossible or improbable, were a force of their own, a power that could never be stopped, no matter what outside circumstances said.

She squeezed Max's fingers without looking at him, not ready for him to see whatever might be revealed in her expression. He made her almost believe the ending she yearned for wasn't completely out of reach.

Dahlia shoved some cash at Vi and tore off two tickets from the roll hanging around her wrist. "Gotta run. I told Dustin I'd be back in fifteen before the next food frenzy starts." Her voice took on a singsong. "Can't wait until tomorrow!"

Vi didn't have time to do more than waggle her fingers in farewell as Dahlia disappeared into the tourists crowding Main Street. She looked at Max. "You've met Brian, right?"

Max's expression went carefully neutral. "I have. Seems like a decent dude. Dahlia obviously loves him."

"Gramps doesn't like him."

His smile returned. "Gramps doesn't like a lot of people."

He had a point.

"And since Brian isn't from Devils Hollow, he never had a chance. Gramps isn't the one marrying him. If he makes Dahlia happy, no one else's opinion matters." He looked beyond her shoulder, his mouth tightening. "Not even Beasley's."

Vi followed the direction of his gaze. Widow Beasley herself marched toward them. The crowd parted for her, as if sensing royalty and afraid to touch even the hem of her calf-length blue coat.

"Max." The purr as she said his name was low and sensual. Her smile faded as she turned to Vi, and she adjusted the stack of papers in her arm. "Miss Keller."

Vi resisted the urge to bow with an obstinate sweep of her hand, thanks to Max's timely pinch at her waist.

"Widow Beasley, always a pleasure." Max took her hand in both of his. "Is there anything we can do for you? I heard one of your cats went missing last night."

It wouldn't be surprising Max knew that bit of information. He was the local spy and seemed to know everyone and everything that happened in Devils Hollow without even trying. Definitely one of the benefits of befriending all the old men and women.

Beasley's face fell, and tears glittered in her eyes. As much as Vi couldn't stand the woman, it was impossible not to feel an ember of sympathy for her. She preferred the company of pets over most people, too.

"Poor Crookshanks." Beasley sniffed. "She slipped out when I opened the door, as she does from time to time. She never stays out more than a few minutes, but last night she didn't come back."

"I'm sure she'll show up." Max's expression was all sincerity and sorrow. "Probably just hunkered down somewhere safe."

"Thank you, Max." Beasley tightened her grip on his hand, her fingers white and bloodless. "I'm not so sure about that. We had trespassers last night on Adams property."

Vi widened her eyes as her heart tripped. "Did you catch them?"

"After causing significant damage to my new hedge maze, they eluded my security team." Her eyes narrowed, as if considering all the ways she'd torture the culprits before beheading them in her basement. "Twice."

Twice? Unless Beasley was counting them both escaping the security guard in the maze and her new sinkhole, someone else had been on her property last night. But who? And why?

"They dared to return not long after Crookshanks slipped out. Be assured that there won't be a next time." She released Max's hand and lifted a paper from the stack in the crook of her arm. Her throat worked as she gazed at the poster bearing a picture of a fluffy orange cat the size of a small panther. "But what could they possibly want with poor Crookshanks? She's blind in one eye and missing half an ear."

Vi's mouth went dry. As much as Max's sympathetic explanation for Crookshanks' disappearance was possible, this was Hallowtoberfest. Adams property bordered Lake Forsaken, where there had been more than a few darker activities performed by more sinister tourists who wanted an up close and personal encounter with things they shouldn't be messing with in the first place — things they'd regret awakening, things whose attention they'd wish they'd never drawn.

Idiots.

"I'm sure Crookshanks will show up as soon as she gets hungry." Max patted her hand and took the poster. "I'll keep an eye out for her in case she ventures near Ward House. We'd be happy to hang some posters for you."

Beasley laid her hand on Max's cheek. "You are so sweet, Maximus." She dragged her fingers down his jaw, far too slow and lingering to be innocent. "If Crookshanks remains missing tonight, I may call on you to assist me in searching for her. Everything is harder in the dark, don't you agree?"

Vi hid a snicker behind a fake cough while Max smiled through it all. *What a showoff.*

"Do you have any tickets left for the haunted house contest?" A man dressed in an amphibian costume, clearly the prince-and-frog awaiting his true love's kiss, looked expectantly at Vi's glowing orange necklace. A gaggle of princesses flanked him, all with tiaras, scepters and flowing gowns. She couldn't wait to run out of tickets so she could remove the glowstick and melt back into the crowd of anonymity.

By the time she'd finished selling tickets, Beasley had departed with her stack of posters. *Thank God for small favors.*

"So, Maximus." Vi bared all her teeth at Max as they returned to Hallowtoberfest headquarters at city hall. "What do you think Beasley is up to?"

"Call me Maximus anytime, sweeting," he said near her ear, lassoing her arm with his and pulling her close. "We'll see how far it takes you."

"Focus, partner." She tried to keep her tone stern, no easy task while her body hummed in response to his gravity. "We have important mysteries to solve."

"Yes, we do." Heat glimmered in his eyes.

"Drag your mind out of the gutter."

"Where's the fun in that?"

She punched him lightly in the ribs, and he laughed. "We need to figure out who snuck onto Adams property last night." Vi lowered her voice. "Besides us, of course."

"Could be anyone." He shrugged. "Tourists are always trying to get a glimpse of the mansion and Beasley's secrets. I think she likes the attention."

"That's not even a question. But what about her jumpy, midnight-hour guest? Greenbeard clearly didn't want to be there. And, to my well-trained eye, it looked like she was paying him off. I've had a lot of practice at watching suspicious transactions. I know a payoff when I see it."

"Imagine that. Violet Keller running a shady tattoo parlor." He arched an eyebrow.

"Kickin' Ink is a well-respected establishment with a zero tolerance for shady doings." She narrowed her eyes. No one, including Max, badmouthed her baby. And what Ruby did in her own private room stayed in her private room. "Be respectful."

"My mistake." If he wasn't so damn adorable, she'd smack the smirk right off his handsome face.

"Back to Beasley and her sabotage. Her theme is summoning Abigail Ward. Greenbeard was the one who got scratched up in the extra-special graveyard walk. Coincidence? After the payoff we witnessed last night, I think not. She wants to stir up the tourists for her own benefit, to increase her odds of winning."

"Maybe." Max didn't sound convinced. "Kudos to Greenbeard for going all in by shredding his arm for cash. He's an excellent actor."

The memory of that night, how Greenbeard's eyes changed color from black to blue, curled like a ribbon of frost through her. Maybe that's why he'd looked reluctant with Beasley. He'd got in over his head and wanted out.

"Whatever the case, we'll figure it out, along with who snuck onto her property after we left and why. If they truly did take Beasley's cat..." Max stopped outside the city hall door. "Then we might have a problem."

The same year Vi had her brush with death at the lake, several local pets disappeared. All of them were later found on the barren shore, victims of what appeared to be dark ceremonies. Beasley was called to identify one of her cats. Being the resident historian, she claimed the remains of the ceremonies resembled a ritual Abigail's sister, Anna, had conducted to raise her spirit from the dead.

"Burning hell... I loathe the riffraff that the tourist season drags in," Max muttered, echoing her thoughts. "Why can't everyone be normal?"

Vi snorted. "How boring would that be?"

"Don't interrupt my whining with your rationality."

"We need a brainstorm session to figure out how we can put the information Greg gave us to the best use." Getting caught last night had at least given them a focus point. That Greg had betrayed Beasley — both in letting them escape and telling them Beasley's haunted house exhibit featured Abigail Ward and her sister Anna — made the mystery even weirder. Beasley had always been a self-righteous pain, but evil went too far. And however Beasley planned to use the local urban legend to win, they needed to twist it to make Gramps' display even better.

Max's slow smile erased all thoughts of contests, Beasley and puzzles. Commiserating took on an entirely different turn, squirmy and steamy, where tongues were used for words...but minimally.

"Meet me in the parlor after corn maze duty tonight." He tucked a lock of hair behind her ear and trailed his fingertips along her jaw. His thumb brushed her lower lip, and every nerve sang in response. The fire in his eyes, promising that she wouldn't regret missing more sleep, thrummed hot and sure in her blood. "I'll be your hero this time and brave the consequences of stealing the whiskey."

She blew out a long breath as he turned for the door. Hero, villain, equal measure of angel and devil... Whatever he was, she didn't care, as long as he wanted her.

Chapter Eighteen

"Isn't it wild that you share a name with your new favorite doll, once owned by Devils Hollow's most famous urban legend persona?" Max couldn't resist poking at Vi's discomfort with the supernatural. Riling her up had always been one of his favorite pastimes. He handed a werewolf cookie, fresh-baked with a pinch of wolfsbane, to a passing tourist headed for the haunted corn maze. "What a coincidence."

"Shut it, Max," she growled, glaring at a stocky vampire as he swiped a cookie from her plastic pumpkin basket. "Hey, there's nothing wrong with asking first, Edward Twinkle Fangs."

The vamp didn't slow, which was probably the one thing that saved him from getting an ass-whooping via Violet Keller's thick-soled boots. She kicked some dust at the departing vampire's cape and pushed her black beanie back, loosening a rebel lock of long, blonde hair to curl over her shoulder. Still growling, she began pacing the black iron fence separating the corn maze from the pumpkin patch.

"You're scaring the tourists." Max laughed, handing treats to a couple of elves that gave Vi a wide berth, lacking the bravery of true elves. One tripped in his haste to escape her black stare. They'd apparently forgotten to practice the telltale unearthly gracefulness, too.

"We're not selling haunted house tickets, so I don't have to pretend to be nice anymore. My friendly well ran dry hours earlier." Vi hurled a cellophane wrapped cookie at a passing pirate with grabby hands. "And just because Abigail's doll was named Violet doesn't mean that the freaky-deaky Barbie we found floating in the lake is *the* Violet."

"Whatever you choose to believe, sweeting." He grinned at her huff of annoyance. "Grab your flashlight. It's our turn to patrol the back forty, make sure no strays wind up in the woods. You know those city folk. Can't figure out the difference between a corn stalk and a tree."

Ditching the cookies with the teenager volunteer manning the entrance to the corn maze, Vi followed the fence line, headed for the unlit recesses of the cornfield bordering the woods tourists claimed was a Devils Hollow haunted hotspot. "The less people, the better."

He couldn't agree more. Since Vi's return, their one-on-one time hadn't measured up. Being alone with her in the dark was not an opportunity he'd ever pass up, whether or not screams and chainsaws rang in the distance.

Max swung his flashlight as he strolled after her, whistling the theme to *This is Halloween*. The orange-tinted light from the lampposts marking the maze entrance faded into shadows and disappeared altogether as they walked through dew-bright grass under a clear, star-spangled sky. Fallen leaves crunched softly beneath their boots, and it wasn't long before even the terrified tourists and roars of motorized weapons faded, too.

Vi ducked a tree branch, and her flashlight beam tripped over a spiderweb glistening with moonlight. A silver moth beat its wings frantically, caught in the trap, a black spider scuttling from the edge. The spotlight swung back to the ground, hiding the moth's fate.

A strange shiver coasted down his back, and he stopped whistling. A hush surrounded them. The scent of overripe blackberries and soil replaced kettle corn and apple-cider. Pale toadstools squished beneath his sole, and a coil of ivy scaling a tree shuddered in a soundless wind. It seemed as if they followed a path leading to a world betwixt and between reality and dreams.

Most volunteers avoided patrolling the edge between the maze and woods as much as possible. No one who resided in Devils Hollow chose to venture into the woods at night unless absolutely necessary. Tourists were another story. Put up a warning sign, and they took it as a notice that secret supernatural happenings assuredly occurred in the area, which was why someone had to keep tabs on the border. And since neither he nor Vi were afraid of anything, it was all them and only them until the maze shut down for the night.

Hours with Vi alone... A grin tugged at his mouth. He couldn't ask for more. And tonight, when they met in the night-veiled parlor with pilfered whiskey, he'd coax her into his arms again. What had started in Beasley's sinkhole—physically, emotionally, spiritually—would come full circle. His body ached just thinking about touching her skin once more, tasting her, tugging her hips against his and—

"Hurry up." She glanced over her shoulder, a dozen feet ahead. "Stop fantasizing about Beasley and her cats climbing all over you."

"Mmm. Beasley wasn't the one I was imagining doing the climbing." He joined her as they reached the back row of the maze. The sliver of moon added a glow to the aisle of moist grass they followed, the shuddering cornstalks on one side and spectral forest on the other. "Feeling better? It's less peoply out here."

"Ask me after I find a tourist to club into submission, preferably a know-it-all witch who has too much time on her hands." She pulled a cookie from her pocket and shook it at him. "Seriously, who makes it their life goal to dig up tragic details of towns and torment people with that knowledge?"

"Don't think Hecate meant it to be personal, sweeting." Max slowed his pace, happy that she matched it, keeping close. "And it's not the doll's fault your parents named you after a creepy toy belonging to a girl who met a tragic end."

Vi stared at him and took a violent bite of her cookie.

"Hecate wasn't threatening you," he said.

"Sure about that? I bet Queen Hecate and her ghost-hunting minions are plotting my sacrifice right now. My death is worth it if it sets Abigail Ward's spirit free."

Max laughed. "Think you might be overreacting. Not enough sleep, coffee or sugar is affecting your judgment. Besides, no one knows for sure the fate of poor Abigail. Town history claims she was clever as all get out. Could be she decided she didn't want to follow in her sister's proper footsteps and get married. Maybe she faked her death so she could see the world on her own—changed her name, joined a safari, and lived happily ever after in the jungle with her wild cat and some version of Tarzan."

Vi looked at him sidelong and solemnly handed him the rest of her cookie. "Clearly, it's not my judgment that's affected. Devils Hollow has trapped you with the illusion of freedom. No matter what you do, you can't—don't even want to—escape. The darkness creeping from Lake Forsaken has infected you."

His humor faded. She had no idea how many times he'd actually thought that after his accident, as if fate had decided his future for him. He'd promised Grams to keep Ward House and the family heritage intact, always planned to assume that responsibility. Eventually—after a long, successful baseball career and Gramps bowed out at the ripe old age of one hundred. But if Vi had asked him to go with her when she left, he would have, no question.

"You might be right. Even though I don't regret being with Gramps, I've considered from time to time what keeps me here. Could be supernatural forces, family ties, the community, my own choices, maybe a combination." He shrugged. "Escape hasn't worked out for me like it has you."

Vi removed her black beanie and squished it in her fist. The moonlight gilded her blonde hair with an unearthly air, as if she were a fairy come out to play until dawn. Her slender throat worked as she swallowed, and she said in a whisper, "May I tell you something?"

He stopped. A step ahead, she turned, facing him. "Violet Keller. You don't ever need to ask me that question. You can tell me anything you want—lies, secrets, truths…anything."

If he didn't know her better, he'd swear the glimmer in her dark eyes were tears, not the shimmer of moonlight and shadows.

"I'm sorry." The words stumbled from her mouth, choked. "For leaving you the way I did, right after—" She rubbed her forehead and closed her eyes. "I should have talked to you first."

"You think?" Not the response he intended. They'd briefly brushed the topic last night, and he'd thought any bitterness had smoothed out. Five years of hurt ruined all sorts of intentions to be gracious and accept apologies.

Her mouth tightened, and she started walking again. "I know asking for forgiveness is too much, but I want you to know I wish I could take it back. I'd trade Kickin' Ink for a shot at a do-over. I'd do so many things differently."

"Like loving me?"

She stopped so suddenly that he bumped into her and had to grab her arms to keep from knocking her over. Her rosebud scent curled around him, intoxicating. The soft press of her fine ass against his groin made him twitch in anticipation. Vi shook her head, her hair tickling his chin. "No." Her voice was hardly more than a rasp of emotion. "Never that."

His heart beating furiously, Max slowly turned her around to face him, half-afraid she'd either shrug free of his light hold or throat-punch him for being too handsy. She allowed him to keep his grip on her shoulders, her gaze fixed on the collar of his jacket, as if she couldn't bear to see whatever might be reflecting in his eyes.

Burning hell... It killed him that she thought he could look at her with anything but respect, admiration, friendship...love. But being less than honest would be a dishonor to them both.

"These past five years without you have been...a challenge." Slowly, careful not to drive her away or break whatever spell that held her near, he tucked the long, loose curl behind her ear. He didn't miss her slight tremor. "I ran through the entire gamut of emotions when you left, not going to lie. One day I would've done anything to have you back, and the next I cursed your name for leaving me, hurting me, finding our relationship so unimportant that you couldn't even bother with a goodbye."

A wind kicked up, muttering through the cornstalks and leaves. In the woods, unseen, an owl hooted, eerie and sad. Vi remained silent, her shoulders tense beneath his hands, as if frozen between the past and future.

"At the least, I thought I deserved an explanation, a phone call, a letter, even a strip-o-gram."

She half-laughed, half-sobbed, and briefly covered her mouth with one hand. "I should've thought of that."

"Yes," he said, somber. "You should have. But you're here now, and even though five years of sludge have passed beneath the bridge that we can't ever get back, I'm here now, too...listening."

He wanted so badly to lift her chin and force her to meet his gaze so she'd see that when it came to rejection or judgment from him, there was nothing to fear. There was nothing she could do that would ever change the fact that his heart was hers — then, now and into the end of days.

But the next move was hers. She had to figure out for herself that she could trust him. She had to remember that in a world where promises and relationships were tossed away like sand, that never applied to him — to them...even if she believed she'd failed him.

Slowly, as if she gathered her courage to face the worst demon, she lifted her dark eyelashes. Vi raised her face, her breath faster than normal, brushing warm on his chin. Finally, she met his gaze. He hadn't been wrong earlier about the shimmer in her eyes. *Tears, definitely*. Whether they were for hurting him or her regret, he knew they were real. Vi refused to cry in public, hated crying in general, believed it made her weak. To him, they were beautiful, a sign of the woman he loved shedding her past to embrace her future.

And he'd be damned if that future didn't include him.

"The night I left," she said, her voice hoarse, "after we..." She cleared her throat. "I saw you and Dahlia together...kissing."

"What? I never... Oh." A memory he'd dismissed as a fluke, a meaningless gesture, a girl's unreciprocated, momentary crush jumped free. He'd been on a high after Vi had confessed her feelings and loved him hard in the field beneath the open heavens. While she'd snuck home to change her grass-stained shirt for the community high school graduation party, he'd waited for her, his heart soaring.

He'd noticed the stars in Dahlia's eyes too late when she'd interrupted him with a quick lip lock. The kiss had ended as soon as it had begun, and he'd made it clear where he stood as gently as possible. Dahlia had been heartbroken for as long as it took for another boy to ask her to dance.

To him, it had been a nothing, a moment, a one-sided kiss. But to Vi, that kiss had been everything, had changed the course of their lives.

Ah, sweet, guarded Violet, who never believed she deserved as much as anyone else.

"You don't have to explain. With me out of the picture, even if you hated me for it, I believed you were smart enough to figure out that Dahlia was the perfect woman for you." Her mouth twisted to one side. "Obviously, I overestimated your intelligence."

"So, you thought you did both me and Dahlia a favor by leaving Devils Hollow." He slid his hands from her shoulders to cup her face. "Vi, you're an idiot."

Her dark eyes sparked like firecrackers. "You and Dahlia are the best people I know. You deserve each other. You certainly deserve someone better than me. If you weren't smart enough to at least explore what you could have had with Dahlia, that's on you."

"Now I'm to blame?" He couldn't help laughing, and when she squirmed to get away, he snared her waist, tugging her against him. "Convenient how you twist your perception to suit your fears, made my choice without even consulting me. But that's not the point. Dahlia's a sweetheart, beautiful inside and out. Any man, including me, would be lucky to have her. Maybe I should have jumped on that boat and sailed it out to sea, never came back."

Vi's eyelashes fluttered slightly, the only sign that his words affected her.

"But *maybe* you should have stopped and considered that I might not want a woman who's sweet all the time." He stroked his knuckles along her cheekbone, enjoying her shiver. "Maybe I prefer a woman who will kick my ass when I need it, a woman who is all-out colorful, exquisitely damaged and incredibly creative — a woman who would misguidedly sacrifice her own happiness for the people she loves, even if it's the most ridiculous knee-jerk reaction to a one-second kiss that meant nothing and went nowhere."

Her slender throat worked, and every fear, hope and dream danced in her dark eyes, a reflection of his own heart to the depths of his soul. Her apology and confession were more bricks carefully removed from the fortress wall she kept fortified. He wanted to be back inside that wall, wanted her to open a window and let him in like she used to. Restraining the raw truth wasn't happening, and if she ran again, he'd be on her heels.

"No one has ever challenged me the way you do, sweeting. No one else has ever reached into my chest, pulled out my madly beating heart, and held it in her hands. No one makes me feel free, inspired and alive like you do, Vi." He cleared the rasp of emotions from his throat and huffed a laugh. "And I completely hijacked your long overdue apology. Please continue."

"*Max.*" Vi fisted his jacket with both hands, jerked him down to her and found his mouth with hers. Her heat, need and ferocity rolled over him, took the very breath from his lungs, and it was all he could do not to take her to the hard ground and feel her body beneath his.

Max captured the back of her neck with one hand and held on tight. The silken slide of her tongue on his strung a steel wire through his body that stiffened, on the edge of painful, with each advance and retreat.

Sweetness laced her soft lips, from the cookie and Vi's own exotic taste. Her fingers tangling in his hair, her gasp as he squeezed her delectable derriere and yanked her hips tight to his stirred the wildness in his blood.

As if sensing how close he was to losing control, Vi broke the kiss and tucked her face into his shoulder. She trembled against him.

"We aren't taking our corn maze responsibilities very seriously," Max wheezed. He drew a deep breath, in no way ready to let her out of his arms. "If Beasley caught us in a compromising situation, she'd assign us to porta-potty duty."

"Doubtful," she said into his jacket, her voice muffled. "She's probably spying on us from the cornstalks now, getting her jollies in whatever way she can." Vi lifted her head, her willpower apparently renewed enough to chain the desire that still shone in her eyes. At least one of them was strong when it counted. "Tonight, you'll be the solo star of her steamy, sordid dreams."

"Why do you have to be so horrible?" He kissed the tip of her nose.

"Honest isn't the same as horrible. She's obviously got the hots for you, and I know you've got a kinky thing for grandmas. Might as well take advantage of it."

Vi's wide smile, real and true, made his pulse pop. That he was the reason for it gave him a surge of hope. November was still a couple of weeks away. He had time to convince her that wherever life took her, she didn't need to be alone.

"Vi—"

She froze, her gaze fixed past his shoulder, toward the woods behind him. Her grip on his biceps tightened, almost painful. Moonlight lent an otherworldly pale to her skin and gleamed cold in her dark eyes.

Slowly, Max turned his head toward the forest. Among the shadows between the trees, the white, filmy sheen of a gauzy dress flickered and disappeared in the scrub. "Burning hell. Stupid tourists." He swiped his flashlight from the ground, fallen and forgotten due to Vi's world-shaking kiss. "Guess we get some action tonight. Ready to chase down an imbecile?"

"Are you absolutely sure that was a person?" With trembling hands, she replaced her beanie, hiding her golden hair.

"Scared we might cross paths with a spirit, sweeting?" He wriggled his eyebrows. "Don't worry. I won't tell Dahlia...or Gramps. Definitely not Beasley."

His challenge worked. She lifted her chin, her eyes flashing. "Suck it, Max."

"Later, I promise, but only if you ask with a pretty please, extra cherries on top." He lowered his voice and held her gaze. "Or wherever else you want them."

She scowled and clicked on her flashlight. The beam shifted and shuddered over the shining grass as she headed for the forest. "Let's go."

Once within the trees, the moon's glow mostly vanished, hidden by thick fir boughs and tangled limbs, bare and gnarled. Moss and pine needles silenced their steps and made it impossible to detect which direction their wayward tourist went. Despite her show of bravery, Vi remained close enough that her jacket sleeve whispered against his, not that he'd ever complain.

Max scanned for a flicker of white among the trees, but nothing moved. No rustle of leaves or snap of twigs beneath soles broke the stillness. Even the owl seemed to have relocated, no white wings coasting in the darkness on a silent hunt. He kept his voice soft, away from unseen ears. "We might have lost them."

Vi shook her head. "There's only one place a tourist would go at this time of night." She whooshed out a resigned breath. "Lake Forsaken."

A cold finger trailed his nape. Despite growing up next to the lake and his decidedly lacking sixth sense, every so often the mere mention of the lake's dark waters triggered a hairpin twist in his chest. He'd never encountered anything supernatural, malevolent or otherwise at the lake. Maybe Vi's phobia of the water rubbed off on him.

But after the Greenbeard graveyard incident, another unexplained tourist accident could affect the entire town. With the exception of a few dimwits, most people wanted the thrill of being scared without the consequences of actual danger. If a mishap occurred on their watch, he knew who Beasley would blame. Keller's Killer Café might be blacklisted. Vi already had enough on her conscience without that potential curveball.

"To the lake we go." He hooked his arm through Vi's and tugged her onward as she grumbled.

Half an hour later, they stopped beside a giant oak with bare branches. The trees broke a dozen yards from the water. Without any vegetation growing on the barren shoreline and only rocks to break the expanse, there were few places for a human to hide. Moonlight spilled over the water, giving it an appearance of smoky glass.

"We should split up," Vi whispered. She kept her gaze on the ground, where her flashlight aimed at a fallen log green with moss. "Meet up at the old gazebo. It's about halfway around the lake, so we'll cover even ground. It will save time and make it harder for anyone hiding to slip away without being seen."

"That's a terrible idea." The thought of letting Vi go off alone, at night, especially near the dark water where she'd almost drowned, made every protective instinct roar in denial. "That gazebo is dangerous. Should've been torn down decades ago. I'll add it to my property management to-do list tomorrow."

"It's a perfectly practical idea." She gave him a look that said he was being an unreasonable man who didn't trust that she could handle a wayward tourist on her own, which meant he stepped into dangerous territory. Pushing Vi in any direction she didn't want to go never ended well.

Max clenched his jaw. How had he suddenly become the wary one? He wasn't even sure ghosts existed, and people could be the worst monsters out there. Vi would never let a human scare her off. Convincing her otherwise would be a wasted effort. "You have your phone with you, right?"

"Don't worry, Maxie." She patted his cheek. "I'll check in with you every five minutes, make sure a rabid squirrel hasn't attacked you and left you bleeding out on the forest floor for the wolves to find." Vi turned on her heel and headed away from him, sticking to the edge of the woods like a wraith bound to the trees.

A chill slid through his jacket and iced his skin. As she put distance between them, he had the distinct sensation that with each careful step she took, he gradually lost her once again. This time, forever.

Chapter Nineteen

With the trees crowding one side and the lake a watchful presence on the other, Vi focused on any sign of trespassers. Just her luck that a corn maze tourist decided to break the rules on her watch. And there was only one reason visitors ever risked traipsing through the woods at night.

Ghost-hunting at Lake Forsaken.

Idiots. She shoved her free hand into her coat pocket and stepped over a log bristling with toadstools, half-hidden in ivy. Why would anyone want to rub eyeballs with a presence they could neither punch nor run from? It was all fun and games until a spirit decided humans were the best toys.

A shiver coasted down her back as a wind stirred across the lake, carrying an echo of laughter. She gripped her flashlight tighter and turned her attention to the woods, away from the dark body of water.

Bearing the tradition of his Ward forefathers, Gramps had kept up with warning outsiders to steer clear of the forest, even if the real danger came more from the dark waters sheltered within the center of the woods. She doubted any of his ancestors counted on people in coming ages to actually seek out stupid ways to be terrified.

But those rules never applied to Max, Dahlia or her. Growing up, they'd been allowed to venture through the woods as long as they stayed on the trails. The lake itself had never been forbidden. Maybe if it had, she wouldn't be scared out of her wits to be within a few feet of the water lapping the black, empty shoreline.

Vi glanced over her shoulder, back to where she'd left Max. Only the silhouette of the ancient oak's bare, pale branches remained visible against the night sky. The emptiness twisted through her, unsettling, a reminder of old nightmares she'd fought so hard to destroy.

She'd told Max the truth when she'd said his kiss with Dahlia had sent her running. It had definitely been the deciding factor. But ditching Devils Hollow and leaving Max behind hadn't been so simple as a knee-jerk reaction to her broken heart or the freedom to follow her dreams.

Splintered images of the nightmare shuddered through her, as if escaped from a trap. Dahlia, sinking beneath the water, her hair floating like tendrils of kelp. Max's unseeing eyes fixed on the heavens as his corpse bobbed on the surface — all while she watched from the shoreline, helpless. She couldn't save them, couldn't do anything, didn't have enough courage to even jump into the water.

Never enough.

Vi took several long, deep breaths, pushing the images away one by one. Dahlia was safe at the café.

Max had been fine for years, rowing his canoe without any trouble. As long as Dahlia and Max weren't with her at the lake at the same time, any premonition from a damaged girl dealing with her fear couldn't happen. The lake grossed out Dahlia, and with Hallowtoberfest in full swing, the odds of her coming to the lake were zero. A couple of more weeks and any danger factor would pass.

Because Vi would be gone.

She paused and briefly closed her eyes. Being close to the water at night messed with her rationality. She'd meet up with Max on the opposite shoreline. She'd make some grumbling comment about tourists wasting her precious time and energy, and he'd laugh. Everything would be fine.

Everything will be fine. The words washed through her, and the tension in her shoulders eased a notch. For the first time in years, she could almost believe that they held more than a grain of truth. All her goals, leaving Devils Hollow without regrets, actually seemed within reach.

She had her little sister back. Handling the Hallowtoberfest duties, giving Dahlia the freedom to run the café, had seemed to do the trick. Payback fulfilled. Whatever sourced the undercurrent of tension slithering beneath Dahlia's surface, they'd work it out. Dahlia had found happiness with Brian. They hadn't talked about November yet, but when she returned to Kickin' Ink, it would include a vow to keep in close contact.

Making up with Gramps had been a cinch. He'd scolded her, she'd apologized and that had been that. If only all her relationships were so easy. Watching him finally win the haunted house contest would be worth every sleepless night and graveyard tour. She hadn't yet got around to telling him how huge he'd been in her life while growing up, but she'd make sure he knew before she left town. She swallowed the lump in her throat. Before he was gone forever.

And Max... Vi touched her lips with chilled fingertips. Her mouth still tingled from his kiss, the warmth of his hands imprinted on her skin like a tattoo—not a temporary henna mark, but a permanent swath of color, impossible to remove. By some miracle, he took all her wrongs, sanded the sharp edges and stored them in the attic of their past. Over and done, time to move on. Even though leaving him while Gramps faded away would be tough, she couldn't let Ruby carry all the duties at Kickin' Ink for an indefinite time. Max had forgiven her betrayal. Hoping for more was a heartache waiting to happen.

Which left one goal—conquer her fear and break the lake's nightmare hold.

Tomorrow. She aimed her flashlight at the smooth water and ignored the corkscrew in her gut. The beam stretched and dwindled against the night cloaking the lake. Tomorrow she'd swim Lake Forsaken. Ruby would ink in the last petal of her tattoo when she got back to work, and any curse, imagined or real, would be broken.

A burst of white broke from the trees, and the owl soared silently over the lake, its wings spread wide.

Vi stopped and tracked its majestic flight, transfixed. The mighty bird made a lazy circle, its perfect reflection following on the lake's surface. With one, powerful flap, it returned to the trees, out of sight.

Her skin prickled. An omen, for sure. But for good or bad?

The night settled again into stillness, and Vi continued her trek around the lake. Her boot scuffed a rock, and the pebble tumbled down the slight bank, leaving a trail in the black soil. She loosened her scarf. Her blood still burned from pressing close to Max. Kissing him hadn't been any part of her plan, but when he'd turned her apology on its head, granted her forgiveness without even a groveling session and whispered all the hidden wants of her heart, she'd been helpless to resist.

Again.

Resisting him had always been her weakness. But no matter the current state of their relationship, he still deserved someone as selfless and caring as himself, a woman who could love him fully, freely, without fear. He needed someone who belonged to Devils Hollow like he did. That couldn't be her, and now that she had Kickin' Ink to manage, staying was even less possible.

But she wouldn't make the same mistake from five years ago—loving him and leaving on the same night, no explanation, no goodbye. This time, when she left, he'd know exactly why she had to go, and she'd find the strength to resist whatever argument he made for her to stay...somehow. Her throat tightened. Being a grownup sucked sometimes.

A flicker of white danced in her periphery, moving across the dark water. Faster than a lightning flash, it was gone by the time she whipped around to face the lake. Definitely not an owl.

Her heart pounded as she searched the smooth surface. Had he, she...or *it* sunk into the shallows? Or hid in the shelter of the trees? No ripples indicated any disturbance. Other than a bone-pale moth flitting away, nothing else moved. The moon reflected bright on the surface, but the depths remained black and endless.

A breeze brushed her face, bringing the scent of moisture and decay. With it came a whisper, as if some distant barrow had cracked wide to the world for the first time in centuries and gasped for air. Every hair on the back of her neck stood at attention. Goosebumps prickled down her arms.

A yell rang out from the woods, and she jumped, dropping the flashlight.

Max.

Vi grabbed her flashlight and leaped into a sprint. Branches clawed at her, and her boot caught on a rock hidden in the moss. She stumbled several steps, regained her balance, and veered onto the less-obstructed shoreline. Fragments of her nightmare flashed again to full, terrifying life.

Max was alone, facing who-knew-what. If anything happened to him, she'd never forgive herself.

Ahead, the lake narrowed into the stream dividing the property between Ward and Adams. The bank steepened into a gaping ravine, the water bottlenecked into a natural lifeline to the lake. Red leaves coated the ground, slick and bright beneath the moon. In the trees across the stream, near where the gazebo nestled out of sight, movement shifted in the shadows.

Please let that be Max.

Vi had jumped this portion of the stream dozens of times, no problem. The drop to the water below had always been part of the thrill for kids looking for adventure. Without slowing, she leaped. The layer of fallen leaves slipped beneath her boot, and as she lost her balance, her stomach lurched. She tumbled down the bank and landed on her back in the reeds and shallows. The banks of the ravine rose above her like the sides of an open grave.

Spluttering, Vi scrambled to her feet and wiped water from her eyes. Wet weeds clung to her hair. Mud squished between her fingers, cold and heavy on her hands. The lake's chill sank through her clothes and seeped into her skin.

She lifted her gaze to the thin strip of sky far above and aimed her flashlight at the banks on either side. Thank God she'd kept her grip on the flashlight. The banks were sheer, no rocks or roots, glistening with moisture. *Perfect.* Climbing up was impossible. The only way out was by wading along the stream and into the lake itself. She'd have to search for a section of bank that wasn't so steep, where she could drag herself out like some twisted, monstrous lagoon creature.

It might all be worth it if Max had caught the idiot tourist who ruined her night by interrupting a smoking-hot kiss. And hopefully said tourist hadn't sacrificed Max to the lake spirits while she'd unceremoniously tumbled into a crevice. She headed for her undignified escape.

"*Violet.*" The whisper drifted from inside the ravine, distant.

Vi froze, a rabbit snared.

"*Violet.*" An answering voice echoed from the lake.

Every instinct screamed at her to run. But stuck between the ravine and lake, there was nowhere to flee. She swung the flashlight beam into the depths of the ravine, the darkness impenetrable.

I will face my fears.

She drew in several shuddering breaths, her heart racing. There was only one way out. Keeping her back to the ravine bank, she sloshed sideways toward the faint reflection of light on water. She grasped the flashlight, its weight a cold, solid comfort in her hand. The yawning blackness felt like inching along the edge of a cliff. One wrong step, and she'd be swallowed up, never to return.

Mud pulled at her boots, and each slow step was a fight to break its sucking grip. Waist-high reeds clawed at her hands, sharp and stinging, but she didn't dare to look away from the glimmer of light signifying freedom. The ravine narrowed into a chokehold. Every breath rasped in her throat, raw. The hiss of her jeans against reeds and stone echoed into the darkness and returned with a sibilant whisper.

"Violet."

Something brushed her shoulder, and she blindly struck out with the flashlight. Light careened off the embankment and settled, revealing nothing more than a dangling root.

"Violet."

Muted light beckoned ahead, water glimmering beneath the moon. *A few more steps.* Her skin prickled and her hands shook. The light trembled in time with her racing pulse.

Vi slipped from the ravine mouth and gasped for air. She didn't slow or pause, her gaze on the safety of the bank. In the minute or so from when she'd tripped, a low fog had set in. Misty fingers coiled through the trees and seethed across the water, hiding the ground more than a few feet away. The moon blended the haze and shadows with silver-gray. It felt so much like her nightmare that she curled her fingers and dug her nails into her palm just to be sure she was awake.

She forced herself to slog quietly through the shallows toward the bank. Reeds muttered and begrudgingly parted, stabbing at her bare hands. Weeds tangled her boots and dragged her steps. Her neck prickled with awareness, a slithering down her back. Someone — or some*thing* — watched her.

The urge to call out to Max fought with the need to be as quiet as possible until she escaped the grasp of the water. She hadn't been in deep water when she'd almost drowned. Not even the shallows of Lake Forsaken were safe.

"*Violet.*" The fog snaking out over the lake seemed to call her name.

Blood pounded in her ears. *Just my imagination.* Nothing more than the wind in the trees across the way. She kept her gaze on the waiting bank so close.

A distinct *splash* came from somewhere in the fog, as if someone had jumped in.

Vi spun and aimed her flashlight at the center of the lake. Mist sparkled in the beam. Her breath clouded in the air. A single ripple rolled toward her.

For a stretching, timeless moment, the past collided with the present. Years ago, she'd watched, fascinated, as a similar wave approached her, just before the water dragged her under with invisible hands.

Screw courage. She turned for the bank and ran.

Chapter Twenty

Vi sobbed as she scrambled up the bank and out of the water. She whirled to face the lake. Mist flowed and gleamed in the flashlight beam, hiding the lake in an otherworldly haze. Whatever had created that nightmare ripple remained unseen.

Another splash came from somewhere in the fog, as if someone came up for a desperate gasp of air, only to slip beneath the surface again. She strained to see something, anything. What if the wayward tourist had fallen in? Or Max?

"Hello? Max?" She crept forward, returning to those dark waters, each step another needle in her chest. Too vividly, she remembered the fear, the helplessness. If Max and Dahlia hadn't been there to drag her up, to save her…

The lake sloshed around her ankles as Vi made a slow arc with her flashlight. Unlike herself five years ago, Max was an excellent swimmer. If he went into the lake to rescue a struggling tourist, he'd already be back to shore, which meant he must still be searching the woods. Whoever was out there wasn't Max.

She was the only one here to save them.

Her heart hammered, blood pounding in her ears. She shivered, suddenly cold, but sweat slicked her palms. Her numb toes curled into her boots, frozen in place. The mist stuck to her, a chilled steam on her skin, stinging her eyes. She couldn't trust her vision. The fog hid everything in a clinging dread that whispered one certainty. Whatever had dragged her into the water five years ago was still there…watching, waiting.

For her.

No. Just my imagination.

The haze shifted, as if trying to take form. Fear rippled up her arms like an electric current, and Vi scrambled back onto the bank. She couldn't do it, couldn't slide into the water, offering herself to what lurked beneath. If she swam in those waters again, she'd never emerge. She'd be dragged under, trapped in water weeds and icy arms, and no matter how hard she struggled, she wouldn't get free. No one would pull her up to the light, to air and life.

Hands gripped her shoulders and pulled her back against a solid, male body. Terror exploded into instinct. Vi instantly threw her elbow back. A grunt followed. She spun and slammed her elbow into a firm ribcage. Only then did her eyesight connect with her brain, recognizing Max.

Max gurgled and stumbled back several steps before falling to the ground. His flashlight tumbled from his fingers and thumped to the ground.

"Max!" Her heart still pounding, hands shaking, she rushed to where he lay on his back. He stared up at the sky, too much like her nightmare. "I didn't know it was you. Are you okay?"

"'Kay," he wheezed and closed his eyes. "Give me a sec."

"I feel terrible." She crouched beside him and ran her hands over his throat to his chest, searching for any sign of blood or damage.

"You should." He squinted one eye open. "Did you scream just to have an excuse to pummel me?"

She hadn't even been aware that she'd screamed. Under the circumstances, not surprising. "Totally." His teasing erased most of her tension and her shoulders slumped with relief. "It was a test that you royally failed."

"Never was much good at pop quizzes. You know that." He laced his hands behind his head. "But I won't complain if you want to keep stroking me."

Vi jerked her hands back, her face heating.

He winced. "Check beneath my coat, where your elbow got me. Not sure, but it feels like maybe I have a cracked rib."

She had his jacket unzipped and fumbled under his shirt in the next second. His skin was smooth and clear, no bruises or red marks. As much as she was relieved to find no visible damage, she couldn't deny a pang of self-reproach. Maybe Max was right, and she should work on her skills. If someone else had grabbed her, she might not be so lucky.

"Lower." He twisted slightly, as if in pain.

Vi dragged her fingers down his ribcage, not that she knew what a cracked rib felt like. She reached his belt and stopped.

"Lower." His voice was nothing more than a husky rasp, and when she lifted her gaze to his, the heat in his eyes nearly burned her alive.

Whatever initial damage she'd caused clearly hadn't debilitated him for more than a minute. *What a faker.* And yet she couldn't seem to find the willpower to remove her hand from his stomach. The smooth skin over hard muscle was both familiar and not. When she'd touched him years ago, they'd hardly been more than children. Max had been wiry, athletic but not filled out into the man he'd become.

He was very much a man now.

A trail of fine, dark hair disappeared into his waistband. Muscles ridged his stomach, firm beneath her fingers. With his coat tugged apart and his shirt pushed up to his chest, it was impossible to miss the state of his arousal, pushing at his jeans.

Her mouth went dry...and *bam*. The bite of desire coiled hot and liquid in her belly, swamping the adrenaline still pumping hard through her veins. The wild need to touch him, claim and be claimed roared to life. Her pulse throbbed in her trembling fingertips as she traced the sharp line of his hip bone.

Prickles skittered between her shoulder blades, a warning, at the same time Max grasped her wrist in a gentle but controlling hold.

"Sweeting," he said in a low, rasping voice, "as much as I sincerely regret interrupting you touching me and looking like you want to use your tongue to investigate every delicious inch of me until we're both utterly undone, we need to go."

A chill swept down her back, as if the lake had reached out to taste her, a taunting reminder of what she hadn't quite seen. Anything could rise from the depths, creep ashore, and she wouldn't have known, distracted by Max.

Using every ounce of self-restraint not to scramble away and reveal how very freaked out she was, she tugged his shirt back down and smoothed it. She did her best to ignore the muscles below the fabric.

"Don't worry, Maxie. I wasn't planning to violate you on the beach in the sight of any lurking tourists." She snorted and smoothly rose to her feet. "You've become a prude in your old age."

He took the hand she offered and pulled himself up. Standing, he didn't release her fingers and jerked her tight against his chest. "I promise to demonstrate exactly what I am and what I'm not in thorough detail," he said in a low, seductive purr, "once we're off the shore. Your powers of distraction, while admittedly fierce, aren't enough to make me forget that someone conducted an unholy ceremony only yards away."

Vi pivoted, searching the strip of black circling the water. Mist hovered over the lake and curled along the ground with white tentacles. Moonlight caressed the landscape in a milky glow. A slight breeze, chilled but not ice-cold, stirred the haze, parting it enough to see what Max had mentioned.

A stone altar had been assembled on the shore. A thin stream of smoke snaked into the air, the dying breath of a fire. Something still remained on the stones. Vi took a step forward before Max stopped her.

"You don't want to see it." His jaw tightened. "Trust me on this one."

A sick ball formed in her stomach, cold and hard. "Did you find anyone?"

He shook his head, tucked her hand in the crook of his arm and led her up the bank, away from the lake and the remains left on the shore. "But I'll need to call Beasley and let her know that she was, unfortunately, right."

"Right about what?"

His breath clouded in the air. "Crookshanks won't be coming home."

* * * *

Vi carefully opened her bedroom door and shut it without making a sound. She glanced once at Max's door before heading through the shadows toward the stairs. Maybe he already waited for her in the parlor.

After wading through Widow Beasley's tears and the full spectrum of emotions ranging from grief to hysterics to rage, Max followed her wishes and let Greg from her security team investigate the crime rather than the local police. Vi understood her reasoning. When it came to the potential damage of tourism, rules were bent.

Disturbing as the night had been, and as sorry as she felt for Beasley and her cat, ghosting Max wasn't going to happen. He'd challenged her to meet him, promised to rob Gramps of his whiskey and take the heat if they got caught, and she wouldn't miss it for anything.

On bare feet, she snuck through the house toward the parlor, her heart kicking up a notch. The thrill of sneaking out of her room and pilfering whiskey was only part of the adventure. Knowing that Max waited for her — hopefully for more reasons than drinking whiskey and talking — set her temperature to scorching.

Neither one of them had made any promises to the other, hadn't discussed the future past October thirty-first. Staying in Devils Hollow wasn't an option for her, and Max surely knew that. She'd tell him all the reasons why before going again, but until then, she'd take as much of him as he was willing to give.

Vi slipped through the doorway of the parlor and paused. The figure standing at the window facing the direction of the lake was *not* Max. Hecate's long, black hair snaked down her slender back in loose tendrils, dark on her blood-red robe. She really did play the part of a witch perfectly.

Before she could retreat without being noticed, Hecate turned. She held a small, leatherbound book in her hands. Her mouth curved into a secretive smile. "Violet. I hope your evening has been pleasant."

Dammit. So much for slithering away, and the private time she wanted — *needed* — with Max would be far less enjoyable with company.

Vi trudged toward the sideboard and leaned against it. The shot glasses winked in the cupboard, taunting her. Maybe she could get rid of Hecate before Max showed up. "I wish."

"Tough night?" Hecate's black eyes glittered like a nocturnal animal's, as if she saw far more than humanly possible.

"Try a tough few nights." Violet wriggled her bare toes on the ancient, hand-woven rug Gramps had found tucked in the corner of the attic years ago, covered in dust. He'd thought he'd hit the jackpot. "If I could get more than three hours of sleep at once, I'd be performing a happy dance on the lakeshore, maybe sacrifice some blood."

"I would not jest of blood or sacrifices at Lake Forsaken, not without proper protection in place. The waters have been unsettled these last days." She cocked her head. "It's as if a long-awaited arrival has awakened a presence deep within the lake's already tormented aura. Sabrina claims it's due to the alignment of the planets. I believe otherwise."

Violet slid into the loveseat and tucked her hands into her hoodie pockets, needing the warmth to counter the cold sliding down her neck. She shouldn't have mentioned sacrifice, especially not after what Max had found on the shore that night. "I grew up in Devils Hollow surrounded by the urban legend of the Ward sisters and the lake." She shrugged. "I guess Abigail Ward is the only one who knows the full truth. Besides, history is so subjective these days. Throw in a bad behavior, and accomplishments get erased as if they'd never existed."

Hecate gazed again out of the window, candlelight drawing out deep blue streaks in her hair. "It is the fearful and weak who attempt to alter history to suit their own needs and beliefs. No one has the power to change the truth, only to hide it."

As much as she didn't want to continue the conversation, maybe an outsider had unearthed details yet unknown to Devils Hollow residents. Maybe Hecate knew something that could help her conquer her fear of the lake and what might lurk in its depths. "You've done a lot of research on the lake, haven't you?"

Hecate nodded and pivoted from the window, every ounce of sly humor gone. "It's a dark and bloody one, as I'm sure you are aware."

"Everyone knows the local Devils Hollow urban legend." Vi drew up one knee and settled back in the chair. "How Abigail Ward, enraged over losing the man she desired to her sister Anna, sacrificed herself in an act of revenge and cursed her sister. The lake formed from her blood. To this day, Abigail haunts the lake, thirsting for vengeance."

"Ah, yes. The tale told by most, that Abigail and Anna were ferociously competitive. When Caleb Adams arrived in Devils Hollow, the girls moved to a new level—passionate jealousy. Abigail lost Caleb to Anna, went mad, sacrificed her soul to evil in exchange for a curse—and Lake Forsaken was born."

Vi nodded politely. Same story she'd heard a thousand times. So much for learning any secrets that might shed light on her own near-drowning, the unearthly voices, what she believed she saw in the water, the nightmares.

Or the dark premonition that haunted her still, like a promise unfulfilled.

"But that's not the version of the story I learned." Hecate set her candle on the coffee table and slid into the opposite chair, her silk robe whispering on the wood. She lifted the book in her hand. "I found this journal. It weaves a different tale—that Abigail and Anna weren't bitter rivals, but sisters of both blood and heart. It speaks of a different course taken by Abigail, one with neither hate nor jealousy."

"No need to be jealous, ladies." Max appeared in the parlor doorway in black pajama pants and a ratty Lynyrd Skynyrd T-shirt. He gracefully jumped over the back of the loveseat and landed in the cushions, slung an arm around Vi's shoulders and tugged her close to his side. "There's enough of me to go around."

Hecate rolled her eyes, and Vi couldn't help liking the woman a smidge more.

"Was there a midnight meeting called to order that I didn't know about?" He looked between them, then to the cabinet with the shot glasses. "Unkind to leave me out. And why hasn't the whiskey been poured?"

"You're late." Vi tucked her knees up and snuggled deeper under his arm, grateful for his warmth. "Hecate was just about to disclose another version of Abigail Ward's history."

"Should I get Violet the Doll to listen in?" Max shifted as if to get up.

Vi wrapped her arms around his waist like a manacle. "Get that doll and I'll hurt you."

Chuckling, he settled back and kissed her temple. "Promises, promises."

"Don't mind him." Vi gave Hecate an apologetic look. "He's immune to the supernatural."

Hecate's fine eyebrows lifted as she studied Max like a seven-headed insect beneath a microscope. "Interesting."

Max squirmed, a fact Vi enjoyed a bit more than necessary. Not many people could make him uncomfortable. "I'd love to hear what you learned." He waved a hand. "Please, continue."

"Certainly." Hecate leaned back, settled the book in her lap, and templed her fingers in a story-telling pose. "The journal claims that when Caleb started courting Anna, Abigail was indeed devastated but kept her feelings secret, never revealing to another soul that she loved Caleb, too. She cared for her sister more than herself and refused to ruin their happiness."

Vi leaned forward. That was a detail no one in Devils Hollow had ever relayed. In all the stories, Abigail cared for only herself and getting what she wanted.

"But when Caleb and Anna announced on their wedding day that they intended to move from Devils Hollow the next morning, Abigail's heartbreak overcame her. She couldn't imagine a life without the only two people she loved. So that night, beneath a Hallow's Eve blood moon while the wedding celebration continued, she took her own life. The blood flowing from her wrists, blending with her tears, formed Lake Forsaken. By morning, the lake had settled where nothing had been before. The salt from her tears ruined the earth around the lake. Only when her spirit is freed will green things grow again."

"That's far more romantic than the legend we grew up with." Vi relaxed into the cushions and Max—and far more boring. A kind, benevolent Abigail Ward wouldn't leave a dark spirit that haunted the waters, searching for retribution, tormenting sixteen-year-old girls with nightmares.

Or deadly premonitions.

"Not the type of story that would draw thrill-seeking tourists," Max added, echoing her thoughts.

"Perhaps it is a tale lost in time, told by a gentler soul to soften a terrible tragedy. But the slivers of information I found during my years of research suggest it holds too many grains of truth to dismiss." Hecate lifted her chin slightly, a challenge that none of her gang would take.

"Don't let Widow Beasley hear about it." Vi wasn't even kidding. Beasley protected the urban legend with everything she had. "She'll have the Devils Hollow townsfolk mob you with pitchforks." The twisted tragedy and the curse were what kept Hallowtoberfest alive and tourism rolling in. Without Abigail Ward's bloodthirsty phantom, Devils Hollow would cease to exist.

"It could be simply that the truth holds a bit of both the urban legend and the kinder version, as the journal proclaims." Hecate paused, as if listening to voices only she could hear. She then said in a voice of midnight and shadows, "Revenge is often borne of great love, twisted by an even greater pain."

A chill brushed Vi's neck, and the little hairs on the back of her neck prickled. She burrowed deeper into Max's warmth, grateful when he tightened his hold.

"Tourists certainly believe something supernatural is going on." Max drummed his fingers on his knee, a telltale sign of nerves. "Not that I've seen anything — or heard, smelled, touched, felt…anything." His disappointment was palpable. He hated being left out — and had no idea how lucky he was. If she could trade her own experience for a void, she'd do it in a nanosecond.

"Oh, Abigail clings to Lake Forsaken, no question. Guilt and violence, anguish and regret, sorrow and betrayal often tether spirits to the mortal plane." Hecate opened the journal and carefully turned through yellowed pages, the translucent parchment crackling beneath her fingers. "Her death, no matter its nature, tied her to this place of mourning. Whether a curse was intentionally cast or was a product of Abigail's despair at the loss of her sister, if one exists, we will cleanse Lake Forsaken of its stain and open the way for Abigail to find her way to the light."

"And what about any evil?" Vi couldn't help but ask. "Does it go to the light, too? Or does the light burn it up?"

"The darkness is more difficult to destroy, and curses aren't easily broken." She spread the journal open on her lap and traced a line with one black-tipped fingernail. "We will do what we can to face the forces of darkness. On the day when the veil between worlds is thinnest, if all goes well, we'll leave Devils Hollow better than when we came."

"And if all *doesn't* go well?" Vi hated how small her voice sounded. Max squeezed her shoulders, too observant, as usual.

Hecate looked up, and her sly, secret smile returned. "Devils Hollow will have more stories to build their businesses on. Either way, someone will benefit from our work."

Vi ignored the icy finger tracing her neck. "In your research, do you ever deal with…dreams? Nightmares?"

"What manner of nightmares?" Hecate leaned forward, new curiosity glinting in her eyes.

Hyperaware of Max sitting so still next to her, Vi hesitated. Some questions were better left unasked, some answers best left unknown. But if someone had solid advice to offer, she'd be an idiot not to find out.

"Drowning." She didn't add that she'd almost drowned herself. Only Max and Dahlia knew about that day. Max knew about her nightmares, only because he'd witnessed them. Neither one knew about her premonition…not yet. And sharing her greatest fear with a woman who took the name of the queen of witches wasn't happening.

"Drowning in Lake Forsaken." The sentence was all statement, not a hint of question. Hecate watched her, seeing far too much.

"I almost drowned in Lake Forsaken." Vi blinked. She hadn't meant to say that aloud.

Beside her, Max released a soft, hissing breath.

"I know." Hecate shrugged when Vi stared at her. "Grandpa Ward told me, but even if he hadn't, I sense the lake's mark on you."

The lake's mark. Vi shivered, suddenly ready to be somewhere, anywhere else.

"Do you believe in fate, Violet Keller?"

Vi shook her head. "We choose our own destinies. How they pan out has everything to do with what we do and how we react to what other people throw at us."

Hecate tsked. "You don't believe in luck, even a little?"

"Bad luck, yeah. Good luck? She's never been much of a friend of mine."

"Until you left Devils Hollow," Hecate said softly, lifting the journal and turning it around. "The near-drowning, the nightmares and the doll risen from the lake's depths merely confirm my suspicions." She pointed to the page.

Holy crap. All the heat drained from her blood. On the yellowed onion skin, a charcoal illustration of a girl beneath a tree smudged the white. If Vi hadn't known better, she'd say it was her in that ancient drawing. At the corner of the page, in tiny, flowing handwriting was a name.

Abigail Ward.

"Burning hell." Max scooted to the edge of the couch and rested his hand on Vi's knee, protective.

"They are all connected to you, Violet," Hecate continued. "Surely you can't argue that. Tonight, at three a.m., we are seeking to communicate with the spirits tied to Lake Forsaken. You must join us. Help us break the cycle for you, cleanse you of the force that claws into your dreams."

Vi hesitated. It was what she wanted, to face the memories and whatever *thing* — imagined or not — she'd encountered at the bottom of the lake years ago. This time, she wouldn't be alone. She'd be with people who knew what they were doing...maybe. At the very least, the Dimensions gang knew more than she did.

Max cleared his throat in the silence. "I don't think that's a good —"

"Will I have to get in the water?" Vi said through the chill snaking into her bones.

Hecate's smile gleamed like knives in the gloom. "Only if you want to."

Chapter Twenty-One

"This is a terrible idea," Max whispered to Vi. He hunched in his jacket and eased closer to her, gloom closing in on all sides. Whatever hocus pocus Hecate and her crew were up to, having Vi involved could lead to nothing good, but she hadn't asked for his advice. And telling her what she should or shouldn't do wasn't his call. All he could do was have her back if she needed it.

He shifted on his feet and scanned the surrounding trees. This wasn't the hot and heavy evening tryst he'd planned with Vi at all. The moon cast a cold gleam over the barren banks of Lake Forsaken and stained the soil the color of old blood. The water seemed to deflect the light, holding its secrets in the dark depths. A chilled breeze lifted Hecate's loose, black hair like a funeral veil as she crouched with the others on the water's edge.

This is such a bad idea. Sure, Devils Hollow depended on the fascination of the supernatural to survive. Even though the most woo-woo he'd ever experienced was an extra frosty draft in Ward House, he'd never faulted anyone for believing in forces unseen, a bit of magic to soften the mundane. He wanted that as much as the next guy. Clearly, there were other forces at work beyond the five senses. There were too many miracles in the world to deny it.

But whether or not his sixth sense was faulty or there was nothing more to spirits than superstition, he hadn't been able to shake the sick coil in his gut after finding the remains of Beasley's poor cat. And putting Vi out there as a sacrifice? His fingers itched with the urge to pick her up, throw her over his shoulder and run as far and as fast as he could.

Running off with Vi anywhere was an exquisite thought, but he wasn't ready for any sensitive parts to be maimed. Manhandling her would not end well for him. As much as he hated the slithering sense of *wrong* up and down his nerves, Vi needed this. She'd never find peace until she figured out how to fight the source of her fear and destroy it for good. And he'd be there, battling beside her.

Vi slipped her arm through his, and he went still, all thoughts of lakes, ceremonies and spirits splintering. His heart squeezed in his chest, and it took all his strength not to pull her to him and wrap her next to his hammering pulse.

For most, so small a move would mean nothing. For Vi to seek comfort was huge. For her to want it from him?

It was everything, the closest thing to a confession he'd get. For now, he'd take it, write it on the permanent pages of his soul.

"Are you ready, Violet?" Hecate looked over her shoulder. Her minions circled her, all dressed in black, necklaces of protective crystals glittering on their chests, iron scabbing their ears and wrists. The excitement shining in their eyes betrayed the somber expressions. Raven had her video camera ready. Clearly, they lived for this stuff.

"Sure." Violet slipped free of his hold, and Max shoved his hands into his pockets to deny the need to grab her wrist and pull her back, safe.

With measured steps, her gaze set ahead, Vi moved toward the giant symbol the gang had drawn into the earth.

"You, too, Max." Hecate's smile was sharp. "All present souls must be within the circle. It's a matter of precaution, a protection should any part of the ritual go…unplanned."

"Wonderful." Giving them authorization to do this, to mess with the lake in the middle of the night, had been a mistake. But when Vi had glanced at him, her dark eyes wide and questioning, he couldn't regret it. Not yet, anyway. Whatever Vi wanted, if he had the power to give it to her, he would.

If only she could comprehend that the offer extended far beyond witching hour shenanigans on the shore of Lake Forsaken.

Max stopped at the edge of the circle etched into the earth. It was at least eight feet in circumference, split into seven equal segments fanning around a circle at the center. An iron bowl filled with liquid hung over a small fire at the center, ready for spells.

Burning hell, he wished his sleepless nights were due to Vi's natural voodoo, not Esmerelda and friends.

"Pick one section of the circle," Hecate instructed them. "Be careful not to break any line or smudge a single sigil. It's very important to remain in your area once the ritual begins. Do *not* break the circle for any reason."

As they each carefully stepped into their respective spots, the wind cut across the lake, carrying the scent of moisture and decay—a barrow. As prickles sparked the back of his neck, Max freed his hands from his pockets. Whatever wicked thing came this way, he needed to be ready.

In the section next to him, Vi seemed completely calm, her golden hair in a tight, prepared-to-kick-some-ass bun, black boots, jeans and jacket. But her skin appeared pasty in the moonlight, her eyes like fathomless holes. His fingers twitched with the need to reach for her, comfort her. He hated the line separating them, but he'd read enough books to know those boundaries were important. He wouldn't do anything stupid to endanger her.

Hecate faced the lake, and a hush fell, even the night listening in. She looked at the moon and shook her hair back. It writhed down her back like snakes as she lifted her hands in a pose of supplication.

Max resisted a sigh. It was a reenactment of every stereotypical horror movie he'd ever seen. He wanted nothing more than a nightcap of apple whiskey, his bed and Vi, not necessarily in that particular order. The second Hecate's nonsense was done and Vi was ready to leave, he'd make it happen.

"Tonight, at this hour when spirits roam closer to the veil betwixt worlds, beneath the waxing moon, we call out to the ancestors of this land whose blood and bones feed the earth. Those sleeping under the water, we summon you."

Hecate cast some sort of powder into the bowl at the center of the circle. Smoke billowed free and curled up to the sky, momentarily hiding the moon's light.

"Abigail Ward, we beckon you from afar with an offer of your favorite scent." Hecate tossed a sprig into the bowl, and the spicy aroma of lavender joined the smoke. "We offer strawberries and apples to remind you of taste." A handful of sliced fruit dropped into the bowl. She released an ivory feather. "A feather so you might fly."

The whirr of flapping wings drowned the hum of the small fire beneath the bowl. A snow-white owl floated through the smoke, there and gone. A chill shuddered through Max.

"There you are," Hecate whispered, her mouth turned into a half-smile.

"What was that?" Raven asked, her camera turned not up, but outward, to the lake.

"I heard it, too." Sabrina stared out at the water, her arms around herself as if she was suddenly cold. The laces of her black boots tick-tick-ticked against the leather, an instrument played by the wind.

"Did you hear anything?" Max murmured to Vi.

Vi wasn't looking at the lake or the sky. She stared, wide-eyed at the bowl in the center of the circle and the smoke curling up from burnt offerings.

All the hair on the back of Max's neck stood straight as an image formed in the smoke, blurred but with enough detail to decipher a feminine nose, mouth, pale hair. The features sharpened. If he didn't know better, if she wasn't standing right beside him, he'd claim it was Vi in the smoke, gazing back at them.

One small, ridiculous segment of his brain laughed hysterically. Finally, after all the years of zero paranormal experiences, he had solid confirmation that the other side existed. The rest of his rational self froze in disbelief and, he wasn't too proud to admit it, no small amount of fear.

Oberon gasped as Raven aimed her camera at the smoke, and Hecate motioned briskly at them to be still and silent. Her black gaze fixed on the image in the haze, like a crow discovering a treasure that it had no intention of relinquishing.

"Abigail Ward, we welcome you to our circle."

At the face so like her own reflected in the smoke, Vi could hardly breathe. Blood roared in her ears, driving her heart to pump too hard. Abigail could be mistaken for a family member, a sister, aunt or cousin. What that meant, she was equally sure she both didn't want to know and needed to find out.

She reached for Max's hand. He caught her fingers before she'd made it halfway between them, his skin warm, his strength the only thing that kept her standing upright.

"Spirit, tell me your true name." Hecate spoke like an enchantress of fantasy novels, confident and practiced, a demon master who expected to be obeyed. "Confirm your identity and speak only truth."

The smoke twisted and writhed like worms as it shifted toward Hecate. "You have no authority to command me, mortal."

Even with her sweater and coat, goosebumps rolled down Vi's arms.

"And yet here you are, summoned by my command, by the combined power of the seven souls here." Hecate lifted her chin. "We demand your name. Speak it."

"I am Abigail Elizabeth Ward." Abigail made a slow spin, taking in each of the gang in turn. When her inhuman gaze fell on Vi, it felt as if an ice pick struck her heart. Cold spiderwebbed out into her bones and blood. Only the warmth from Max's hold kept her tethered to the present. The world blurred and wavered, as if she stared out from a thick layer of ice.

Or water.

"Why are you here?" Abigail's question ripped through her, sharp as a serrated blade. "Why did you not heed my warning?"

Vi's vision shimmered and returned to normal. She sucked in a deep breath of air, her lungs burning. It took all her strength not to break the circle and hide from the spirit's intense gaze. Violet Keller might run, but she did *not* hide from anyone but Gramps.

"She's no one to you," Max answered with unexpected authority. For his initial supernatural experience, he handled it surprisingly well. She'd panicked her first time. Not much had changed. Even with the protective circle and Max beside her, she shook in her boots. "And you need to let her go."

Abigail went still and cocked her head, as if listening to a beloved voice from far away. Slowly, almost reluctantly, she faced Max. "Caleb," she whispered. "Have you returned for me at last?"

"I'm not stupid enough to give you my name, but it sure as hell isn't Caleb." Max lifted his hand as if to push the spirit back with flesh and blood. "And I'm definitely not here for you."

The spirit moaned and doubled over as if in pain. Black oozed on its chest and spread, a wound opening anew. "Why can you not leave me in peace?"

"That's why we're here," Hecate cut in. "To set you free so you may find peace."

"Only *she* can give me peace. Only *she* can give me freedom."

"*She?*" The word was out before Vi could hold her tongue. She hadn't intended to speak, had no desire to regain the phantom's attention, but she had the distinct impression Abigail didn't mean Hecate, a woman willing to give her spirit peace and freedom. Someone else imprisoned Abigail. But who?

Abigail once again met her gaze, and there was nothing but bleakness in her expression. "Beware." Her image in the smoke blurred, voice fading. "Beware."

"Who do you speak of?" Victor demanded, black eyebrows drawn in a fierce frown. He jabbed a finger at the smoke, iron rings gleaming on his fingers. "Answer before you depart, spirit!"

Abigail threw back her head and wailed, a prey shriek. The noise must have startled the owl from its roost, for it circled them once before flapping away in a flurry of white wings.

Abigail's image disappeared. The smoke thickened, expanded, a storm gathering strength. Once fragrant with lavender, the scent turned toxic, rotten. A wind ripped through the circle, clawing at hair and clothes. Vi shielded her eyes from the grit pelting her face. She gripped Max's fingers tight, afraid if she let go, she'd tumble out of the circle. Across from her, Victor stumbled and righted himself with a curse.

"Cease, unholy spirit." Hecate stood firm in the blasting wind, her hair whipping across her like stripes of night, her long skirt wrapped around her legs. She held out her hands as if readying to cast a wicked spell.

A gust roared through the circle, and the fire winked out. The wind died as suddenly as it arose, taking the smoke with it. A deep, aching silence stretched as they stared at one another. Vi's breath puffed quick, temporal clouds of white. Everyone seemed afraid to break the stillness, as if they might all shatter with the smallest noise.

Between heartbeats, Victor gagged, choking. He clutched his throat. His eyes rolled back in his head.

Blood dribbled from the corner of his mouth, bright red on his pale, fake-vampire skin.

"What's going on?" Sabrina whispered.

Hecate sliced her hand through the air, a warning to be quiet. Raven never stopped filming.

Victor straightened and dropped his hands to his side. The temperature slid to winter-cold as he lifted his gaze. Something *other* looked through eyes that had turned milky white. "What mortal dares disturb us?" Distant and echoing, a woman's voice emerged from his mouth. "What manner of suffering do you wish upon yourself?"

That voice. Chills raced across Vi's skin and her pulse skipped like a broken record. It was the same voice that haunted her nightmares, the same voice that had called her name from the depths of the lake.

"Speak your name." Hecate's words were clear and unwavering, but the hand fisting her skirt trembled.

Victor's face stretched into a wide, plastic smile, as if he was endlessly amused that Hecate expected an answer. He paused. A glob of blood dripped from his chin and landed in the bowl at the center. Slowly, Victor turned his head and stared straight at Vi. "Sister."

No matter how much she wanted to, Vi couldn't look away. A buzzing filled her head, the droning of a thousand angry bees, and when the wind slammed into her back, she couldn't keep her balance. Her knees hit the hard earth in a jolt of pain. Max's hold on her hand vanished. The night blurred, and the world fell away.

Water surrounded her...heavy, suffocating. She couldn't breathe. If she opened her mouth, only the lake would flood in, black and lifeless. Slick weeds stroked her legs, brutally soft. Icy fingers wrapped around her flailing ankles. She clawed for a surface she couldn't reach.

"Sister." The disjointed voice rattled in Vi's skull. "Why did you forsake me?"

Vi violently shook her head, desperation a cornered, snarling beast. But no matter how hard she kicked or thrashed, she sank deeper. Her limbs weakened, the cold water sapping her strength as her lungs burned, burned, burned for oxygen.

"Join me, sister."

Vi opened her mouth to scream, a protest, a violent denial. Only bubbles emerged, rising to the air she needed to live, surrendering one by one. The lake rushed into her lungs and darkness took her, deep and final.

"Violet Keller, return!" Hecate's voice thundered through the black.

Gasping, Vi opened her eyes to Max staring down at her, panicked. A sky full of diamond stars and silver moon glittered behind him.

Holy crap. It hadn't been real, only a nightmare. She sucked in another breath and somehow resisted sobbing. *It wasn't real.*

"Vi." Max stroked her hair back, his hands shaking. "You fainted."

Sure. Fainted. That sounded reasonable, far better than the alternative. "I didn't faint." She forced herself to sit up. The night spun for a second, and she wrapped her arms around her knees until gravity settled into place. "Fainting is for wimps."

Max grinned, which did nothing to add color to his complexion. "There's my girl."

Hecate crouched close. "What do you remember, Violet?"

Darkness, water, bone-crushing cold. A terrifying whisper. Sister. Why did you forsake me?

"Nothing." She squinted as the rest of the gang surrounded her. Sabrina rubbed her arms as if she couldn't get warm. Raven seemed to have forgotten her recording duties, the video camera at her side, filming the ground. Victor sprawled in the circle, spread-eagled like a sacrifice. "What happened?"

"Anna Ward happened." Hecate's smile sharpened to feral. "It appears we have more than just Abigail's spirit to exorcise."

Chapter Twenty-Two

An hour after returning home and settling in for the last hours before dawn, Max still couldn't sleep. He blew out a breath and stared up at the ceiling, the familiar angles of his bedroom in the gloom a small comfort. When he closed his eyes, Violet filled his vision, lying in a funeral pose, her skin corpse-pale, not breathing. *Burning hell.* He couldn't get the image out of his head, couldn't calm the fear that he'd lost her — not to distance but to death.

And the thing that had used Victor as a personal puppet? Goosebumps prickled down his arms. As much as he'd dreamed of a paranormal encounter, if only just so he wouldn't feel like an outcast in his own hometown, he wasn't sure it was worth the cost of his peace. After witnessing Anna Ward looking at them from the other side through Victor's eyes, there was no going back.

The doorknob to his bedroom clicked, turning slowly, and his heart jackhammered. The door creaked open an inch, and he sat up fast, wielding the cross he kept hidden beneath his pillow. If either Ward sister followed them from the lake and thought to find an easy victim, she had another thing coming.

Vi peeked in, her blonde hair tousled, only her lovely face visible. Her gaze flicked to the cross. "Expecting company?"

He drummed up his cocky smile as his pulse kicked higher due to altogether different, and much more compelling, reasons. "Just hoping you'd eventually show up in my room to take advantage of me."

"Then exorcise me?" She arched an eyebrow.

"Exorcise you, sweeting? Never. Can't blame a guy for being prepared for any extreme." Max casually shoved the cross back under his pillow. "Are you — ?"

He'd barely got the words out before she'd launched across the room and onto the bed, landing on top of him. She wrapped her arms around his ribs and held on tight, as if he alone anchored her in a storm he couldn't detect.

"Vi, angel." He stroked her hair and kissed her temple, inhaling her floral scent deep into his lungs to ensure he wasn't dreaming. "You're safe. I promise not to let any summoned ghost, witch or tourist get you. They have to go through me first. In case you hadn't noticed, I'm not the scrawny kid too weak to stand up for himself anymore."

"I can't get her voice out of my mind," she whispered into his shoulder, her breath warm on his bare skin. "I'm afraid if I close my eyes, I'll stop breathing and wake up beneath the water again."

Max eased back and gently lifted her chin, meeting her gaze — haunted, scared, vulnerable — three qualities he rarely found in her dark eyes and hated with a vengeance. She should always feel safe, untroubled, treasured. "Tell me what you saw tonight. I know you lied to Hecate."

Her slender throat worked as she swallowed. She hesitated, her brow wrinkled, a sign of uncertainty that killed him. If she couldn't trust him enough to reveal what bothered her after such a strange night, what hope did he have of convincing her to take a chance on a lifetime love with him?

The next heartbeat, her shoulders sagged, and he released the breath he hadn't even known he'd been holding. All was not yet lost.

"Since returning to Devils Hollow, my nightmares have made a comeback." Her mouth tightened. "Viciously. I haven't got more than a few hours of sleep any night for the last two and a half weeks."

He'd never forgotten the nightmares that plagued her after she nearly drowned in the lake. On nights they'd sneak out and meet in the field, talking while the stars burned until they drifted to sleep, she'd wake up and burrow into his side as if she could climb beneath his skin and hide. She'd worn the same, spooked expression she had now. *I'm an idiot.* Even if years had passed, he should have recognized the signs.

"You should have told me...or Gramps. You know he'd mix up a remedy for you."

"Been there, done that. I raided his cabinet on day two."

He laughed softly. "Of course, you did."

"I didn't want to worry anyone." She rubbed one eye, and when she dropped her hand, the tired crescents smudging her skin seemed darker. "Nothing works, Max. The nightmares only go when I'm out of Devils Hollow, but I can't leave. I promised Dahlia. I can't let her down again."

Damn it all to hell. Another motivation for her to ditch him again. His stomach twisted. Somehow, someway, he needed to erase every single reason keeping her from staying. He refused to let her go without a struggle, not this time — not when he finally had her in his arms where she belonged.

"We'll figure this out." He cupped her face and looked her dead in the eyes so she'd understand he meant it with every mote of Maximus Carter stubbornness and determination. He hadn't been named after the character in *Gladiator* for nothing. Missing a sword did not make him any less deadly. "I promise. You aren't alone, Vi. We'll fight this, defeat it…together."

Tears swam in her dark eyes, and before he could move, she pressed her mouth to his. The kiss started out soft, gentle, a thank you between friends. But when she trailed her fingers down his shoulder, planted her palm directly over his wildly beating heart, he couldn't deny the need to return the favor, to keep her in his arms, her lips tangled with his.

Max lassoed her waist with one arm and jerked her tight to his chest. He didn't mind that she fell onto his lap, that her knees straddled his hips, how her surprised gasp only heightened every sense.

"Vi." Between kisses, he said her name like a prayer, a desperate wish. "Stay with me. Let me make you forget the nightmares."

Breaking free of his mouth, she eased back, her palm still pressed to his heart. Her lips were swollen from kisses, a blood-red bow against her pale face in the gloom. She studied him with grim misery, as if she could read his past, present and future and couldn't decide if she wanted to be around for any of it.

"We don't have to talk about any deep subject if you don't want to. We don't have to do anything you're not ready for. If you just want to snuggle, I'm down for that. You can choose what to keep for tomorrow and forget the rest. Whatever you want." He tried for his lopsided smile and suspected he royally failed.

"What I want..." The words hardly counted as a whisper. "What I want doesn't matter."

"You're wrong." He brushed her hair from her face. "What you want *always* matters to me."

Still watching him, she bit her bottom lip, and every single cell in his body jerked to attention. If she didn't want to fool around anymore, he'd stay true to his word. But damn, he wanted her mouth on him, her hands, any part of her body she was willing to spare. Hell, he'd settle for her pinkie toe scratching his knee.

Since Vi's reappearance, all his focus and thoughts — with the exception of Gramps — revolved around her. He was so in love with her he couldn't see straight. When she was near, he felt half-drunk and hot all over, as if he'd swigged a half-dozen shots of stolen whiskey. Every dream and hope realigned at her return, entwined in her. It was terrifying, the enormous power she held over him, how little control he had over it. The thought of not having her in his life nearly brought him to his knees.

Slowly, as if second-guessing herself, she lifted her hands and loosely hooked them around his neck. Vi sat very still and held his gaze, her expression revealing nothing.

He'd wasted years harboring his feelings for her, and by the time he'd found the guts to tell her the truth, it had been too late. Their romance had been too new, too fragile to overcome childhood wounds. Maybe nothing had changed. Maybe he couldn't convince her that they could face and conquer anything as long as they were together. That fear didn't matter. He was in deep, over his head, and if he were going to drown, he'd rather die fighting than sinking without a struggle. If Vi left again, it wouldn't be because she didn't know how deeply and desperately he loved her.

"Violet." His whisper was rough with longing, all the emotion he held inside spilling out in one name.

Her chin trembled, betraying her control. How could he not love this woman who melted for him when he least expected it?

Gently, he twisted his finger around an escaped strand of golden hair. The tress drifted over his skin like the finest silk as he released it, sleek and rich. "Just...stay."

"I couldn't bear it if anything happened to you." Her voice cracked, raw and vulnerable. Tears glittered in her dark eyes. "I need to know you're safe, alive, well and happy. If I lost you..." She squeezed her eyes shut.

"Why are you worried about that? Nothing is going to happen to me, sweeting." He pulled her tight. "And losing me isn't even possible. Whether or not you want it, I'm yours, no matter where you go...always."

Vi burrowed into him like she used to after one of her nightmares and pressed her face into the hollow of his throat. Her mouth brushed his pounding pulse, and every protective instinct flared to life. She didn't need him to defend her, bore the scars to prove that she was a fierce force all on her own, a survivor. But he'd do whatever it took to make her feel safe when she needed it most, let her know he was always on her side—had her back then, now and always.

"I'm not the gem you think I am," she murmured against his neck. "You deserve so much more than I could ever give you. I thought you'd figure that out by now."

"I've already figured it all out, made a plan and set it into motion." He slid his hand up her spine, enjoying the responsive shiver beneath his palm. "That's the beauty of being smarter than you."

She bit his neck, hard enough to sting.

He laughed. "Very well, *slightly* smarter. Here's the thing, sweeting." He leaned back and cupped her chin, holding her gently captive. "I've loved you for the entirety of my miserable life, since the moment you looked at eight-year-old me with those big, beautiful eyes as if you could see my scars and they were merely a part of who I am, not the tragedy they were. My love might be dumb and blind, but it's also so deep and powerful that sometimes I feel like I'll explode if I keep holding it in. I'll never get over you, Vi. I've tried. Life without you just doesn't work right for me. Bring me the salt and iron. I'll battle an entire army of spirits for you and never regret it."

She shook her head, and he pressed his mouth over hers before she could say any damaging, final words, a sweet, lingering kiss to remind her of all the reasons she had to stay. He wasn't ashamed to use whatever devices were at his disposal to distract her, to keep her close for as long as possible.

Forever.

Max broke the kiss and caressed her cheekbone with the back of his knuckles. "I didn't tell you all that so you'd make promises or confess your undying affection, although I won't protest if you insist." Gently, he grasped her hip with his other hand, anchoring her to him. "Just know I'm here for you. Near or far, I'll always be here for you."

Chapter Twenty-Three

Vi muttered a curse beneath her breath, a prayer for strength. Why did Max have to make everything so easy and simultaneously so hard? Maybe it had been a mistake to sneak into his room like she used to, but being alone in the Raven Room with her sketches of the lake on the walls, shadows watching from every corner and Anna Ward's voice in her head had threatened to bury her alive. As much as it would hurt, she had to tell Max the truth. It was the only way he'd understand why he had to let her go.

"After I almost drowned, besides the nightmares, I had a terrible vision—of you, of Dahlia. You both died…because of me." The words flew from her mouth, fast as bullets. If she spoke too slowly, she wouldn't be able to get them out. "It was too vivid to dismiss as anything other than a premonition. I knew, just…*knew* it was a warning to leave Devils Hollow, to prevent the three of us being together at the lake. And after tonight, I think it came from Abigail."

"A premonition" — Max lifted his eyebrows — "from Abigail."

She poked him in the chest — his firm, bare chest — and tried her best to ignore the need to trail her fingers over his pectoral to the plane of his shoulder, down the tempting curve of his arm. As much as she longed for a distraction from the phantoms clinging to her soul, she couldn't use Max that way. It would only complicate...everything. "You aren't allowed to poo-poo any supernatural event, not after last night."

"Maximus Carter does not poo-poo." He dropped his chin and narrowed his eyes, an attempt to be intimidating. The sparkles in his eyes gave him away, and she loved him even more for adding a hint of humor, chasing the fear back. "Name one time I've ever not believed you."

She couldn't do it. Even if she'd made up monster stories or cried werewolf a thousand times, he would've followed her into the woods with only a pocketknife and searched through every shrub, just to make her happy. New tears burned her eyes. *Shit.*

"You should have told me." His voice softened to a low rumble that glided along her nerves, playing counterpoint to the slide of his fingers skimming the bare skin of her hip bone at the waistband of her silk bat sleep shorts. "We could have figured it out together."

"At your expense? And Dahlia's?" She shook her head, banishing the hint of tears. "I wasn't going to take that chance." She shrugged. "Besides, I'd always planned to leave Devils Hollow, just not so soon or in such — "

"A dumbass way?" Max's lopsided smile came to life at her glare. "I already accepted your apology. Life is too short for five-year regrets, sweeting. You're here now." He slipped his hand up her ribs, igniting tiny sparks on her skin. "And that's all that matters."

It wasn't all that mattered, but Vi couldn't summon a rational argument when his lips found her throat.

"Whatever tomorrow brings, we'll take it one day at a time. We'll figure this out."

Her eyes drifted shut, tendrils of pleasure melting in her bloodstream, weakening her limbs. "And on November first?" Her voice rasped, needy, and she tipped her head back, offering her neck. "When I go back to my life waiting at Kickin' Ink?"

"One." He nipped her shoulder. "Day." Erased the sting in a long, silken lick. "At a time." Max trailed hot, open-mouthed kisses up her neck. "Fair warning, Violet. Until November first, I'm going to do my absolute, very best to convince you that, no matter what you decide or where you go, that I'm a necessary part of your life."

Already knew that. She shuddered as he nibbled on the shell of her ear, the unwanted spike of joy at his words almost immediately erased by the dark stain on her soul left by the lake. That reason was exactly why she had to leave him. She couldn't live in a world where Max didn't exist, and the longer she stayed, the more of a chance they'd all be at the lake at some point in time.

"Denying me isn't an option. And don't even think about ditching me without a goodbye again." A warning snarl entered his voice, as if he'd read her thoughts. Hell, maybe he had. "I'm yours, Vi, and I won't let you go."

The decent part of her whispered that she should break away from his amazing mouth, escape from his strong arms and capable hands while she still had a chance of operating with a clear mind. He adjusted her on his lap, and his hard heat hit her in the most sensitive spot.

That small, sensual shift, and the rest of her selfishly shoved decency aside and melted with a moan of surrender. *Just once more...* She was only doing what Max asked, to let tomorrow deal with itself, leave regret behind and live each day to the fullest. *Just once.*

Whatever consequences came tomorrow were entirely his fault, and the pain would suck for them both, but until then...

Vi threaded her fingers in his hair and held on tight as his lips worked their magic on her neck. Honestly, she had no chance of resisting him, not after he steadfastly defended her, shielded her when she needed it, saw all her flaws and still wanted her now, tomorrow. Her heart hitched. *Always.*

A future with Max was a dream, a fantasy she couldn't dare entertain long, but with the shadows clinging to the walls, the lake whispering from afar and only his touch shutting out the fear, she didn't have the strength to fight it anymore.

She buried her face in the crook of his neck and wrapped her arms around his ribs. It seemed that for the first time in hours she could finally draw a full breath as the tendrils of doubt and worry loosened from her heart.

A growl rumbled in his chest, and Max tipped her head back, his mouth finding hers once more. His bedroom with its baseball trophies, old-time family pictures and untidy shelves of books faded into the background. The aroma of fresh laundry blended with the outdoor scent of Max's skin, an aphrodisiac absorbed into her organs. Vi gripped the back of his hot neck, and his embrace tightened to crushing, as if he tried to tattoo her on every inch of his skin.

Just once more. She'd take these memories away with her, nestle them deep in her soul and set them free only when the loneliness became too heavy to bear. She'd hold them close as the days passed and Max finally moved on, found someone who fit him perfectly and brought him happiness, a partner who wanted nothing more than a Devils Hollow life. Maybe, if she pretended really hard, she could find shreds of purpose in her art, a sliver of joy, some faded echo of what might have been. It would be enough. It had to be.

The ancient, windup clock on his dresser ticked in the quiet like a gong, drowned by the relentless beat of her own heart. Desperately, as if every passing second might steal this moment away, she kissed and kissed him, pushed him down until his back hit the mattress and he was beneath her, all hardness and heat.

Max broke the kiss and trapped her face between his hands, holding her still. His chest rose and fell in ragged breaths. "Vi." His voice was low and raspy. "Be very sure that this is what you want. I don't want you to have any regrets."

With one finger, she traced the curve of his jaw, the morning stubble lusciously rough on her skin. She trailed his throat, down to his powerful shoulder, awed anew by the man he'd become. He was beautifully built, his body a masterpiece of toned muscle, sinew and silken skin. She briefly planted her palms on his firm chest, the wild beat of his heart vibrating beneath her hand, and drifted to the hard, rippled plane of his stomach.

"You're all I want." In case he hadn't figured that out yet, she rocked her hips against him, and he sucked in a shaky breath. "You're all I've ever wanted."

"Burning hell." He released her face, trapped her wrists and dragged her down to him. "You have no idea how long I've waited to hear those words from your sweet, lovely, wickedly perfect mouth." His lips found hers again, and liquid heat spiraled low in her belly. With a quick tug, he swept her camisole over her head and tossed it into the darkness, baring her torso. The delicious slide of skin on skin lasted only a second as Max sat up with her still in his arms, her knees straddling his hips. Her nipples contracted in the cool air, and when he filled his hands with her breasts and brushed his thumbs over the tender peaks, she gasped.

"*Max.*" The whine in her voice didn't even phase her, the fever in her rising, destroying all restraint. She wriggled on his lap, the need to be closer a savage beast that only he could tame. "I can't handle teasing right now. I need you." Passion blinded her, erased all worries of tomorrow, premonitions and darkness. Only Max and the rest of this night mattered, and if this was all she'd ever know of his love, she'd savor each second to the fullest. She wanted his weight on her, inside her, to be filled with him until she couldn't think straight.

As if sensing what she wanted, in one quick move, Max flipped her onto the mattress and stretched his body over hers in heavy, exquisite possession. Vi nearly sighed at the sensation of finally being right where she belonged.

With Max. Always with Max.

With a shaking hand, he brushed the hair from her face. His fiercely tender expression made her heart swell and push at her ribcage. "Vi, you completely undo me." He bent his head and kissed the unfinished rose on her shoulder, reverent. "Every inch of you is perfect, an artwork of ink and flesh. I wouldn't change a single shade."

She reached for his cheek, and he trapped her hands above her head on the pillow with a shake of his head.

"I need to be in control. If you touch me more, I'll lose all dignity."

"I'm definitely okay with that." She bucked her hips, and he made a pained groan. She wriggled to free her hands. The hard shape of him pressed against her sleep shorts, taunting, and stroking him there became a burning need.

Max kissed her furiously, almost hard enough to bruise her lips, and in the next second, his weight was gone. Vi opened her eyes with a snarl of protest. If he intended to tease her as some sort of vengeance...

All thoughts dissolved as she found Max standing beside the bed, his thumbs hooked in the waistband of his boxers. A hint of mischief curved one corner of his mouth as he watched her like the star of a show waiting for the audience to settle before the performance of a lifetime.

Who was she to deny him the pleasure? She rose onto her elbows while dragonflies fluttered in her stomach, wild with excitement. *Damn.* She'd had enough steamy musings of him over the years, but reality didn't do her imaginings justice. The shadows softened details, making it seem as if he stepped from the dream world just for her.

The muscles of his stomach contracted as he slowly pushed his boxers down. Her gaze followed the agonizing disrobement to the sexy V she'd admired too many times to count, the fine trail of hair leading to the parts of Max she'd only met once. That single meeting had both ruined her for any other man and fueled her fantasies for the last five years.

His boxers dropped to the floor, and her mouth went dry. *Holy crap.* The fantasies *definitely* didn't do him justice, and her memory must be fading because she didn't remember him being so...endowed. Standing proudly at full attention made it difficult for her to look away.

Max spread his arms in a *what do you think* pose, and Vi managed to drag her gaze to his face, her cheeks heating. He lifted his eyebrows. "Speechless, sweeting?"

She opened her mouth, shut it, opened it again. Nodded, and when his smile widened to brilliant, she couldn't regret stoking his ego.

"I've been working out."

She cleared her throat and forced her attention to stay on his eyes, not the needy part bobbing with his every move. "Hard work pays off, it seems. But just so you know, I liked you just as much when you were a wiry teenager who had no idea what he was doing."

All humor drained from his expression, and she cringed. Maybe she shouldn't have said anything emotional. Those were words better said in the afterglow of sex, not before. Then, she could have something to blame it on.

Without a word, fire gleaming in his eyes, he prowled the two steps to the bed, grabbed her bare ankles and pulled her across the mattress to him in one hard tug. Another yank, and her sleep shorts were off her legs and thrown over his shoulder.

"Do you know how many times I've dreamed of you in my bed, Vi?" Raw need rumbled in his low voice, and her stomach clenched. "All the dark, dirty things I've wanted to do to you?"

Now, she truly was speechless, trapped in his web like a weak, trembling butterfly.

He kissed and nipped his way up her calf. "To make you beg for my touch? To make you plead for my forgiveness?" He slid onto the bed between her knees, the stiff hair on his legs tickling her inner thighs. "To punish you with pleasure until you were on your knees at my feet, clinging to me as if I alone could give you enough oxygen to breathe?"

Her heart pounded, deafening. Oh, he *definitely* wasn't the teenage boy who'd been her first everything. The Max she'd grown up with had been mischievous but cautious, more invested in what other people thought, concerned about what other people needed from him, not the other way around. This new, dominant side of him rocked her to the core, made her throb in anticipation.

In one quick move, he pulled her onto his lap and settled her directly over his erection, her knees on each side of his hips. The tip of him teased her entrance, and when she wriggled to get to what she wanted, he gripped her waist, holding her fast.

"Not so hasty, love. This time, I'm in control, and I plan to make it last for a while, at least long enough to hear you moan my name and beg for more."

"*Max.*" She gripped his shoulders, wrestling for dominance. "Is that enough of a moan for you?"

He laughed, short and brutal. "Not even close."

Max hooked his hands beneath her arms and lowered his head to kiss the spot between her breasts. Vi threaded her fingers in his silken hair and gasped as he closed his mouth over her nipple and sucked. Soft, hot strokes of his tongue made her squirm on his lap, the twitch of him beneath her frustrating, too far away. He switched to the other breast and bit her gently, tugging at her throbbing flesh.

A noise she didn't recognize rose from her throat of desperation and need. She slid lower, dragging her damp breasts over his chest, the sprinkling of his hair a delicious friction on her overheated skin. Never had another man brought her to such vibrant life, where every inch of her clamored for his hands and teeth, mouth and tongue. Maybe she'd second guess her surrender in the bright spotlight of morning, but for now there was only Max, his lean, muscled body, his naughty mouth on her skin, and she was going to luxuriate in every single sensation with him.

Max slipped his hands to her ass, and he squeezed, each touch a mix of reverence and desire. His movements turned leisurely, lazy, drifting over her limbs with agonizing slowness.

"Is this your idea of punishment?" The words were little more than gasps as he trailed hot, open-mouthed kisses over her breasts while controlling her body by his grip on her butt. "Because it's totally working. Whatever you want, I confess." Her breath hitched as his finger brushed her where she needed it most, a tempting, flirting promise.

Max laughed again, soft and sensual. "I want you, Violet—all of you, every day. In my arms, by my side, stretched out and moaning in my bed or yours, the meadow or barn, doesn't matter where." The slide of his tongue along her lobe made her shiver, and when he followed with a bite, she gasped. It was as if he had a roadmap of her body and knew right where to touch her, taste her, to make her squirm with growing desire. "Confess you want that, too, and I'll consider giving you what you want."

She bit her lip as he rocked his hips up, once, just enough to brush her most sensitive spot. Not moaning his name was one of the hardest things she'd ever done. He drew a fingertip across the delicate crease of her thigh and groin, avoiding where she needed his touch most.

Vi dug her fingernails into his back, his arm beneath her bottom holding her captive, keeping her from taking what she wished. "This is coercion, and nothing I say will count."

"I never promised to play fair in the bedroom." He leisurely circled the feathery whorls of hair, making delicious circles with his thumb. "All of you, every day. Say it."

As he toyed with her unmercifully, Vi pressed her face into his shoulder. She'd had a zillion fantasies of Max over the years, but she hadn't counted on him developing this confidence or command. It exceeded every dream, day or night.

"It's so easy, sweeting." His breath warmed the shell of her ear, his voice rough. "Tell me you know I'm right, and your wish will be my pleasure to fulfill." He pressed his thumb in a spot that made all of her muscles tighten and twitch with anticipation.

Her skin too hot and tight, she squeezed her eyes shut. What could it hurt, really, to say a few words that they both knew were true? "I want you, too."

He laughed, low and wicked. "Not good enough, love." He slipped a finger inside her, and she bit his shoulder, needing the anchor to not float away. "If you expect me to make good on my promise, I need specifics. What, exactly, do you want from me?"

"All of you." She gasped, his fingers circling, pumping, tormenting, stoking the storm inside her to a twisting frenzy. "All day. Every day."

"That wasn't so tough, was it?"

A garbled noise came from deep in her chest, her best and only response. He sounded calm and collected, but his shoulders rose and fell with his rapid breaths. The tautness of his body beneath and around her was impossible to miss, and moisture gathered on his skin. She licked away the bead of sweat slipping down his neck, and it was his turn to groan.

Max's hold beneath her loosened, and she jerked as he allowed her to lower an inch, to finally sample the hard, scorching heat of him against her dampness. He shifted on the bed, spreading her legs wider, and eased in deeper. Vi hissed in a breath. *Holy hell's bells.*

"Okay?" He studied her face, his expression strained. His legs trembled between her thighs, a testament to his restraint.

"Frickin' fantastic." She cupped his jaw and kissed him, hard and long, communicating with her lips and tongue how fine she truly was. His answering groan, the silken slide of tongue on hers, the drive of his hips in full possession, drowned every worry beneath bliss. Vi couldn't get close enough. She tangled her fingers in his hair, threw her head back and clamped her legs around his hips. Riding out the storm Max brewed in her body and stirred in her soul was all she could do.

Max furrowed his brow and closed his eyes. He grasped her nape and brought her mouth back to his, claiming her lips. His free hand squeezed her hip and guided her to his own hedonistic rhythm, primal and insistent. The deep, fast thrusts mimicked the tempo of his tongue, offering, plundering, devouring her with frantic heat.

Sweet, liquid tension burgeoned low in her core, and she tightened her hold on his shoulders, muffling her moans into his neck. Vi squirmed harder against him, lost in a barrage of sensation. The bristles of his unshaven jaw scraped her cheek in delicious abrasion. The coarse hair on his legs tickled her inner thighs. The flex of his muscles as he worked her into a frenzy, the plunging length of him inside her, his soft lips and stinging teeth on her breasts, his hand cupping her ass as she rode him all gathered into a wrecking ball of fever.

Her limbs locked and pleasure exploded in a tidal wave. Vaguely, she was aware of Max murmuring her name, the upward drive of his hips, wild and wanton. She shuddered, and her body spasmed in surge after blinding surge until she collapsed, weak and spent in his arms.

With one last, desperate thrust, Max buried himself to the hilt with a growl. He groaned her name as he toppled over the edge with her.

Reeling as if she'd downed an entire bottle of Gramps' apple whiskey, Vi couldn't even argue as Max loosened his hold, his breathing choppy. She throbbed with aftershocks, his length still inside her.

"My sweet, amazing Violet." His whisper cracked with emotion. He pushed her tangled hair from her face and gazed into her eyes. "You've undone me once again. Why that continues to surprise me, I have no idea."

Warmth spread through her, unstoppable. She'd never get used to the way he looked at her, with a love and devotion that she could never hope to be worthy of, as if she alone set his moon into motion. In her mind's eye she still was, and maybe always would be that broken, rebellious girl who'd never fit in.

Yet, Max had always seen a beauty in her darkness when no one else could. And when he studied her with such knowing intensity, as if he adored every jagged piece of her, it was enough to make a girl feel like maybe she could be enough.

Vi couldn't decide whether to laugh or cry — probably both. But when Max rolled her onto her back, his warm weight trapping her against the mattress, she couldn't protest. He kissed her again, his mouth both tender and hungry, his hands worshipful and demanding, and she closed her eyes in helpless surrender.

Tomorrow. She'd save her doubts and decisions for later. For this moment, she'd pretend that love was enough, and she could be the girl Max needed.

Until then, tomorrow could go screw itself.

Chapter Twenty-Four

The gray touch of dawn filtered through Vi's eyelids, and she resisted the call to wake up. For the first time since returning to Devils Hollow, she'd slept without a single nightmare. Whatever dreams she'd had receded into the ether, leaving footprints of only rest and peace.

Burrowing deeper into the warm blankets, she hugged her body pillow tighter. When she shifted, her thigh brushed something hard, hairy and definitely not made of feathers. She opened her eyes and froze, her heart on immediate flatline as memories of last night burned back to full life.

Max faced her, one arm slung over her waist, his features relaxed in sleep and so frickin' handsome that she couldn't draw a full breath. He might have more hair, but he was five times the snuggler her body pillow could ever hope to be. She tried to remain perfectly still, to simply savor the moment, to drink in every detail and ink each particular color, every plane and curve landscaping his face permanently on her heart.

Last night, he'd been everything she needed — friend, comforter, lover. He'd made her forget the lake and its spirits, the life waiting for her in November. In his arms, the nightmares, goals and responsibilities in Devils Hollow had disintegrated into unimportant. He'd regenerated every memory of their time together, as if five years had never passed at all.

Max had made her believe that somehow, someway, it would be all right. That hope clung to her even now, a candle flame kindled in her heart, expectant and unquenchable.

She fisted the blanket to deny the tender urge to stroke his stubbled cheek. As much as she should regret her weakness, could see no way of how this might work out without everyone being hurt, she'd do it all over again simply for this moment of being in his arms, watching him sleep.

Loving him.

Her heart ached. She didn't believe she could love him more than she already did, and he proved her wrong. Leaving him behind again would destroy her beyond recovery, which was why she needed to sketch him on her brain and later on paper, to remember him clearly in days to come.

She took in the straight line of his nose, the delicious curve of his mouth, her face warming at how those lips had teased and tempted her. Before she could think on that too long, she forced her gaze to the powerful column of his throat, the corded bulge of his shoulder, the delicate line of his collar bone, to the sprinkling of hair on his sculpted chest.

A surprising splash of color on his pectoral peeked from the blanket, a sliver of purple, too delicately shaped to be a bruise. Vi bit her lip. He'd mentioned he had a tattoo, had been so mysterious about it at the time, and in all the pandemonium, she'd forgotten about it. The gloom of night had hidden it while he'd been driving her mad with passion, and she had other, much larger objects on her mind at the time. But now, with sunlight drawing out the color, she had to know.

Careful not to wake him, she eased the blanket down an inch, two. Her breath caught. Tattooed right over his heart, the fragile petals of a single, tiny violet bloom shone with rich, vivid colors. A vine with vicious, black thorns took the place of a stem.

It felt as if a blade pierced her heart. The organ stuttered, stopped and restarted with a ragged beat. Tears burned her eyes. *Oh, this man.* Even though she'd hurt him, he'd printed a permanent reminder of her on his skin. How could she ever deserve him?

"I did it as a reminder that you'd come back to me, eventually." Max's sleepy voice broke the quiet. He watched her, wearing his sexy, irresistible, lopsided smile. "And it obviously worked."

She swallowed back the emotions swirling too close to the surface. If she set them free, they'd never return to the cage where they belonged. "So it seems."

He tightened his arm around her back and pulled her closer. "What it seems to me is that you might like me, at least a little." He nibbled on her neck, shooting tingles everywhere. "Why else would you still be in my room?"

"Didn't want to wake up Gramps by sneaking out." She closed her eyes and pressed her lips together to prevent a moan.

He chuckled against her throat. "I might believe you if I didn't know you could sneak into his room, steal his pillow from beneath his head and leave him dreaming, none-the-wiser."

"I'd never."

In one quick, nimble move, he flipped her onto her back, and she gave an embarrassing squeak. He gazed down at her, his eyes bright with heat. "No need to lie to me, sweeting. You forget that I know you." He brushed her nose with hers. "Intimately."

Despite everything they'd shared, both five years ago and last night—multiple times—her face heated. She played it off by snorting. "You know only what I want you to know. *Maxie*."

The challenge in his smile kicked her pulse into gear. Maybe she shouldn't have said that.

"What *I* know is that you make a delightful noise when I kiss you here." He nibbled just beneath her ear, and she couldn't control the half-groan, half-gasp that broke free. "Or how you squirm when I bite you here."

As his teeth grazed the cord between her neck and shoulder, her back arched in response, uncontrollable.

"Or the way you wriggle when I touch you...here." Max slid his fingers down between them.

Her eyes fluttered closed of their own accord. Every sensitive nerve in her body seemed to ignite at once, and she bucked her hips against his hand. Yeah, so maybe she knew exactly what she was doing when she decided to challenge him. Every point of contact between them was pure, unadulterated bliss.

A knock sounded on the bedroom door, and they both froze like guilty teenagers.

"Max, get up." Gramps' cracked voice boomed from the hallway. Vi held her breath as the doorknob rattled but didn't turn. Sometime in the night while she slept, Max must have locked it. *Thank God.*

"Give me a sec." Max scrambled up and grabbed his jeans from the chair. He pulled them up, going commando.

Vi's mouth went dry. The sight of him hastily buttoning up, hiding half of his perfect parts, sent new heat through her veins—but not enough to forget that Gramps was on the other side of the door. If he caught them together, they might as well get engaged. His shotgun would be ready to go, helpfully guiding them down the aisle.

Gramps knocked again, shaking the door. Vi pulled the blankets over her head and curled into a ball, hoping if he managed to get in, she'd be mistaken for a messy pile of fleece and flannel.

"Hurry up, son. Time's wasting."

From beneath the blankets, Vi held her breath as the door clicked open. *Please don't pay any attention to the extra-big pile of blankets...or my pajamas scattered around Max's room.* She shut her eyes. Holy hell, there was no getting out of this.

"What's the rush, Gramps?" Max's voice filtered through the material, calm and casual. Vi hoped he blocked the doorway so Gramps wouldn't come in. "Need help with breakfast? Hecate need extra shampoo or Victor missing his moisturizer? Oberon lost his towel again?"

Gramps grunted. "Nothing so pressing. Meeting in the breakfast room." His voice faded, as if he already headed away. "Ten minutes...or Duke gets your bacon."

Vi sighed and relaxed. Maybe this was the day her luck turned.

"Oh, and, Max?"

"Yeah?"

"Tell Violet to drag herself out of your bed and be there, too. We'll be having a discussion, the three of us."

Vi didn't bother hiding her groan as Gramps' heavy footsteps tromped down the stairs. She flung the blankets off and found Max still by the door, grinning like a fool.

"Shut it, Max." She rolled out of his bed, pulled a blanket around her bare body, and strode for the door with as much dignity as she could muster.

"I didn't say anything," he said, a laugh in his voice. "But since I'm already accused, I do have something to tell you."

She stopped at the doorway beside him and arched an eyebrow, giving him her best glare. "Be very, very careful with your words. And make it good, worth getting pummeled."

His eyes darkened with heat, and before she could retreat, he had her up against the wall, the full length of his body pressing into hers. "Best." He nipped her neck, and she bit back a groan. "Night." As his hands slipped beneath the blanket and reverently cupped her breasts, her breath snagged. He kissed her, long and slow. "*Ever.*"

When he released her, she nearly stumbled, held up only by his hands on her elbows. His satisfied chuckle did nothing for her pride.

"Hurry up and get dressed, sweeting." He guided her out of the door and swatted her bottom. "Bacon waits for no man or woman."

"Not hungry."

"Miss breakfast after Gramps told you to be there, and he'll have your hide."

Throwing him a one-finger salute over her shoulder while he laughed, Vi trudged to her room and slammed the door. Go hungry and deal with a grumpy Gramps later or choke down crepes while smiling and plotting her escape.

Leave Devils Hollow with no regrets. She tossed the blanket aside and headed for the shower, her chest tightening. Maybe some goals were beyond reach, wishes that only came true in fantasies.

* * * *

Somehow, Max didn't beat Vi to the sunroom. A fog had curled in from the woods, filling the windows with gray and fuzzy silhouettes of shrubs and statues in the landscape beyond, a perfect setting for the season. The delicious aromas of coffee, bacon and croissants filled the air, making his stomach growl. After last night, he could use an eight-course meal to replenish his energy, make sure he'd be ready for the next round with Violet, hopefully sooner than later. Max plopped into a cushioned chair and reached for the coffee carafe on the table.

"Not so fast." Quick as a striking snake, Gramps smacked his hand with his cane, sharp enough to smart. "We have matters to discuss, and I won't have you distracted by drink." He took a sip from his own cup, glaring over the rim.

"But—"

From the next chair, Vi kicked his shin without looking at him, her heavy boot leaving a sting. Hands clasped in her lap, she focused on Gramps. She smelled of soap and roses, her wet hair in a hasty bun at the nape of her neck. Black yoga pants and zip-up hoodie hid all the delectable parts he'd touched last night—tasted, loved. His heart thumped hard, and his body tensed in anticipation. Maybe he should have punished her longer, but he couldn't regret a single second of surrender.

"Listen up, boy. You need to hear this, too." Gramps thwacked his cane on the floor like a gavel. Lying on the rug in front of the hearth, Duke lifted his head, looked blearily around and promptly went back to snoring.

Sighing, Max leaned back in his chair and tried his best to give all his attention to Gramps. It was impossible. Vi was too close, an orchestra dismantling his focus on every level. From her scent to the smallest twitch of her pinkie on her thigh, it was all he could do to keep his gaze ahead and on Gramps.

"The shipment of decorations for the haunted house contest was canceled due to shortages or some other such nonsense. Unless someone wants to fly to China and return with a truckload of glow-in-the-dark skeletons and other delights, I have to alter my plan for the victory."

With the whirlwind of happenings in the last couple of days, Max hadn't taken the time to tell Gramps what he and Vi had learned while spying on Beasley. Honestly, he hadn't figured out exactly how to tell Gramps the information without letting it slip that they'd trespassed on Adams property, been caught and had only escaped thanks to Greg's betrayal of his employer.

"We've got you covered. Vi and I had already been discussing alternative ideas." Max nudged Vi's boot with far less enthusiasm than she had kicked his shin. "Right, Violet?"

"Absolutely." Vi flashed him a blank look before giving Gramps a saccharine-sweet smile. Burning hell, he loved how she always had his back, always trusted his plans, even when she didn't know what they were.

Gramps harrumphed. "Don't recall asking for your opinion."

"Hear me out, Gramps." Max continued as Gramps folded his arms over his flannel shirt, his mouth pressed into a vicious line. "Through avenues best left unexplained, Vi and I did some recon. Beasley's theme this year is the summoning of Abigail Ward. We can play off that, beat her at her own game. All we have to do is—"

"Zombie apocalypse," Gramps interrupted. "Complete with graveyard, shooting simulator and lasers. All the whippersnappers are talking about it on the internet."

"But, Gramps—"

"Mark me, I have no inclination to lower myself to Beasley's standards." He swiped a hand through the air, cutting off all protest. "I'll win on my own terms, and if I lose our bet, it won't be because I stooped to her level."

"Bet?" A ribbon of ice curled in his gut, and Max leaned forward, every iota of attention now on Gramps. "What bet?"

He lifted his chin, defiant as any toddler. "Beasley and I made a wager. Whoever loses the contest this year deeds their property to the other."

For a full ten seconds, Max froze, unable to believe his ears. Gramps' entire life revolved around Ward House, maintaining the family heritage, protecting the fragile history that his ancestors bled for to found Devils Hollow. And if he lost Ward House to Beasley, how could Max ever keep his promise to Gram, that he'd do everything in his power to keep Ward House in the family?

Max surged to his feet. He had to fix this before it was too late. "I'll go talk to Beasley. She'll listen to me. I'll tell her you haven't been feeling well, weren't thinking straight when you made that bet."

"You will do no such thing." Much slower than Max, he wobbled to his feet and used his cane to straighten to his full height while Vi watched with wide eyes, her expression seemingly calm. "This is my year, Max. My last year. I know it, and even if you refuse to say it aloud, you know it, too."

The lump in his throat made it impossible to respond.

"Beasley may be an uppity, conniving, know-it-all pain in my bony ass, but if I'm not around anymore, I know she'll treat Ward House proper."

Max flinched, as if he'd been physically slapped. "You don't think I can?"

"Don't be a knucklehead, Max. That's not the issue." Gramps' bushy eyebrows lifted. "Make no mistake. The upkeep of Ward House is a burden, a full-time, lifelong endeavor. Grams and I accepted the responsibility willingly. By all means, your mother should be the one here preserving the history, listening to the stories of our ancestors whispered in the bones of the house and the earth beneath."

Instead, his mom had abandoned all things family — Grams and Gramps, her heritage...him. No matter how much time passed, the scars ached at the mere mention of her.

"I know you lost your dreams when your baseball career ended before it even began. That's the thing, Max. Ward House must be loved to be preserved. It is like a child that must be taken care of with great attention to detail, and as much as you've honored both Grams and I by staying, Ward House is not your life purpose."

"Actually, it is." Max slowly sat down and ran his hand down his face. "It wasn't, at first. I hated this house and what it represented — the family I no longer had, the life I'd been ripped from. But I was just a scared, lonely little boy who had no idea where he fit in. You and Grams changed that for me." He glanced at Vi. "The friends I made in Devils Hollow changed me. It took a while, but Ward House became my home." He rotated the wrist he'd broken in his motorcycle accident, the bones cracking and throbbing. "And yeah, baseball was the dream of a starry-eyed, idiot teenager who thought happiness could be found in approval, that everything would be fine as long as I was someone everyone looked up to."

Gramps snorted. "Baseball star or not, I'd still whoop your scrawny behind if you smart-mouthed me."

"As you should. What I'm saying is the accident was a gift. It showed me that what matters most in life is the people you have in it. Ward House is your legacy, Gramps, and will one day be mine. You're part of its history. I won't let Beasley take over."

"Well, tarnation, son. You should've piped up before. Then again, maybe I should've had the gumption to ask over shots of apple whiskey instead of assume." Gramps huffed and scratched his scruffy jaw. "I suppose there's only one thing left to do."

"Exactly." Vi answered immediately, as if she'd been waiting for precisely the right time to speak up.

She bared her teeth in a scary smile, and said in a sweet voice, "Zombie apocalypse for the win."

"Damn straight." Gramps' shout was loud enough that Duke rolled to his feet and barked once, looking startled.

His grandpa's wild, excited grin made Max's heart ache, and even though a win grew less likely by the day, he refused to ruin the moment. Vi's laugh lightened the moment another degree, and he couldn't help but love her even more.

Hope. Why couldn't she see how much hope she gave them both, just by being here?

"You kids eat. I've got plans to sketch out." Gramps shuffled for the door, Duke waddling on his heels. As he passed through the doorway and into the hall, he stopped, hooked one thumb in his overalls shoulder strap, and faced them. "Meanwhile, I suggest you start figuring out what the two of you are about. Before I put my second foot in the grave, I want to go knowing you're both happy, and if you can't follow that your happiness is tied to each other, let me know. I'll knock you each in the noggin with my cane until you get it."

Vi kept her expression blank, but a lovely pink infused her cheeks. Max bit the inside of his cheek to hold back a grin as Gramps shuffled onward.

"And," he called over his shoulder, "if you pilfer another sip of my whiskey without permission, I'll tan both your hides."

Chapter Twenty-Five

"The zombie apocalypse idea is outdated." Vi handed Dahlia a waiting plate piled high with demon eggs, complete with splattered blood, unholy toast and its signature mark of a melting butter cross. It smelled almost as good as her waiting coffee. "No way will it beat out Beasley, not when she's using summoning Abigail Ward as her theme."

Dahlia huffed, stirring a loose curl by her chin that had fallen free of her clip sometime during the breakfast rush an hour ago. She packed some straws in her apron pocket and reached for a handful of clean cutleries. "I'm sure between Gramps and Max, they'll come up with something amazing."

"But not enough to win." Just saying the words felt like a betrayal, even though they were true.

"Gramps loses every year to Beasley." Dahlia shut an ajar cupboard with a bump of her hip, never slowing. "I'm sure he can take another."

"Not this time." Vi hooked her fingers through five coffee mugs. "He has to win."

Dahlia paused and studied her with lifted eyebrows. "What aren't you telling me?"

Gramps didn't want anyone else to know about his failing health, didn't want to spend the last of his days being pitied and pampered. If he hadn't told Dahlia, it wasn't her place to change that. "He said this is his last year to enter the haunted house contest, and if he loses..." Gramps hadn't mentioned whether or not his bet with Beasley was a secret, but since even Max hadn't known until this morning, she wouldn't be the one to leak that information, either. "It will break his heart not to win even once."

Her stomach twisted at the memory of Max's shocked, hurt expression when he'd learned that Ward House was on the betting table. She'd always known he belonged in Devils Hollow, but until that moment, she hadn't truly understood how deeply his roots had sunk into the eccentric little town.

She'd always known a life with him was an illusion, that Max would never leave Ward House, but when Gramps had made his announcement, for a second, her heart had jumped. With Ward House out of the equation, Max could be truly free. That fragile fragment of hope had died at Max's sincere, emotional response.

He'd never leave Devils Hollow—and she could never stay.

"Silly men and their competitive natures." Dahlia continued to study her, those dark eyes seeing far too much. "If he gives up the contest, I'm sure he'll find another dozen ways to antagonize Beasley."

Not if he's gone. Vi grabbed the coffee carafe with her free hand and led the way toward the café dining room.

With any luck, Dahlia hadn't seen the tears shining in her eyes.

"Hey, I have an idea. If Gramps is set on the zombie apocalypse, what about combining that with local history?" Sliding past her, Dahlia spun and walked backward. She pushed through the double doors between the kitchen and café without slowing. The babble of lively conversation replaced the crackle of cooking in the kitchen. "Isn't there a movie where some historical figures fight off zombies? Maybe it could be the Ward ancestors fighting off zombies with axes and bows and arrows. Everyone can don period garb, speak old-timey. Might be fun."

The very idea of chasing after tourists with an ax brought goosebumps, and even though the best night of her life had morphed into a gloomy morning, she couldn't hold back a smile. "Dahlia, you're a genius."

"Obviously." She rolled her eyes.

"I'll run the idea by Gramps and Max." A thrill ran down her spine as she imagined the costumes, the screams of tourists and Gramps having the time of his life serving apple whiskey in iron tankards while in top hat and waistcoat. "I bet they'll think it's brilliant, too."

Dahlia handed off her plate to a customer dressed in halo and horns at the bar, his black, glossy wings hanging over the barstool and almost brushing the floor. She waited until Vi had filled his coffee cup before resuming the conversation. "Speaking of brilliant, don't forget dinner with Brian tonight." Sparkles danced in her eyes, and her smile was bright enough to compete with the overhead lights. "I can't wait for you to meet him. If Max tries to get out of it, tell him Ward House laundry, grocery and landscaping duties can wait. It'll be like the double date we never had. You know, because you left."

"Subtle, sis." Putting 'Max' and 'date' in the same sentence reminded her exactly how right she was about how things changed with the reality of daylight. Last night had been the best. Being in Max's arms, letting his words of love warm her soul and fill the empty corners of her heart had been the peak of her life.

But this morning, what he'd said about Ward House and Devils Hollow only confirmed what she'd known all along. Max belonged in Devils Hollow, and no matter how much Gramps wanted it, no matter how much *she* yearned for it, she couldn't stay with him, not when that darkness still clung to her like pond weeds.

Max wanted to fight that invisible enemy with her. Letting herself believe it was possible, not feeling so alone for a few hours had felt fan-frickin'-tastic. But she wouldn't risk his life for anything...or Dahlia's. And if her only hope was in Hecate and Dimensions...? *Yeah. I'm screwed.*

Vi looked up from the coffee carafe and met Dahlia's gaze. She must have hesitated a little too long. Her sister's knowing smile was wide and wicked.

"You sneaky little colorful witch." Dahlia grabbed her sleeve and dragged her around the corner, where the ice cream machine hid them from most of the café customers. "No wonder you didn't text me back last night. You were with Max, weren't you? I want details. Hot, dirty, specifics."

Dammit. Her face was already burning. "Not going to feed your sordid imagination."

Dahlia crossed her arms and arched an eyebrow. "You owe me years of sordid details, so spill."

"You're never going to let me live it down, are you?"

"Only after you make up for the five years we missed." She batted her eyelashes, hooked her arm through Vi's and dragged her back to the kitchen. "And as part of your sacrifice to make amends, you're required to follow me around for the rest of the morning giving me every juicy second of last night's happenings."

"Oh, you mean the encounter we had with the ghosts of both Ward sisters?" She shrugged. "Sure." Even spirits were a better subject than talking about how Max had awakened every cell in her body and melted her like wax in his warm, capable hands.

Dahlia laughed. "Nice try, Vile. No cigar. I want specifics. Is Max sweet or sinister between the sheets? Did he make you scream and — ?"

Vi clapped a hand over her sister's mouth. "I'm seriously scandalized. You're supposed to be the wholesome Keller sister." Dahlia licked her hand, and she jerked away, unsurprised to find an unrepentant grin. "What Max does or doesn't do in his bed — alone or with someone else — is none of your business."

"You used to be fun." Twirling like a ballerina, Dahlia pushed back through the swinging doors into the kitchen.

"And you must not have heard me. We had a close encounter of the Ward kind last night. Even Max experienced it. Anna Ward used poor Victor like a meat puppet. He's so traumatized he forgot to wear lace to breakfast this morning." As much as she tried to keep it lighthearted, the sudden chill in her blood made it impossible. She'd be remiss to pretend Anna Ward hadn't scared her silly — or that the danger was very real.

Dahlia's eyes widened. "You're serious."

"Very."

"You saw her? Anna Ward?" Dahlia lowered her voice to an awestruck whisper. "Abigail?"

Vi nodded. She couldn't bring herself to say the names aloud, wanted no reason to draw attention to herself. If either Ward sister was summoned again, it would be on Beasley's head. She couldn't think of a more deserving person to experience Anna Ward's black-hold stare.

Dahlia scowled. "I miss out on all the fun…always."

"'Fun' is definitely not the adjective I'd use. I know I don't have the right to ask you for anything, but will you promise me something?" Vi leaned her elbows on the counter as Dahlia handed Dustin a handful of orders. Bacon sizzled on the grill, and Dustin's spatula on metal made a rhythmic click and scrape melody, enough background noise to give the semblance of privacy.

"Sure, on one condition." Dahlia faced her, every trace of mischief and humor gone.

She couldn't answer flippantly, not while Dahlia watched her with an intensity that rang every alarm bell in her head. Whatever Dahlia wanted — demand, sacrifice, act of penance — would be worth it as long as her sister stayed safe.

"Anything." Vi held Dahlia's gaze, steady and sure. "You know that."

"You first. What holy vow do you want me to keep?" Dahlia lifted her chin, and a chill she hadn't heard since returning to Devils Hollow entered her sister's voice.

Vi ignored a shiver. "Promise me you'll stay away from Lake Forsaken — at least for the rest of the month."

Dahlia's eyes narrowed slightly. "Why?"

Revealing her vision, the underlying fear that drove her to ditch Devils Hollow and the people she loved most, in the kitchen in between orders wouldn't do it justice. "I'll tell you tonight, after dinner. It's a longish story."

After a moment of lip pursing, Dahlia shrugged. "Never liked the lake much, anyway. Leeches, pond scum, bugs. *Ick*." Her dark eyes glittered. "I definitely got the easy end of this particular bargain. Sucker."

Great. "What embarrassing deed of atonement am I facing now?"

The iron bells above the café door jangled and several new voices joined the conversations already in play. With every day closer to Halloween, the café got increasingly busier. From breakfast to evening coffee and dessert, the rush went on until closing. It wouldn't be long before Dahlia's only shot at a break was when Vi could escape from festival duties.

"I'll tell you tonight after dinner — and only if Max is with you." As Dahlia headed out again with two plates balanced on each arm, she flashed her teeth. "And since you have a few minutes before heading out to do Beasley's bidding, if you really want to prove how sorry you are, the bathroom could use a good scrub and restock." She winked and disappeared through the double doors.

"Crap." Vi slumped and glanced helplessly at Dustin through the wait-station window. "I bet you know exactly what she wants, don't you? And zero chance you're going to tell me."

He arched one black eyebrow, jerked his head in the direction of the bathroom and went back to cooking.

"Dahlia loyalist," she muttered and stalked toward the storeroom. She wasn't too far away that she didn't hear Dustin's low cackle over the snap and hiss of frying food. Tonight was going to be a perfectly splendid evening of torture.

But as long as Dahlia stayed far away from the lake until after she was gone from Devils Hollow, she'd pay any necessary price.

Chapter Twenty-Six

"I still smell like splattered pumpkin." Vi sniffed her coat as she walked beside Max, headed for the café. The evening had been spent dodging catapulted pumpkins while gauging distance traveled before impact and the ensuing explosion of orange flesh, strings and seeds. The lucky winner and guest had received a night in the abandoned mortuary. "Do you know how much I hate pumpkin anything?"

"With the force of a thousand suns." Max pulled her closer, his fingers tangled with hers. "Luckily for you, I love pumpkin spice everything."

"I always knew there was something wrong with you."

"Never denied it." He dragged her to a stop, and before she could so much as squeak, he dipped her back and kissed her, long and sweet. By the time he pulled her straight, she was breathless and tingling everywhere.

"Nothing wrong with that," she wheezed.

His grin was all mischief and masculine satisfaction, and when he slung an arm around her shoulders and continued their walk along the dark streets of Devils Hollow, an image played out in her head—lazy summertime strolls, arm in arm, a relaxed dinner at the café, joking with Dahlia while she tested her latest brilliant cooking creations on them, walking back to Ward House beneath a sky full of icy stars, a warm breeze on her skin, Max keeping her close and safe.

Home.

Her heart missed a beat and thumped again, hard. The dream that could never be, and no matter how powerful Max's persuasion skills, she couldn't let that fantasy take root.

A buzz came from her coat pocket, and she fumbled for her phone. Her favorite picture of Ruby shone on the screen, a sharp needle in her hand and a sharper smile on her pretty face, Kickin' Ink's logo in the background. Vi answered the call and resumed walking.

"Hey, Ruby. Please tell me there hasn't been a fire, murder or tragic face tattoo gone awry."

"Two out of three isn't bad."

The lack of humor in Ruby's voice brought her to a halt. She glanced at Max, who raised his eyebrows. "What happened?"

"Emma happened. She grew three heads, horns and a tail while you've been gone. Normally, I'd be okay with that, but the girl's more of a monster than I am. My ass can only take so many pokes with her pitchfork before my inner Wednesday Addams erupts in a black, wicked hurricane of destruction. I can't have another crime on my record. I need her gone."

Vi forced her feet to move again, her stomach twisting. If interior problems brewed at Kickin' Ink, the business could implode. Ruby was the heart of the business, Vi the head, but she couldn't turn her back on Emma, at least not without hearing both sides. If no one had believed in her or given her a shot when she'd been a rebellious kid out on her own, desperate and alone with only her sketches for company, her life could have been very, very different.

"Em lives in the loft above the studio. She has nowhere else to go. I can't just kick her out."

"Bet I can convince her the streets are a safer place to be." The sweetness in Ruby's tone made the words all the more menacing. "I haven't yet out of respect for you, Vi, but I'm walking the razor's edge here. She had a party after hours, and we lost some inventory. Last night, I found her practicing her nonexistent tattoo artist skills on some loser she picked up at the pub down the street, using *my* equipment, in *my* room, on *my* chair...naked. That's my gig. There's only room enough at Kickin' Ink for one Magic Mamba. Someone's getting out, and it's not me."

Crap. Without Ruby, she'd be scrambling to find anyone even remotely close in both skills and charisma to replace her. Losing her would be a disaster for Kickin' Ink. But giving up on Emma the second she slipped up would make her no better than her father. Everyone at Kickin' Ink had made mistakes, some more serious than others.

She shook her head. Managing the situation from Devils Hollow without someone losing an eyebrow and half their hair would be tricky, at best. But leaving with only a week and a half to go, so much still unresolved, another promise to Dahlia broken...she couldn't do it.

Once again, her bad luck rose from the dead, awakened from its Devils Hollow grave upon return. Until now, Ruby and Em had never locked horns or had a single problem. Em had been the model student, learning the business behind Kickin' Ink, generating her own art, her curious nature perfect for learning. She observed every detail from cleaning needles to Ruby's method of mixing color. It couldn't be a coincidence that discord stirred now, when so much was at stake.

Max slipped an arm around her shoulders and squeezed. The I'm-here-for-you gesture was so sweet, unexpected and *needed* that tears blurred her vision. She blinked them away. This was no time to morph into a pansy. She'd worked too hard to make Kickin' Ink a success. Losing it wasn't an option, just as leaving Devils Hollow before November first wasn't happening.

"I'll call Em and talk to her. I'll be back in a week and a half. Can you manage not to kill her until then?"

"No, I can't." The words were more of a growl. "If Emma doesn't stay out of my way and out of my sight, I'll lose the last link chaining my control. Put your protégé on a leash, Vi, or I'll be outta here by the time you get back."

The line beeped out into dead silence.

"Hell." She stuffed her phone back into her pocket. The café was only a block away, and they were already late to dinner with Dahlia and Brian. She'd have to call Em afterward and do some serious damage control. She'd made it two-thirds of the way done with her Devils Hollow venture. Surely, she could last ten more days without the darkness taking everything from her. *I have to.*

"I couldn't help but overhear." Max kept his gaze ahead. "Ruby sounds…delightful."

"She is, actually." Vi shook aside the dark thoughts, eternally grateful for the distraction. "As long as you don't crack open her bad side."

"And without you there, whatever hairline fractures already there have turned into canyons."

"Yeah." She sighed. "Something like that. Ruby's the best tattoo artist around. Not only is she beyond talented, but her charisma also draws in customers and keeps them coming back. Without her, Kickin' Ink wouldn't be the success that it is today."

"So modest of you to give her all the credit, but I know you, sweeting. Whatever you set your mind to, you don't stop until your vision comes to full, vibrant life."

Vi shrugged, warmth curling around her heart like silk ribbons with his words. Besides Dahlia, Max had always been her biggest supporter, had always believed in her, no matter what. That he still did was a fact she'd treasure always. "Ruby and I hit it off right away. We're a great team. I'm the behind-the-scenes girl with the sketches, and she's the face of Kickin' Ink with the needle skills. But Emma is still a teenager, an aspiring artist with nowhere else to go. She doesn't have anyone positive in her life, and if I let her go for screwing up, that might destroy her. The thing is, I get why she messed with Ruby's stuff, even at the risk of Ruby's — wrath — her dreams of being something more than she is."

Max tucked his hands into the pockets of his jeans. The movement was casual, impersonal, but the loss of his heat around her felt like she sank slowly into chilled water. "Dreams make people do a lot of reckless things they regret later."

"Stupid things, too." Like how she left Devils Hollow without saying goodbye or telling both Dahlia and Max why. "And not always possible to fix."

"Sometimes stupid and reckless are exactly the same." He slid her a knowing glance. His follow-up wink immediately made her feel better.

"I doubt you've ever done anything that qualifies as stupid. I mean, since you're smarter than me, according to rumors from some unreliable sources."

"*Slightly* smarter. And I wasn't always the super-genius you know and love today. Ask my deceased motorcycle and ache-with-the-weather wrist. They'll tell you the sad facts."

Vi looped her arm through his, needing the contact, and when he squeezed her to his side, her worries about Ruby and Em took a back seat. *Ten days.* She couldn't decide if she wanted those days to fly like a mad witch on a high-speed broom or inch by to savor every delicious second. November first would be hard, one way or another.

Keller's Killer Café came into sight, and her steps slowed at the darkness inside. Dahlia usually kept at least a few lights on, dimmed so anyone could see that the café wasn't momentarily open but would be later. But only one, tiny light burned — in the small window of the attic.

"So much for leaving the porch light on for us. I know Dahlia's a stickler for being on time, but we're not that late." Max frowned as they crossed the empty parking lot. "Are you sure she meant tonight? The only thought that got me through avoiding catapulted pumpkins was knowing that a Vampire's Eternal Kiss waited for me at the end of the night. Dahlia's signature cocktails give Gramps' whiskey a run for the money, not that I'd even think those words anywhere near him. I'm feeling robbed."

Vi barely heard him as she unlocked the door and stepped inside. The light in the attic window tightened the knot already in her stomach from Ruby's call, turning it into a cold, heavy rock.

Every booth and table were empty, coated in shadows. Silence weighed heavy, no clanks of dishes from the kitchen or even the low music of Dustin's favorite station. A hint of cooked food lingered, nothing fresh to indicate a celebratory dinner of the first double date in Keller sister history.

She locked the door behind them, kicked on the lights and circled the counter. Dahlia's red tennis shoes were tucked neatly beside the door leading to the kitchen, skulls-and-crossbones socks folded on top. While Max took a seat at the bar, she poured him a shot of whiskey and pushed it his way. "Do you mind waiting here for a few? I think I know where she is."

Questions swirled in his eyes, but instead of asking them, he took the drink he offered and raised it in a salute. "Take as long as you need. I'll be here, waiting. I know where Dahlia stashes the good stuff, so I'll be fine."

I'll be here, waiting. She gave him a grateful smile and headed for the kitchen instead of leaning over the counter to kiss him like she wanted to. Max always seemed to know exactly what she needed and gave it to her freely, even when she screwed up. Letting him wait for her while the future held so many unknowns felt wrong, no matter how much he denied it, how hard he resisted or how much either of them wanted it. How could she ask him to wait for what might be forever? Or never?

The kitchen was empty. That it was clean and tidy tightened the writhing mess in her gut. This wasn't from plans interrupted by an unexpected event but one that had closed shop before it even began. If Dahlia had gone home, she wouldn't have turned off all the main lights and left her shoes and socks behind, which meant she could only be in one place. Vi headed for the storage room and the ladder leading to the attic.

The café roof had always been where Vi and Dahlia could escape, speak in private and dream of better days. She grabbed the flashlight they kept by the door and climbed the wooden ladder. The rungs creaked beneath her boots, louder than she remembered.

She hadn't eaten *that* much of Dahlia's cake. Maybe she should see to getting them repaired while she was still in Devils Hollow, before Dahlia was on her own again.

Guilt, always familiar and perfected over her lifetime, stabbed her. But this was a different level of emotion. When she'd left Devils Hollow, Dahlia still had Dad and Mom, wasn't in charge of the café and dealing with the stress, work and duties alone. Sure, the responsibility of the café was a given for Dahlia, who never wanted anything else. Her dream had always been to take over, to release her culinary creations into the world and live happily ever after in Devils Hollow, their father's pride and joy. But neither one of them had ever thought she'd be handling it alone at the tender age of twenty-two.

Vi jerked the pull-string of the lone attic lightbulb as she ducked beneath the sloped roof. The click offered no light, either burnt out or no longer operational, another small repair Dahlia probably hadn't had time to deal with.

Note to self—add 'fix attic light' to my goal list before November first.

She turned on the flashlight and ignored the abundance of dusty spiderwebs hanging from the low rafters, too close to her head. Bypassing the stacks of pots and pans, broken appliances and surplus cutlery, Vi reached the end of the roughed-out attic floor. She tucked the flashlight in the back pocket of her jeans. Several bare beams stretched over insulation, and the single, stained-glass window from the original building waited across the way. The clasp had always been broken. Even better, the window led to a private nook on the roof, a secret Vi and Dahlia had discovered as girls exploring, trying to stay out from underfoot of their parents at work.

On hands and knees, she crawled along the beam leading to the attic window. A cobweb brushed her cheek, and she swiped at it, somehow managing not to tumble into the insulation and through the thin plank of the café ceiling.

The glow from her flashlight jerked with each move and sent shadows crawling up the walls. Beneath her hands and knees, the beam shuddered, a whole lot thinner than she remembered. If she fell through the ceiling, leaving a ragged hole for customers to look at while they devoured pastries and sandwiches, Dahlia would stain her hometown sweetheart reputation to destroy her.

Vi made it to the window and paused to wipe the moisture from her forehead. The broken clasp was lifted, the window open a sliver, the sign she'd both expected and hoped she wouldn't find. Once they grew older, Dahlia only went on the roof to cry.

There was little worse than seeing Dahlia lose her sunshine. She deserved to be happy all the time.

Moonlight filtered through a film of fluffy clouds and offered enough light to see. She edged along the gutter to the steep angle of the gable, to the fenced-in ledge of roof hidden on three sides. They'd learned early on that people rarely looked up, including their parents.

Dahlia sat on the roof, her knees tucked to her chest, feet bare, staring up at the moon. Tears glistened on her cheeks, and she'd taken her hair out of its ponytail, leaving it to flow down her shoulders. She looked like a fairy from the summer court, longing for her home.

"Hey," Vi said softly, not wanting to startle her.

Dahlia's smile was sad. She didn't look from the moon. "I figured you'd find me here."

"Some things never change." Vi settled next to her and blew out a breath. I don't remember it being so hard to get onto the roof." She leaned over slightly, her gaze on the shrubs three stories down, and quickly leaned back. "Or that the ground was so far away."

"Things always change." Dahlia rubbed the tears from her face. "It's the only thing you can count on. You sure as sugar can't count on people."

"No argument here." Bittersweet warmth skittered over her as Dahlia rested her head on Vi's shoulder, exactly like they used to when they were girls, when Dahlia leaned on her strength. "Want to talk about it?"

"Brian dumped me." Dahlia wriggled her finger, now empty. "We'd always talked about staying in Devils Hollow. He knows how much the café means to me, that I never wanted to quit the family business, leave Mom and Dad behind, ditch my hometown. He *knew* that. So when he told me he accepted a job offer across the country, I asked him how that was going to work." She laughed, low and without humor. "That was the problem. It *isn't*."

"Damn. I'm sorry, Dahlia. Do you want me to stab him for you?"

"I'll think about it and let you know." New tears rolled down her cheeks. "The worst thing is he didn't even discuss it with me first. He expected me to follow him wherever he went, give up the other parts of my life and go. He didn't give me a choice."

"Jerk."

"That's another terrible part of it. He *isn't* a jerk. He thought my love for him would trump my goals, dreams, family, that I'd be so excited that he has this opportunity that I'd abandon it all. So, actually, maybe *I'm* the jerk for not loving him enough to leave everything behind."

Ouch.

"Did I do the wrong thing, Vi?" She tilted her chin, meeting her gaze. "Or was it right, caring more about my own dreams than my future husband's?"

"I'm not anywhere close to being qualified to answer that." She squeezed Dahlia's hand. "You have to do what's right for you. If Brian can't see that, can't support that, maybe he's not the man for you."

"But maybe he is. Maybe letting him go is the biggest mistake I'll ever make." Dahlia scooched around at an angle, facing her. Her eyes held an earnestness that reached into her soul and staked it. "Did you ever regret letting Max go?"

So many times.

"It's not the same. Max and I were never engaged. We weren't a couple when I left Devils Hollow." But they might have been — *would* have been if she'd stayed. The vision of Max floating in the water, face up, his blank eyes staring at the sky twisted through her, unbidden.

"But you were best friends who did everything together. You shared dreams with each other, made plans. Max always wanted his future to be with you." Dahlia threw back her head and gazed again at the stars, as if hoping the heavens would offer the answers Vi didn't have. "Am I going to be the female version of Max? Left behind in Devils Hollow because I wasn't strong enough to chase after the person I love? To let the love of my life go without a huge fight?"

Her breath caught. Not once had she considered that Max hadn't been strong enough to chase her, to track her down. Did he feel that way? That her leaving Devils Hollow was somehow a failure on his part?

But she wasn't Dahlia, who had everything to offer. If Brian was idiot enough to ditch Dahlia, she was better off without him. Brian's departure left the door wide open to the future, to an epic love worthy of her.

Vi looked to the sprinkling of stars in the black velvet sky, searching for the right words, some way to help Dahlia so she wouldn't make the same mistakes or have the same regrets. She released a shaky sigh.

"Every morning after I left, I questioned if I'd done the right thing. And every night when I went to bed, I knew that I had. What I regretted is how I left, not why. I was afraid if I told you — or Max — you'd change my mind." Her intention to tell Dahlia exactly why she'd left faded beneath her sister's heartache. She didn't need any more darkness in her life, not tonight.

"I knew you planned to leave Devils Hollow." A breeze stirred Dahlia's golden hair, tugging a loose lock across her face, where it gently waved like a weed in the water. She didn't bother pushing it away. "I just always imagined Max would go with you."

"Max belongs in Devils Hollow, now more than ever." The words burned her throat. "You both deserve the best. If Brian isn't willing to sacrifice anything and everything for you, he's not the best."

Dahlia shook her head. "Shouldn't that be a mutual drive? Why should he be the one to sacrifice everything and not me? If you love someone — truly, madly, deeply — shouldn't respecting that love, making sure it's nurtured and preserved, be your number one priority?"

The answer to that question sliced like a bladed star in her chest. At the time, she'd believed one hundred percent that leaving had been best for both Max and Dahlia. She understood why they saw it as a betrayal. They'd all made sacrifices in one way or another.

But she'd been the one who'd lost both her sister and Max in the trade. She'd been the one who spent five lonely years away from the people she cherished most. Whether or not it had been the right decision, the reasoning behind it had been born of love and respect.

"Maybe," she said carefully, "the very best possible act of love someone can do is to walk away."

"Hold up." Dahlia straightened and blinked several times. "You don't think love is worth fighting for? That the people you love don't deserve a battle to the bitter end, aren't worth the bruises and broken bones that go with it? That *I'm* not worth it to Brian to stay, to duke it out instead of walking out?"

"That's not what I meant — "

Dahlia ripped her hand free and stood, her silhouette blacking out the stars. "No, I get it. You don't believe that anyone is worth sticking around for, especially when it gets hard, when it hurts so sharp and fierce that you fear you'll shatter into a thousand pieces."

"Dahlia." A plea threaded through her sister's name. "That's *not* what I said."

"That's *exactly* what you said five years ago when you ditched us, Vi. It's a whole lot easier to leave than struggle through it day by day until you drown, isn't it?" Tears glittered in Dahlia's eyes, trapped by the moonlight. "Do you know what I planned to ask you to do tonight?"

Vi didn't have time to even shake her head before her sister pointed a finger in her face.

"I was going to ask you to forgive me for kissing Max all those years ago, to forget the space between us and focus only on the future. But you know what? I'm *glad* you saw me kiss him, because it exposed you for what you really are."

Without knowing how or when, Vi was on her feet, her hands fisted, nose to nose with her sister. For five years she'd made excuses for Dahlia, run through all the possible and rational reasons Dahlia might kiss Max, had believed she'd forgiven her if not forgotten. Maybe she'd been fooling herself. Blood pounded in her head, trembled in her throat. "And what am I, Dahlia?"

"A coward." Dahlia held her gaze, not backing down, no longer the sweet, vulnerable younger sister who once upon a time only looked up to her. "If I hadn't kissed Max, we both know you wouldn't have left so soon. And do you know what I wanted more than anything?"

Vi shook her head, not trusting herself to speak.

"I wanted you gone."

Chapter Twenty-Seven

I wanted you gone.

Vi recoiled as if she'd been slapped. Dahlia's words sliced through her, scattering her fury and leaving behind an emptiness, cold and aching. Not once had she suspected her sister longed for her to be away from Devils Hollow, that Dahlia had kissed Max not because she had a crush on him, but to crush *her*.

"Why?" Her voice cracked. "Why did you want me to leave?"

"I was sick of living in your shadow." Dahlia crossed her arms, her chin lifted — old, hidden wounds boiling free. "You got all the attention because you made a battle out of everything. All I got were leftover crumbs of energy. You always did whatever you wanted and didn't bother noticing that you left me to pick up the pieces. I did my best to smooth things over, make everyone happy. Sweet, considerate, steadfast Dahlia — the perfect daughter didn't have the luxury of running away."

All Vi had ever wanted was to protect Dahlia, to give her the best opportunity to find joy, while her sister had been harboring a jealousy so deep that she'd purposely hurt her to drive her away. Had those emotions always been there? How had she not seen it?

She swallowed the sawdust in her throat. "I left Devils Hollow for you, Dahlia."

"For *me*." She laughed, brittle, the meanest sound Vi had ever heard from her mouth. "That's the best lie you've told yourself yet. While I stayed behind and dealt with the chaos, you were following your ambitions...free. Your annual Christmas card proving that you were still alive didn't do much to warm the heart. But thanks...so much. Without you, where would I be today?"

"Holy hell, Dahlia, if you'd just listen—"

"Save it." Dahlia sliced a hand through the air, vicious. "What you think doesn't matter, not anymore. Do you know how much I used to look up to you? How much I wanted to be like you—brave, strong, independent, not giving a flying frickin' pumpkin what anyone else thought?"

If only. She'd been terrified of failing, known she'd never fit into the Devils Hollow box, no matter how she tried. It had been easier to pretend that she didn't care, even when she'd been alone in the world, without a clue of where to go and what to do, scrambling to put one foot ahead of the other. And she'd always needed both Dahlia and Max. Time and distance had never changed that fact.

Dahlia continued before she could say any of that. "So many times, I dreamed of following in your footsteps, throwing everything else to the wind and just going for the life I wanted."

Vi forced herself to say something, anything to keep the conversation going, turn it a different direction. Dahlia needed to vent, a target for her hurt. If a temporary punching bag was in order, she'd take the blows. "I thought you always wanted to take over the café, stay in Devils Hollow."

"Dad won't give up the reins until he's dead." She snorted. "And he's stubborn enough to outlive me, but that's not the point. I'm not like you, Vi. I've *never* been like you, which I finally understand is a good thing."

The knife in her heart cut deep and cold, so sharp that Vi winced.

"There was another reason I kissed Max. I wanted to know, for a hot moment, what it felt like to be you — to go for what I wanted just once, consequences be damned." The strangest smile curled on Dahlia's pretty face, small and secret with a hint of cruel. "And maybe in the process show Max that he sold himself short with you. He's no slouch at kissing, even when he's taken off guard."

Anger and hurt steamrolled through her, as if the scar from that night had been pierced and the old wound ripped open. As kids, Dahlia had always saved her best manipulations for when they were fighting, but never like this, never so vicious, so brutally personal. Vi fisted her hands and took a step toward her sister.

"Gonna hit me, Vile?" Dahlia tapped her chin, a dare. Her eyes glittered like obsidian, cold and bright.

Vi drew a long breath, her heart racing. Not once had she struck her sister, and she had no intention of starting now. As good as it might feel to let off some steam, Dahlia needed the release more. Brian had hurt her, and she had years of chained emotions spilling over, freed from the lid always locked tight. She forced her hands to relax at her sides. "Of course not."

"Don't pretend it doesn't bother you. Rejection is a painful, powerful beast that rages for months, years." Her grin turned sly. "Max may deny it, but he liked kissing me. His tongue in my mouth said enough."

Calm, Violet. She took two more breaths. "I didn't leave Devils Hollow because you kissed Max."

"But it was the icing on the cake, wasn't it? Made your decision to leave everyone you claimed to care about behind, insignificant baggage that didn't fit with the bright future, right?"

The fight slowly drained from Vi. There was no winning in this conversation. Dahlia said she'd wanted her gone and blamed her for going. No matter what she said, it would fall on deaf ears. There was no changing her sister's mind, not tonight. And telling her about the vision, her nightmares would only seem like another excuse.

"Why don't we continue the discussion in the morning? I'll take you home, get you something to drink. You'll feel better after some sleep."

"Typical Vile. Taking off when things get too hard." Dahlia stepped around her, toward the open window, her bare feet soundless on the roof tiles. "That's the difference between us. I believe the people I love are worth it—the heartache and struggle and pain that go with caring. Even though the man I love wants me to drop my dreams for his and I may lose my heart in the process, I'm not selfish enough to quit when things don't go my way—not like you."

Tears burned her eyes. That her sister, her best friend from childhood, believed she was so selfish and uncaring, didn't know her well enough to see the tiniest crack through her actions? It hurt more than leaving her family behind without an explanation, more than keeping her distance from the people she loved most, more than the loneliness and fear of the last five years.

"As much as I resent being dumped like week-old trash, as much as I despise smiling when I'd rather snarl, if trading my own happiness prevents ruining the people who are there for me, I'll gladly make that sacrifice." Dahlia stood straight and regal, an ice queen limned in moonlight, her expression one of pure contempt. "If I die alone, scraping gum from under tables of a café that will never be mine, at least I'll kick it knowing that I was always there for the people I love, especially in moments when they weren't perfect."

Something inside her crumpled, caving in her chest. Vi couldn't draw a single gasp of air.

"See you tomorrow." She arched one eyebrow, mocking. "If you dare." Without looking back, her sister slipped through the window and disappeared into the darkness.

And all Vi could hear was Hecate's voice, quoting from Abigail Ward's journal.

"Revenge is often borne of great love, twisted by an even greater pain."

Chapter Twenty-Eight

Vi scrawled a red 'X' over October twenty-ninth and set her colored pencil on the desk. The click of wood on marble echoed in the silence, loud and empty. Two more days in Devils Hollow. A week had blurred by after Dahlia's revelation that she'd been as relieved as much as hurt about Vi leaving town. If her sister thought she'd give up again so easily, at least now Dahlia understood breaking her vow to stay until November first wasn't happening.

No matter how awkward it might be at the café.

But part of her pulled at the chains, wanting to get back to sketching in the back at Kickin' Ink, quietly running the business while Magic Mamba entertained the masses. And she couldn't deny the insistent tug to run away now before the darkness lurking in the lake broke free. Before her premonition, her nightmare, came to life and she lost both her sister and Max.

She'd never been one to hope for happily ever after. That fantasy had died when she left Devils Hollow. But for a few days, pretending she could have a future with Max and a close relationship again with her sister had been a dream come true.

Reality couldn't be ignored forever. She'd known that, and still let herself be sucked into the illusion. At Kickin' Ink, the pressure to live up to anyone's expectations only to ultimately fail them was minimal. Maybe it was due to her confidence in her sketches, turning a client's vision into tattoo art. It kept her alive. Here, she slowly sank beneath the water, stagnant and useless.

Vi took one last glance in the mirror and straightened her Nevermore scarf. Had to look good for another morning of discomfort and delight. She'd promised to come in early this morning while Dahlia made the last preparations for her secret culinary creation. The orders had gone through the roof, all to be ready and delivered on Halloween—and the cash raked in would be enough to carry Keller's Killer Café into next October.

Maybe it would be enough for Dahlia to truly forgive her, too.

Grabbing her keys and purse from the bedside table along the way, Vi headed out. She opened her bedroom door and shut it noiselessly behind her. Some people might not mind waking up the entire house with their three a.m. seances — *ahem, Hecate and Dimensions crew* — but she wouldn't disrespect another's sleep, especially since she didn't get much of it.

Vi turned and gasped. Max leaned against the wall beside his bedroom door as if he'd been there the entire time. Maybe he had. Her sleep deprivation brain fog made her miss a lot lately.

"Good morn, sweeting." With his hands tucked into his jeans pockets, his dark hair shower-damp and a black sweater stretched across his shoulders, he looked ready for a commercial for...damn. Anything and everything she'd want to one click and immediately have in her hot little hands. "Sleep well without me?"

She smiled instead of cringing at the stab of regret and guilt. "Sorry. It was a long night on the phone talking Ruby down then convincing Em to apologize...again."

"For the record, no matter how late or early, I'll always be waiting for you, especially in bed."

He gave her a wicked smile that sent heat curling all the way to her toes and tripled the lingering regret. She had zero doubt that whatever she'd missed out on last night, he'd make it up to her—with some degree of Max's version of sweet torture for staying in her room instead of going to his. She had no idea how she'd manage returning to a life without a daily dose of Max.

"Think it'll stick, the apology?" He pushed from the wall and joined her as she made for the stairwell.

"No one has died...yet. So there's that."

"A victory."

"You have no idea." She sighed. What she wouldn't give to drag Max in the other direction, go back to his bed, pull the covers over their heads and pretend like the rest of the world didn't exist for an hour...or eternity. "Kickin' Ink is falling apart beneath my distant nose. I'll be lucky if there's anything salvageable in the wreckage when I get back. And Em is a mental mess. If she sticks around until November first, I'll be pleasantly surprised."

"Em must be special if you're willing to risk the future of your parlor for her."

"She doesn't have anyone or anything else. I know what that feels like, to believe you're on your own against the world." She didn't dare look at him. "Even if it's more of a stubborn choice than a fact."

"Sounds like a couple of Keller sisters I know."

"Don't start."

For a few seconds, only the thud of their steps descending the stairs filled the deep quiet of the sleeping house. Shadows clung to the corners, dawn little more than a silver line on the horizon. She should definitely still be in bed—and definitely with Max. His heat at her back, the hint of his shampoo and aftershave curling around her, eroded her sense of duty and practicality. A week ago, Dahlia might have understood the delay, even applauded it. Now? A single minute late and she'd see it as another broken promise. Breakups could cloud the brightest sunshine, whether those beams were fake or not.

"As I folded sheets and guest towels in the dark before dawn, I had a thought," Max said as her boot hit the floor.

She didn't slow, passing through the foyer toward the door. The way he said it, so casually, set all of her alarms off. Whenever Max said, 'I had a thought', it was a warning that the subject at hand was one he'd been pondering for quite some time, dissecting possibilities and outcomes until he came up with the perfect plan. That he said those words to her? She shivered.

"Whatever it is, I don't want to know." She reached the front door and opened it. "Ever since my argument with Dahlia after her breakup, smoothing out our relationship has taken my meager supply of patience, compassion and spare energy. All the prep work we've been doing to get Gramps' historical zombie apocalypse set up in time for tomorrow is all I can handle at the moment, especially with Beasley watching with her beady eyes, hoping for a clue. The only thing keeping me going is the anticipation of chasing tourists and making them scream in terror."

Max grinned, trailing her outside. "It's going to blow even Beasley's knickers off."

"*Ew.* Only you'd want to see that."

He leaned close to her ear, his breath warm on her skin. "I only want to see your knickers, sweeting. You know that."

She did. Yet another reason she had to leave Devils Hollow in the dust on November first. Max's single-minded devotion to her was everything she wanted, needed, and she'd already spent too much time pretending it could happen for them. He wouldn't be content with a long-distance relationship, might believe he could eventually convince her to settle down in Devils Hollow, the one place she couldn't. Sometimes, loving someone completely meant letting them go.

Dahlia still didn't understand that truth.

Vi managed a smile when he slipped an arm around her shoulders and pulled her against him as they walked to her waiting truck. She gripped her purse strap to prevent her hand from disobeying her commands and curling around his waist anyway, kept her shoulders straight to deny the natural urge to lean her head against his arm and rest in his strength. She loved being a capable, independent woman, but sometimes it was nice to let someone else carry the tough bits for a while.

And she couldn't let Max be that for her, not when she couldn't give him everything he wanted.

Only a few steps separated her from her truck. Maybe she could escape without hearing his devilish plan. She hit the unlock button on her key fob and reached for the door.

"Open another Kickin' Ink parlor in Devils Hollow." Max pivoted and leaned his back against the truck door, blocking her from slithering away without answering. "The closest tattoo artist is twenty miles away. You'd be a hit—and not only during October." He gently pushed the end of her scarf aside and revealed the unfinished rose on her shoulder. Slowly, he traced the petals that were there, the empty spot waiting for completion, and her skin tingled beneath his touch. "You would become a Devils Hollow legend, a must-see for all the tourists, and the fact that you'd only have time for a select few would make you even more sought after. And better, during the hours before, after, and in between, we can create our own magic together."

Her heart squeezed at the scene he inked to life before her unwilling eyes. How perfect would it be to wake up in his arms every morning, roll out of bed with a pot of cinnamon-laced coffee, sketch her days away while Ruby lured customers in? Spend her free time with Max at Ward House, helping out Dahlia at the café? Family dinners and campouts, sipping Gramps' whiskey on the porch while watching the mist curl around the trees?

Too perfect. It wouldn't last, *couldn't* last—not in Devils Hollow, not with her vision clinging like water weeds.

Her throat tightened. She couldn't let this fantasy go on. It wasn't fair to either of them, no matter what her heart claimed, no matter that he believed a curse could be conquered with love. Risking Max to fulfill her own desperate yearning for home and life and...*him* would make her as selfish as Dahlia accused. She pretended to study her keys while the tears faded. Devils Hollow would just have to go on without her.

"You're killing me, Vi." He cupped her cheek and forced her gaze to his. "Your thoughts are spinning worlds of answers and questions in your eyes, and the fact you aren't sharing them with me is making me wonder if I need to step up my game."

Before she could reply, he brushed his lips against hers, tender and coaxing, luring her to soften. Her eyelids fluttered closed of their own accord, and the tension in her shoulders loosened, as if merely waiting for his touch. What started out gentle morphed into tongues and teeth, hands in her hair, on her back, sliding under her coat for the skin on skin contact she'd missed last night. She moaned into his mouth, couldn't get enough of him. She'd *never* get enough of him.

By the time Max broke the kiss, she was bodily crushing him against her truck, her fingers fisted in his jacket, her breath choppy. She blinked twice to clear her vision as the world spun, dizzying.

He picked her up beneath the armpits, pivoted, and settled her back on the ground beside her truck. Her legs wobbled, and he grinned as she leaned against the solid support of the door. "Just think about it, Vi. That's all I'm asking."

With a wink, he strolled back to the house, his hands tucked into his back pockets. Before trotting up the porch steps, he turned, gave her that same wicked, heart-stopping smile and went inside.

Holy hell. She pushed away from the truck, managed to open the door and force her shaking legs to climb in. How she'd ever tell him no, she hadn't a clue, not without breaking both of their hearts again.

* * * *

The five minutes it took to drive to the café didn't reveal any answers to all her problems, and without her morning coffee fix, figuring out anything was hopeless. Vi trudged up to the back door of the café just as a white delivery van pulled up. She paused as the driver hopped out of the back with two unmarked boxes.

"Need me to sign for something?" She wasn't about to interrupt Dahlia for approval of an order drop off.

"That would be great." He set the boxes beside the door, pulled a device from his back pocket and handed it to her. "I have thirteen more for you."

"Perfect number for the season." She scrawled her initials on the screen as he unloaded the delivery and traded him for the last box.

"Happy Hallowtoberfest."

"Same to you." *Time to put on the friendly mask.* She pasted on a smile, and with a box under each arm, went inside.

The kitchen smelled like heaven—all caramel, cinnamon-sugar, and pure, devilish baked deliciousness. The clank of pans and whirring beaters joined the Digital Daggers song playing in the background. *Can't Sleep, Can't Breathe.* She snorted softly. Seemed appropriate.

"Special delivery," she announced, setting the boxes on the edge of the counter, the only empty spot. Bowls, utensils and ingredients filled nearly every space, and knowing Dahlia, each station was set up in perfect order for the culinary confectionary masterpiece she was making this year for the elite Hallowtoberfest finales throughout Devils Hollow.

Dustin didn't bother to acknowledge her presence. Good Lord, the man could hold a grudge on Dahlia's behalf.

Flour up to her elbows, her hands busy kneading a doughball the size of a small mountain, Dahlia glanced over her shoulder. "Finally, and just in time. I was worried my secret ingredient might be delayed, forgotten or sabotaged. That would be a complete disaster."

"Aw, and here I thought you might be worried about me." Vi sharpened her smile, in case her sister detected the hint of vulnerability beneath the teasing. "I'll bring the rest in."

Dahlia wiped her hands on her apron and headed her way. "I'll help. That's a lot of boxes, and I don't want my competition to get the smallest hint of what I'm making."

"The nondescript white van was a genius move." Dylan nodded in approval and went back to measuring.

Vi rolled her eyes. He had such a crush on her sister. "I think I can handle thirteen more boxes before Beasley or the new owner of Slices and Dices has time to spy."

Dahlia froze, her hands twisted in the apron, eyes wide. "What do you mean by only thirteen more? I ordered fifty. I *need* fifty."

Cold shot through her. "He dropped off fifteen, not fifty."

"No." Dahlia rushed for the back door.

Vi considered staying in the kitchen with Dustin to avoid the fallout but forced herself to go outside.

"*No, no, no, no.* This can't be happening." Her sister clutched her head and stared at the stacked boxes as if they leaked black widows. Flour dusted her golden hair, and bits of dough clung to the strands.

"What can I do?"

Dahlia was still and silent for so long, Vi wondered if she'd heard her speak. In the quiet, her heart thundered a quick, hard beat, louder than Dahlia's ragged breaths. Maybe she could jump in her truck and track down the white van. It couldn't have gone too far, and it was early enough that traffic was minimal. But that wouldn't solve the problem of a mistaken order of fifteen instead of fifty.

"You've done more than enough." When Dahlia finally looked at her, tears glittered in her eyes, sharp as uncut diamonds. "Instead of checking with me, you signed off on the delivery. Instead of for once considering that maybe, possibly, you don't know everything, you did what you thought was best. This will ruin me."

Each of Dahlia's words snapped like a whip, leaving welts in the air, on Vi's lungs. The scarf around her throat seemed to constrict, tight enough that she couldn't breathe.

"I promised to deliver hundreds of my Pastry to Die For to the biggest Hallowtoberfest parties. I signed contracts. We'll be lucky if we're not sued, but the flood of complaints we're sure to get?" Her gaze swept over the boxes, too few. "Beasley will blacklist the café from Hallowtoberfest. We're doomed."

"You don't need Beasley." Her voice scraped her throat like sandpaper, raw and rasping. "You've made the café what it is, Dahlia. *You're* the one who draws customers with your culinary skills and charm. Hallowtoberfest or not, the café will be fine. I'll take the blame. I'll personally apologize to each and every —"

"No, you won't." Dahlia pointed a shaking finger at her. "I don't want you anywhere near my customers. If you give the tiniest flying frick for the café or for me, you'll go home before we're all nothing but bloody bits of flesh hanging from bones." She stormed back into the café.

The door slammed shut behind her, the lock clicked and Vi gasped. It felt as if her heart had been struck and helplessly tangled, like a dying sparrow in the grille of a truck. She turned toward the slender, silver line of misted sunrise on the horizon as if it could offer the wisdom she didn't have. Tears blurred the light into a wavering, depthless pool.

Her phone chirped from her back pocket. Instead of ignoring it like she wanted to, she wiped the moisture from her eyes and pulled her cell free. A text from Ruby scrawled across the screen.

I just bailed out of jail and yes, Em was involved. She's still in the slammer. I love you, Vi, but I'm done. I'll lock up Kickin' Ink until you get back, put a sign on the door. It would be best for us both if you keep any response to yourself, at least right now. Don't text me back. Don't call. Neither one of us will like that conversation.

Vi dropped her hand to her side, lifted her face to a sun that wasn't there and closed her eyes. She'd been an idiot to believe she could skirt beneath the radar for an entire month in Devils Hollow without disaster striking.

One more day.

If Gramps didn't depend on her to play the part of zombie-killing Abigail Ward for his exhibition, she could take Dahlia's advice and leave before something worse happened. But he didn't have anyone else to fill that role at the last minute, and it was his final year for...everything.

One day. She'd already lost her sister, killed the family café, probably had only ruins left of Kickin' Ink. Breaking the news to Max would shatter the last shard of her soul. Her heart had been condemned since the second she'd stepped across the city line.

There was nothing more she could possibly lose by staying in Devils Hollow one more day. Nothing at all.

Chapter Twenty-Nine

"Gramps, take a load off." Max grabbed a shovel from where it leaned against the iron gate and handed Gramps the thermos he'd brought with him from the house. "Warmed up with an extra shot of apple whiskey, as you instructed."

"Ain't no time for taking loads of any size off." Gramps ripped the bandana from his head, wiped the moisture from his brow and took a long swig from the Thermos. His thin hair stuck up in wild, white tufts, and the chilled breeze made the strands seem to float like weeds on a gentle current. He wiped his mouth with his sleeve. "If we don't get it done today, it ain't I' done."

"Which is why you're lucky to have me around." Max picked up where Gramps had left off digging up a mound of dirt to make it appear like a fresh grave. Duke played sidekick, snuffling in the freshly turned earth and snuffled. The robotic zombie tucked behind the accompanying gravestone would pop up when it would be most effective to scare unsuspecting bystanders. Hallowtoberfest tourists had a deep love for cemeteries, and he'd make sure their impromptu Ward family graveyard lived up to expectations.

"Son, don't I know it." Gramps leaned on the shovel handle, his shoulders hunched. "I don't say it nearly enough, don't want you getting all misty-eyed and mushy on me, but without you, I would've had to give up Ward House to Widow Beasley a decade ago when your Grams passed on into glory."

Try as he might, Max couldn't stop getting misty-eyed. He looked away before Gramps caught him and instead focused on the hole he dug. "There's nowhere else I'd rather be, Gramps." Another shovelful of upturned soil joined the pile already there. "And Grams would figure out how to ditch heaven and haunt me just to chap my hide on a daily basis if Beasley got her bony fingers on Ward House."

Gramps snorted. "She'd focus her wrath on me first, make no mistake. Wouldn't have enough energy left for you."

"Don't underestimate her. I bet she wields a mean spiritual rolling pin."

A smile cracked his grandfather's face, and the lump in Max's throat cleared. Their remaining time together might be another day, another week or a year, but if those minutes were spent smiling and dreaming of once upon a time and what was yet to come, it would be enough.

The rumble of a familiar diesel motor interrupted the quiet, and Max paused. Vi wasn't supposed to be home for another few hours, just in time to put some finishing touches on costumes and test out the shooting simulator before heading to their last gig as part of

Team Orange. Her black truck appeared around the bend and parked at the edge of the field next to Hecate and gang's sketchy green van.

"Good. Violet's back early. She can help you finish up while I see about my stillery. If my signature Dead-End cinnamon-apple whiskey doesn't make enough of a lasting impression for any waffling voters, abandon all hope for society as we know it."

Max didn't stop Gramps from wandering away, Thermos clutched in his fingers. Duke trailed him, looking like a kid who'd found the stash of chocolate. If the old man focused on a less strenuous activity, one that made him happy, all the better. Between digging and tossing shovelfuls of soil, he kept watch on Vi's truck, waiting for her to hop out.

Minutes passed, and he went onto the next hole, alert to any movement. A tiny knot formed in his gut and grew with each dip and lift of the shovel. Vi knew how much they had left to do before the exhibition tomorrow, and she was never one to avoid work, wasn't afraid to get her hands dirty. Even if she took another call from the drama at Kickin' Ink, she'd have the phone in her hand while taking on whatever needed doing. The longer she sat in her truck, the tighter that gut instinct wrenched.

Something was wrong.

Max abandoned his shovel beside the half-dug grave and strode through the makeshift cemetery toward Vi's truck, past headstones with haunting words from the otherworld and glittering cobwebs strung with strangled moths and black, lurking predators. He hopped over the three-foot iron fence, avoiding the spiked finials and followed the tug on his soul to his girl...his heart. Burning hell, he'd never get tired of having her close, in his arms, his bed, anywhere. Wherever she was, that's where he wanted to be.

And as soon as the Dimensions crew finished up their work in Devils Hollow and gave the Ward sisters their long overdue final farewell party and taking any darkness, bad luck, and curses — real or perceived — with them, Vi would have no valid reason not to stay. No matter how much she denied it, she didn't really hate Devils Hollow. It was the bad memories tied to the town that pushed her away. The rest of their memories together would be nothing but fierce and fearless, no more regrets.

Max approached her truck and tapped the tinted window. After a long pause, the window rolled down an inch, two, just enough to see Vi's beautiful eyes. She'd clearly been crying. *Shit.* He pulled the door handle and found it locked.

"Vi, darling." He curled his fingers over the top of the window. If there was enough room, he'd climb in through the window to get to her. Hell, maybe he'd do it anyway. Broken glass could be replaced. "Let me in."

Her eyelashes lowered briefly, as if she bore the weight of the universe and couldn't take another second without resting. When she lifted them again, any shimmer of tears was gone.

"Opening the door is a mistake." She shook her head. "I never should have in the first place. I knew that, and I did it anyway. That's on me."

Whatever door she referred to, he suspected it wasn't so easy to open as one leading to the interior of a badass truck. And if it impacted him, he'd shove his foot in there so fast she wouldn't have a chance to shut it. A cracked bone or two from a slam and an ensuing limp were sacrifices he was willing to make.

"It's never a mistake with me, sweeting." He kept his voice calm, a lull to her brewing storm. She hadn't erupted yet, but he sensed it rising from the deep, savage and boiling. "Talk to me."

She released a short breath. "I screwed up and ruined Dahlia's creations for tomorrow. She won't be able to complete all the orders made, which means—"

"Beasley will make sure Keller's Killer Café is banished from any future Hallowtoberfest activities." *Burning hell.*

"Yeah. Dahlia told me to go home…permanently."

"Sweeting, she didn't mean it."

Vi met his gaze. "Yes, she did. Until I returned to Devils Hollow, she was fine. The café flourished, she'd fallen in love, was engaged. Not to you as I first thought, but she was happy. That's all I've ever wanted for her. Since I've been back, she's lost her fiancé, second-guesses everything she thought she wanted and now I've killed her dreams for the café. We all know that no business in Devils Hollow survives long without being a part of the official Hallowtoberfest program."

It was, unfortunately, true. Without the marketing push, the backing of the Hallowtoberfest committee and the tourist cash that came with it, businesses either died or relocated. Gramps had always complained about the unholy power wielded by the committee. One black mark—or bias of a committee member—could ruin lives. Devils Hollow folk fought to keep the town small and quaint, and the committee did its best to push outsiders at least a pitchfork length away.

"Everyone adores Dahlia. Not even Beasley is immune for long." If she was out of the truck, he could

310

hold her hand, pull her close, assure her everything would be okay. The lock, steel and fiberglass served as an impassable barrier between them. That Vi chose to keep it in place awakened pinpricks of cold in his chest. "She'll get through this and come out the other side better than ever. Trust me."

Vi's fingers on the steering wheel made white, bloodless stripes on the black leather. "One of the reasons I left Devils Hollow was to give her the chance to find happiness without me being in the way."

"Dahlia and I were never going to happen, Vi. *Are* never going to happen. I'm in love with *you*, have been since grade school. That's never going to change." *Please look at me, Violet.*

She stared out of the windshield, into the forest hiding the lake and continued as if he hadn't spoken. "The other reason was to make sure my premonition never came true. Maybe it was stupid, nothing more than residual fear from almost drowning or a superstition, but for me, it was too vivid to forget. If something had latched onto me from the lake—whether bad luck, curse or the phantom of either Ward sister—I wanted to keep it away from her. Away from you both." Her slender throat worked. "I had thought, *hoped* that with being gone five years, it would be gone, too. I thought if I faced my fear of the lake, I could conquer that nightmare. At the very least, I told myself that nothing too terrible could happen in a single month."

"Hecate and her faithful crew are putting all their focus, knowledge and skills into demolishing any negative energy that clings to the lake. Abigail and Anna will both be sent off to the next life, light or dark, whether they want to go or not. After tomorrow night, you'll be free," he told her.

She shrugged, as if ridding herself of the lake's touch no longer mattered or that she no longer cared what wickedness came her way. "I only returned because Dahlia needed my help. I couldn't sit back and let her lose the café. It was a risk, but I figured Hallowtoberfest was too busy for either one of you to be hanging out at Lake Forsaken, especially together. She may want me gone now, but I promised to stay until November first. I have no intention of breaking her trust again for any reason. If she can't find it in herself to forgive me, it won't be because I didn't try, didn't keep my word."

"There's my girl," he managed to say. It was exactly what he needed to hear, so why did his throat feel as if invisible fingers tightened, slowly strangling, stealing his oxygen?

"And I'll play my part, do my best to get a win for Gramps tomorrow. He deserves every bit of joy for the rest of his days."

"Agreed." The word rasped, dry and guttural. She still stared into the woods as if she spoke to a phantom he couldn't see, not a flesh and blood man who needed her to look at him, to promise him that no matter what obstacle landed between them, they'd battle through it together.

"I also made a few vows to myself while I was in Devils Hollow. I determined to tie up loose ends, to leave with all unfinished business from five years ago wrapped up, to conquer my fear and find what forgiveness I could." Her voice trembled. "So I wouldn't ever have to come back."

"Violet—"

Finally, she looked at him over the window's rim, and he almost wished she hadn't. The bleak determination in her eyes, the distance, squeezed his heart. "I know you have this hope that I'll stay, that we can be together, build a life in Devils Hollow and live happily ever after. But some love stories aren't meant to last, no matter how epic they might be."

As much as his heart threatened to collapse, even though he wanted to argue, he held his tongue and waited for her big finish. She wouldn't listen until she'd said all she had to say. But he'd be damned before letting her walk out of his life again, no matter how hard the road ahead may prove to be. If he had to chase her back to Kickin' Ink, commission her to create the artwork and tattoo violets over every inch of his body just to stay close to her, he'd do it. He'd let her walk away once. If she opted for a second time, he'd go to war for her.

"Today just reminded me of the truth. Some of the things we do might be forgiven, but they're never forgotten...not really. They leave a stain that can't be bleached out by time or colored a different shade to blend in with the present. I don't belong in Devils Hollow—never have, never will."

Max hated that she'd convinced herself of that lie.

She rested her forehead on the steering wheel. "Give me a few seconds, and I'll put my game face on. If Gramps loses tomorrow, it won't be because of me."

He watched her, silent. Finally, she lifted her head and met his gaze. When he still said nothing, she arched an eyebrow.

"Are you done?" he asked quietly.

"For the moment." Straightening, she opened the door and hopped to the ground. "I'll go change. Meet you in the cemetery."

He hooked her arm with his as she turned away and forcibly pulled her back around to face him. "You're not getting off that easy, sweeting."

He should have known better. Faster than he thought possible, his leg flew out from under him, courtesy of her foot behind his knee, and he landed hard on his back. The gray sky spun for a second before Vi blocked his view, leaning over him.

"I'm leaving for you, too, Max. I wish you could see that." Tears glittered in her eyes. "You deserve so much more than I could ever give you, and you'll never find that as long as I'm around."

Before she could walk away, he grabbed her ankle, held it hostage with both hands, and hoped she liked his pretty face enough not to kick him. "You're wrong on so many levels. Just because you never saw your future at the family café doesn't mean that your choices wouldn't lead you back to Devils Hollow. No one is left untouched by their past, and forgiving doesn't erase the mistakes. It simply gives us the power to move through them, for both ourselves and the people we love."

A few teardrops slipped free, shining silver as they trembled down her cheeks. That she didn't try to escape gave him a sliver of hope. If she listened, as long as she stayed, he could get through to her.

"You've always belonged here, with me." He kept his voice soft, the lulling drawl that always drew her in. "And with Dahlia, no matter what she says. Popular opinion has never stopped you from doing what you want, going after what you want. Don't let fear steal that from you. It's one of my favorite qualities."

"What I want is for you and Dahlia to be happy, free and safe." She sounded so lost and desperate. All he wanted to do was pull her down to the ground with him and hold her until November.

"I hate to break this to you, sweeting, but for that to happen, we both need you."

She shook her head, and her mouth tightened, the moment gone. "You're not getting it."

"You're the one who isn't getting it, Violet. What about what *I* want? You don't get to decide what makes me happy. That's on me. And whether or not you believe you belong in Devils Hollow, there's one fact that will never change. You belong with me. We belong together. We've *always* belonged together."

"So you're willing to leave Ward House? Break your vow to Grams for me? Let Beasley take over Ward House once Gramps is gone?" She snorted softly, giving him no time to formulate an appropriate response. "Max, I love you. You know that. But some fantasies just aren't meant to be." She ripped her ankle free of his hold and stalked toward the house.

He rolled onto his stomach and watched her go. It was the first time she'd ever said those magical three words to him, and instead of joy, all he felt was despair. Love should conquer all, not surrender to the mountains in its way. The Vi he knew would never surrender.

Unless she believed it was the best solution for the people she loved.

She'd scratch and claw, trade her very soul away for him, for Dahlia, but for herself? His girl wouldn't battle for her own happiness. She may have the career she wanted, but not the life she dreamed of—not the happiness she believed she didn't deserve.

Max jumped to his feet and ran, catching up with her at the front door. "That's your solution? You're just going to leave again? I lost five years with you, wasn't given the chance to voice my opinion, was robbed of the opportunity to fight back. This time, at least give me the courtesy of listening to what I have to say about it. You owe me that, Violet."

Vi spun on him so fast that he backed up a step. Her dark eyes gleamed, almost feral, and when she poked him in the chest with one finger, it hurt. "I fail everyone close to me. Whenever I try to do something good in Devils Hollow, it backfires and turns to dust. Maybe this darkness, this curse, is God's way of telling me to stay away. I don't know. All I know is that everyone is better off without me here."

That she believed what she said opened up a well of anger, deep and dark. He'd managed to shut it off years ago, thought he had drained it dry, but now, those emotions that Vi had left behind for him to deal with on his own raged to the surface.

"One lie after another, Violet." He straightened and loomed over her. "What's sick and sad is that you refuse to see reality. You claim you want me to have all that I deserve."

"I do."

He snorted. "If that were true, you'd stop hiding behind all the excuses, take a good, hard look in the mirror and admit that you're afraid of me."

She held his gaze, her mouth tight. "I'm *not* afraid of you."

Laughter broke free, low and mocking. A wildness rolled through him, a desperation to force her to open her eyes and acknowledge what should be obvious. "You're so terrified you'd rather believe a curse, abandon your family and face an unknown future alone than risk your heart on me. You'd rather base your life on a premonition than let me help you fight it off. You'd rather sacrifice happiness—both yours and mine — than admit that you need me as much as I need you."

A hard edge to his voice sharpened the words into weapons, chopping through her armor to remove the blinders and gut punch her with the vulnerable truth. From the tears gleaming in her eyes, the color draining from her beautiful face, he'd struck home. As much as he didn't want to hurt her, sometimes facing the truth required pain on all sides. And if verbal violence was all that worked to get through to his Violet, he'd go down to the grave swinging.

"I'm done letting you pretend, Vi. I'm done patiently waiting for you to be the brave, badass woman I know you are and slay any demons standing in your way. If you walk again, it will be with the full knowledge that it's not any lingering curse or Devils Hollow bias that keeps you from being happy. It's *you*."

Before she made any response, he spun and marched across the lawn toward the forest, focused on Lake Forsaken lurking unseen behind the trees. He'd make sure she had nothing left to lean on, no defense to hide behind, even if he had to dredge the entire blasted lake of spirits himself.

Chapter Thirty

Vi tried not to squirm as Sabrina jerked the silk laces of her corseted dress tight. The full-length mirror in the Raven Room reflected Sabrina's struggle to squeeze her properly into the exquisite costume for the Hallowtoberfest haunted house finale. Where Gramps had found the garment, she had no idea.

Black, scrolled leather crawled over blood-red chiffon like a gate offering glimpses to another distant world. Ebony roses clung to one hip and thorned vines crept up the side. Layers of hand-painted ombre chiffon to match the corset made up the floor-length skirt, so lightweight it felt like a purposeful contradiction, a reminder of the clamp around her ribs. It was every Gothic girl's dream of a gown and clashed perfectly with her black Doc Martens.

And each cinch felt like a noose closing around her throat, the final stretch of failing to fulfill her obligations in Devils Hollow. In a few hours, she'd be on the road, another disaster left in her wake.

What a joke, thinking she could reverse the curse, heal old wounds, find some peace for her haunted memories in the hometown where she'd never quite fit in. Of her list of goals, the only one she'd truly made good on was hugging Gramps and making sure he knew how much he meant to her. Dahlia had refused to even acknowledge her presence at the café this morning. Max had ghosted her after their disastrous conversation yesterday. Regrets and sorrow would still be clinging to her coattails when she left.

Again.

You're afraid of me. Max's words whittled a bloody design on her heart, keeping rhythm with the rain on the roof. His furious expression remained burned on her brain. The accusations fluttered in the pit of her stomach, trying to escape like bottled flies. Max could believe whatever he wanted about her as long as he was safe, alive and happy.

Maybe, years down the misbegotten path of her life, she could take some comfort in knowing she'd at least tried. Dahlia may not forgive her, but her sister knew she was sorry. Max knew she loved him, even if she couldn't stay.

Her heart cracked, a pulsing, aching mess that left her lightheaded. Without the wrapping around her ribs, she had the sensation she might fall apart.

She managed to draw a short, shaky breath through the constraints of her corset. But there was one final act she could control, even with sweating hands and pummeling pulse. In the morning, with her truck packed to go and dawn rising from the dead, she'd make that fateful swim across the lake, earn the last petal of her rose tattoo. If nothing else, she'd ax that fear and leave it in the Devils Hollow dust or die trying.

The Ward sisters could suck it.

Vi winced as Sabrina gave the corset a particularly brutal tug, bringing her painfully back to the present. "Thanks for helping me out. Getting into this costume by myself would have been a total — "

"Bitch," Sabrina finished for her. She wrenched one final time, hard enough to make Vi's bones creak, and secured the strings. "There's no escape for you now, Violet."

The tiny hairs on the back of her neck lifted. Sabrina's words had been light and teasing, no ominous meaning to them. It must be the electricity in the air, the anticipation of the upcoming haunted house exhibition in an hour. Twilight stirred in the rain beyond the windows of Ward House, calling to fallen leaves and shifting shadows.

"It's finally Halloween." Sabrina settled her hands on Vi's bare shoulders, her fingers cold, and met her gaze in the mirror. "When the veil between worlds dwindles to the barest thread, and the dead emerge to dance with the living. And the worst possible night to be stuck inside babysitting weak vampires."

"Poor Victor." Vi had hardly seen the vampire impersonator since his fateful encounter with Anna Ward. In the past week, he'd kept to his room and only allowed Hecate in with holy offerings of blessed tomato juice. Not that she could blame him. Coming face to face with the Ward sisters would make the snarliest creature of the night want to hide under the covers until spring. Being possessed by Abigail could drive even the most passionate bloodsucker to trade his lace and fangs for a briefcase, tie and normal nine-to-five.

"He's a pathetic excuse of a parasite." Sabrina rolled her eyes before turning her attention out of the window to the darkening woods beyond. "Almost as pathetic as me, bowing and scraping to Hecate just for the privilege of being included in her monster-hunting squad. I thought she'd appreciate the arrangements I made on my own, applaud my ambition. It took a lot of work to raid the enemy and steal a sacrifice without getting caught. Instead, I'm punished."

Vi went still. Surely, meek Sabrina wasn't responsible for trespassing on Beasley's property and the fate of poor Crookshanks. Was she? "Sacrifice?"

Sabrina continued as if she hadn't spoken. "Bloody stars, Hecate even invited Max and your sister to join in."

Ice rushed through blood and bones, erasing all thoughts of stolen cats and sacrifices. Vi spun, facing Sabrina. "Dahlia refused the invite, right?"

"If she had, the circle would be short one body and I'd be out there instead of in here. See? Punished." Evil laughter erupted from Sabrina's cell phone, Vincent Price at his best, and she groaned. "Excuse me. I have a dark spell of my own to cast in a crystal glass of tomato juice. If Victor checks out early, don't be alarmed. No one will find his ashes."

Vi barely noticed as Sabrina slipped out into the hallway. Her pulse vibrated hard on the bodice of her dress, and she pressed a palm over her heart to keep it in. Dahlia and Max, both at the lake, together. Her nightmare unfolded, raging to vivid, horrifying life.

This can't be happening. She had her skirts hitched up and fisted in her hand, made it halfway down the stairwell before her mind caught up with her body. Gramps wandered into the foyer, dressed in top hat, vest and coattails, the creepy doll from the lake beneath his arm, as she rushed down the last steps.

"I'll be back in time for the exhibition, Gramps. Promise."

"What in tarnation—?"

"No time to explain." Vi shoved open the door and stumbled out into the storm. Rain pelted the roof like bullets, forming puddles in the grass between the house and tree line shielding the lake. Max's boot prints left a trail of muddy indentations, a trail easily followed, headed in the direction of the lake.

Headlights turned into the driveway and flickered on the trees, but she didn't slow. She squinted against the deluge as she ran and slipped on the saturated grass, her heart louder than the distant roll of thunder. How could Max be so stupid? Even if he believed he was somehow immune to anything supernatural, he'd listened to her own experiences, understood her deepest fears. He'd been present at Hecate's unfortunate ceremony. He *knew* Lake Forsaken was far from ordinary, yet he chose to challenge both it and the premonition that had driven her out of Devils Hollow.

And now Dahlia was there, too.

My fault. Vi choked on a sob. If she'd kept her mask on, held her secrets and intentions closer until she was gone again, neither one would be at the lake now, tempting fate. They'd both be safe, even if they hated her. She could deal with that, as long as they remained brilliant lights in the world.

Her heart caved in, as if hollowed out for so long that it could no longer take the pressure. She'd rather the one to die than lose either one.

Lightning forked across the sky, white-hot and wicked. Electricity tingled down her neck, along her arms. The scent of ozone filled the air. Three heartbeats later, thunder boomed, shaking the ground beneath her just as she reached the trees.

She grabbed a slick fir branch to keep her footing, her pulse a rabid beast rattling her ribcage. Sucking in a breath, she shook off her sorrow for tomorrow, when she could curl up into a ball and cry for days alone. As much as she loved storms, being on the lake in this would be like a human lightning rod begging to be struck down.

The thick bower of limbs provided some measure of protection from the punishing rain. Vi's boots squelched in the growing mud as she ran, her drenched gown clinging to her legs. A gust of wind howled through the trees and flung her wet hair in her face like clinging tentacles. She slipped and stumbled, collided with a ragged stump scaled with white mushrooms. Cursing, she righted herself and pushed onward.

Fingers of mist curled among sharp-edged ferns and fallen logs, thickening as she drew closer to the lake. Ozone stung the air, sharp and bitter. Leaves shuddered and branches twisted as if great beasts raged on all sides as Vi hurried on, shielding her face. The five-minute walk to the lake from Ward House seemed to take hours. At last, the woods reluctantly spat her out onto the lifeless beach.

Raindrops drilled the water, making the lake appear to boil. Fog gathered thick and concealing on the water and shore, and anything beyond a handful of yards in any direction remained hidden. The trees made dreamy silhouettes on either side of her. Chanting rose from sources unseen, muted by distance and the clinging film, the hint of burning herbs announcing Hecate and the Dimension crew's presence nearby.

The haze shifted and a temporary window opened across the lake. Like a phantom fading into twilight, the silhouette of Max rowing his canoe away appeared. In the next second, the gray swallowed him whole again.

Movement stirred in the water itself, and Vi's heart stopped. Wreathed in mist, wearing an old-fashioned gown of white, Dahlia stood chest deep in the water, her head tipped back as if contemplating why the sky wept. Before she could call out to her sister, a few feet behind her, someone — *something* — broke the surface just enough to reveal hell-black eyes and long hair slick with water and weeds.

A chill poured down her back. She'd recognize those eyes anywhere.

Anna Ward.

Vi dropped to her knees on the bank. She couldn't look away from the direct line of her sister and Anna to where Max had disappeared. A dizzying sense of déjà vu made her wobble, as if this were a summer day set in reverse and she could only watch helplessly from a mirror as Dahlia took her place, as her premonition came to violent life. She knew that in only a few moments, ice-cold hands would pull her sister under, exactly as they had her, years ago. She also knew, down to her bones, that when Dahlia resurfaced, she wouldn't come back up alive.

Her premonition was one hundred percent real — not the irrational fear of a girl traumatized from almost drowning, nor a vivid teenage nightmare faded by time as she'd secretly hoped, but real. True. Now. She had to stop it.

She had to stop Anna Ward.

"Don't." Vi dug her fingers into the barren earth and held Anna's burning gaze. "Not her. Take me."

Anna slipped soundlessly back beneath the water, an alligator hiding in the depths, waiting to strike.

"Dahlia! Get out of the water! *Now!*"

Dahlia finally looked at her, as if just now noticing her presence. Her expression of wonder frosted over. "No. If I want to help with a black magic Halloween ritual by wearing a beastly dress in the lake or swim naked beneath the full moon and fish for crawdads, I'm going to do it. I'm sick of being the good Keller girl, always working, doing what's right and expected of me, always giving up what I want to make everyone else happy."

"Please." Vi's heart pounded all the way to her fingertips, so hard and fast she shook. Of all the times for Dahlia to go rebel, this was the absolute worst. And if they survive this, she'd kick Hecate's ass for putting her sister up to this. "I can't." She swallowed the gravel in her throat. "I can't lose you."

The mask slipped, and Dahlia softened into the sister she'd always known—her best friend who understood her heart, who had the patience of a saint and a secret wicked streak that she shared with only a select few. That Dahlia trusted her with that private side was an honor she'd never take for granted.

"That's what you don't seem to get, Vi." A hint of sadness ruined her small smile. "The people who truly love you can never be lost, no matter what words are exchanged, no matter how much distance you put between them or how much you believe you don't deserve them—even if you think they're better off without you."

"Let's hash it out on the bank, where it's safe, before lightning strikes again. Being near water during this storm is just asking to be zapped." As much as she wanted to warn Dahlia about Anna, she had the distinct sensation that announcing the specific name would propel the spirit into action.

Dahlia didn't take the bait. She lazily swept her hand over the surface, as if it were a hot day off work and she had nowhere to go for hours. Her drenched hair clung to her skull and neck like water weeds, the thin material of her dress molded to her arms and shoulders. "The other night, I was brutal on you."

Vi shook her head once, curt. *Come on, Dahlia. Walk toward me.* "Everything you said was true."

"Most of it...maybe." She shrugged. "But my delivery could've been better. My choices don't make me more valuable as a human being. I'm not a better person than you for staying and doing what you were never meant to do. I'm sorry if I made you feel that way."

"But you are a better person." Vi's eyesight blurred, and she swiped both tears and raindrops away. "You inspire smiles and sunshine. That's not me. It will *never* be me."

"And that's the way it should be, idiot." Dahlia released an exasperated sigh. "Our differences are exactly perfect. If everyone was the same, what a dull, unbalanced world it would be. I will never have the power or skills to impact the same people that you do."

Vi snorted.

"*Violet Keller.*" She pointed, all humor gone, and moved closer to the shore a step, maybe two, mist swirling around her. "Don't do that. Don't dismiss who and what you are. You might not inspire sunshine and smiles, but the people who harbor stars and shadows recognize those same qualities in you, are drawn to you because of who you are. Do you honestly believe I'd ever feel at home hanging at Ward House with Gramps, Max and all the ghosts that haunt those walls?"

At the mention of ghosts, she scanned the water for any sign of Anna. The drilling rain made it impossible to determine anything beyond the boiling surface. The fog kept the rest of the lake close, hidden.

"Do you actually think I share any of the same enthusiasm for the supernatural that all the tourists who come here do?" Dahlia continued, drifting a few inches closer to shore. "I'm a fake, Vi. I *loathe* all the hoopla around Halloween, but I put on a grin, hang out the welcome sign, and instead of the fancy cuisine I want to prepare, I bake monster cookies and concoct lunch specials that appeal to the blood lust and creepy-crawly desires that customers demand. Even worse," her voice dropped to a whisper, "I'm *scared* of leaving Devils Hollow."

For a moment, all Vi could see was her little sister, small and vulnerable. "Scared of what?"

"Here, I know what to expect, where I fit. I know that if I cater to the tourists and Beasley, smile and suck up to whoever needs it, that the café will survive, that Mom and Dad will be proud of me, that I'll make everyone happy. I'm frickin' sick of making everyone happy." Her shoulders slumped. "You're not the coward, Vi. I am."

"Not even." She hated witnessing her sister break down. Someone like Dahlia should never have cause to break down. "I'm the one who snuck off and went AWOL for five years, remember? I left you behind without even considering how it might impact you."

"No, a coward would stay in a life she doesn't want because she's too afraid of disappointing others."

"That's called selflessness. There are far too few people in the universe who would be willing to put aside their own wants and needs for someone else."

Dahlia snorted, exactly as Vi had moments ago. "As much as I envied you, enough to give Max a jealousy kiss, I never wanted you to leave."

"Never?" Vi arched an eyebrow.

"Well, maybe for a day—a week, tops." Dahlia's smirk faded. "Definitely not for five years. I love you, Vi. I need you in my life, and by that, I mean more than an occasional postcard. Don't bail on me again, not for any reason."

"I won't...ever."

Her sister nodded, and the knot in her chest that had formed years ago, so ingrained on her soul she'd become accustomed to it, loosened and untangled. They both had their own hopes and dreams, fears and frustrations—different, but with the same power to affect every nuance of their lives. Maybe she'd been so focused on her own issues and failures that she hadn't been able to see—truly *see*—her sister.

"Do you finally get it now? We're both screw ups in our own ways." Dahlia scooped up some water and splashed it her way, missing by a mile. "So stop playing the sacrificial victim."

"Fine. As long as you stop being the Keller family martyr."

"Deal. Forgiven?"

"Always."

"Same. I just needed a groveling session to get over it." Dahlia's wicked smile shone through the storm, bright and pure. Her gaze slipped past Vi. "We have an audience."

Vi pivoted toward the trees behind her. Dozens of people spread along the shore at a careful distance, as if watching a movie already in motion. With the continuous noise of the rain and fear stealing her attention, she hadn't noticed their arrival.

The headlights coming up the driveway as she'd run from Ward House into the woods clicked into place. *Frickin' Beasley*. She must have adjusted the time for Gramps' exhibition time without telling them. The tourists must have seen her and followed, believing she was all part of the competition.

The chanting, going on so long that it had faded into the background, suddenly stopped. A girl wearing a skeleton bodysuit and crown of bones gasped and pointed toward the lake.

Vi swung back to Dahlia. Behind her sister, the water rippled. "Get out of the lake." She scrambled to her feet and waded into the lake, ankle deep. The water sucked at her feet like tar, a tether holding her back. "Hurry!"

Dahlia's smile froze in place. She glanced over her shoulder, and when she looked back, the whites of her wide eyes gleamed. Frantically, she pushed toward shore, her dress trailing her in a bridal veil.

Lightning split the sky directly above the lake, painting the surrounding trees in neon-white, and a tourist screamed. Mere inches behind Dahlia, Abigail rose from the lake, tangled in weeds and shadow. Her black-void eyes fixed on Dahlia's back she struggled toward safety.

Thunder rattled the ground. Vi fought to take another step. She reached for Dahlia, almost close enough to touch her sister's outstretched fingers.

With a cry, clawing for Vi's hand, Dahlia flew backward. Water churned around her as she was dragged toward the center of the lake, propelled by an invisible motor.

"Dahlia!" Vi could only watch from the shore as her sister drew farther and farther away at inhuman speed. The mist dwindled with her passing, a curtain opening to the final act of a long overdue play. Dead center in the lake, still in his canoe, Max slowly stood, a book in his hand.

Halfway between the shore and Max, Dahlia shrieked. Between one blink and the next, she slipped beneath the surface.

Gone.

Chapter Thirty-One

The rain suddenly ceased, leaving a heavy, aching silence. Not a single noise came from the hushed tourists witnessing Vi's life completely unravel in a matter of heartbeats.

She dropped to the ground and loosened her boots as fast as she could, sobbing when the laces knotted beneath her fumbling fingers. The mist dissolved with the rain, nothing more than wisps curling on the lake's surface. Vi kicked her feet free and scrambled in.

Icy water closed around her ankles, then knees, hips and thighs, claiming her for its own. Her choice. A willing sacrifice.

For Max, for Dahlia...anything.

The muck on the lake bottom slipped beneath her bare soles and slithered between her toes like eels as she splashed forward. Once the water reached her waist, she plunged in, surrendered to the lake.

For a second, the chill paralyzed her. Losing the steady ground beneath her feet awakened the memories, tangled in water weeds, trapped by icy hands, her lungs burning for air. Her breaths came too hard, too fast. Her sister was down there now, reliving the same terror. The only difference is they now knew who — what — to blame.

No. Not today, Anna. Not ever.

Vi swam into the depths, toward the spot where Dahlia had vanished only yards from the shoreline but a world away from safe. She kept her head above the water, maintaining a modified breaststroke in case Dahlia resurfaced. The terror slid free with each kick, each breath she took between strokes. A calmness erased any panic and tamed her thoughts into one focal point. If her entire life had been leading up to this moment, where faith and fear collided and she permanently tipped to one side or the other, lost the rest of her days to the Devils Hollow darkness, so be it. Either way, she was done being afraid.

White streaked across the sky, the resident owl vivid in the fading daylight as it circled on silent wings. Max rowed furiously toward her in his canoe, whatever task he'd been given by Hecate apparently set aside. She wanted to yell at him to go back, to get off the water, but it would be a waste of energy. He wouldn't listen. No matter what she said, any present danger or the sins of her past, he'd have her back.

Always.

God, I can't lose him, too.

Lightning ripped over the lake, cracking like a whip, blinding. Thunder roared as the electric-white burn faded. Vi blinked the reflection away. Her vision cleared, and she stopped swimming, treading water.

Dahlia reappeared between her and Max, nose-deep in the water. Her hair was slicked back, dark with water and tendrils of waterweeds. Moisture glimmered on her pale skin like crystals. Dahlia's eyes had turned black as oil, focused like a snake, unblinking, unfeeling.

That's not *Dahlia.*

Back in the cemetery, during the ruined graveyard walk, she'd seen those same eyes in Greenbeard after he'd been tossed atop Abigail Ward's grave, then again in Victor at the botched witching hour ceremony conducted on the lakeshore.

Anna had taken possession of her sister.

Dahlia slipped back beneath the surface, out of sight in the muddied water.

Max glided nearer in his canoe, close enough to see the determined line of his mouth and the fear in his eyes. The paddle slid in and out in a strong, steady rhythm.

"Maximus!" Hecate's voice carried from shore. "Burn the journal! Now!"

He didn't stop, his gaze set on Vi.

Whatever Hecate had planned to rid Lake Forsaken of spirits, it was Dahlia's only hope. Vi couldn't let Max risk her safety for everything else. He drifted near, cutting off her view of the shore. She ignored his outstretched hand and hooked one hand on the side of the canoe. "Do it, Max. I'm fine."

"You're not safe in the water. Get in." He grabbed for her.

Vi pushed away from the canoe, avoiding his hand. "Only after you burn the journal and save Dahlia."

"Burning hell, Violet." Glaring, he pulled the journal and a lighter from his pocket and stood in the canoe. He held the tiny tongue of fire beneath the edge of the journal. "Anna Ward," he said in a commanding voice, "with this flame, be *free*."

Smoke curled from the leather as it slowly caught ablaze. Vi searched the water for another sign of Dahlia, of Anna. *Come back to me, sister.*

A shout of warning came from the shore. On the opposite side of the canoe, white fingers slithered over the rim. Death-black eyes peeked over the edge.

The canoe jerked violently and tipped. Max toppled into the lake, the journal with him.

"Max!" Vi fumbled around the canoe to where he'd fallen, only water on all sides. Anna had taken Dahlia, and now she had Max, too. She righted the canoe and clung to the freeboard, shivering, refusing to cry. Water lapped the sides of the canoe, a brutally gentle lullaby.

This can't be happening. Her grip tightened to painful. She hadn't sacrificed five years with the people she loved most, hadn't worked to conquer her fear of the water, hadn't returned to face her mistakes only to lose everything to a spirit who was too filled with hate to let go and move on to the next level.

"Anna Ward! You can have me, but not Dahlia — not Max, not *them*." Her voice rose to a scream. "Show yourself, you fugly bitch!"

"Who are you calling fugly?"

She released the canoe and spun. Several feet away, Max treaded water, his dark hair hanging in his eyes. She choked back a sob. "You're alive."

The crooked grin he always saved for her came to life. "If I'm going down, it'll be due to the mountain of apple pie I plan to eat over my lifetime, not any ghost."

"But the journal…Dahlia. Anna has her."

His smile faded. "Shit. The journal."

"It's the only possession we have of Anna's," Hecate called. Wading into the water at a march, she wore a grim expression. Her skeleton Dimensions crew and

334

the tourists gathered behind her, a rapt audience. "It must be recovered. We cannot free this plane of her presence otherwise." She slid into the water and swam toward them without a single gasp or wince from the cold.

"You keep watch for our friend." Max swiped his hair from his eyes. "I'm going under."

Vi latched onto his arm before he could dive back beneath the black water to search for the journal. "If you're at the bottom of the lake, you might as well sacrifice yourself to her. No way. I'll do it."

"*I'll* do it." Hecate bobbed several feet away, her black hair slicked off her face, her skin pale in the fading light. "She'll be too distracted by the two of you to take any notice of me." Not waiting for an answer, Hecate drew a deep breath and dove. One slender foot peeked above the surface, and she was gone, leaving only a ripple.

"That sounds...ominously exciting." Max grimaced. "I say we get out of the water and distract the spirits from dry land. I'll get the paddle."

Vi considered suggesting just heading for shore as fast as they could, but Max was already off. She wasn't going anywhere without him. While he swam to the paddle, she stood guard, her heart thundering in her head. The lake was too quiet, too still. Dahlia had been beneath the surface too long to be without oxygen. Anna's possession better give her inhuman powers, otherwise...like Anna herself, she'd face a future without her sister.

Please, God. Don't take her away.

Hecate popped free, and Vi choked back a shriek. The witch gulped a huge breath and disappeared beneath the surface again.

She exhaled roughly. *Dammit.*

"Got it." Max nabbed the paddle and turned.

Slipping noiselessly from the water, Anna rose behind him.

Max. She only had time to think his name as Anna's bone-white fingers wrapped around his neck and squeezed.

Max dropped the paddle and fumbled for the chokehold on his neck, clawed at the fingers stealing his life. The paddle floated from his reach, toward Vi. Had it been Dahlia at his back, he would have had little trouble escaping, but possessed by Anna, she clenched with supernatural strength, her expression cold. She didn't seem to feel the fingernails digging into her flesh, didn't struggle to control a man twice her size. Emotionlessly, she waited for Max to die.

Ice swept through Vi. She knew what came next. Max floating in the water, his lifeless eyes staring at the sky. Anna would then drown Dahlia and leave her body to resurface, her sister gone, too. The premonition…final.

Vi pushed toward the paddle, the only weapon close at hand, but what could a plastic stick do against a spirit? What could she possibly do to save the two people she loved most in the world?

Revenge is often borne of the greatest love, twisted by an even deeper pain.

Hecate's words. She believed that Anna and Abigail weren't bitter rivals as the legend said, but sisters of both blood and heart.

All the slivers of information she'd learned about Anna and Abigail Ward from Hecate's journal and her days since returning to Devils Hollow stitched together into a delicate, detailed picture of sorrow and pain, shaded by words of truth from both Dahlia and Max. Anna didn't hate Abigail. No matter the strife between them, she loved her sister as deeply as Vi loved Dahlia. And when Abigail took her own life, leaving Anna behind…

Vi sucked in a steadying breath and forced her gaze to Anna's instead of Max slowly suffocating in her stranglehold. "Sister, hear me."

Dahlia's oil-slick eyes focused on her. From the corner of her eye, she caught movement—Hecate noiselessly swimming toward shore. She had to buy Max enough time for Hecate to burn the journal.

"I'm sorry it took me this long to return to you. Forgive me for being too thick-skulled to figure it out until now. All this time, I thought you hated me for being everything you weren't, for letting the affection of a boy come between us, allowing my jealousy to poison our relationship."

Max suddenly drew a deep breath. Vi didn't dare acknowledge him. Her fingers still around his throat, Anna studied her intently, still as death, water gently lapping at her bone-pale shoulders.

"I didn't leave you because of any of those reasons. I did it because I believed you'd be better off without me here, interfering in the life you always wanted. I thought if I were gone, you'd be free to be truly happy." From the shore, the fire popped, the only noise beyond Vi's heartbeat and Max's harsh breaths. Subtly, slowly, she drifted closer, the paddle in her loose grip.

"I never stopped to consider the impact my actions would have on you." Briefly, she dropped her gaze to Max, just long enough to note the gleam of understanding in his eyes. This apology wasn't only for Anna, but to Dahlia…to him. "That was inexcusably selfish of me, and I regret, deeply, causing you a single pinprick of pain. Love puts others first, and I absolutely blew it when I left you. I am so sorry, sister."

Anna watched her, unblinking, the water weeds tangled in her hair glistening in the last few minutes of daylight. Her long fingers remained wrapped around Max's throat, a warning. Each word had to be careful, perfect...true.

"But I understand now. You're angry because I departed this plane without even a farewell. I was wrong, taking that choice from you, making the judgment call for all of us." Vi's throat tightened as she floated nearer. The blood pounded, pounded in her head, pushing her to reveal the darkest corner of her heart, to crack open her soul and set them all free.

"That was a lie I told myself, a deception so deep and tangled that I couldn't see the truth before. I left...for myself." The words came out rough, raspy. "Beneath my bravado and confidence, I was afraid. Afraid that, in the end, when the dust settled, my love wouldn't be enough for you. Afraid that I wouldn't be enough. Afraid that, ultimately, I didn't matter enough. And by letting that fear cripple me, I failed the people I love most."

Tears burned her eyes, blurred the images of Max in Dahlia's grasp — the two people she loved most, the two people she'd completely failed. "Instead of truly living, I spent my time wrapped up in worst-case scenarios until they were the only probabilities I could consider. I surrendered my happiness, my family, my love, my life. Instead of moving through the fear, I clung to it and gave it the power to control my destiny."

The current pulled her nearer as she spoke, close enough that Max's body heated the water between them. The words continued in a rush, a river dammed up for so long that once freed, it couldn't be stopped. Anna faded into the background until there was only Max, only her. She held his gaze as tears spilled, blending with the lake.

"You've always loved me as I am, *despite* who I am. It took me a while, but I finally figured it out. Faith is the antithesis of fear, and you never lost faith in me. I finally get that no matter what I do, what I say or where I go, you'll always love me anyway. You'll always need me." She cupped his face with one hand and stroked his cheekbone with her thumb. "Like I need you. Love you. I'll *never* leave you again. My destiny is with you…here. You belong in Devils Hollow, and wherever you are, that's where I want to be, too."

"Wherever, whenever," Max croaked.

At Max's voice, Dahlia stiffened, the spell of Vi's emotional words broken. Her lip curled in a snarl, and her hiss sounded like steam from hell's deepest pit. She squeezed Max's neck with one hand. With the other, she pressed against his head, forcing it an angle meant to break.

"No!" Vi raised the paddle. "Let him go!"

A streak of white flew across the sky, and the owl divebombed, straight at Anna. The bird's outstretched claws tangled in Dahlia's wet hair, jerking. Powerful wings flapped in her face, and the piercing shriek that broke from Dahlia was of pure, endless rage. She released Max to grasp the owl by the neck, and the flapping of wings turned frantic. Coughing, Max struggled to stay afloat. Vi clung to him like a life preserver.

"Spirit, be gone!" Hecate's command cracked like thunder as she hurled the journal into the waiting fire.

Both the owl and Dahlia ceased struggling, and for a piercing moment their gazes held, black on gold. The fire hummed, consuming paper and leather. Between heartbeats, the owl vanished. All that remained in Dahlia's hands was a cloud of sparkling dust. Then that, too, melted into the fading light.

"Abigail," Max wheezed. "The journal belonged to Abigail, not Anna."

Anna threw her head back. The howl that came from her mouth sounded as if several voices cried out together, unearthly, unnatural...utterly terrifying.

"Max." Vi could barely get his name out, panic a living, breathing force in her blood. "Swim." He tore his gaze away from Dahlia, and Vi grabbed his arm, dragging him with her. "Swim!"

There was no way they'd reach dry land before Anna caught them. Vi kept her gaze ahead as a deathly chill raked her spine. Max swam beside her with strong strokes, unwilling to leave her behind. Her toes hit the soft bottom of the lake, too little too late. Hecate and crew crouched before the fire in some last-hope ritual. The crowd shouted, pointing, needless warnings. She knew the fate awaiting Dahlia and Max...her.

"Out of my way." Gramps pushed through the tourists as Duke growled a warning. He cracked a horned fairy on the thigh with his cane when he didn't move aside fast enough. The Doll hung beneath his arm, limp and bedraggled. Without hesitating, he flung his prized possession into the fire.

A gasp came from behind Vi, and she spun, Max with her. Mere feet away, Dahlia's mouth opened wide in a soundless scream. The whirring of insect wings erupted as a host of black moths broke from the lake, circled Dahlia, momentarily blocking her from sight.

The moths swarmed toward the fire. Together, the insects flew into the flames, surrendering to death.

Gramps removed his handkerchief from beneath the costume top hat that had somehow remained on his head and wiped his face. In the stunned silence, he snorted. "One thing about this infernal lake I never could fathom." He tossed his ruined handkerchief into the fire and watched the flames consume it. "All the damn spirits."

Chapter Thirty-Two

The blood pounding in Vi's head dulled the crowd's applause to a discordant buzz as she turned back to the lake and Max. He cradled Dahlia in his arms. Her eyes remained shut, her skin pale as death, a mirror of the premonition.

No. Not Dahlia. Not my sister.

Suddenly, Dahlia jerked like a puppet brought to life and coughed. Max lifted her upright, and she retched in long, racking heaves. She leaned over his arm, the tips of her loose hair brushing the water.

Vi covered her face with her hands and breathed, just breathed. Dahlia was alive. They were all alive.

It's finally over. The Ward sisters were gone, the curse broken.

Max waded ashore, and Vi scrambled to help him support a still coughing Dahlia to dry land and safety.

As they broke free from the lake's grasp, the tourists surrounded them, pressing suffocatingly close. Max swayed as if he barely had the strength to stand, let alone keep Dahlia upright. Vi didn't have the energy to respond or a cane to beat them back. But Gramps did.

"Stand aside, fiends, or risk being hexed." He elbowed his way through and stood in front of them like a guardian, ready to beat the crowd back singlehandedly. With his cane, and Duke as backup, he probably could. "Curiosities will be satisfied back at Ward House during the formal consumption ceremony of the Ward family signature Dead-End cinnamon-apple whiskey and Heart Scream pie, straight from the hellfire ovens of Keller's Killer Café." He shook his fist at a man dressed as a horned demon with black lips and a too-tight red bodysuit. "I don't give a hoot about Widow Beasley's misaligned schedule. Take your sorry tail-ends back to Ward House before I kick you all out for disturbing sacred ground."

"If you'll please follow me to the house." Victor, who must have accompanied Gramps to the lake, separated from the shadows and smiled, sharp with fangs. "Along the way, I'll share with you the true fate of the Ward sisters and their shocking past. I narrowly escaped with my life while discovering this information." Victor held an iron lantern in one hand, a blood-red rose in the other, and when he swept toward the woods, his black cape swirled around him like...

Moths.

Vi shuddered.

"Mark me," Gramps said, watching them go. "Never trust a witch named Sabrina. By the by, she's locked in the cellar. Confessed to crucifying Beasley's pet. Wager she was fixing to polish off the vamp, too. Can't say I entirely blame her for that one, though."

Dahlia sank to her knees on the barren soil, and both Vi and Max went with her. Thankfully, the tourists trailed after Victor, lured by the promise of secrets, scandal and pie.

"It's over." Hecate doused the fire, and smoke curled up into the heavens, bleeding with the night. She laid a dry blanket around Dahlia and handed one to Max. "Both Anna and Abigail Ward are free."

"The lake is cleansed," Oberon added as he tucked rocks used for their ceremony into a leather satchel.

"The curse broken." Lifting the hood of her cape, Raven's eyes glittered. Clearly, she'd found the night more exciting than frightening and undoubtedly had it all recorded, ready to upload for their next viral video.

"And you are free as well, Violet." Hecate kneeled before them. Her hair, usually sleek as silk, fell over her shoulder, the strands dull and frizzed, a reminder of the part she'd played in the battle. "Do you feel it?"

Whether it stemmed from the Ward sisters or the breaking open of her own soul, she couldn't deny she felt emptied, lighter, like she could sleep for a week without a single nightmare. Max slipped the blanket around her, and when he laced his fingers with hers, her heart squeezed. *Home.* She was finally home, this time for good.

"I don't aim to let strangers have free rein of my house and limited-edition whiskey. I wager that was Beasley's plan when she bussed 'em here an hour early, to steal my whiskey and my win." Gramps straightened his top hat and gripped his cane, his eyes ablaze, Duke guarding his heels. "If you kids are done messing around with your hocus pocus—"

"We prefer to call it 'abracadabra', Mr. Ward." Raven snaked her hand into the crook of his arm and pressed close. *Smart girl.* Close quarters made it more difficult for Gramps to smack her with his cane. "Come along, Oberon. We have tourists to enchant."

"Maybe we'll get a lead for a future Halloween site." Oberon slung his pack over his shoulder, hitched up his black velvet pants and followed. "But a shot of cinnamon-apple whiskey sounds almost as welcome as a Warlock's Elixir with a sprig of mint."

"Warlock's Elixir?" Gramps harrumphed. "Adding a fancy name doesn't make a mojito any better. Once you taste my special blend Dead-End whiskey, your eyes will be opened to the nature of a *true* elixir. Mark me." He paused and glanced at Max, his white eyebrows bunched together like caterpillars ready to fight.

Max answered before he could ask a question. "We'll be there in a minute, Gramps. Maybe two, but we'll be there. Promise."

Left alone on the beach with only Max, Dahlia and Hecate for company, Vi refused to let go of her sister's waist. She hadn't said a word since reaching land, her face downcast. Vi gently removed a water weed from her tangled hair. "Dahlia?"

"I could see, hear and sense everything, but I felt...nothing," Dahlia whispered. She rubbed her chest, right above her heart and slowly found Vi's gaze. "Until you spoke. It was like the shades of a dark room lifted inch by inch, allowing sunlight in." She grasped Vi's hand. "I knew you wouldn't leave me to Anna."

"Never." Vi hugged her tight. She smelled of lake water and musty vegetation, but her skin was warm, and her shaking arms locked around her back.

"Come, Dahlia." Hecate's voice held a surprising gentleness. "Let me take you back to the house. You have been through much this night and will need specific instructions and tools to process and move forward."

"And forget?" Hope trembled in Dahlia's soft words.

Hecate's expression softened. "The memories will temper in time, dearest, and it will help knowing that your suffering is not without great value. You helped set two spirits free and rid this plane of darkness." Hecate gently disentangled Dahlia from Vi's hold and drew her to her feet. "That is an honor few may call their own."

The tiniest smile curved Dahlia's mouth. She squeezed Vi's hand once and let go, allowing Hecate to lead her away. "Chef Dahlia, Destroyer of Dark Things. I can absolutely work with that."

Vi sighed and leaned into Max. Her sister was going to be okay.

Max waited until the trees and deepening night hid Hecate and Dahlia from view before speaking. "I heard everything you said, too, Vi. Can't argue that they had the same effect on me." He snorted softly. "Would have preferred to hear them on dry land without an angry spirit determined to choke the life from me, but after five years of waiting, I'm not one to quibble."

Pressing her face into his neck, his skin still damp from the lake, she smiled. And when he curled his arms around her and held her close, she couldn't bring herself to care that the hush of water on rock blended with Max's heartbeat or that the odor of scorched herbs and humus feuded with his autumn-outdoor scent. She was with him, he was alive and that was more than enough.

"Tell me you meant every word," he murmured into her hair. "That this isn't the part where I wake up and realize it's November first, you're gone and I have to live unhappily ever after without you...again."

Vi went still. The desperate hope and longing in his voice tangled in the deepest corners of her heart like webs. The love he'd awakened in her decades ago simply by being Max, a love such an integral part of her that she couldn't imagine existence without it, swept through her, warm and overwhelming. Her ribs stretched beneath the pressure, and she drew a ragged breath.

Meeting his gaze, she pressed her mouth to his, moth-light, soft as the chilled autumn air. "I know where I belong now. I'm not going anywhere. I love you. I've always loved you."

He closed his eyes as if he struggled not to fall apart. "Say it again."

"You're my home, Max." She dragged her fingertips over the stubble of his jaw, the heaviness on her soul drifting into the sky to join the first stars winking through the thinning clouds. "I love you, until forever. Wherever —"

"Whenever," he said before she could finish. And when he held her tight and took her mouth with his on the barren shore with the lake whispering a discordant lullaby, October shielding them in its biting embrace, she'd never felt more free.

Epilogue

The hum of the needles stopped. Vi released the breath she'd been holding and forced her shoulders to relax into the leather chair. No matter how many tattoos she got, how little time it took or how much she knew what to expect, she always went into wimp mode while getting inked. It was ridiculously embarrassing.

Em grinned down at her, a devilish sparkle in her brown eyes. She wielded the tattoo gun like a weapon, twirling it in her fingers.

Vi's throat went dry. Emma had completed her schooling, had performed enough tattoos under Magic Mamba's tutelage to earn her begrudging approval. Her transition to Devils Hollow's first tattoo parlor had been seamless. Her inked artwork was in high demand with nothing but praise. So why did her heart pound too fast?

"Behold." Emma handed her a mirror. "My latest masterpiece."

"Masterpiece? I asked for a single rose petal, not a masterpiece." Vi refused to take the waiting mirror and instead held Emma's gaze. "What in tarnation did you do, girl?" Channeling Gramps popped right out as if her five-year absence from Devils Hollow was nothing but a forgotten dream. A year back home, and the life she had anywhere else went scurrying out of the back door.

"Don't you trust me, boss?" Emma assumed a wounded look that Vi didn't believe even a little.

"Not since you chased Beasley out with the broom."

"After she threatened me. I don't care how much clout she carries. She can take her committee and suck it all the way to November."

Vi couldn't hide a smirk. Kickin' Ink's second parlor had thrived in Devils Hollow, despite being blacklisted for not participating in Hallowtoberfest. October had been their biggest month yet. The exclusive, private location in the famous Ward House sunroom didn't hurt. "But you stole one of her cats."

Emma's gaze slid to the black cat curled up in what had once been, not so long ago, another beloved pet's pillow. The first slice of morning sun drifted over the sleeping feline and the empty rocking chair in the corner. "Cats choose their owners. Everyone knows that. I can't help it if he keeps coming back."

And when Beasley found out where her precious Nigel ran off to every morning? She shuddered.

"Come on, Vi. I'm dying here." Em shoved the mirror at her. "Take a look."

She swung her legs over the edge of the chair and swiped the mirror from Em's fingers as she headed for the full-length mirror on the wall. Cowardice was *not* a characteristic she entertained for any reason. Not anymore. She reached the mirror and pivoted, lifting the hand mirror to see her freshest body art.

Her breath caught as she gazed at the design Em had inked on her shoulder, the last petal of the rose that represented her regained courage, the conquering of her fears. True, she'd asked for a simple rose petal to match the others, but she couldn't be angry at Em's creativity. The silhouette of an owl blended with the crimson, its spread wings brushing the edges of the petal. Each line was so delicate and subtle that only by looking closely could she see that the bird appeared to be descending into the rose itself.

"I love it." Max's voice, unexpectedly close, made her jump. Completely enamored by the tattoo, she hadn't even noticed him slip into the sunroom studio. "It's perfect."

Vi turned into his arms, and he swept her into a kiss that had her head swimming and her blood pounding. By the time he was done kissing her, she was breathless, and Em was nowhere to be found.

"What were we talking about?" She clutched his shoulders, needing the support while her knees stopped shaking. A year with Max, and she still wasn't immune to him. She had a sneaking suspicion he would always be her greatest weakness — and strength.

"Burning hell. I have no idea." He rested his forehead against hers, his ragged breath warm on her lips. "But I have some new thoughts I'd love to share with you — with my mouth, my hands, my tongue."

Every inch of her tingled in anticipation. "Do tell."

"There's no telling." He grinned, slow and wicked. "Only showing."

"There is a strict no-show-and-tell policy in the Devils Hollow branch of Kickin' Ink," Em called from the corridor in a singsong voice. "I'm heading to the kitchen for coffee, and you'd better be gone by the time I get back. If not, I'll show you out with a crack of my whip."

Max lifted his gaze to the black whip Em kept on display above the hearth. As far as Vi knew, she'd only used it twice—and once on Max. "She's a tyrant."

"Why we love her." Vi batted her eyelashes.

"Why does everyone seem to forget that this is, technically, *my* house?" he grumbled, tangling his fingers with hers and leading her across the gray river rock floor. "The guests have no trouble remembering these important facts. The tattoo patrons and resident artists? Dahlia and her café crew? Not so much. I should be able to do whatever I want, wherever I want."

"Much to Beasley's deep, eternal disappointment." She stopped beside the supply cabinet, carefully laid some adhesive over her new design and topped it off with a bandage and tape.

"Burning hell. Did you see her new list of rules and regulations for the haunted house competition?"

"Nope," she said happily. "I let Dahlia keep her copy this year."

Max rolled his eyes and followed her into the corridor. "And the clause specifying that if a house is not involved, the participant shall be eliminated? The woman should be appreciative. I let her keep Adams House."

"It was only right, after what Sabrina did to Crookshanks."

"True, but she should learn to lose gracefully and give Gramps his due. He won, fair and square."

"He ruined her perfect record." Vi grabbed her Nevermore scarf and coat from the hook and followed Max into the crisp October air. "She'll never forget. He'll be a black mark on her memory forever."

"Pretty sure that was why he was smiling when he went on to join Grams." Max zipped up his jacket and paused on the porch. A hint of sadness invaded the humor. "You ready?"

She took his hand again and squeezed. "Ready."

The path leading through the trees to Lake Forsaken hadn't changed during the last year, all fuzzed moss logs, vibrant fallen leaves and toadstools. A slight breeze carried the odors of humus and water, a herald to the location where everything had changed.

They walked in silence along the shoreline until they reached their destination. Vi kneeled before the marble cross marking Gramps' grave, the granite statue of a dog where Duke rested beside him. "I still don't get why he wanted to be buried here instead of the family cemetery plot."

Max remained standing, his hands in his pockets. A moment passed before he spoke. "I think he meant to mark the end of an era. Look."

Vi followed the direction of his gaze. At the foot of Gramps' grave, a tiny purple bloom broke free of the barren soil. A shiver swept through her as she recognized the flower.

A violet.

Tears blurred her vision, unbidden. Where nothing had grown before, beauty rose from the ashes. Where once agony and anger had stained the waters lapping at the shore, new life took root at its feet, its colors sharp and vibrant against the darkness.

A feather drifted from the sky and landed gently on the mound of soil covering Gramps' bones. Vi looked up. A gray owl circled them once before veering away and disappearing into the trees. When she looked back down, Max kneeled on one knee, a small box carved with roses resting in his palm.

"I may not be the brightest crayon in the box, but I recognize the confirmation signs when I see them." His crooked smile came to life and the wobble there stabbed her straight in the heart. "Vi, will you be mine? Eternally, no matter where we go or what we do? In this life and the next?"

She tackled him to the ground as he laughed and kissed him until she couldn't tell where she ended and he began. And when he wrapped her close to his heart and held her captive, the lulling whisper of waves brought only peace.

Devils Hollow. There was no better place to be.

Want to see more from this author?
Here's a taster for you to enjoy!

Music, Love and Other Miseries:
Every Breath
C.J. Burright

Excerpt

Weddings suck. Gia Hellman trailed her finger around the rim of her second-round wine glass and tried not to feel jealous or sorry for herself.

Endless strings of twinkling white lights peppered the country club's vaulted ceiling with imitation starlight. Soft, sublime, romantic music performed by professional musicians, all friends of the groom, blended perfectly with the sweet scent of roses lacing the summer air. The food made her wish she had an appetite instead of the twisting pit in her stomach.

In the center of the dance floor, her best friend Adara melted into her new husband. She'd never seen Dar so happy. The fact that anti-romance Dar had followed through with a formal wedding ceremony and until-death vows should've made Gia all weepy in a good way.

It should be me.

She slouched in the cushioned chair and rested her chin in her hand. It wasn't that she wanted Dar's husband, Garret. It was the 'happily ever after' fantasy she wanted, would have had by now if fate hadn't been an unfeeling witch. But her 'happily ever after' had vanished a little over two years before, when the love of her life had been ripped from the world too soon.

Joey. He was irreplaceable.

"Dance with me, Ms. Hellman." The smooth, low voice brushed her ear and sent tendrils of warmth through her, more intoxicating than the wine in her bloodstream.

Gia twisted in her seat and lifted her gaze to the ridiculously sexy man standing behind her, his hand out, waiting with annoying confidence. He knew she wouldn't say no, even though she absolutely should. Ian O'Connor was her co-worker and the off-limits man of her darkest fantasies—breaker of hearts, hater of love, lawyer for the right price. And the groom's oldest friend. Avoiding him was impossible, resisting him a full-time pursuit.

"Have you already made your way through the throngs of willing women?" She batted her eyelashes. "Must be a new record."

"I strive for perfection." Ian's cool, blue eyes gleamed, his hand still out, expectant. The lights danced in his dark hair and gave his every line a magical edge. He always looked good, but in a tuxedo, the tie loosened at a rakish angle? *Devastating.* "You can't blame me, Princess. I had to do something to make the time pass while you made your own, more elegant way through the ranks of men slavering on your heels, waiting their turn to cop a feel."

"Classy." She set her glass on the table and stood, facing him. "All my dance partners tonight have been nothing but respectful." Gia planted a hand on her cocked hip and lifted an eyebrow. "Not all guys are like you, Sugarpop."

His smile was pure wolf. "No wonder you look bored out of your mind."

She sighed and slipped her hand into his, ignoring the tingles that ran up her arm at the contact. Dwelling on them would only bring trouble, and she'd had enough man trouble for a lifetime. "One dance. That's it."

"One is perfect," he murmured, pulling her close to his side as he led her onto the dance floor.

One. She repeated the word in her head instead of dragging in a full breath of Ian's spicy cologne. One was his rule. One night, no more. One night of fun, then on to the next woman who wanted nothing more than casual. There seemed to be an endless supply of women who'd settle for a single hookup with Ian O'Connor.

But she wasn't fling material, not anymore. Still, as he slid his arms around her and pulled her tight against his solid heat, it was hard to remember why.

"Nice dress." His breath caressed her earlobe as he skimmed his fingers over her bare shoulders, drifting all the way to the base of her spine. "At least Adara and I agree on one thing—this dress, on *you*. Off would be even better."

The responsive shiver was impossible to hide, so she narrowed her eyes at him. "Careful, O'Connor. She hasn't officially lifted the ban on you."

Nearly a year and a half before, Gia had drunk one too many margaritas at the annual law firm Christmas party, and in her state of missing-Joey inebriation, she'd been too weak to resist Ian's charms. Adara had come to her rescue, ripped Ian a new one, reminded Gia why she should stop at two margaritas and the Ian Threat Act had been established.

"It's a risk I'm willing to take." His focus flicked to where Adara slow-danced with Garret, oblivious to the outside world.

Gia kept her gaze on the dancing couple, the pit in her stomach expanding. The last thing she'd expected was Adara dealing with Joey's death before her, let alone finding her true love and getting hitched. When Joey had fallen sick, he'd made Gia promise to drag Adara out of solitude—a brother's desperate way of looking out for his introverted older sister when he would no longer be around to do it. Now her vow to Joey and her obligation to Adara were finished, and instead of being happy, a longing for what used to be rose from the deep, unstoppable.

That was why she couldn't keep up the fling routine. She wanted what she'd had with Joey again—more than a mere physical connection, to be someone else's favorite person. She wanted to find someone who made her sun shine brighter, even in the rain, to give her heart to the man who deserved it, a man who had enough sense to notice her excellent taste in shoes.

Basically, the full-price fairy tale, with no discounts.

She slid her hand from Ian's sculpted shoulder to the hard curve of his biceps, a last, torturous hurrah. She was tired of falling for halfway. She wanted it all, and no matter how he made her neurons sing, surrendering to Ian's charms was another dead-end. She had to escape before his melody became an orchestra her body couldn't deny.

"Thanks for the dance." She tried to twirl free of his hold, but he tightened his arms around her. Planting her palms on his firm chest, her push was weak, ineffective. "Gotta go."

"That was only an eighth of a dance, at best." His fingers were spread over her bare back, warm skin on skin, holding her gently captive. "Don't short-change me, Princess."

"Oh look, it's Karen from accounting." She pointed over his shoulder at some random wedding guest who definitely wasn't Karen. "She's asking for you."

"Karen can wait." Not falling for it, he brought his mouth closer, close enough that his breath mingled with hers. "You pressed against me is all that matters for the next two minutes."

She couldn't resist a smile. "Two minutes? That's it?"

"Two minutes is all I need to convince you that the next twenty-four hours should be spent with me...in bed. On the couch, the stairs, the counter..." He brought his lips dangerously close to her jaw. "I promise my hands are slow, my tongue enchanting and, as for the rest of me" — he brushed her earlobe with his nose — "the best things are only definable through experience."

She let her eyelids droop as tingles swirled in the emptiness inside. It would be so easy to surrender just for one night, let Ian work his magic, make her forget. Her gaze drifted to the happily married couple. Adara smiled at something Garret whispered in her ear, her smile so much like Joey's that Gia's throat closed. She ripped from Ian's hold.

"Have to pee." Without looking at him, she escaped the wedding party before she exploded, nabbing her wine glass along the way. She swept through the open double doors and into the hallway, her sparkly silver stilettos clicking a quick cadence on the tile, the raven skirts of her taffeta dress swishing against her legs, while the corseted bodice made it hard for her to breathe. *Leave it to Dar to choose black as one of her wedding colors — Gothic matrimony at its finest.*

She smiled politely at a wedding guest coming the other way and propelled her feet into the banquet room, where vows had been said and lives forever joined. Red rose petals still flanked the black runner leading to the podium, sweetly infusing the air. She flounced onto a front-row chair and drained her wine.

Joey's picture stared back at her from where it still sat on the stand from the ceremony, Adara's way of including her absent brother in her wedding.

"Don't look at me like that." She waved her empty glass at him. "It's only my second." But if someone happened to overhear her talking to the picture of her dead boyfriend, she'd totally blame it on the wine.

His fierce gray eyes stared back at her, holding a secret smile.

"I know, right? Adara...married. It's a miracle." Tears blurred the lines of his handsome face. "I think miracles maybe only happen once in a lifetime. The one we had together turned out to be a complete bust." Aching emotions clogged her throat. "I miss you, Joey...so much."

As if a small part of him were there with her, a sense of comfort curled around her and she smiled through the tears. "Don't worry. Adara reminded me who I am, so you can cross haunting her off your 'unfinished business' list. You were right that I'd forget, but when you're not here to remind me every day how loved I am, it's hard." She released a shaky sigh and pointed at his picture. "So, I'm waiting for another you. I get that he won't be you—no one ever could be—but you promised me he was out there. And I know love slams into you when you're not looking for it, because that's what you did to me. So I'm checking out of the dating game. While I'm waiting for my fairy tale, I'll figure out how to make an impact on the world, like you would have."

She blew out a long breath, feeling like she'd made a sacred vow of her own. And if she was making vows, she might as well get back up. She lifted her gaze to the rafters. "If I'm on the right track, give me a sign—a clap of thunder or flickering lights. *Something.* Throw me a bone or even a fingernail. I'm not picky."

Joey's picture clattered to the floor, so fast that she didn't see it, landing face-up.

"Get. Out." Gia pressed her palm to her hammering heart. "Joey?" She searched for a shimmering phantom or fluttering orb, maybe a ghostly whisper, but only the distant strains of *Death of a Bachelor* softened the silence. If Joey was there, he didn't reveal himself.

On wobbling legs, she climbed the two steps to the podium and picked up his picture. "I can take a hint. Let the quest begin."

About the Author

C.J Burright is a native Oregonian and refuses to leave. A member of Romance Writers of America and the Fantasy, Futuristic & Paranormal special interest chapter, while she has worked for years in a law office, she chooses to avoid writing legal thrillers (for now) and instead invades the world of paranormal romance, fantasy, and contemporary romance. C.J. also has her 4th Dan Black Belt in Tae Kwon Do and believes a story isn't complete without at least one fight scene. Her meager spare time is spent working out, refueling with mochas, gardening, gorging on Assassin's Creed, and rooting on the Seattle Mariners...always with music. She shares life with her husband, daughter, and a devoted cat herd.

C.J. Burright loves to hear from readers. You can find her contact information, website details and author profile page at https://www.firstforromance.com

Home of Erotic Romance

Sign up for our newsletter and find out about all our romance book releases, eBook sales and promotions, sneak peeks and FREE romance books!